W9-AOA-279

THE MIDNIGHT FEAST

THE MIDNIGHT FEAST

A NOVEL

LUCY FOLEY

wm
WILLIAM MORROW
An Imprint of HarperCollinsPublishers

This is a work of fiction. Names, characters, places, and incidents are products of the author's imagination or are used fictitiously and are not to be construed as real. Any resemblance to actual events, locales, organizations, or persons, living or dead, is entirely coincidental.

THE MIDNIGHT FEAST. Copyright © 2024 by Lost and Found Books Ltd. All rights reserved. Printed in the United States of America. No part of this book may be used or reproduced in any manner whatsoever without written permission except in the case of brief quotations embodied in critical articles and reviews. For information, address HarperCollins Publishers, 195 Broadway, New York, NY 10007.

HarperCollins books may be purchased for educational, business, or sales promotional use. For information, please email the Special Markets Department at SPsales@harpercollins.com.

FIRST EDITION

Designed by Michele Cameron

Library of Congress Cataloging-in-Publication Data has been applied for.

ISBN 978-0-06-300310-1 (hardcover)
ISBN 978-0-06-335786-0 (international edition)

24 25 26 27 28 LBC 5 4 3 2 1

FOR KIM, FOR TEN
WONDERFUL YEARS
WORKING TOGETHER.
THANK YOU FOR
EVERYTHING!

THE MIDNIGHT FEAST

THE WOODS

An engine idling on the edge of the woods at night.

A message left in a hollow tree.
A summoning.

Prologue

A FOX, BROWSING IN THE *dead beech leaves for the trail of a rabbit, stops still. Raises its head, ears pricked, paw raised, before turning and fleeing. The owls halt their night-time chorus, lifting as silent pale ghosts from the branches to find another patch of woodland. A small herd of deer scatters more noisily, crashing through the undergrowth in its haste to get away.*

Something is moving through the trees now, disturbing the normal night-time harmony. Shadows with form, with substance. Rustling through the leaves, treading upon the woodland floor, snapping twig and bracken.

Deep in the woods they gather. The same clearing they have always used; and their forebears before them, since the legends began. A strange flock. Black-robed, beast-headed. Born of the unknown depths of the wood: an image from a medieval woodcut, a dark folktale to frighten badly behaved children. In the modern world, a world of busyness, of speed and connection, they make no sense. But here among the trees, hidden from moonlight and starlight, it is as if the modern world is the fairy tale: other and strange.

A short distance away, the old man sits in his study in the woods: a converted cabin surrounded by ancient trees.

The door is ajar to the elements. Now that darkness has fallen there's a chill to the air. It creeps in at the open door, it rifles through the papers on the desk.

In front of him is a single feather, its black down ruffled by the breeze. The old man doesn't pay it any attention.

He doesn't pay it any attention because he is dead.

Bella

IT'S OPENING NIGHT OF THE Manor, the "new jewel of the Dorset coastline." The drama is all out front: soaring ocean views, emerald lawns stretching to the cliff edge, the Owen Dacre–designed infinity pool. But on this side, the landward side, there's another world. A bristle of dense ancient forest behind the main building, which guests can access via a series of gravel paths that wind between the "Woodland Hutches." One of these is mine.

I close the door. Follow the sound of music and laughter through the purple twilight to the welcome drinks, which are taking place on the very edge of the trees. I step into a chic take on a woodland grotto. Hundreds of lanterns hang from branches. An actual harpist plays. Antique rugs and huge scatter cushions have been strewn about the forest floor with bohemian abandon. I sit down on one, gulp back a "Woodland Spirit" cocktail—"a dash of locally harvested birch bitters and rosemary infused gin."

My fellow guests loll around, chatty and giddy with the anticipation of a weekend in the sun beside the sea with nothing to do but eat, drink, swim, and make merry. Many of them seem to know one another: wandering about shrieking as they bump into old friends, some reclining on the rugs and calling to acquaintances to join them. The vibe is relaxed, albeit spiced with a faint note of social competition.

No one needs the ultra-soft woolen blankets provided because—though the sun is setting—it's still warm enough to wear only a single layer of linen (there's a lot of linen). The first flare of the impending heatwave.

In the middle of the scene, like a fairy queen—like Titania on her woodland throne—sits the owner of The Manor. Francesca Meadows. Radiant in a pale rose, off-shoulder fantasia of washed silk, hair rippling down her back, face aglow with candlelight. *The culmination of a dream*: that's what she said in the article. *I'm so excited to share this place with everyone.* Well, everyone who can afford it, anyway. But who's quibbling?

I look around me. I suppose it's all pretty idyllic if you're part of a couple or larger group, if you've come here for a weekend of escaping the city. Maybe it's just me for whom it doesn't feel quite so mellow and chummy.

I wait for the alcohol to hit, my gaze flitting toward the deepening shadows between the trees, to the ragged ceiling of branches uplit by the lanterns, down to my own outfit: linen, yes, but with the tell-tale creases that show it's just been pulled from a packet. But the one place my eyes linger time and again—I can't help it—is on the face of Francesca Meadows. She looks so zen. So very fucking content.

Suddenly there's a commotion, deep in the wood. Her gaze snaps in that direction. The guests fall silent and peer into the gloom. The harpist stops playing.

Suddenly a group of newcomers bursts into the grotto. Not dressed in linen. A raggle-taggle bunch in hiking boots. Mainly women, a few piercings and tats, untouched gray roots. Francesca Meadows doesn't move, her smile doesn't snag. But a member of the staff—a small blonde woman in a white shirt and heels, perhaps a manager—walks toward them, as if dispatched by silent command. She speaks in a discreet murmur. But the leader of the raggedy pack is having none of it.

"I don't give a flying fuck," she says. "There's been a right of way through here for centuries—before that house even existed. *You're* the ones trespassing. Local people have always walked among these trees . . . using their wood, their flora and fauna. There's a unique convergence of ley lines here. Keeping people away from the land—from *their* land—like this, it's evil. It's a kind of murder."

She looks over the woman's head and straight at Francesca Meadows as she shouts: "I'm talking to you, by the way! I don't care that you clearly paid off the council, whatever it was you did. As far as we're concerned these woods belong to *us* more than they ever will to you. So you can just let us carry on through here, or we can *really* make a scene. What's it gonna be?"

The manager takes a step back, uncertain. There's a split-second glance toward the owner. Perhaps the tiniest inclination of Francesca Meadows's golden head. Then the manager mutters something to the little crew. Whatever it is it seems to work because after a moment's deliberation they carry on their way. Straight through the clearing—looking around in distaste. Beneath the force of their glares the lounging guests sit up a little straighter, rearrange their rumpled clothing. One of the trespassers tips a cocktail over with her foot and the group departs to the sound of breaking glass.

The harpist resumes her playing, the barman picks up his cocktail shaker.

But I can feel it. Something in the air has changed.

The Day After the Solstice

THE FISHING BOAT GOES OUT just before dawn, wake shining silver in the halogen lamps. The fishermen are heading for the deep water, tracking a wide berth around The Giant's Hand, five limestone stacks that stick out beyond the line of the cliffs like four huge fingers and a thumb. It's a little before five in the morning. This is almost the earliest the sun will rise all year: the day after midsummer, the longest day.

Already the sky is pinkening from violet to mauve. Something strange this morning, though. A second streak of color has appeared, like a duplicate sunrise but in the opposite direction, over the land. A paint spatter of livid scarlet.

Later, they will say they could actually feel the heat of it. Even there, all the way out to sea. The hot breath of it on the backs of their necks like the warmth of a second sun.

"What's that light?" The first to notice points it out to the guy next to him.

"What, mate?"

"There: right there above the cliffs."

Now the other guys turn to look, too. "That's not a light. That's . . . what *is* that? Oh. Shit."

"That's a fire."

"Something's burning. Right on the coastline."

As the wind shifts they smell the smoke, too. Flecks of ash appear in the air, dancing around them, settling upon the deck, the waves.

"Jesus. It's a building."

"It's that place. The hotel that just opened . . . The Manor."

They cut the engine. Stop and watch. All of them fall silent for a moment. Staring. Horrified. Thrilled.

One guy takes out a pair of binoculars. Another takes out his phone. "Can't feel all that bad," he says, snapping a few shots. "The shit they've been up to. Feels like just deserts."

A third man snatches at the phone. "Nah—that's not on, mate. People could be dead in there. Innocent people . . . members of staff . . . locals."

All of them fall silent as this possibility sinks in. They watch the smoke, which is beginning to billow in huge ashen clouds. They can smell it now, acrid, scoring the back of the nostrils.

One of the guys gets on the phone to the police.

The light changes again. The smoke spreads like ink in water, spilling fast across the blue-white of early morning, blocking out the newly risen sun. It's as though the darkness of night is returning, a shroud being drawn across the sky. It is as though whatever is happening back there on the cliffs has canceled the dawn.

Eddie

OPENING NIGHT

IT'S JUST BEFORE MIDNIGHT. NEARLY the end of my shift. All the guests are still at the welcome drinks so the inside bar is empty. I'm unloading glasses from a crate onto the shelves and listening to Rita Ora on my headphones. The guys on the rugby team used to give me crap for my music tastes, but "I'll Be There" has really been getting me through the mountains of dirty dishes and glasses—stacking and unloading and rinsing and doing it all again as they come down from the Seashard (the restaurant here). I saw the food when it went out: it looked amazing. But it's like stuff you'd feed to pigs now. I'm hungry but not even tempted to steal a bite.

It's my first proper shift, now the hotel's full of guests. I still haven't got the hang of the sprayer hose thing: I've managed to soak my shoes twice. All the staff wear trainers here at The Manor, because the whole vibe is "casual," but they're Common Projects, which I'd never actually buy myself because they cost about three times my weekly pay.

I jump as someone lifts one of the cans from my ear. But it's just Ruby, my mate from reception.

"All right Eds? Come to grab a Coke." I reach into the fridge and hand her one. "Need some caffeine. Frigging knackered from smiling all day."

Ruby's moved down from London. Most front-of-house jobs were taken by non-locals, like her, with experience (she worked somewhere called Chiltern Firehouse) and the right accent.

A guy wearing a pale pink suit and posh trainers wanders in. "Got any Macallan twenty-five in here?" He peers at the shelf behind me. "Only eighteen? Huh." He huffs off, clearly unimpressed. Ruby takes a slug of her Coke. When he's out of sight she says, "Do you feel like there are men whose entire personality is 'rich white douche'?" She takes another sip. "Think most of them are staying this weekend."

Ruby's one of the few members of staff here who isn't white—her dad's Trinidadian. When she's not in uniform she wears a leather trench and little Matrix-style glasses and I'd find her too pretty and cool to chat to if she wasn't also super nice and a bit geeky—she's starting an English MA at Exeter soon. Besides, there's no way she's into Dorset farm boys who are miles thicker than her, so I don't have a chance to blow in the first place.

After Ruby's gone I turn my music up and get into a rhythm stacking tallboys, tumblers, martini glasses, champagne coupes. There's a little game I play when I put them into the dishwasher: trying to guess the cocktail from the smell and the color of the liquid left behind. Maybe it sounds lame, but I think of it like practice. I feel like a good bartender would be able to work it out. The indoor bar special is "The Manor Mule": grapefruit, ginger, vodka, and a dash of CBD oil—that stuff seems to be in everything here.

Turns out working summers on your dad's farm doesn't qualify you for more than washing dishes. But everyone has to start somewhere, right? And if I "prove myself" over the next couple of days, the manager, Michelle, says I can help out at the feast on Saturday night, serving drinks and that. I want to be a bartender, to escape Tome and have a whole new life in London. In a way the ACL injury was a relief. I didn't want to play rugby at that level. It wasn't fun anymore, there was too much pressure. I don't want to go to uni, either. And I definitely don't want my dad's life, to take over the farm. My brother was meant to do that.

I catch a flicker of movement out of the corner of my eye. Just manage not to swear when I see a dark figure approaching the bar. Where did she appear from? She moves nearer, into the light.

"Hi," she says. "Can I get a martini?"

She looks like London and money. Blonde, reddish lipstick, smells of smoky, expensive perfume. Kind of old. Not mum old but definitely a lot older than me. But she has a pretty face, nice normal eyebrows. Loads of scary eyebrows around these days. My ex-girlfriend Delilah went through a stage of drawing hers on with a Sharpie.

I wipe my damp hands on my jeans and clear my throat. I'm not supposed to make drinks. If Michelle caught me . . .

But I can't say it. I can't bring myself to tell this woman that I'm just the guy who does the dishes.

"Er . . . gin or vodka?" I ask.

"Which would you choose?"

Isn't someone like her meant to know how they take their martini? I notice there's something jumpy about her now I look more closely. She's fiddling with the stack of cocktail napkins, tearing one into ragged little strips. I clear my throat. "I guess it depends what you like?" To sound more confident, I use a line I heard Lewis, the head bartender, use: "But it's gin for the win, if you ask me." Like I make hundreds of them a day. "And I can do dirty or with a twist."

She smiles almost gratefully. "Gin it is, then. I trust you. Two gin martinis, please. What does dirty mean?"

I blush. Hopefully it's dark enough in here that she can't see. "Er . . . it means you add olive brine."

"Dirty then, please."

Is she flirting? Delilah always said I was totally thick about girls coming on to me: "Fuckssake Eddie. They could come over, flash their tits, and dry hump you and you'd be like: 'Oh, that Jenny's friendly, isn't she?' "

"Two dirty gin martinis coming right up," I say, as confidently as I can. Do I sound like a knob? Like a West Country farm boy trying to be something he's not? Well, guess that's exactly what I am.

"You know what?" She slides off the bar stool. She's shorter than I imagined, but then I'm taller than pretty much everyone. "Could you bring them to my room? I'm in Woodland Hutch number"—

she fishes a key out of her bag, checks it—"eleven. The one nearest the woods."

"Er . . ." I think. If Michelle caught me going to a guest's room she might actually murder me. Ruby told me yesterday she thinks Michelle has "crazy Liz Truss eyes" and that: "you don't want to get on the wrong side of her. She'd cut you in your sleep."

"I'd be so grateful," the guest says, and flashes a smile. There's something kind of needy about it.

The guests are always right. Michelle literally told us that last week in training. Especially guests who stay somewhere like this.

"Sure," I say. "Coming right up."

I KNOCK ON the door to Woodland Hutch number 11 ten minutes later. It's a pretty long walk to the Hutches along the lamplit gravel paths with a tray of drinks, especially while keeping an eye out for Michelle. The welcome drinks must have finished: there's no music or voices, all I can hear are the owls and the sound of the wind in the leaves. This Hutch is the farthest away from the main building, pressed up against the trees, branches curling round it like they're trying to claw it deeper into the woods. You couldn't pay me to sleep here.

These rooms are called Hutches because rich people like to pretend they're roughing it when really they're tucked up in super kings with their own outdoor bath and rain shower. They're the cheapest ones, without the sea views of the Clifftop Cabins round the other side of The Manor. Cheap relative to the others, that is. The new Treehouse rooms, I suppose, will be for rich people who want the same sort of experience but also to sleep several feet off the ground.

"Hey," the guest says as she opens the door. "You were quick." Somehow in her husky voice it sounds kind of dirty, like Nigella talking about sausages or melted butter (Mum and I used to watch a lot of cooking shows together; Nigella was my first major crush). Her lipstick's a little smudged and she's taken off her shoes.

I want to say something cool or clever, but all I manage is: "Yeah, no worries."

"How about you set the drinks down in here?" She holds open the door to the room. "Come in."

As I shrug off my soggy shoes (I've been hardcore trained in this sort of thing by Mum) I sneak a look around. I've haven't been inside any guest rooms yet. I don't know what I was expecting but it's even posher than I'd imagined. It's small, but there's a big four-poster bed at one end draped in white linen and a couple of dark green velvet armchairs at its foot, a glass and gold coffee table between them. The fact that it's a wooden cabin somehow makes all the fancy furniture look even more fancy. And it *smells* expensive, like the rest of The Manor. They've been diffusing a "signature scent" through all the spaces. Ruby says it gives her a migraine.

I set the tray down on the coffee table. I'm expecting a husband or boyfriend or the like to pop out for the second martini, but there's no one. The guest sits down in an armchair, takes one of the glasses. The breeze must have picked up because the branches are scrabbling against the windows now.

"And the other drink?" I ask. "Shall I just leave it here?" Yeah, I'm hovering a bit as this could be my first chance—my only chance?— for a tip.

"That one's for you," she says.

"Er—" I've already crossed a line here but I reckon that would be going about several thousand miles beyond it. "I don't—"

"It's nearly midnight. There's no one else in the indoor bar. You'll be fine. Keep me company?" She pats the seat next to her.

There's something about the way she said that last bit. Her voice changed. She sounded suddenly—what? Lonely? Afraid? Like she doesn't want to be left here by herself? I sit down on the very edge of the armchair, feeling seriously uncomfortable.

Another scrabbling of branches against the roof and I see her wince.

"This was the last room they had," she says. "I guess I just didn't think about what it would be like being here on my own, after dark."

I do get off shift pretty soon. Also, I'm not really sure how to say no. Most of the people who stay at places like this are very used to getting their own way.

She picks up the martini glass, sloppily, and some liquid sloshes over the rim. "Oops!" A nervous little laugh. She takes a sip and says, "You were right."

I blink at her, no idea what she's talking about. "Excuse me?"

"Gin wins. The drink. Try yours."

I take a sip, because again I can't say no. Another line crossed: well done, Eddie. It tastes how I imagine lighter fluid would, like being drunk for the first time. I can't even tell if it's good, but she seems happy so I feel pretty proud. It looks professional, too, with the olive garnish.

"What did you say your name was?"

"Eddie."

"Hi Eddie. I'm Bella. So . . . you're from around here? Your accent . . ."

"Uh, yeah. Nearabouts." I'm not going to tell her I come from the farm down the road because I've already heard a couple of guests complain about the smell. The staff have been laughing about it, too: it's one reason I haven't told most people I work with, either.

She's watching me closely, like she's trying to work something out. I can feel myself blushing again.

"Sorry," she says, realizing she's staring. She glances away, reaching for her drink.

There's a sound from outside. A moan. That isn't what I think it is, is it? I can feel my blush getting worse; I'm glad it's dimly lit in here. Many things at The Manor are state-of-the-art—but maybe not the soundproofing in the Woodland Hutches. Another sound: a squeal . . . then a groan. Oh God. Oh no. Somewhere pretty nearby—maybe even only a few meters away—someone has started having really loud, Pornhub-style sex.

I don't know what to do with my face. Then she laughs, which is a relief because I can copy her and pretend I'm not totally mortified. When the laughter dies away I can't think of anything to say. Maybe she can't either because the silence stretches until it would be really difficult to get any words into it. There are some more yelps and a rhythmic thumping. I couldn't cringe any harder. It feels even quieter in here by comparison.

"I don't really know what I'm doing here," she blurts out, suddenly. Almost like she's talking to herself.

"What, in this room?" That makes two of us, I guess.

"No . . . I mean here, at The Manor. I booked it on impulse, you know?" She seems sort of anxious. Almost . . . afraid? "And now . . . well, now that I'm here I'm wondering whether it was such a good idea—" She breaks off. "Shit, sorry. I'm rambling. It's the martini, I guess." But she doesn't sound drunk. She sounds wired.

I don't really see how it could ever be a bad thing, being able to afford three nights in a place like this . . . where all you need to think about is whether to go to the pool or beach, what to eat for breakfast. Rich people problems. Ruby says they manage to make everything into a drama because when you have no real difficulty in your life you end up creating your own.

"I mean . . . it seems like it would be a pretty nice place to stay?" I say.

"Yeah," she says. "Yeah, I suppose it would be. If—" She stops again and smiles. "I definitely think I'm a little tipsy." She holds up the martini. "This is dangerous stuff!" But she takes another long drink, anyway.

When I next glance at her she's looking at me so intensely I don't know what to do with my face.

"Sorry," she says. "There's something about you that reminds me—" She trails off, lifts her hand. "Maybe it's your mouth. The shape, here." Now her finger is tracing the outline of my top lip. I can feel the skin tingling. Is she coming on to me? Is this actually happening?

There's another moan from the cabin nearby.

It's been ages since I had sex. Suddenly even bad sex noises seem a turn-on.

I can smell the booze on her breath. She is fit, even if she's older. And there's something kind of intense about her and this whole situation, which is also pretty hot.

She smiles at me—but it's not like before, when we were laughing. I smile back.

Somehow, we seem to have moved a little closer.

I think I know what's about to happen but I still can't quite believe it.

And then it's happening. She's kissing me. Or we're kissing each other . . . because I definitely seem to be kissing her back. Am I into it? I mean, I'm hard. But then I'm also a nineteen-year-old guy, so most things make me hard.

Except . . . there's also the whole power dynamic which makes me feel weird. Am I going to sleep with a guest because I'm too polite to say no? I've only slept with one other person before this. Does that mean I'll be rubbish? When we broke up Delilah said that she "faked it half the time." I think about that way more than I'd like to.

I squeeze my eyes shut and try to drown Delilah out.

And then it's over. She's pulling away. I open my eyes.

She's staring at me. I have the impression that she's surprised to see me sitting here, that she was expecting someone else. "Oh shit," she says, after a few seconds. "I—God, I'm sorry. I have to go—er, I have to go to the bathroom."

When she gets up, she staggers a little bit and I realize she may be more than a "little tipsy." As she disappears into the bathroom I spot the half-empty bottle of sparkling wine on the dressing table.

I sit here in this posh room waiting for my hard-on to go down, wondering what to do next. Awkward doesn't even begin to describe it. If she's drunk and I'm not . . . well, that's pretty bad, isn't it? That really doesn't look good at all.

I just want to leg it now. I could do it easily while she's still in the bathroom. But that would be really rude. It might make it worse, too, if, I dunno, I make some sort of enemy of her by doing it. She could get me fired on my first proper day of service.

I step toward the door and manage to knock against the chest of drawers. A folder falls to the floor and a load of paper spills out. Bollocks. I get down on my hands and knees to shovel it all back inside, but then I stop short. It's a load of articles, cut from magazines and papers. They all seem to be about Francesca Meadows, the boss of The Manor. Loads and loads of them. One about her wedding to the architect Owen Dacre a couple of months ago. I read the big quote at the top of another: *"I wanted to create a place for our guests to escape their super stressful lives in the city, somewhere they can find peace. I know some might say that the average person can't afford it, but I wanted this place to be perfect and perfection is expensive."*

On the page just beneath there's a photograph of the boss holding a very groomed white cockerel. The word *CUNT* is written across it in biro. The letters have been pressed so hard they've ripped the paper.

The handle to the bathroom door is turning. I feel like I've seen something I shouldn't. I dump the pile of papers back on the desk and just manage to dive out of the front door before she steps back into the room.

Francesca

OPENING NIGHT AT LAST. I'VE waited for this moment for so long. The Manor is teeming with guests for the first time and I'm feeling *blessed*. That's the word I've written in my journal, which I write in every day to root myself in the now (I'm really good at living in the now). I'll let you in on a little secret here: *blessed* is actually the word I write most days. I know it's become something of an Instagram cliché. But it's true for me and that's the important thing. Authenticity is key, isn't it?

I'm sitting in my meditation space in our apartment at the top of The Manor, looking out through the windows. It's still gloriously warm. Climate change is a terrible thing but one has to stay positive and you can't deny it's good for business. The sky's as clear as I've ever seen it, the stars so bright and close the night sky reminds me of the black opal that's set into a gold ring on my left hand. My crystals never fail me. They're so important, actually, that every one of our rooms here has a little selection of hand-picked stones in them, to help meet our guests' needs. It's touches like that, I know, that set The Manor apart from the rest. Black opal signifies purification for the body and soul, did you know that? "Not that you need it," my new husband, Owen, told me. Oh, and it provides you with a shield against negative energy.

I felt the need for that a couple of hours ago. That little scene at the welcome drinks—those trespassers stumbling across the beautiful woodland idyll we'd created. I'm not going to dwell. But really, you would think by now they would just accept that they lost, fair and square. It's the countryside, for goodness' sake—they've got plenty of space to ramble about in without having to trample over private land.

I run my fingertips over the black stone. *Breathe in, breathe out.* I look down at the lawns and the shimmering silver of the sea beyond, bathed in the light of the gibbous moon. My queendom.

Everything here is utterly perfect, save a couple of niggles. The first is Seaview Farm, just down the road. The farmer . . . I don't want to speak ill of anyone—it just isn't in my nature—but my goodness, he's such a wild-looking brute and the farm is an eyesore, too. And don't get me started on the smell! The animals look sad, like they're begging for a better life. They honestly do! It's the last thing one would expect to see before turning into our gates. The things I could do with it! Think super clean and beautiful: Soho Farmhouse meets Daylesford Organic. Our guests could wander across in the special wellies we provide, take tours and feed baby lambs from bottles and select their own eggs for breakfast. All just a dream right now—but I came across some interesting documents among my grandfather's papers suggesting there's a question over the man's ownership of a large chunk of that land. I've had a little chat with my lawyers, lodged something with the local council. So, watch this space! I've got a couple of new friends on the council now. Nothing's impossible: I learned that when I got the footpath rerouted.

You see, I've always found that everything works out for me in life, better than works out. Take this place: fully booked for six months from the day we opened reservations! We're starting as we mean to go on, with a magnificent celebration. When I realized our opening weekend fell over the solstice it felt fated. Here was our way to say we'd arrived, with something curated, experiential. An alfresco "midnight feast." It's not enough these days to offer all the creature comforts and top-quality food. Guests expect something more. A little *magic.* Something they can feel part of, something they can talk about when they return home, something, yes . . . to stir envy in friends and family, social media followers (though officially we do discourage use of phones here, to make sure our guests really connect and ground themselves). A little healthy envy, we can work with that!

And there's a lot of local pagan history that I want to tap into, old rural traditions of celebrating the seasons . . . but with a fresh, modern touch. Nothing macabre, you know? Some of the local legends are a little on the darker side. And nothing *crusty*. "Pagan chic," you could say. I have this vision of Saturday night's celebrations taking place outside under a clear, starlit sky. The forecast suggests I've manifested my desire. See? I always get what I want. It's going to be fabulous. I can feel it.

I close my eyes to truly experience the moon's energy on my face. It's so important to engage all your senses, to check in with your environment. But it's only now that I become aware of the *thump thump thump* of distant bass. A shout, some laughter. It's coming from the beach below the hotel, I know it. They're back. I didn't think they'd have the audacity to trespass once The Manor was actually open. That's *my* beach.

I pick up my phone and call Michelle. "Hello, lovely," I say, lightly. "It's happening again. Can you sort?"

"You've got it Francesca. No problem!" Michelle. So eager to be of service. I can hear she's practically vibrating with excitement at this opportunity to prove herself. She has been by my side every day for the last six months in the run-up to opening. As loyal and obedient as a trained spaniel.

"You're a *star*," I say. "You know that, don't you? Thank you."

Another thundering of bass, just as I hang up. And *whoosh*—a flame of pure rage leaps up inside me so fast it leaves me breathless.

No Francesca. Inhale. *That's not who you are. You are so much bigger than this. Reach for the light. Find the still place. Exhale.*

Bella

OH . . . SHIT. WHAT WAS I thinking?

I step out of the bathroom. I've just splashed a load of cold water on my face and feel a lot more sober. I mean, still drunk, yes, but now painfully aware of every detail of what just happened.

The Hutch is empty, the front door banging on its latch. Eddie the bartender has gone. I'm relieved, but also mortified. Did he feel like he had to run away?

Jesus. I'm a mother, for God's sake. Maybe even old enough to be his?

The thing is, I didn't want to be alone here beside the woods.

I booked this place months ago. I've been thinking about my stay for so long. But now I've arrived I'm riddled with doubt. I can't believe I'm really here. I'm not sure I'm brave enough.

I take a long, hot shower. Then I sit down at the dressing table to try and collect my thoughts. I'm wearing the soft forest-green gown provided: *THE MANOR* embroidered on the pocket, same as the typeface on the little stationery kit they've left in the room. There's a sage stick, too, for "cleansing" the space. A branded box of matches beside it, which seems brave. Also a "bespoke selection of crystals." Very The Manor: woo-woo, but still chic. As the young woman on reception explained, they come with a little velvet pouch and gold chain, fashioned by a hot young jewelry designer, to wear round your neck for the duration of your stay. I pick up one of the stones—small and black, smoothly polished—and roll it inside my palm. The little booklet on the table tells me, "Your crystals all come ready charged for your use and healing," and I wonder how you go about charging a crystal. I think of my own soul-sickness. A chronic condition, one I've lived with since my teens. Somehow I don't think crystals are going to cut it.

I glance in the mirror and get a shock. I don't recognize the person reflected there. In the dim light my lipstick is a red gash. My eyes have a black glitter.

The thing is, tonight was an experiment. I don't think I've ever ordered a martini before in my life. And everything with the bartender was totally out of character, but that makes a sort of sense because I am *in* character. This person in the mirror, this room, those clothes hanging in the closet . . . even the name on the booking are not mine. One of the quirks of The Manor: I had to send a biography over in advance. "We like to know who we're welcoming into our family here." Putting it together reminded me of how I once enjoyed creative writing at school, the diaries I used to keep. It was almost fun, constructing a new persona around my rented wardrobe. The woman in the mirror works in an obscure part of film production. She's the sort of person who has so much self-confidence she's happy staying on her own in a hotel for a weekend. Apparently she's also someone who enjoys seducing members of staff.

I glance at the velvet armchairs and think of how we sat, the two of us, with our drinks. And the moment I realized that Eddie was waiting—waiting even to take a sip of his drink, his full glass held awkwardly in one hand. It was up to me to set the agenda. This is how men must feel, I realized. Older men, wealthy men. The power felt alien. Dangerous. He seemed like a sweet guy, too. There was an innocence, a goodness, there. They don't make them like that anymore. Or at least, I thought they didn't. I knew a boy like him once, with that same lack of edge.

I grab a tissue and dash off my lipstick. I never wear red, or this much make-up full stop, and the foreignness of my own reflection is freaking me out. When I take the tissue away, I see lipstick has smeared beneath my mouth on one side. I look like an evil succubus that rejuvenates herself by drinking the blood of young bartenders. I also look drunk and several years older than I am.

I put my head in my hands and try to think. Try to breathe normally.

What the fuck am I doing here?

I glance toward the dressing table, see all the clippings piled haphazardly on top. So Eddie saw them. I try and work out just how weird it would seem through his eyes. Maybe it just looks like I really do my research before I stay somewhere? But I suppose the image with *CUNT* scrawled across it kind of puts paid to that idea.

The photo of Francesca Meadows comes from the *Harper's Bazaar* article. Her hair combed into buttery pre-Raphaelite waves, spilling over gleaming bare shoulders. She appears to be entirely naked, but the photo's cropped below the elbows and her torso is obscured by the white cockerel she's cradling in her arms, its feathers as lustrous as her hair, its crest the same strawberry-stained red as her lips. The headline: *MEET THE CHATELAINE OF YOUR NEW COUNTRYSIDE EDEN.*

Someone sent it to me. That's the really strange part, the thing that's kept me awake at night since, wondering: who? Why?

I remember the post hitting the doormat. Picking it up while chewing on a slice of toast. Opening the envelope, pulling out the article.

By now I can practically quote it.

"Such happy memories of my time there . . ."

"Idyllic summer days . . ."

"Such larks. Midnight feasts and parties in the treehouse. I want to capture the adult version of that."

The strange fizzing sensation in my ears.

I remember gagging as the toast stuck in my throat. For a moment I thought I might vomit.

"Bookings open in a few days' time," the article read.

My daughter, Grace, upstairs, crying because she'd woken from her nap.

Shit, I realize I forgot to check if bedtime went OK. She's staying with Mum while I'm here on my "work trip." My "Team Bonding Weekend." Because receptionists in estate agents' offices really get invited on this sort of thing. This is the kind of place our clients would stay—the ones who come in shopping for a second home in the countryside. Not little old me. What would Mum say, if she knew where I was?

I shouldn't be here, shouldn't be doing this.

Shouldn't be charging around making drunken passes at barmen. Shouldn't be doing anything that takes me more than a few centimeters from that warm, chubby little body, those small, grasping, surprisingly strong hands, those serious dark eyes that seem to stare into my soul with a kind of ancient wisdom: *who are you?*

This isn't my place. It's such a strange feeling. Like I'm playing truant from my own life.

No, I remind myself. This is *the* place. This is necessary. In a funny way I'm doing this for her, for my tiny helpless daughter. What will I pass on to her? Who do I want to be for her?

But I should be honest: I'm doing it for me, too.

The branches scrabble against the roof again. I can see them through the windows, pressing against the glass. I get up and draw the curtains, but it doesn't make me feel all that much better.

The questions I've been asking myself since I first read about the opening of The Manor come to me again. Who sent me that article? Why? And more importantly, most important of all: what do they know?

The Day After the Solstice

THE FISHERMEN HAVE TURNED THE boat round. Come in closer for a better look at the ruin of the building. Smoke still pours from it as it burns to the bones: a huge black skeleton squatting above the cliffs.

Then one of the men frowns. Steps closer to the bow of the boat, shielding his eyes. Points to something a little farther along the coast. "What *is* that? Down there. See it?"

"Where?"

"Near the bottom of the cliffs. Beneath the farm. It looks like—" He catches himself, unwilling to say it before being sure.

"Fuck," one says, under his breath.

It's not the first time they've come across a body. You see all sorts out at sea: everything that can find its way into a net, that can float up to rest on the surface. But this is different. The blood, for one thing. You don't see any blood with a drowning victim. And by then the corpses seem barely human—poor bloated creatures risen from the deep, transfigured by the salt water into something other and strange.

The horror of it appears to them in fragments. An outstretched, bloodied arm: the fingers of the hand pale as limestone in the early morning light. The limbs lying at improbable angles. Hair gleaming in the first rays of sun. The rest of the head—no. Too horrible to contemplate for longer than a few seconds. The impact of the fall. The face completely gone.

Francesca

OPENING NIGHT

I STEP ONTO THE MOONLIT, dew-wet lawn in bare feet, the better to connect myself to the earth. I can still hear the tinny whine of music from the beach, the buzz of the speakers. I close my eyes, release myself from caring. Michelle is on the case.

There's just one little thing I need to do before this weekend begins in earnest. Another sort of release. A purging. A quick glance behind me to check I'm not being observed.

In one hand I hold the urn containing my grandfather's ashes. His original wish was to be scattered beside the Orangery where his old Labrador Kipling was buried, but I didn't want to risk any macabre vibrations beside what is now our treatment center. I'm sure he'd understand. He was pragmatic above everything.

Granmama died before Grandfa and it turned out this place was actually hers. She left it to me in trust. I suspect it was a little redress to Grandfa for his many indiscretions, to my mother for barely setting foot here in adulthood, to my older brothers for running roughshod all over the place. Evidently she saw me as its rightful inheritor.

I suppose she might raise a perfectly groomed eyebrow at my opening the place up to paying guests. But one has to move with the times. Besides, our guests are carefully curated. They're the right kind of people. That's why I like to call them our "family."

I open the jar. In graceful, sweeping motions I scatter Grandfa's earthly remains into the warm breeze, which carries him out over the cliffs and out to sea.

There. Gone. A weight lifted.

One of the first things I did after darling Grandfa finally went was to get rid of his woodland study. He had his fatal heart attack in it, so it had some unpleasant associations. He went a little *odd* toward the end, sadly. He spent all his time in there, thinking he was still doing important governmental work. It seemed harmless enough and of course it wouldn't have been right to shuffle the poor old dear into a home as soon as I inherited . . . though I did start to apply for planning permission, that sort of thing.

The last time I came down to visit him (and hand-deliver a very special bottle of whisky to a new friend on the local council) he had one particular obsession. "You must keep the birds happy," he kept saying. "Don't upset the birds." Over and over like that. Such a shame: he once had such a great mind.

"Yes, Grandfa," I told him. Poor old thing. Clearly he'd gone a bit gaga, started believing in local nonsense.

But then he sat up in bed and grabbed hold of my wrist so hard it hurt. "You must not upset the birds. Do you understand?"

"Oh dearie *me*, Arthur," his nurse said, coming back in, "not the birds, *again*."

I cast the final handful of ash onto the breeze. Check that the jar's empty. Check again that no one has witnessed my secret midnight ritual. There. It feels ceremonial, fitting. Drawing a line under what has gone before.

I've always been good at letting go of the past.

Eddie

"OH, THERE YOU ARE, EDDIE," Michelle says. I'm back at the bar, and trying not to look like I've just jumped out of my skin. Michelle has this way of appearing from nowhere like she's trying to catch you slacking off.

I sneak a look at her face. She looks pissed off about something. I wait for her to tell me she knows what I've just been up to, that I'm fired—on my first proper day!—but then she sighs and says, "I've just had a couple on the phone begging me to move them from their Woodland Hutch to one of the sea views—*obviously* none are available, what do they think we are, a sodding Travelodge? It's opening weekend! I almost told them they shouldn't have been so stingy in the first place!"

It's all "we" with Michelle. She's totally bought into "The Manor family" stuff. And I suppose she's allowed to talk about the guests like this, to bitch about them, but if I said anything I'd get sacked on the spot. Even with the discount for the construction work, the Woodland Hutches still cost hundreds of pounds a night. I can take a guess at what Michelle gets paid—more than me but not that much more. But I suppose working at places like this kind of messes with your idea of what's normal.

She comes behind the bar and I get such a strong hit of her perfume I step back. They've got us wearing the fragrances that are available in the onsite shop—The Manor Market—as it's "so important in creating ambience" and it smells like Michelle has chucked the stuff on, like she thinks that will show everyone just what a loyal employee she is. She rummages around in the fridge, pulls out a bottle of white, and sloshes it into a glass, pouring so it's almost full to the brim.

"You holding up, Eddie?" she asks.

"Yeah," I say, carefully. During the pre-opening training period I noticed Michelle sometimes acts like she's your best mate, other times like she's queen of the universe and you're something caught on the sole of her shoe. It's hard to keep up and it's best to play it safe.

She takes a big gulp and half the wine seems to disappear in one go. She's gripping the glass so tight I'm worried the bowl might break. I suppose this must all be pretty stressful for her. I'm not going to be the one to remind her that she has to drive home (most of the staff drive). It's different in this little corner of Dorset. People drink and drive all the time on these country lanes, like it's the seventies or something.

"Why did they want to move so badly?" I ask.

"What?" She frowns at me over the rim of her wine glass.

"The guests: why did they want to move out of the Woodland Hutch?"

"Oh. They said they didn't like the"—she makes little quote marks with her fingers—"'atmosphere.' That the trees were closer than they'd imagined. But they also kept going on about hearing strange sounds from the woods, seeing lights, that sort of thing." She rolls her eyes. "Don't know if that was before or after they'd drunk their complimentary bottle of sparkling Bacchus. Know what I'm saying?"

I don't blame them, not that I'm going to say that to Michelle. Mum always warned me not to play in the woods after dark. "It's not safe," she said. "You never know who might be prowling around in there." I always assumed it was her being super-paranoid, after everything that happened with my brother. But local people believe stuff about these woods. Lately I've gone back to doing what I did as a kid: closing the curtains carefully at night, so there's no gap. Otherwise it feels (I know how stupid this sounds) like the woods are watching me.

"You're off your shift now, aren't you?" Michelle's looking at her watch.

"Er, yeah," I say, "finished at midnight."

"Well. There are some youths down on the beach again." The way Michelle says "youths" makes her sound about eighty, even though I reckon she can only be about thirty-five. "Francesca has alerted me to it. Now we're open, she's extremely concerned about it."

The way Michelle says Francesca's name: it's like she gets this thrill from it. Ruby reckons she's a little in love with our boss. "Or in something, anyway. Doubt Francesca even knows her name," Ruby says. But she's wrong. The boss seems to know everyone's name. Even though she seems to float around, smiling at everyone . . . I don't think she misses a thing.

"So, Eddie," Michelle says, back in scary boss mode, "could you go and have a word with them?" She's quite small, Michelle, but you know you don't want to mess with her. She's all sharp angles: that white shirt with its pointed collar, the square blonde bob, the spiky shoes.

"Er . . ." I say, "I don't think—"

"You want to work behind bar, right?" Then she smiles. She's scarier when she smiles. "Let me spell it out. You do something like this, it doesn't get forgotten." She taps the side of her head with a finger. "*Think* of that appraisal, Eddie!" She looks me up and down. "You're a big boy. I believe in you. I've chosen you specially because I think you know this area better than most. Am I right?" She eyeballs me until I drop my gaze. Does she know I faked my address on the job application? That I actually come from next door, from Seaview Farm? I wouldn't put it past her to have found out somehow. I also wouldn't put it past her to use it against me if I don't do what she says.

"Er—"

"Good," Michelle says, even though I didn't actually agree to anything. "Sometimes as staff we have to go above and beyond. We have to do things that make us feel uncomfortable. I'm sure you understand."

I WHEEL MY bike out of the shelter behind the main building and leave it by the gate at the cliff edge. The moon is nearly full, and a way off the coast the limestone rocks of The Giant's Hand are lit up so they look like huge silver fingers reaching out of the black water. Beyond that, across the dark space of sea, I can make out the faint lights of the Isle of Wight. The stars are really clear, too. My brother knew a bit about stars. That's one of the last memories I have of him. "There's the Great Bear," I remember him saying. "That's me. And there's you, the Little Bear." I know if I searched for them now in the sky I'd be able to find them, but mostly I avoid looking.

There's a shout from down below. I so don't want to do this. But you don't say no to Michelle, so I plug in the code to the gate that leads to the steps down to the beach. This is the only way to reach the beach from land, via the front lawns of The Manor, so the local kids must've come by boat. Yeah: I can just make out a small inflatable dinghy pulled up on the sand. They've lit a big bonfire in the middle of the beach. I can see a load of figures sitting around it, hoods pulled up, the little orange dots of their blunts glowing in the dark. Stormzy's blasting out of a speaker. I take a deep breath and head down the steps.

Once I'm on the sand I call out. "Hey! Guys?" Not that loudly, though. What am I meant to say to them? There's, what, like twenty of them and one of me? And it's a free country, they're allowed to be here. The music's the problem, I guess. That's what Michelle would say. But I doubt they'll be like: "Oh yeah, sure, Eddie, sorry mate! Whoopsie! Whatever you say!"

I could still go back up the steps. I don't think any of them have noticed me. I'm in the shadows here. I could just tell Michelle I tried—

The hit comes out of nowhere, from behind. And then I'm sprawled on the ground, sand gritty in my mouth and nose, ribs aching like I might have broken something. All the breath knocked out of me.

Francesca

I HEAD BACK INTO THE apartment, cleansed. My darling Owen is back from his gym session—he often exercises late at night to help his sleep.

"How were the welcome drinks?" he asks. He's a man of few words, expressing himself through his creations (he's behind all the architectural innovations here).

"Oh, simply *magical*," I tell him. No point in dwelling on the negative and mentioning our trespassers. "Come here and let me look at you, my beautiful man." I reach for his face and hold it between my hands, study the dark lines of his brow and hair, the sharp hook of his nose, the high cheekbones. I've always been drawn to beautiful things and people. Broken ones, too. And Owen is definitely a little broken. His mother walked out when he was a teen. I mean, from what little he's told me, she was clearly unhinged. Sorry: *struggled with her mental health*. I just wish he would share more. I want to help him heal. Besides, I can empathize with absent mothers: it's honestly a wonder I turned out as emotionally intelligent as I did.

But I'd be lying if I said his darkness wasn't attractive to me. It was something I noticed at our first meeting in a London members' club, to discuss my vision for The Manor. I saw the way people turned to look at him. Drawn by his raw magnetism, his presence. The sense of mystery. I caught sight of us in the large mirror opposite and couldn't help but notice how fantastic we looked together. His darkness to my light. A worthy match.

"So," I remember asking, as I sipped my sparkling tea, "what attracts you to the project?"

He thought before speaking. My love's sentences are as precisely and economically constructed as his designs. "I was going to turn it down at first," he said, "when your office called me. I haven't worked in the UK for years. But I couldn't stop thinking about it." I intuited a world of meaning—and damage?—beneath the restraint. And also something that didn't quite make sense.

"My office called you?" I said, confused. There was clearly some misunderstanding: they'd done no such thing. *He'd* made the first contact, surely, when he sent over his pitch? But I didn't make too much of it: I could feel the hand of Fate at work. Besides, as he talked through his plans, I felt myself practically levitating with excitement at the vision and scale. He shared my ambition, knew exactly what the place needed. It felt like the two of us—this partnership, professional as it was then—was meant to be.

We married only a couple of months ago after a whirlwind courtship. When you know, you know. You know?

"Ready for bed?" I ask. I let the vintage silk gown slip from my shoulder. I anoint myself every day in sweet almond and rosemary oils: in the dim light, I know my skin looks like satin.

He nods, silently.

I beam at him. "Just one little thing I wanted to check first. The trees *are* coming down tomorrow, yes?"

He nods. "In the morning. We'll start excavating later."

"That's wonderful news," I say. It is, though I do wish the Treehouses had been completed on schedule. I did try and tell Owen how important they were to me! We shouldn't need to have construction vehicles here on this very special weekend. It's not a good look. But, ever the optimist, I opened up bookings for the autumn and now we haven't a day to spare.

Calm, I remind myself. Serenity and calm. That's what everyone expects of me, including Owen.

I take his hand and lead him through to the bedroom, feeling the calluses on his fingers. Not what you'd expect of the hands of an architect, really.

As we approach the bed, I spot something on the pillow. A single black feather. Bizarre. The windows have been open, so it could have blown in. Still, I'll try to have a word with housekeeping tomorrow as it's a little sloppy of them to miss it.

For now, I'm going to exist in this moment. I brush the feather onto the floor. Then I let my robe follow, a whisper of silk against the boards.

Now I can *really* be myself.

Owen

I LIE LISTENING TO THE ragged sound of my own breathing. My right shoulder aches. Christ. I feel wrung out. I feel . . . used. A little brutalized. But in a good way. At least, I think it is?

The way Francesca is in bed—she's completely different from how she operates in every other aspect of life. You'd think it would be all candles and soft music, staring into each other's eyes, maybe a little tantra. *Making love.*

It's nothing like that. It's fucking. It couldn't be called anything else. It certainly doesn't feel as though love comes into it. This is wild, dark. Often a little violent. Her, not me. I'm her (mostly) willing victim.

I didn't finish tonight. I was too . . . what? Unnerved? I can feel the sting of the scratches she left with her nails . . . I think she might have broken the skin this time. Yes, when I turn my head to check, I see the marks on my right shoulder bear tiny dark beads of blood.

It's a thrill, I guess. It's certainly more to my tastes than candlelight and tantra. But it still throws me. Makes me wonder if there isn't another side to my partner. One I only glimpse in the bedroom, in the same way that you see another side to some people when they're drunk or high; some hidden part of them liberated. Fran doesn't drink or take anything, of course, so maybe sex is the only outlet. But maybe it's just sex. Maybe I'm reading too much into it.

Fran turns toward me and takes my face in both hands. "That was glorious, my beloved. Was it glorious for you?"

And just like that, all traces of the wild animal of a few minutes ago are gone. She gazes into my eyes, unblinking. I'm first to look away, always am. There are things I haven't told her about myself.

I don't think you'd call them secrets. Omissions would be more accurate: omissions of those aspects that don't fit the version of myself I present to her. But don't we all do that, to an extent? Curate ourselves? I suppose being an architect doesn't hurt. The attention to detail. When you put it like that, perhaps I am my most masterful construction.

"Isn't it crazy," she says, "how the universe brought us together like this? It's like I asked for you and you walked into my life. Do you ever think about that? How Fate drew you to me?"

Well, not quite Fate. I had a telephone call—"I'm ringing from the office of Francesca Meadows . . ."—inviting me to pitch for the renovation project. Fran seemed confused when I mentioned it at our first meeting; told me they'd done no such thing. I've tried to remember anything about the voice of the person who called me— but I barely even registered if it was male or female, because I was so fixated on what they were saying. *Tome Manor. Dorset coast. Had I ever heard of it? Would I be interested? We think you'd be perfect for the project.*

I hear a crackle of laughter from the beach, a few shrieks, and, unmistakably, the thump of music, perhaps even louder than before. Dead-beat local wasters with nothing better to do. The thought of them depresses me. They've been turning up most nights since the beginning of summer. Francesca sends staff down early every morning to clear the sand—of the burned wood, the tiny glass popper vials, the empty cans of Tennent's and white cider. Sometimes I help out because I'm always the first down there: I take my morning surf not long after dawn.

Fran pulls her silk robe back around herself and drifts toward the windows to look out. "Michelle assured me she has it in hand," she says.

That woman. I make a face.

"I know you can't bear her, my love. I can't understand it. She's a godsend."

"She's a busybody. And she's a little tacky, surely, for the sort of impression you want to promote here?"

Fran wrinkles her nose. "I *will* have to have a word about those highlights. I could even get my stylist to come down here and work on several of the staff in a day; a few others could also do with some help." She smiles. "But you have to admit, she is so efficient."

The smile leaves her face as another shriek issues from the beach: more animal than human. She sighs. "Why can't they just respect what we've created here? I've tried with them, I really have. We even welcomed them at the locals' evening. You remember?"

"I could hardly forget." It was only a week ago, after all. An appeasing, peacekeeping mission. I absented myself for various reasons but I heard all about it. Drinks were "half price" (though I happen to know Fran ordered cheaper stuff in for them—suspecting they wouldn't appreciate the premium mezcal and artisanal gins). They came, got legless, took the piss out of everything, ran amok. It ended with someone leaving a shit in the pool. An actual human shit. Can you imagine? Fucking animals.

"It was just so . . . disappointing," Fran says. "And you know I don't want to make it about class. I really don't. But you just *can't* with some people."

Yeah, class shouldn't matter, in 2025. But it does. Maybe more than ever. And my wonderful wife—while practically perfect in every way—is perhaps a little bit of a snob. It's OK. I get it. Maybe I've become one, too. Living in this world.

Fran's always saying she wants to really *know* me. She wants me to "be vulnerable" with her. She's a very sensitive person (outside the bedroom). And I have shared with her, in my way. She just doesn't know how selectively. I've told her the bare bones: that I had a shitty, neglectful childhood, and it doesn't sound like her mother was God's gift to parenting either, despite the privilege. So that's something we have in common.

I pull the sheets up over me, then realize that their pristine whiteness is marked by flecks of blood, presumably from my scratched shoulder. It's OK. More where these sheets came from, finest Belgian linen and all. Because this is my life. It's crazy. Some part of me still can't quite believe I sleep here, wear £400 suede trainers, drive a James Bond car—a birthday present from Francesca. That I wake up every morning in this place, like some latter-day Lord of the Manor.

I'm such a fucking fraud.

Eddie

I SPIT SAND OUT OF my mouth. I feel like I've just taken a really hard tackle on the pitch. I roll onto my back and look up.

"Eddie Eddie Eddie. Oi Oi Oi!" He's crouching on his heels, looking down at me.

Shit. Nathan Tate. Everyone my age knows him, mainly because he's the guy who supplies dodgy gear to any house party or rave for twenty miles and because if there's any kind of trouble you just know he's not going to be far away. Once upon a time he kicked around out with my big brother; now he's still hanging out with nineteen-year-olds, even though his black shoulder-length hair is going thin at the temples. He's wearing a black hoodie that says I AUTOEROTIC AXPHYXIATE ON THE FIRST DATE. He catches me reading it. "Confused, Eddie mate? Guess you guys were all tealights, Ed Sheeran, and missionary. Am I right?"

He must be talking about Delilah. I scramble to my feet. I should shove him back for that. But after a beat I let it go. Guess I let most things go. That's why, even though I'm a big guy, I've never been in a proper fight beyond a bit of argy-bargy on the rugby pitch (never started by me). "My gentle giant," is what Mum says. "You can't even kill a fucking spider," is what Delilah said, pissed off, when she asked me to squash the one under her bed. Still, I guess everyone has a limit. I've just never found mine.

Tate's grinning away, but his eyes don't match the smile. I can see the dead brown canine tooth that he seems almost proud of, his grin snags up at that side. Same side as the three gold hoops he wears in his earlobe, which he probably thinks make him look like Johnny Depp in *Pirates of the Caribbean*. They don't.

"How you *doin'* Eddie Eddie Eddie?" My name sounds totally stupid like that. "Where did you just appear from?"

I glance over and see the rest of them at the bonfire have turned to watch.

"The Manor," I mutter.

"The *Manor*?" he says, using a la-di-da tone. "*Very* posh! You staying there, Eddie mate? Penthouse suite?" I don't answer. He's holding a lighter in one hand: clicking it every so often, the flame flickering. "Heard they're having some sort of bullshit solstice celebration? Mate of mine works for an organic cider farm, says they've put in the biggest order ever. Can just see it now. City wankers letting their freak flag fly for the weekend. So . . ." He does a little fake scraping bow. "What brings you down to our humble kingdom?"

I think of that promotion Michelle talked about. No more soggy trainers. Mixing my own cocktails. I stand a little straighter. I've got half a foot on him. "I—I've come to tell you to leave the beach. The music . . . you're disturbing the peace."

"Oh yeah?" He smirks. "Look at you, Eddie! All growed up. Nah, mate . . . they can go fucking whistle. King's land, *innit*?" He uses words like that, like he's from some inner-city London scene, which sounds a bit weird with a Dorset accent. "See they've tried to fence off the land access, all of that, but they can't do shit about us arriving by boat." He turns and looks over his shoulder. "Oh, look who it is! Come join us, babe."

I look past him and see that someone else has broken away from the group. As she comes nearer, I see—oh crap—it's Delilah. It took me a moment as she's dyed her hair from bleach blonde to a dark reddish color. She comes to stand next to Nathan, arms folded.

"Hey . . . Lila," I say, trying to sound friendly.

"Eddie," she says. Definitely not friendly.

"You look different."

She tosses her head, smirks. I know I'm staring. "Take a good long look at what you're missing, fool."

I broke up with Delilah last year. At first, I couldn't believe she chose me to get off with at that party. That she wanted to *keep* getting off with me—and the rest. Then the fitness influencer stuff got really boring. I don't miss being a TikTok boyfriend. Maybe I'd have respected it if she'd actually done any exercise, but she'd just cover herself in olive oil and Lycra, get me to take thousands of clips of her twerking in her workout gear, then lie back down on the sofa with a Pot Noodle to watch *Selling Sunset*. All those creepy comments, probably from fifty-year-old pervs. It's not like she made any money from it, just got sent cheap leggings and dodgy supplements to plug. Thing is, Delilah is mega fit but there are thousands—millions even—of other really fit girls on the socials and they got there first and built up their followings. "I just need my big break," Delilah said. "I am low-key positive it's only a matter of time till PrettyLittleThing come knocking."

"These tits will ruin you for life," she said to me, when I told her it wasn't working. "You won't find better."

But I want more than tits, I thought (even though they are amazing). I want someone I can have a laugh with. Make plans with. Also, someone who doesn't think Khloé Kardashian is #lifegoals.

It wasn't really any of that though. It was what happened in the woods. What we found. Every time I saw her I remembered. Every time we had sex I thought about how we'd been about to do it in the woods when we heard that sound. The scream.

Tate slides a hand onto her bum. Gross. I look at Delilah. *Nathan Tate, really?* I ask, silently. *I fucking* dare *you to say something*, her expression replies. I swallow. I'm probably more scared of her than I am of Michelle.

Tate turns to her. "Aiit babe?" Then he sticks his tongue down her throat. I look somewhere beyond them, to the bonfire. Eventually Tate breaks it off with a disgusting wet pop. "She's got a beautiful fucking voice, my Lilo," he says. "Joining the band, aren't you, babe?"

I don't know what's worse. That he just addressed her as an inflatable sunbed and she seems OK with it—or the crap about the band. We used to laugh at Tate. How he behaves like he's Tome's celebrity because he and his band supposedly once played off off *off* the main stage at Glasto, but that was over fifteen years ago and he's still hanging out here, pretending he's this big deal.

"I thought you were a fitness influencer," I say to Delilah.

"I'm nineteen years old," Delilah says. "I can be whatever the fuck I want to be, Eddie. And it's none of your business anymore, if it ever was. You're not the only one who wants to get the hell out of this place."

Tate turns to Delilah. "Eddie here was just telling me we aren't allowed on this beach. Telling us to clear off."

Delilah arches an eyebrow. "That's 'cause he thinks he's better than us. Just because he works at that place. You know what he does there?" She giggles. "He's the frigging dishwasher." She shakes her head at me, faux-sadly. "That ain't *it*, Eds."

"I've been promoted, actually," I say, "bartender." But it comes out sounding pathetic, like the lie it is.

"Ooh, well done," Delilah says. "*Bartender*. Bet that makes you feel really special."

I know Delilah applied for a position in the spa: she went to beauty college in Poole after school. She didn't get it. Now I work at The Manor I know she never had a look-in. Apart from Julie—an experienced local lady (Dad swears blind she's actually a "witch")—all the spa staff have come from exclusive wellness retreats and swanky hotels in Ibiza, LA, London, and St. Barts (wherever that is). Any front-of-house staff come from farther afield, or they've concealed any trace of having come from around here. Ruby's sure Michelle's had elocution lessons.

Click—the little flame of the lighter in Tate's hand sparks to life again, then dies out. He's like some pyromaniac twelve-year-old kid.

"So, what's it like," he asks, "working for all those rich twats? You know it doesn't make you one of them, right?"

"Yeah, but he wants to *become* one of them," Delilah says. "That's his little plan."

She's playing with a gold chain around her neck. I think it's new but I don't want to look too closely in case she thinks I'm staring at her boobs.

"Do your folks know you're working there?" she asks, watching me.

"I dunno," I say, shrugging like it doesn't matter.

She narrows her eyes. "Yeah, see . . . I don't think you've told them. I saw your mum in town the other day? She said she was glad we were getting on so well and wasn't it nice we were spending so much time together." Another blood-freezing look—yup, Michelle has nothing on her. "What did she mean by that, Eds? Sounds to me like you haven't told her where you've really been going?"

Please, I try and tell her silently. *Don't tell Mum about this.* It would really mess things up for me.

Tate cuts in now, like he thinks he's due some airtime. "What's brilliant, right, is that they want this to be a private beach for the guests. Look—" He points to the wooden steps they've built down from the lawn and the line of white-and-green-striped huts they've put next to them, like something the Victorians used to change in. "They bulldozed the old path we used to use, the one that connected to the cliff footpath. And they've put a fucking keypad on their steps. But this is our beach. They're not gonna take it away from us. Not like they took my dad's caravan park—" His voice cracks. For a moment all the swagger seems to go out of him and I have to look away. I heard these days old Graham Tate stays every night at The Crow's Nest until he's falling off his stool and they refuse to serve him any more.

Yeah, I know what it means to have your dad fall apart in front of your eyes.

"Fuck that place," Nathan says, geeing himself up again. "Fuck that Francesca Meadows. You know what I reckon? It's time someone turned the tables."

There goes the lighter again. Click click click. He's jittery, eyes darting all over the place. Looks high as a kite. Did he drive the boat over here? Delilah and I might not be together anymore but I still care about her. "Lila?" I ask. "Could I have a quick word?"

She shakes her head. "Don't call me that anymore. You don't get to call me that."

"Nah nah nah," Tate says. "It's Tate'n'Lyle now, isn't it babe?" Then "Hail" by Kano blasts through the speakers by the campfire and he turns round to face his mates and fist pump the air, shouting out the words.

I look at Delilah: *Tate'n'Lyle? Are you kidding me?*

Maybe Delilah's finding it a bit cringe too because she's not meeting my eyes. She goes to flick her hair over her shoulder and her hand snags on the chain around her neck. It flips out of her top and a coldness goes through me.

"Delilah," I whisper, staring. "What the hell?"

"Oh." She looks down. "It's a feather, Eddie. It's not a big deal."

"But it's the one . . . it's from when we found him, isn't it? The one that was on the desk."

"Yeah. Well. He's not going to miss it, is he?"

"We should have left it for the police."

"Oh for fuck's sake Eddie. You know what they said. Heart attack." She looks at me and for a moment I just know she's remembering that night, how horrible it was. I'd swear there's a flicker of fear. Just as quickly it's gone and she says, "Wait. You aren't telling me you actually *believe* in them?"

Tate turns around again. "What're you two gassing about?" He can't bear not to be the center of everything.

"Eddie's freaking out over my necklace," Delilah says. She's holding her hand over it protectively.

"I'm not . . ."

"He's frightened of the Birds," she says. "He actually believes in them."

She's mocking me now. But I saw how scared she was, when we found the dead old man with that horrible look on his face. The door creaking on its hinges in the breeze. *Oh my God, Eddie. Do you think . . . do you think . . .*

Tate pulls up his black hood so his face is totally in shadow. "Burn to the bone," he rasps. And even though I know he's larking around it gives me a chill. Then he tilts his chin up so all I can make out are his crooked teeth, that dead brown canine, his deranged grin. "Don't tell me you're afraid of some little birdies, Eddie boy?"

Bella

I'M LYING ON THE MOST comfortable mattress I've ever encountered but I've never felt less like sleeping.

"I have to make you aware that you'll be very close to the woods," the receptionist told me when I phoned to book, after transferring a chunk of my modest savings into my current account. "And there will be construction work during your stay, near those Hutches. But we're offering a substantial discount."

"How much?"

"Fifty percent. But I should also let you know that this particular Hutch will be closest to the noise."

I took a deep breath. "I want it."

It's not the impending construction work: I can deal with that. It's the feel of the woods hemming me in, the trees pressing against the windowpanes as though they're trying to have a good look at everything.

Giving up on sleep, I scroll through Instagram until I find the official account for The Manor. Every image or video has a kind of sunlit haze to it, like it's a dimension slightly more perfect and beautiful than our own. And every gorgeous image of the surroundings—the Georgian main building silhouetted by the setting sun, the light glinting off the pool, the herb garden in full bloom, the woods with the dawn mist rising off them—is interspersed with a photograph or Reel of Francesca Meadows looking equally picturesque: a wicker trug filled with rosemary looped over one arm, bending down in a trailing linen shift to tickle an improbably clean pig behind the ear, picking barefoot through the wildflower meadow like something from a perfume ad. These images, the ones of her, always seem to get the most likes, the most views. I scroll and scroll until my eyes ache. But I can't stop looking.

A sound, outside. I glance up, suddenly alert. The phone slithers onto the floorboards with a clatter. Out there in the dark, coming from the direction of the woods: a low, guttural groan.

And then . . . nothing. Over in a second. But the silence seems to reverberate. I slide off the bed and grab the robe from its hook, pull it around me. My nerve endings bristle. My eyes, when I glance at myself in the mirror, look wide and scared.

I unlatch the door. The warmth of the air is almost foreign. It's almost completely silent outside, just the faintest hush from the trees as the breeze moves through them. The sky is a deep, velvet, countryside black and the stars seem crazily bright and near, as I've not seen them for many years. The sound is gone. Already it's hard to remember it properly, grasp exactly what I did hear. Or perhaps it didn't come from the woods as I'd thought, but one of the other cabins. Perhaps the loud sex couple are back at it. I don't think so, though. I'd hate to think what sort of sex would produce a noise like that. It sounded like something in pain.

And then something catches at the edge of my vision. Like a trick of the eye at first, like those little silver specks that appear if you stand up too quickly. Little pinpricks of light moving between the trees. The welcome drinks will be long over by now; it can't be that. As my eyes adjust, I see the lights look more like flames, flickering, moving around at head height or perhaps higher.

And now I catch sight of something else. A figure at the very edge of the woods. Possibly wearing some kind of hood. Maybe fifty feet away, just caught by the perimeter lights. Standing so still that if I hadn't looked in exactly the right spot I might not have noticed it. I say "it" because I'm not totally sure that what I'm seeing isn't a trick of the eye. If it is a person it's difficult to tell where they start and the shadows begin—and if it is a person I can't make out a face. I squint into the darkness. I think I see some kind of movement there now. But again it could just be a trick of the wind, the shadows rearranging themselves. Or it could be another guest having a quiet smoke in the night air.

But something is clawing at the edges of memory. Something I don't want to let out of its cage—

I shut the door quickly, then lock it. My heart is thumping in my chest. A ditty playing on repeat in my head. Vaguely following the lines of that old children's song "The Teddy Bears' Picnic," with its warning of creatures meeting in the wood.

Except in the version I learned, there was something much worse than teddy bears lying in wait.

The Day After the Solstice

THE FISHING BOAT DRAWS CLOSER still—as close as the fishermen dare without running aground; the submerged rocks along this stretch of coast are infamous.

Now they can make out the body a little better, the spreadeagle of the limbs.

"Must have fallen from the cliff path," one says.

"That's quite a way down."

"Makes you wonder. How long you'd be conscious of falling—before you hit the bottom."

"Jesus, mate. Don't say shit like that."

The breeze has picked up. A section of material lifts and billows like a sail: the white fabric crazed with streaks of blood.

"It's one of them," says another. "Got to be. From that place. They had their opening weekend do there last night, didn't they? Could hear the music down in Tome."

The relief of it. Not a local, then. One of *them*. The alien species. The invaders.

"Tide's gonna take 'em soon," one says. "Or should we—"

"Fuck no. Not going any nearer. We've called the cops. We've done our bit."

Smoke continues to fill the sky to the west. "It's got to be connected, right? To what's going on at that place."

"There was chat in the pub last night," one guy interjects. "About the Birds."

"Pull the other one, mate."

A shrug. "Just telling you what I heard from Joe Dodd."

"Oh, old Joe. Right. Well he does like his fairy tales. Few pints of bitter down, was it?"

"I dunno. Maybe. But there's been talk for a while of locals sorting 'em out. Could be someone finally snapped . . ."

They stop talking at the sound of sirens and a sudden cavalcade of flashing blue lights above the clifftop.

"Well, here they come. Not our problem anymore. Wonder what they'll make of all this."

They all fall silent again. In spite of all the blood, the hair might actually be the worst thing. It's the way it moves. Ruffling in the breeze, giving the false impression of life.

Eddie

OPENING NIGHT

MUM IS IN THE KITCHEN when I get home, wearing her old terry cloth robe and slippers and holding a mug of tea. It's nearly two a.m., I hadn't expected her to be up. But maybe I should have. She's had trouble sleeping ever since I was little. Since everything with my brother, probably.

"Where have you been, Ed?" she asks.

"Just out . . . down on the beach, with Lila and the others." It's not a lie.

"Drinking?"

"Nope."

"You came back along the road? Not through the woods?"

"Yeah, Mum."

"Good. But you still need to be careful. The guests going to that place have been roaring along the road since mid-morning, driving like maniacs."

"It's fine, Mum. I'm always really careful."

"*Good Housekeeping* did a piece about her. All that earth goddess stuff. It's total crap. You don't go destroying people's livelihoods and cutting off their rights of way. If you ask me, there's something evil about her. This heatwave coming . . . heard tomorrow will be the hottest day in sixty years. Hope it melts the lot of them, don't you?"

It's pretty shocking to hear Mum say "crap"—it's the closest she'd ever get to swearing. This is exactly why I can't tell my parents where I work. "Yeah," I say, noncommittally.

"You want some Horlicks, love?" she asks. "To take to bed with you?"

I won't drink it as it's still about twenty-five degrees out and definitely not Horlicks weather but I know she likes making it, looking after me. "Yeah, sure. Thanks."

In the kitchen she warms the milk on the old range cooker, which stinks of oil and undoubtedly makes my small room, just above it, even hotter than it already is. She slams the cupboard as she takes out the jar of Horlicks and when she turns round her cheeks are bright pink. I get it from her, the blushing, except she's not blushing now: she's angry. Dad simmers all the time, so you get used to it. But Mum is just mild, kind Mum . . . until she blows up out of the blue. "She's so nice, your mum," Delilah said once. And she is. But she's also pretty terrifying when you get on the wrong side of her.

"They've got some so-called farm shop there," she mutters.

"Have they?" I had a look the other day. You've never seen a strawberry so shiny and tiny and perfect (they come in these little wicker baskets) or granola with so many different "superfoods" in it (a tenner a box). Saw guests coming out today with these huge paper bags of stuff, like they'd gone for their weekly shop—I don't understand what they can be doing with it as they'll all get room service or eat in the Seashard restaurant.

"They had this whole thing about how they were going to be selling local produce."

I get a sinking feeling. "Oh—"

"Yes, I told your dad. Because what could be more local than the farm next door? He was obviously anti at first, but I think in the end he got quite enthused." I try to picture Dad "enthused" about anything these days and come up blank. "You know, what with the supermarkets messing him around, taking smaller and smaller orders, all of that. He went around with a load of cheese and milk."

I have this sudden awful image of Dad trudging into The Manor in his huge muddy work boots, stained jacket and big salt-

and-pepper beard, a sackload of produce over his back like some budget Santa.

"He showed them what he'd brought and they said" (she puts on a hoity-toity voice for this bit): " 'Oh, we have our suppliers already, thank you. And we're only doing organic.' They didn't even bother to ask him if *our* milk was organic." (It isn't: too much red tape, Dad says, and he can't afford to make the switch anyway.)

"I guess they're just stupid snobs, Mum," I say.

She passes a hand over her face. "They're worse than that, Eds."

"What do you mean?"

"Your dad hasn't kept very good records over the years. Land registry stuff . . ."

"What do you mean?"

She shakes her head, like she's thought better of saying anything. "Don't worry. I'm sure it'll come to nothing."

It doesn't sound like nothing, but I can tell from the thin line of her mouth she's not going to tell me any more.

"Did Dad turn in a while ago?" I ask.

Mum's back is turned to me as she stirs the Horlicks. "No. He's not got in yet."

Where the hell is he at this time of night? There's nowhere to go in the whole of Tome after twelve. Mum pulls her robe tighter around her even though there's no way she can be cold. We look at each other and I know we're both thinking about that day years ago when Dad locked himself in the tractor shed—

"Right," Mum says, like she's chosen not to think about it anymore. She puts a steaming cup of Horlicks in front of me. Just looking at it makes sweat break out on my forehead. "Night love." She reaches to ruffle my hair. Then she turns and shuffles up the stairs. I feel bad for her, stuck waiting up for the two of us, wondering where Dad is, when she's already spent the whole day here on her own. She must get so lonely. As I watch her climb the steps, shoulders rounded, I think: she looks old. Mum and Dad had me quite late.

Mum told me once (after too much Christmas sherry) that I was an accident. "But a happy one!" They didn't even think they could have kids anymore. There was a thirteen-year gap between my brother and me. It's why I never really knew him.

I HEAR THE front door creak back on its hinges an hour later. Dad's back. I wonder if Mum hears it, too. I've stayed awake listening out for him while scrolling through Delilah's socials: she's deleted all her old fitness influencer stuff and there's just a black and white picture of her on Instagram with her new darker hair, looking moody and mysterious. The text beneath reads: *Watch this space. Something MAJOR soon!* Same on her TikTok, too, except in this one she's turning to the camera and doing a long slow wink.

Nathan Tate, I think. *Really?!*

I can hear Dad stumbling about in the hallway, swearing as he struggles to take off his boots. He wears the same pair of boots year round, rain or shine: the kind you could drop an axe on without leaving a mark. I creep out and watch him from the shadows on the landing as he sways slightly. I think he must be drunk. But he can't have been at the pub, or not recently, as it shut hours ago. Does that mean he's driven from somewhere? I don't think I heard an engine outside.

He starts climbing the stairs. I reverse back into my room, I don't really want to see him when he's like this; it'll be embarrassing for both of us. And then—shit—I sneeze. It's probably Dad who's set me off because he spends so long round the cows, covered in their spit and hair.

"Who's there?" Dad says. "Eddie?"

"Er, yeah Dad. Hi." I step onto the landing. The little nightlight blinks on.

He appears at the top of the stairs. I wait for him to say where he's been, or ask what I'm doing up so late. But his eyes slide away. He looks kind of shifty, guilty even.

"Well," he says gruffly. "Night, son. Let's not stand here chit-chatting. Don't want to wake up your mum."

I watch his back as he carries on up the stairs to my parents' room in the attic. No explanation of where he's been for the last couple of hours, nothing.

Owen

I UNLOCK THE DOOR TO the storeroom, looking for a nightcap. This is where the big ticket items are kept: wine and booze and anything else the lower-wage staff can't be trusted with. Fran doesn't keep anything more alcoholic than kombucha in the apartment and I couldn't sleep.

I spy a bottle of English Pinot Noir (apparently the latest big news in wine, and Fran likes to stay on-trend), reach to lift it down from the shelf.

"Good evening."

"Christ!" I knock the bottle, just manage to catch it mid-flight.

It's Michelle, Francesca's lapdog, who has just appeared out of thin air like a rogue fucking genie. I don't know how she managed to be so quiet in those shoes when she usually click-clacks around like she's announcing her presence as loudly as possible. Why *does* she wear those prissy little heels when all the rest of the staff wear trainers?

"Oh, it's you, Mr. Dacre," she says.

"Owen," I say, "please." Less because I want the intimacy of first names than because there was something off about the way she pronounced my surname. Perhaps it's just because her accent's vowel chowder: Queen's English strewn with chunks of broad Dorset. As a key member of front-of-house staff, Fran had her take elocution training; she felt the local accent "wasn't quite right for the ambience." With Michelle it's only half paid off and the result—a mutant pick-and-mix of pronunciation—is almost worse.

"Owen," Michelle says. "My apologies." She's standing too close and I don't like it. I can feel her studying me, her eyes tracking over my face. I'm glad of the dim lighting in here. "Do you know," she says, "I think this is the first time we've properly met, you and I."

It's definitely the first time we've ever been in such close quarters. I've managed to avoid her, up until now. I take a step back.

"She's so capable," Fran said. "And so eager. She really *wants* this job, you can tell. She'll be so grateful for it." If I didn't know my partner better, I'd say she also wanted someone she could totally control. "Besides, my darling," she told me. "It's so important to have a sprinkling of locals on the staff. Councils love a local employer and I do so want them to look kindly on our future plans."

Michelle nods to the bottle, which I've been trying to hide behind my back. "Ah," she says, "I wondered why the inventory wasn't adding up. Assumed it was a member of staff." She taps the side of her nose, smiles. "Don't worry—your secret's safe with me."

I scowl at her. For God's sake. Now I'm annoyed that I took any pains to conceal the wine. I feel like a truant who's been caught smoking round the back of the bike sheds by a prefect. And yet I'm her superior—her boss, to all intents and purposes. If I want to take anything from the store I bloody well will.

"I've got nothing to hide."

"No. Of course not." She shakes her head earnestly, cheaply highlighted hair spilling around her shoulders. Can't Francesca see how tacky she is? Then she smiles. "Local, right?"

"What?" I snap.

She nods at the bottle. "One of the local reds, isn't it? Just don't think it's a match for the French stuff. Always tastes a bit fishy, if you want my humble opinion."

"Yeah? I don't think I do." It comes out even harsher than I intended. Her eyes widen. I realize my hand is clenched around the wine bottle, my shoulders up like a boxer readying for a fight. I force myself to relax. "Sorry," I say. Stupid, overreacting like that.

"No worries," she says, but she still looks a little shaken. And then: "Would you mind . . . ?"

I realize I'm standing in front of the door, blocking her exit. I move to the side.

Our eyes meet as she passes. Her expression a mix of wariness and intrigue. I drop my gaze first and she slips out the door.

It's only when the bottle slips from my hand and shatters on the stone, wine hemorrhaging across the tiles, that I realize quite how rattled I am.

Eddie

THE DAY BEFORE THE SOLSTICE

"HAVE YOU FED THE CHICKENS, Eddie?"

"Yeah."

"Good boy." Mum pours me a cup of tea while I shovel Rice Krispies into my mouth. I clock on soon—I'm working a split shift today. Dad sits in silence between us like a bear with a sore head. He should have started the milking a couple of hours ago but he's only just got up. He smells of booze. He's also wearing his work jacket, which is setting off my allergies. I've been trying so hard to hold in a sneeze that when it finally comes it's even more explosive and Rice Krispies shoot across the table.

Dad glares at me. I look down at my bowl, cheeks hot. Why do I have to be allergic to cows, of all things? No one's allergic to cows.

"You don't need A levels to drive a tractor," Dad said, when I enrolled at college. He wasn't even joking. My brother was meant to take over the farm. He would have been great at it. "Drove the tractor when he was twelve years old like he'd been driving it all his life," Dad said, once. He never talks about my brother; I guess that's why it's stuck with me. That and the fact it made me feel like such a loser.

"Yeah," I wanted to yell, "but he's gone. You're left with me, sorry. Stupid allergic Eddie who can't get anywhere near the herd."

There's a knock on the door; it's Kris, one of the two farmhands

(Dad had to let the other five go because of Brexit and labor costs). Kris got citizenship—he's originally from Poland.

"Good morning, everybody," he says, politely. And then he turns to Dad. "Harold, Ivor is missing. He's not in the field, or the barn. The barn gate is open. Do you know anything about this?"

Dad shakes his head.

"Then I think," Kris pulls a face, "he may have been stolen."

Ivor is the farm's ancient bull. He's probably had sex with about a thousand cows, and in the past I've thought about how that's nine hundred and ninety-nine more than my tally—except obviously I'm talking about having sex with people, not cows, whatever they say about Dorset.

"Why would anyone steal Ivor?" I ask.

"They might not know what's wrong with him," Mum says. Ivor's got a congenital disease that's causing him quite a bit of pain so Dad'll have to take him to the knacker's yard soon enough. "And he's still a rare breed and a valuable animal. But if someone stole him, surely we'd have heard an engine, seen lights or something. Ivor weighs more than half a ton—you don't just pop an animal like that in your boot." She turns to Dad. "Did you hear anything, Harold? While you were out?"

"Nope." Dad's gaze meets hers and then slides away.

Mum sighs. "Well, I suppose I better notify the police. Leave it with me. Though whether they'll take much notice is another matter."

It's only ten minutes later when I'm upstairs, brushing my teeth, that I think: why wasn't Dad raging about Ivor being missing? Ivor might not be the bull he once was but I'd still expect Dad to be livid. Maybe even to find some way of blaming it on The Manor. He once blamed Francesca Meadows for the milk going sour: "I tell you: it's some sort of hex," he said.

"Oh, for goodness' sake, Harold," Mum told him. "Please join us back in the twenty-first century. I think it's got a lot more to do with your decrepit refrigeration system than it has with any black magic."

BOTH MUM AND Dad have disappeared by the time I get down-stairs. They barely talk when it's just the two of them. The silences are worse than any argument. Sometimes I wonder if they even like each other at all. I vaguely remember when they laughed together and hugged and stuff. But that was a long, long time ago. Before our family fell apart. Before Dad locked himself in the shed that time with the tractor engine running and Graham Tate (in the days when he still ran the caravan park and wasn't a drunken mess) had to smash down the door with an axe.

It's only seven a.m. but it's already hot out and I can feel my T-shirt turning damp under my arms as I cycle the short distance to The Manor. I heard on the radio it's going to be "a scorcher" this weekend. I cycle past a load of women in yoga gear heading onto the lawn. Some of them give me a quick up and down, lingering in a few places—on my face, then my shoulders and some of them on my, er, package. This has only really started happening in the last couple of years. I still haven't got used to it.

I'm wheeling my bike round to the back of The Manor near the staff entrance for the kitchens when I see her coming in this direction: the woman from last night, carrying one of the hotel's dark green tote bags. In the light of day and without her red lip-stick she looks different, a little older, but still pretty hot in that rich, slightly older woman way. When I woke up this morning it blew my mind that I'd gone back to her room like that and . . . yeah, everything else. I'd been hoping we wouldn't bump into each other again.

She's coming closer. I guess she must be lost. There's nothing for guests round here—just a wooden sign saying STAFF ACCESS ONLY, which I suppose she must have missed. Hard to see how, when it's right there in big capital letters.

I should go and offer to help, shouldn't I? Play it cool and professional, just step out and point her in the right direction. But I can't face it. I don't know what I'd say. I can feel my stupid blush rising just thinking about it. So before she spots me I drop my bike on the gravel and jump behind one of the big blue kitchen waste bins. I'm definitely going to be late for my shift now.

I hear the crunch of gravel as her footsteps get closer and closer. It must be obvious by now she's in the wrong place: it's just bins and generators and then beyond that the stone archway that leads round to the courtyard beneath Francesca and Owen's private lodgings. The footsteps stop. I risk peering out: she's looking at my bike. The back wheel's still spinning. She glances about, like she's seeking out whoever dropped it.

She presses on, stepping into the courtyard despite the massive wooden sign that reads PRIVATE. I shift out from behind the bin and creep a couple of paces forward until I'm at the edge of the stone arch, so I can just about peer in.

There she is at the bottom of the steps that lead up to the private apartment, her back to me. She's looking round in every direction like an animal sniffing the air, checking for a predator.

I should do something. Tell her she shouldn't be here. But then there's what happened last night. Yeah, she came on to me, but the blame would land on the member of staff. I'd totally be fired if she said something.

She's climbing the steps that lead to Francesca Meadows's private quarters. Is she going to knock? She glances over her shoulder as though checking to see if she's being watched. She seems to be fishing something out of her shoulder bag but I can't get a proper look.

Now she's coming down again. I jump back behind the bins and a minute later she hurries past me, muttering: "Shit, shit, shit."

What did she just do?

I check my watch. Bollocks. I'm fifteen minutes late. I'm just going to have to make a break for it. I'm concentrating so hard on not being spotted by Bella that I'm not really looking where I'm going and I almost crash into a cleaner coming out of the staff entrance, cap pulled down low and pushing one of those big carts they use to service the rooms.

"Hey," I say. "Morning!" I've noticed already that some of the staff treat the cleaners pretty badly, like they think they're above them or want to emphasize there's some sort of huge difference between the work they do. But I was brought up better than that.

"Eddie?"

The voice I've just heard makes no sense at all. Staring back at me is the last person I would have expected to see here. Or maybe the second last. It's . . . "*Mum*?" I say, in disbelief.

She looks just as surprised—shocked—to see me as I am to see her. "What the hell, Mum?" I say. "What are *you* doing here?" I feel almost angry: this is my turf. Then, finally, I process the cleaner's uniform, the cart . . .

"You're *working* here?" I say, at the same time as Mum says, "I *thought* you'd been spending a lot of time with Lila this last couple of weeks."

We both stop and stare at each other, lost for words.

"You can't tell your father," Mum says, quickly. "This . . . it would destroy him. You know how he feels about this place."

"I know!" I say. "I knew Dad would be livid. But *you* hate this place, too!"

Mum's face flushes a deep pink. "Well . . . things are hard, Eds. Your dad could do with help on the finance side, but he's too proud. Besides, I don't want to sit around idly and your father won't let me help on the farm." A few years back Mum had half the bones in her foot crushed by a rogue bullock and ever since Dad has decided it's too dangerous for her. I've often wondered if Mum feels as useless as me where the farm's concerned. "So I've told him I got a job at

the Spar. He never goes in there and I've got Mags covering for me."
Mags is Mum's old friend, who works behind the till.

"But why *don't* you work at the Spar?" That would be much better,
I think. I don't like seeing Mum in a cleaner's uniform. I know that
sounds kind of snobby. Maybe I'm no better than the other members of staff after all.

"They don't need anyone else right now. Not with the new au-
tomatic checkout. Look," she says, fiercely, "it doesn't mean I like
this place. Far from it. But we need the money. And beggars can't
be choosers." She looks genuinely disgusted. "So here I am, airing
other people's dirty laundry."

I glance at the cleaning cart. There's a tight bundle of grubby-
looking sheets on the top. "Is that . . . blood?" I ask, spotting a small
stain.

Mum purses her lips. "Honestly, Eddie. You would *not* believe.
Doesn't matter how much money they have. Quite frankly they
make farm animals look like models of cleanliness." Then suddenly
she laughs. "Look at the two of us," she says. "I think this is one of
those moments where you have to laugh or you'd cry. Come here,
love." She opens her arms. I check over my shoulder before stepping
forward for a quick hug. And then she steps back, hands resting on
my shoulders. "But you never said: what sort of work are *you* doing
here?"

I'm about to say that I'm a bartender but I can't lie to Mum, and
she'll probably find out anyway. "I'm on the dishes," I say. "And
some odd jobs. But I'm working up to be a bartender."

Mum reaches out a hand, ruffles my hair. "Well, I'm proud of
you, love." And then, softly, "I know Dad is, too. Even though he
doesn't always show it."

I'm mortified to feel my eyes pricking. I cough and blink, hard.
"Thanks, Mum."

"And this," she gestures between us, "is our little secret. We're
agreed, yes? Because if he found out, it could kill your dad—" She

stops, clocking some guests walking in our direction. "Anyway," she says, quickly. "What I mean is, there are times when it's better to keep a secret from our loved ones than to hurt them with the truth. Right?"

"Yeah." I think of Dad coming in so late last night. Long after the only pub around here had closed. Seems we're not the only ones keeping secrets.

Bella

I HURRY OUT OF THE private courtyard and round the back of The Manor, heart thumping. I wind through a small car park, which must be for staff. Even I know the gleaming silver convertible is an Aston Martin. The numberplate reads: D4CRE.

I cut through the walled garden—a perfect patchwork of vegetables: the vivid green and blood red of lettuce heads, frondy explosions of carrot tops waving gently in the breeze. Everything from the restaurant is apparently "organic and locally grown or foraged." At one end I spot a stone Gardener's Lodge that (for several thousand pounds a night) you can rent for you and your friends to live out your Mr. MacGregor fantasies.

Out of the garden gate and onto the main drive, which snakes between emerald lawns sparkling with dew. A few people sit in a circle on the grass, heads bowed. That must be the "morning meditation" I saw advertised in reception. Beyond is the sea, and the cliffs that drop down to a strip of sandy beach. I know that without the help of the hand-drawn map I received at check-in.

On the other side of the drive, behind the hedges, I can make out the top of the tennis court netting, hear the *thwock* of a tennis ball being hit even though it's so early. I can imagine the beautiful people playing behind that hedge, all tanned limbs and glossy hair, whooping and laughing and high-fiving. I feel like a scholarship pupil at some ultra-posh rural boarding school.

I wait for the great ironwork gates to open and release me from The Manor's grounds. Each stone gatepost is topped by a statue of a seated stone fox, spotted with lichen. Beneath, carved into the stone, are the words: TOME MANOR.

In front of me the road curves away from the sea, cutting inland.

I find the sign for the footpath that peels off in the other direction, toward the cliffs. TOME, it reads: 1 3/4 miles. I walk through a corridor of hedges so full with midsummer growth I can't see anything beyond them: just leaves and then sky, gas-flame blue. For a moment I stop still and sniff the air like an animal. That smell. So distinctive—so familiar. The soapy smell of cow parsley mingled with the hot tang of cow shit.

Suddenly I'm at the cliffs. In the bright clean light the sea has a Mediterranean glitter. The wind punching at me is warm. Looks like someone got up even earlier than I did: a kitesurfer's already out on the water.

The road joins the cliffs again by a place called Seaview Farm. The place looks half-abandoned: bowed corrugated iron roofs, broken fences, a rusting mess of farm machinery. Black tarpaulin snickers in the breeze and flea-bitten chickens scratch about in the yard. I have the feeling of being watched. Maybe that's the whole herd of cows in the nearest barn, following me with their big dark eyes.

I hurry on: not wanting to linger. The air round this place tastes of sadness. Or maybe that's just me, projecting.

Round the next bend I approach a holiday park: a hundred or so mobile homes set back from the sea behind a picket fence. The paint on the fence is peeling, the caravans stained and empty, weeds tangling round their feet. Across the dirty magnolia wall of the nearest one someone has daubed in blood-red paint: YOULL PAY FOR THIS YUPPY CUNTS.

No . . . no, this isn't right. There should be hanging baskets and salty wetsuits drying in the breeze, the yells and thuds of kids kicking a football about, the scent of charred sausages on the air, the chatter and clink of cutlery and life.

"Jesus!" I startle. I've just spotted a figure sitting there in an old deckchair. So slumped and crumpled that, at first, it looks like some kind of bizarre scarecrow. Until the head turns my way and I see the red drinker's face beneath the knotted handkerchief he's wearing on his head. I can't stop staring. It can't be—

"What are you looking at, girlie?" he slurs, whisky sloshing out of the open bottle in his hand. "Come to gawp at poor old Graham? Fuck off with you."

I hurry on, shocked. Can't believe what's become of him . . .

Now I'm in the right spot. I take a deep breath, then veer off the side of the path. To anyone watching it might look like I'm about to jump over the edge of the cliff. But there's a route down if you know what you're looking for: bramble-choked, winding down the limestone face.

When I get to the hidden cove I take off my shoes and socks to feel the wet grit of the sand between my toes. The tide is out and has left behind little pools of salt water among the flattish rocks, on which someone has left a backpack and a small pile of clothes. I clamber over to the nearest pool, the rough pumice of the barnacles and slither of seaweed beneath my soles, and look into the glassy surface. A whole universe is contained inside. I watch for a flicker of life among the weeds: a crab or tiny fish. A little distraction while I work up the nerve to do what I need to.

And there it is, behind me: the cave. Just where I remembered, set into the steeper rocks on the far side. The dank cool of it as I step inside is such a contrast to the heat of the morning. The dim interior feels full of ghosts.

I don't want to go any farther, but this is why I'm here. I walk right to the back of the cave, where it's even darker. My phone's torch gives me just enough light to see the opening in the back of the cave wall, level with my sternum. I brace myself against the rock and lever myself up. I don't know if this is going to work. I'm slim but the girl who climbed in here before was a waif. I manage to haul myself up into the mouth of the tunnel. Then I crawl, lizard flat, on my stomach, trying not to think about the solid rock pressing in all around me. I grope in front with one hand. It seems insane that it might still be here. At the same time, if it's not, what then? What would that mean?

Finally, my fingers brush something. Something small, plastic-wrapped. My heart's beating so hard I think I can hear the echo of it against the stone. I tug the package free. Shuffle into reverse, dragging it with me.

Back outside, blinking in the sunlight, I look at my find. It might be wrapped in several plastic bags but there's something ancient-looking about it, like something just dug from the ground. I pull off the first plastic Spar bag—ripped, discolored—and the second, which has survived better, and the third, which is a little damp but basically like new. And there it is. The cardboard cover a little stained and damp, the pages warped by water. But not nearly as bad as I would have expected. Mostly intact after all this time.

I'm about to open it when a flash of color catches my eye. I look up and see a bright green kitesurf sail. I watch as the kitesurfer hits a wave and the board soars up into the air. I realize I'm holding my breath. If you fell off at that speed, hitting the water would feel like smacking into concrete, but he lands perfectly, carving a white swathe in the waves.

He turns toward the beach and comes in, springing gracefully into the water and towing the whole lot up onto the beach. He hasn't spotted me and I feel like a voyeur as he reaches to undo the zip of his wetsuit, shrugging off the top half. I see his wide brown back and the large black shadow of a tattoo which reveals itself to be a bird of prey, wings outstretched, each tip just touching each shoulder, fitting the canvas of his skin perfectly.

He's pulling the wetsuit lower now and I see two things: one, that his whole body has the same even, amber tan, and two, that he isn't wearing anything underneath the wetsuit. He really must think he's alone. He turns his head to the side and I see the proud profile, the Roman nose. It's Owen Dacre. Hotshot young architect, the "talent of a generation" according to the press. Owner of that Aston Martin convertible, presumably. The guy who designed all the modern extensions to The Manor. Francesca Meadows's partner in both senses. They made a striking couple in the wedding shoot I saw. He looked like Jim Morrison kitted out by Mr Porter. His dissipated look contrasting with her radiant wholesomeness. And the way he gazed at her in those photos. Like he was totally under her spell.

He turns fully round—Christ—and strides up the beach, butt naked, toward the rocks and what I realize now must be his backpack. I crouch back, frozen in place, knowing I should look away but unable to. Watch as he dries himself with a towel, pulls on his clothes, shoves the kitesurfing gear into his pack. Finally he turns this way. He has to see me now. He starts, then mutters something under his breath.

I raise a hand in greeting. "Hey," I call.

He's standing very still but with a kind of coiled energy, like a fox disturbed during a kill.

"What are you doing here?" he asks, abruptly.

"I'm staying at The Manor," I say.

He scowls at this. "It's not safe for you to swim here—there are hidden rocks off this beach. And the climb down—"

"It's fine," I say, nettled by his patronizing tone. "I've been here before." I catch myself. Was that stupid? It just slipped out. But I'm probably being paranoid. It's a popular enough part of the coast.

I watch him leave the beach for the cliff path, until I'm completely sure I'm alone. I take a deep breath. Then I lift the notebook back onto my lap. Before anything else I turn to the back, willing my trembling fingers to work properly. There it is. A scrawled map, drawn in biro. The house, the cliffs, the wood.

X marks the spot.

Time to drag the past screaming into the light.

I flip back to the front. I read the first line. Feel a sudden sting of tears.

Stupid little fool.

Summer Journal

THE CARAVAN—TATE'S HOLIDAY PARK
JULY 23, 2010

Met this girl on the beach today. Never met anyone like her before.

Dorset for the summer cos my folks have the school holidays off from teaching. Mum and I voted for the Algarve but the budget didn't stretch. The weather isn't as crap as I thought it might be though. Got this naff "Summer Journal" in a service station on the way down as I always need somewhere to write my thoughts. That's being an only child for you.

I found a fossil. But it's like it found me.

While Mum and Dad unpacked I came down to the beach, had a poke around in the rockpools. Sixteen is too old for rockpools but the beach was packed with all these kids with bodyboards and tans who knew each other and I didn't want to sit on my own like a loser. Or like the only other solo kid there: twelve or thirteen, skinny with home-cut dark hair.

I was watching him when I felt something against my toe. I looked down and this thing was looking back up at me. Trapped inside a lump of rock: an eyehole and what looked like a beak, or jaw. Tiny jagged teeth. <u>Super</u> creepy. Maybe I yelped or something? Cos suddenly there was this voice next to me saying holy shit, never found one like that and it was one of the guys who'd been mucking around with the body-boards. Couldn't look at him straight on cos I'm a total loser round boys (Streatham High for Girls does that to you), especially fit boys, but he had toffee-colored hair and smelt like salt and sweat (a good smell on the right boy).

Then his mates were coming over to see and most of them were looking at the fossil but one of them shouted over at the small dark-haired kid: all right Shrimp, tell your mum I can't give her one tonight cos I'm busy. Know she's gagging for it. Some of the others sniggered but the boy with the toffee-colored hair said: don't be a dick, Tate. I liked him for that. The kid didn't say anything back. Just hunched over himself.

Then this hush and everyone started moving aside for three other people. A girl, two older twin boys. Like they'd beamed down from another planet. And like you could just tell the Shrimp kid was poor, you could tell they were rich. Their hair, their teeth, even how they stood. The girl came right up and said in this deep, posh voice: that's fucking cool. Put out her hand. I gave it to her without think-ing. She had big black sunglasses with PRADA on the arm in silver letters and a belly button piercing. I had to <u>beg</u> Mum just to get my ears done.

Hey, she said, holding the fossil. Can I take this? Before I said any-thing, she goes: and you can come to The Manor tomorrow, if you like. Granmama and Grandfa have a pool. It's so much better than the beach. No locals.

She touched my arm then. It would be fun, if you came. She smiled at me, although I couldn't see her eyes behind those big sunglasses.

I said: yeah, sure. No idea why, but out of all the kids on the beach, she chose me.

JULY 24, 2010

You know in that Narnia book, when they go through the back of the wardrobe? Today was like that. Started out in a caravan, ended up in a palace. Or a manor . . . but still.

Dad drove me over in the Corsa. This sounds bad but I wished the car wasn't so small and old. He stopped at the closed gates: two big pillars topped with stone foxes and TOME MANOR carved on one. You couldn't see the house, just the driveway stretching ahead. Dad was like: did she say it was a bloody great estate? I don't want to get shot with some local lord's twelve-bore.

Then the gates creaked open and we crawled up the drive and finally you could see this <u>huge</u> house appearing, sea on one side and dark, spooky-looking woods on the other. And maybe this sounds naff but I had the idea that the fossil was this magic amulet that had let me into another world, like in a fairy tale.

Dad cut the engine halfway up the drive and said something like: look, love. People who live in places like this, they're not like us . . .

He doesn't get it. That's kind of the whole point. When would I ever get to go hang out somewhere like this in Streatham?

It's only to swim in the pool, Dad, I told him. So he carried on driving until we saw the girl waiting for us in front of the house, standing with one hip cocked in a hot-pink bikini and cut-off denim mini. I waved and she didn't wave back but she had her hand shielding her eyes from the sun so maybe she didn't see me.

Well, Dad said. Off you go, love. It's your funeral.

JULY 27, 2010

I've been to Tome Manor every day and it has been <u>literally amazing</u>. The pool is so nice. Frankie (that's her name) is super generous . . . she gave me a bikini to sunbathe in (still had the tag in . . . £40!!!!!!). She was like: it's too small for my boobs but you're pretty flat, so it's perfect. And anything's better than that horrendous tankini, Sparrow (she's been calling me that for the last few days cos of my skinny legs). She says I have to sort my "pube sitch" out too. She's given me some wax strips but I've been too chicken to use them.

Frankie is always going on about how boring it is here, how there's nothing to do. But it's AMAZING. The house has more rooms than I can count! It has a library. A cellar. Like, twenty bedrooms. Then there's this wood full of trees that are thousands of years old.

You want to behave yourself in the woods here, Frankie told me, when I stayed the other evening and we watched <u>Blair Witch</u> together (her favorite film). Especially after dark. Or they'll come for you. They don't like outsiders.

Who? I asked. Who doesn't like outsiders?

She burst out laughing. Look at your face! I was just kidding. It's not real. Just local peasant gossip, Granmama says.

Granmama is posh, thin, and scary and spends all her time gardening. I met Grandfa today while we were lying by the pool reading mags. This shadow fell over us and this guy stood there: tall with smoothed-back white hair and kind of a mean mouth. Old but this powerful vibe about him. Like the picture of a Roman emperor I saw in a museum, but in red cord trousers. Has a Labrador called Kipling. He said something like: so you're Francesca's new playmate. You summer here too, then?

I was like, er yeah, we're at the caravan park.

Ah, he said. Graham Tate's one of our tenants. Then he peered down at me (wished I was wearing more than my Speedo then) and goes: I suppose that means we're hosting you two times over.

I just smiled awkwardly. What was I meant to say?

When he'd gone Frankie rolled her eyes at me. Don't mind him. He's only just back in the good books. Had an affair with his secretary. I must have pulled a face, thinking of a guy that old doing it, cos Frankie was like, yeah, gross right? Anyway, he's put it back in his pants. Thank God as Granmama was talking about selling up, moving into a flat in Marylebone. It's boring as fuck but I dunno what I'd do if I couldn't come every summer, specially as our cow of a mother's too busy sunning herself in the Med to bother with us. It's home, you know?

JULY 28, 2010

Today Graham Tate, who owns this caravan park, popped round to shoot the breeze with Mum and Dad. He's this big sunburned guy who wears a tied hankie on his head like in a cartoon and wanders round all day chatting to everyone. He likes ribbing Dad about Palace (Dad's team) being crap at the moment.

Dad pointed at me when I stepped out of the caravan and went, this one's been hanging out at The Manor (pronounced in this la-di-da voice). Graham went: Tome Manor, is it? You watch yourself there, girl. Can't say more as I'm a tenant. But I wouldn't trust 'em. Don't care about our sort—never have. Back in the day the lord kept some thoroughbred white horses. Didn't train 'em properly, so they were half-wild. One day he went hunting and cut along a footpath in the woods and there was a local girl there picking flowers. The horse reared up and struck her. Killed her. But a few days later he was overheard complaining to his rich mates about how the fox got away. No compensation for the family, nothing.

Mum was all like: oh, how awful! And I guess it is but I don't really see how some ancient story has anything to do with the place now or that girl and her brothers. Even if it's real it was hundreds of years ago?

That's not all, Graham Tate said, in this spooky voice. One night when the mist was coming thick off the sea, the stables were opened and the horses got out. Next morning it turned out they'd all gone over the cliffs. Every single one.

So someone did it? Mum asked. Someone led them over?

Not someone, Graham said, in this ominous voice. Something. The Birds.

<u>Birds</u>? Dad asked.

Not just any old birds round here, Graham Tate said and tapped his nose. Can't say more than that.

JULY 29, 2010

Spoke to Frankie's brothers today—the twins. Hugo has a white streak in his hair and is louder than Oscar, but they're both pretty loud. They dress in posh-boy sportswear: trackies with RUGBY 1ST XV down the side. On the beach they seemed like Abercrombie models, but up close they're tall and muscly but not that good-looking. They laugh like the hyenas in <u>The Lion King</u>. Today they came into the kitchen while I was waiting for Frankie to find some nail polish (to sort out my "rank" toenails). They smelt of Lynx, old sweat. They chugged milk straight from the bottle, one after the other. The kitchen was smaller with them in. Hugo reached right across my belly to grab a knife from the drawer.

Like the bikini, he said.

Part of me wanted to disappear. Part of me didn't. You know?

So you're the latest, he said.

I was like: latest?

Latest in the collection!

I did this stupid nervous laugh and was like: er . . . I don't get it?

And he went: yeah, you know how other people like collecting things? Like football cards? Birds that collect shiny things for their nests? Lil sis likes collecting people. He pulled this fake-sad face. Mummy never gave her enough love.

Both of them were grinning. I smiled to show I got the joke but it wasn't really funny. Actually, it made me feel like I was the joke?

Guess you're flavor of the month, Oscar said.

Yeah, Hugo said, till the next one comes along.

I was glad when Frankie came back in. She shook the dark purple bottle at me: here it is, Sparrow. Midnight Lagoon. Which reminds me, we could have a midnight feast soon. Fancy it?

Sure, I said, sounds good (though a midnight feast sounds weirdly babyish for Frankie?). The twins looked at each other. Yeah, we'll come along too, Hugo said. Gave his hyena grin. Know what I want to feast on.

Owen

HEADING BACK FROM THE BEACH I cut through the walled garden toward the private courtyard that leads to our apartment. There's a guy in expensive-looking workout gear doing an affected little jog along the paths. Bloody idiot. He's got the whole estate to run around, what's he doing here? I hope he trips and brains himself on a raised bed, drowns in the carp pond.

It felt like an invasion, yesterday, when the first cars began gliding up the driveway. I didn't build any of this for them—it's all for her. Think I managed to convince myself they'd never actually arrive. Well, here they are. Less than twenty-four hours and already it feels like they're tarnishing this place. Leaving greasy fingerprints on the glass in the Seashard, scuffing the finishes, dumping their towels in damp mushrooming piles around the pool, ungainly bodies thrashing about in the water, blurring the clean lines of the design. It feels like a personal insult. I know they're a necessary evil. I understand that they're the point of The Manor. But if you ask me, it was a whole lot better before they moved in. When it was finished and perfect, our vision fully realized and unspoiled. I created something transformative here. Not just for this old building, not just for Fran, but for me, too. Something that began to heal me.

The guests are like an infestation. They're insatiable. And why do they all look so fucking miserable? Faces like smacked arses, my dad would say. The faces of people waiting for a bus in the pissing rain. They're staying in "the hottest new rural getaway." They've paid hundreds—some thousands—for the privilege. They have everything they could ever need.

Christ . . . and there'll only be more of them, soon. It's why we're building into the woods with the Treehouses, which are already booked out for the autumn despite being massively behind schedule. My stupid fault . . . I kept fucking up the designs. Strange, but every time I went into the trees to visualize them my thoughts just scrambled. Didn't realize Fran had already opened up the calendar. We have to begin construction now and not a moment later. I know she's less than thrilled about it happening during opening weekend but I've tried to persuade her it could work to our advantage. The celebrations will provide a distraction for the guests while we do the loudest of the work: excavating the deep roots of the felled trees to make way for the new foundations. This way we haven't had to close bookings at all. Fran may look like a free spirit, but she's an extremely canny businesswoman.

My walk back from the beach took me past the sad spectacle of Tate's Holiday Camp: a blot on the landscape. I can't wait to get cracking on Fran's plans there—a glamping experience, picturesque shepherds' caravans with outdoor rain showers. But we're charging more for the Treehouses, so they took precedence.

Running guy's now doing stretches on one of the ironwork benches between the beds, really lunging into them. His shorts are smaller than any bloke's should be. I'm sure I'm about to be assaulted by the sight of a sweaty, free-swinging ball.

Not even the hidden cove is sacred from the guests, apparently. That woman on the rocks just now. How the hell did she find her way there? Half the locals don't even know it exists or if they do they don't bother with it because of the hairy descent. In the mornings I have it to myself; that's how I like it. It's the only place beyond the grounds I really like visiting.

When I first learned The Manor was looking for an architect I knew there was no way I could do it. I'd barely worked in the UK full stop. Recent builds included an Icelandic actor's holiday home in the Western Fjords, a hotel in Costa Rica. But I couldn't stop thinking about it.

"Don't you feel," my therapist said, "it might be worth exploring why you say you 'can't'? Sometimes doing the things that scare us is how we conquer those fears."

"I'll send a brief pitch," I said. "I'll do that much."

I went to that first meeting braced to meet my demons. But instead I met my angel: caught in a ray of sunlight through the window, golden hair rippling around her shoulders.

A few sessions later, I told the therapist.

"The way you talk about her . . . is it fair to say you've been searching for a mother figure?" she asked.

"She is *nothing* like my mother," I spat. "Fran's perfect."

"Is anyone?" my therapist mused. "That's a difficult label for any human being to wear."

Cereal box pop psychology crap. I canceled my next sessions. I didn't need a therapist by then. I had Fran.

Oddly, though, when I'd calmed down, I could see that there *were* things about her that reminded me of my mother's better attributes. The beauty. The big dreams. But unlike my mother, my wife is all positivity. All *purpose*. When I look back, I can't be certain which I fell in love with first: the project, or Fran. I've certainly never been so connected to my work before.

Behind one of the espaliered pear trees I stop, check quickly that I'm not being observed, then tug a loose brick out from the wall. Tucked into the recess is my emergency stash of baccy. I make a sloppy rollie. In spite of everything I still buy the same Benson & Hedges rolling tobacco. Nothing else tastes right. Fran thinks I gave up ages ago. I doubt she's ever even tried a cigarette: that's how pure she is. Well. Except in the bedroom.

When I walk into the private courtyard I stop, frown. Something's hanging from the door that leads up to our apartment. Something white and ragged. Small sections of it are half detaching and fluttering in the hot breeze.

The taste of the tobacco is suddenly rancid in my mouth.

I step closer. My flesh is crawling all over, though I'm not yet sure what I'm looking at.

Another step. I can smell it now and I know that smell in the animal way we probably all do. It's a dead creature.

Jesus Christ. The realization of it shrieks through me. It's a bird. Someone has nailed a dead bird to our door. Not just any bird—it's the white cockerel from the run in the walled garden. The one Francesca was photographed with in *Harper's Bazaar*.

I'm not squeamish, but I take a step back when I notice a maggot crawling from one of the empty eye sockets. Jesus. My first thought is: I need to get rid of this thing before Francesca sees it. She's got too much on her plate.

I start trying to free the dead creature from its nail, bile rising in my throat at the stink of it. The heat won't have helped. I look down to inhale and see a small white envelope tucked beneath the bottom of the door. I bend down, shove it into my pocket, then turn my attention back to the bird. The things I do for Fran. But then I do everything for Fran, because she's everything to me. Without her I am nothing.

"Hello, Owen."

I swing around.

Oh for Christ's sake. Not again. I turn unwillingly to catch Michelle's gaze sweeping over me.

"Warm, isn't it?" she says—I feel like I'm in some bad porn, all of a sudden. "Bet you wish you were still out on the water."

On the face of it there's nothing particularly odd about her words. It's hardly a secret that I'm out on my board early most mornings. But something rankles me.

"Oh, goodness." She's looking at the thing on the door behind me.

"Yeah," I say. "Someone clearly has a really twisted idea of a practical joke." Though I can't help but feel it's not a joke, not at all.

"I'll go and get Francesca," she says. "She should see this."

"No you won't." I almost shout it. This is the last thing Francesca needs. Surely the stupid woman can see that?

I rip off my shirt. Italian linen, I have a whole wardrobe of them now. Then I gather up the grisly bundle and carry it to one of the big waste bins outside the staff entrance. When I dump it inside, blood is already oozing through the shirt fabric.

I turn back and have to resist a shudder: Michelle's watching me, a slight frown on her face. "You've got something," she says. "Just there." She snatches out a hand before I can duck away, runs a finger along my collarbone. I feel her nail lightly score the skin. She holds out the fingertip to show me a smear of crimson.

Francesca

LITTLE SCRATCH. I PUSH THE needle into the vein. Close my eyes. Here it comes, the high. My head falls back against the cushions.

Yes.

I'm experienced enough to self-administer the IV drip now and, besides, I don't quite trust anyone else to do it right.

I thrill at the thought of the cocktail of vitamins surging into my bloodstream. I need to be on top form this weekend and especially for tomorrow's celebratory feast.

It's the most perfect morning. The promised heatwave will soon be upon us. A couple of days ago we put in a rather urgent order for some handheld white-feather fans, to keep our guests stylishly cool tomorrow evening. The coronets have been delivered to the rooms. The wicker sculptures, made by a visionary artist in Hackney, will be delivered later. I looked at a few local artists, honestly I did, but there was just no comparison. This guy did an installation for The Vampire's Wife recently. He. Is. Amazing. And the people staying here expect London quality, if you know what I mean, albeit presented in a rural setting. The same sort of elevated spiritual aesthetic as our crystal neck pouches. It's going to be *stunning*—and just amazing for socials. The gift that keeps on giving.

I ease out the needle. The IV bag's nearly empty. I can already feel its contents nourishing me, making me new.

But this—I switch on my laptop—may be the thing that nourishes me most. I click on a little icon of a lens. If you didn't know what it was it might look like the black shiny orb of a crystal ball. Which in a way I suppose it is! I rather like that: it gives a magical, mystical air to the whole thing. I know technology is the root of all evil and blue light is the work of the devil . . . but this is different.

I key in the first password, then the second. It's a mercifully secure system. Now they materialize before me: hundreds of tiny thumbnails, each relating to a different feed. The cameras set up throughout the hotel are teeny tiny—barely visible to the human eye. You'd never spot them anyway because they're so well concealed. It was all done by a man who used to work for . . . well, let's just say people who really know about this sort of thing.

No one else at The Manor knows this exists, not even Owen. I had everything installed while he was away on another project and before the interior designers moved in. The other thing about the guy who installed it: he isn't the sort to talk.

I start clicking through the icons: a few feeds each for all the public spaces—to capture all the angles—and a single feed for each room.

I know it may not be totally, strictly *legal*, having cameras fitted in people's rooms. But it comes from a very good place, honestly. It was one of Grandfa's rules (taken from his experience in government, no doubt): prepare for the worst and it will never happen! I want to keep The Manor the safe, happy environment it is. I want our guests to feel we trust them. There's nothing worse than a place of this caliber patronizing its clientele with theft-proof clothes hangers and dire warnings about not filching the shower gel. Hence the full-size bath oils in glass containers, the matches left on the dressing tables. At the same time, one really has to have a contingency plan. And ultimately, this place is so much more than a hotel. It's a *home*. One has a right to protect one's home, doesn't one?

I watch my guests going about their business. A whole world of human activity! Many are at their toilette, a few are making love (one pair in the most astonishing position; I didn't know anyone's legs could bend at that angle!). In one room a couple are clearly in the throes of an argument. I frown: we don't really want those sort of vibes here! Oh goodness—there's my brother Hugo, with that *awful* woman he's brought here. I'm sure she's some sort of escort. I do hope he doesn't show me up this weekend. Oscar's a little better house-trained. The two of them are in on this project with me too, strictly on the money side. I thought it would only be prudent to make this a family affair and give them a chance to do well out of this place, seeing as Granmama overlooked them in leaving it to me. Besides they're well connected in that regard—they've got a couple of investor friends staying this weekend. Anyway. I click quickly on, not wanting to see anything unsavory.

There's just one room that's single occupancy, a woman. I watch as she enters her Woodland Hutch, carrying one of our beautiful dark green tote bags over her shoulder, taking from it a towel and some sort of book. Funny. Almost everyone else staying is part of a pair—we even have a throuple. I wonder what she's doing here on her own. I mean, all power to her of course! But it's the opening weekend . . . celebratory and social. Something about her doesn't quite fit. I look up the name in the bookings. Bella Springfield. Pretty, if a little common. If she is a media person as her bio suggests *I* haven't heard of her. Odd.

Anyway. Here they all are at last. My guests. Here, in this magical kingdom I have created for them. If I were driven by ego I'd say it gives me a feeling of great power. But I'm not. I've worked on myself over the years. So let's say it's a kind of maternal love I feel for them all. It's what I keep saying: we're one big happy family here!

I check the outdoor feeds next. There's the pool, the walled garden, there's . . . I pause. Click back to the frame of the courtyard. What on earth is Owen doing talking to Michelle? He detests the woman! And why is he shirtless? I zoom in. There's something oddly intense about their body language.

I close my eyes. In two three four, out two three four five six seven eight. Ah. And there we go. All better now. It's a *good* thing if Owen and Michelle are getting along better. It's important to me that everyone is in harmony. Like I say, we need to be one happy family.

I open my eyes at the sound of footsteps on the stairs, glance back at the screen to see that Owen has disappeared from view. I just manage to slam the laptop closed before he pushes open the door.

"Hello beloved," I say. "How was it out on the water?"

"Fine," he says.

He doesn't look like a man who's come back refreshed from his early morning exercise, though. He looks jittery. And he brings with him a stink of smoke. He thinks I don't know about his secret stash, but there are very few things I don't know about here. What *he* doesn't know is that I swapped the disgusting cheap stuff he had in the bag for a low-tar, organic variety. That has to be better than the alternative, right?

As Owen takes a shower I begin to painstakingly apply some very light make-up. People need to believe I use nothing but sunlight, eight hours' sleep, and antioxidants to look like this. It's part of the package. I try to be completely authentic in all things, you know? But sometimes you've got to give people what they want. They don't *want* to know about tear trough treatments, lasers, and the occasional teeny pinprick of Botox, do they? I'm not naturally beautiful, you see. There: I can say it now without rancor. I think most people would be shocked to notice, on second glance, that I am right. My eyes are a fraction too close together, my jaw too heavy. It used to upset me. But I've learned that with tweakments (oh so subtle) and the right make-up you can fake it. Of course what shines from within is most important, but dermal fillers have their role, too.

Owen comes out of the shower, drying his damp hair with a towel. I watch the muscles in his back move beneath the skin, giving the huge eagle tattoo inked across his shoulder blades the appearance of life, of readying to take flight.

My beloved doesn't walk to the dressing room to take out his clothes—he *prowls*. The linen shirt he selects (he is very particular about his clothes; his taste impeccable) tames him a little. Or it covers up the tattoo, at least—but there's still the impression of an animal beneath the fabric, a wolf in sheep's clothing. I watch as he slams the dressing room door. He looks like a man with something on his mind.

"I hope you don't mind me saying, my darling, but you don't look well. Anything bothering you?"

Owen shrugs. A tiny hesitation. "No. Just tired from my surf, I suppose."

"Well, it's going to be a busy couple of days. I'm so glad you had that time to yourself."

"Not quite to myself. We should warn guests off going down to the hidden beach."

I frown. "What do you mean?"

"A woman climbed down this morning."

"You sure it wasn't a local?"

"Definitely a guest. She was carrying one of our tote bags."

As a highly visual person I can't help picturing the scene. The two of them on that secluded beach. I find myself wondering whether he found her attractive. An image shimmers in front of my eyes: two figures on the sandy cove, moving together, embracing . . . and with it a feeling of loss that mushrooms quickly into something darker, angrier—

I blink and it disappears from view, like seawater sinking into the sand.

Goodness. What is happening to me? I take another deep breath. No. I've evolved beyond petty feelings of jealousy these days. It's so liberating. We are all creatures of Gaia and attraction to other beautiful creatures is in our organic make-up. Besides, this is Owen we're talking about. *Owen.* He worships me. He is, for want of a better word, completely obsessed with me. Not in an unhealthy way, you understand. Just in the sense of his soul being inextricably cleaved to mine.

My tone is oh so very light and breezy as I lean toward my reflection and say: "I wonder how she found her way down there. After all, I summered here every year and I didn't find it until I was a teen." I fit the eyelash curler's bracket gently over my eyelid.

"Well, she said she'd been here before, so she knew the way."

"Ow, shit!" I wince with pain: I seem to have caught the skin of my eyelid in the little metal clamp. As I blink away the tears I catch Owen's look of surprise. Francesca Meadows *never* swears. "Oops." I smile, to reassure him.

I think of the woman I just watched entering her Hutch with her green tote bag. The solo booking. It was her on the beach, I'm suddenly sure of it. Now I think about it, the name niggles at me—though I can't think why.

As Owen shrugs on his jeans I make a little mental note to look into this Bella Springfield. Just to satisfy my curiosity. Nothing more than that.

DI Walker

DETECTIVE INSPECTOR WALKER PARKS THE Audi at the top of the cliff beside the old caravan park. He catches his eye in the rearview mirror; runs a hand over the newly buzzed bristles of his hair. Early thirties and already flecked with gray. When did that happen?

He takes out his flask of coffee and pours espresso into the cup. His hand shakes just a little; the adrenaline. A knock at the window and scalding liquid spills onto his thumb. Shit. Detective Sergeant Heyer peers at him through the glass. They've met a few times now. She was born in the early noughties and makes Walker feel ancient.

He slides on sunglasses, steps out of the car.

"Hey boss." She sounds breathless. "Like the shades."

"Thanks."

She frowns at him. "You live in the New Forest, right? Must have taken you, like, an hour to get here. No one closer?"

Walker shrugs. "I'm an early riser. Suppose I spotted it first. You all right?"

There's adrenaline coming off Heyer, too. It's the gleam in her eyes, the way she's bouncing on the balls of her feet.

"Yeah . . . I mean. I guess you got more of this in the Met? We don't get a lot of this sort of thing down here."

"What, death?"

"Not like this. It's all accidents with farm machinery, pensioners falling down the stairs. One of my first was an old bloke having a heart attack in his study. That kind of thing. Nothing like this."

"Well. We don't really know what 'this' is yet, do we? But tell me what you've got so far."

"So, some fishermen found it," Heyer says. "They're waiting on down below. SOCO are about to start on the scene. But the cliffs here are really steep—we'll have to walk down to the next beach along and get them to collect us by boat. This wa—"

"You'll never catch 'em," a voice slurs, near at hand. Heyer jolts with shock, swears under her breath. Walker turns to see a figure leaning against the peeling fence of the caravan park, squinting in their direction. Bottle of Bell's clutched in one meaty paw. Purple blotched cheeks of a heavy drinker. A stained vest, tied handkerchief askew on his head. Walker can smell the booze coming off him from here. Jesus.

"What's this?" the old man crows, pointing at Walker's shades. "Miami fucking Vice?" He lets out a cackle, which turns into a phlegmy cough.

Walker ignores this. "You said something just now," he says, "did you—"

"What's that accent then? Where'd you come from?" The man leans forward, peering at him. If it wasn't for the fence taking the weight of his heavy forearms it's doubtful he'd be able to stay upright.

"Here and there," Walker says, noncommittal. Best to remain as impersonal as possible. "Look . . . did you see something? Last night?"

"Yeah," the old man drawls. "Saw it all. Sitting right there the whole time." He turns and with a wild sweep of one arm gestures to a faded deckchair a few feet away, the derelict caravans beyond. He cackles. "Welcome to my kingdom, son. They want to destroy it. They want to take it from me. Over my dead body. You hear me? Over my—" He breaks off as another hacking cough takes over him.

"When you say you saw it all?" Walker prompts.

The man turns back to Walker slowly now and meets his gaze. His eyes have changed. They're nearly black: all pupil, like he's just stepped out of the dark. His voice when he speaks is a low rasp. "Yeah," he says. "I saw *them*. One of them, anyhow."

"Them?" Walker asks, carefully.

A slow nod. "One of the Birds."

Walker frowns, unnerved by something in the man's expression. "When you say the birds—"

"Tall," the old man says, gesturing with both hands. " 'Bout your height, mebbe. All in black." Now he passes a hand down his ruined features. "No face. Big fucking beak, like this. Sharp as a razor. Wings like this." He spreads out his arms, as wide as they'll go. "Saw 'em clear as I'm seeing you now. It was them 'at did it. Course it was."

"Can I ask what you mean?"

"They've killed before. Old Lord Meadows. Sure it was them who did for him in the end. They'll kill again."

In spite of himself Walker feels a chill. "And what did you see this . . . ah, *bird* do?"

"Chased 'em off the cliff," he says, like it's obvious. "And then," he says, darkly, "it flew away."

Walker hears Heyer give a little sigh. "It . . . flew away?" he prompts.

The old man gives a slow nod, dead serious. "That direction." He points along the cliff path, toward the place where smoke still seeps into the sky. "They can fly an' all," he says. "Course they can. They're birds."

"USED TO RUN that caravan park," Heyer says, once they've taken Graham Tate's details and left him to his whisky. "His son Nathan's something of a local troublemaker: bit of possession, petty theft, that kind of thing. Thought for a moment there he might actually have something useful to say. But people in these parts believe some weird stuff. Besides, he's clearly off his rocker and pissed as a newt."

"Well, who knows," Walker says. "Could still be useful. Perhaps a grain of truth in it somewhere."

"Or maybe . . ." Heyer frowns.

"What?"

"Well. I just thought . . . could he be more with it than he seems? Like, does he even have an alibi? Might seem like a good idea to pin it on some local folklore."

"Good thinking," Walker says. Heyer stands a little straighter, looking pleased. "Let's bring him in, when he's sobered up."

Heyer grimaces. "Not sure that's gonna be any time soon."

"Now let's get down to our victim." Walkers moves off toward the cliffs, then stops. "Look here. See those brambles, along the cliff, how they're snapped, trodden down? We'll have to get SOCO up here to tape them off."

"Yeah."

"Really crashed through. Not being careful about it. Makes you think, doesn't it? Look at the size of those thorns. You'd have to be in quite a state. You'd have to really want to throw yourself off that cliff. Or, it's like Graham Tate said. Someone was in pursuit."

"Shit." Heyer grimaces. "Of all the ways to go. None of them are good, right? But being chased off a cliff"—she shudders—"that's got to be up there. Oh—" She squints at the brambles. "There's something caught in them, there, look."

Walker does. And sees it now: a small piece of torn black fabric. "We'll have to get SOCO up here, too," he says.

Then he steps nearer the cliff edge. Peers over. Senses that strange pull one often feels in high places to jump. He can see officers clustered down there on the beach. A couple of RIBs anchored out to sea. There's an outcrop of limestone about halfway down, a rust-colored stain on the white. Must have hit that on the way to the bottom. Maybe it made for a quicker end. Then he spots it. An arm:

the only part of the body visible from here. The palm of the hand up, fingers reaching out to sea, as though pleading for mercy.

He catches himself. *Get a grip, Walker.*

He cranes even farther forward. One more step and he might just be able to—

"Jesus Christ, boss!" Heyer shouts as he nearly loses his balance and has to scramble backward, sending a few loose stones scattering into the void. A couple of the officers on the beach glance up. Guess it'll have to wait. He moves along the clifftop, finds a place where the vegetation has been worn away. Turns back to Heyer.

"Here, look. Where the gorse is worn away. It's a path."

Heyer swallows. "Looks pretty dangerous. The others all got here by boat."

But Walker's jittery with impatience. "You can wait here if you like. But this is how I'm getting down."

When they finally reach the sand Heyer turns to him. "Just so you know, boss—that wasn't a path, yeah? That was a frigging death slide." She bends over, hands on her knees. "Man. Too early in the morning for that sort of thing. Thought I was going to lose my breakfast on the middle bit."

"Sorry. It was steeper than it looked."

The two of them begin the short walk across the sand to where SOCO swarm around the body. Walker is impatient to see now. The protective-suited officers make a visual screen as they busy back and forth: he catches only glimpses of the splayed limbs, the bright bloom of blood.

And then Heyer shouts and points. She's looking at a spot several meters ahead of them, a short distance from the body. There, half-submerged in sand: a broken bottle of Bell's whisky.

Bella

THE DAY BEFORE THE SOLSTICE

HOUSEKEEPING HAVE BEEN IN MY room already. Everything's spick and span, the cocktails from last night cleared away. And on the dressing table they've left a writhing arrangement of green-leafed branches, bound into a circle. It gives me a brief jolt, it looks half-alive. I pick it up, read the note attached to it:

Join us tomorrow for our midnight feast. Dress code: woodland coronets and white.

For a moment I just stand and stare at the note. Midnight feast? They're actually calling it a midnight feast? *How fucking dare she.* Of all the sick, evil, twisted—

A second later I glance down and realize I've torn both the note and the "woodland coronet" itself to pieces. Leaves and scraps of paper litter the floorboards. I sweep them into the bin. Let housekeeping make of it what they will.

Twenty minutes later, sitting at breakfast, I try to look as casual as I can scanning the Seashard restaurant. Like I'm taking in the scene, just another guest enjoying her breakfast on a sunny morning in the countryside. It's difficult, though, when it feels like every nerve is standing on end, primed on a hair trigger. Waiting for a sighting. It doesn't help that I feel so conspicuous: surrounded by oh so many couples, holding hands like they can't bear not to touch while they pick their way through their Bircher.

Slightly in contrast to the studiously zen interior of the restaurant there are people chatting at the tops of their voices, almost as though they want to be overheard by the tables around them.

"We're going to have this, like, huge event in the metaverse. It is going to be so sick. We're like . . . internet memes, but make it Banksy. Elon is one of our biggest collectors. Who says exploding kittens can't be art, right?"

Or: "You know, I actually spent most of lockdown in Tulum. It was crazy! There were *so many people there*. It was super-social. I went for a week and ended up staying for months! You just had to watch out for the cenotes because they were a total corona breeding ground."

Or: "Microdosing is where it's at, my man. But not acid, and forget any of that pharmaceutical crap: it's all about the organics now, all about mushrooms. Lion's mane in my smoothie in the morning and then if I need a boost a little sprinkling of the old psilocybin. It has changed. My. Life." The guy actually speaks like that, like there's a full stop between each of the words.

I go for seconds at the breakfast table so I don't have to listen to any more. It's a cornucopia of delights. A huge pyramid of fruits, some of which I couldn't even name and—I think—local produce from the hotel gardens. Burnished golden pastries that nobody seems to be eating; I take a fat croissant.

There's enough food to feed everyone here several times over, especially judging by the average BMI. They're going to be chucking stuff away. Yet everyone is emitting a low-level hum of panic, clustering around the offerings as though they're about to run out. These people can't relax—even while they're here in the Dorset countryside. But then maybe it's *especially* while they're here, considering this is the "new place to be seen." They're the queue-jump, turn-left, I'm-a-member strata of society. I'm familiar with the type, from work. They're the ones who came into the agency to purchase second homes when the pandemic hit, who were ushered into the special private meeting room to "discuss your requirements" (read: exactly what digit goes at the front of that seven-figure budget).

Back at the table my phone buzzes. Mum. Shit, I totally forgot to call. I pick up.

"How is she?" I ask, guilty.

"Taking the bottle like a dream. And she slept through till seven."

I let out a breath. "Great. Phew."

"Is that—hang on, is that a seagull I can hear in the background?" Mum asks. I curse the open windows. Mum has always had irritatingly batlike hearing.

"Yeah," I say, cautiously. "Didn't I tell you? My work thing's by the sea."

"No," she says. "You haven't told me much at all, actually. Where by the sea?"

"It's near . . ." I think, wildly. "Southampton!" That's feasible, right? A big city, good links to London.

"Right," she says. "Southampton." Does she not believe me? It's not like I can tell her the truth. What would she say if she knew I was back here?

Besides, it's not *unlike* a work trip. It's been a bit like a second job, over the years. Keeping tabs. Especially since Francesca Meadows inherited this place. My job on reception isn't that taxing for someone who once had a place waiting for her at a top university (never filled). It's left me with the time and space to get on with other things, with research.

"I better go, love," Mum says. "She's just—"

I just catch myself from asking Mum if Grace is missing me. It's like wanting to press on a bruise. The guilt is real enough already.

I hang up and take a sip of my flat white (I had to beg for dairy, it was like asking for an illegal substance) while I look around the room.

And then I spot her. Sitting in the middle of the hubbub. The image of calm, everything revolving around her still center. She's haloed in light, almost too bright to look at, like an angel in a medieval painting. Then I realize that she's positioned exactly under one of the skylights, morning sun radiating down through the glass. Coincidence or design? She wears a serene half-smile as she lifts a glass of something to her lips: a drink that is exactly the same sunshine yellow as the off-the-shoulder linen dress she's wearing.

I read about how she went on a pilgrimage: how she "found my-self" and "healed myself" while meditating at some ashram in the foothills of the Himalayas. It detailed how much "work I've done on myself." About how, rather than some holy visitation, she found the clarity she needed for what to do next with her life: start running high-end wellness retreats for women with excess cortisol and money. And then, of course, she opened this place.

I watch her, riveted. I'm not the only one. Many of those who aren't focused on guarding the pastries they're never going to eat are keeping an eye on her. There are three or four famous faces here: a couple of actresses, I think, and one man-child who might be a singer. But somehow right now they pale in comparison to the radi-ant Francesca Meadows.

Then she turns and, for a few seconds, meets my gaze. There's a trembling of something in the air between us. Her smile remains in place and she continues surveying the room. I dip my face beneath my hair. But she saw me, I'm certain of it. A shiver passes through me. It's the feeling they say you get when someone has walked over your grave.

Summer Journal

THE CARAVAN—TATE'S HOLIDAY PARK
JULY 31, 2010

Super hot today. Lay by the pool with Frankie and we listened to The Cure on Frankie's pink iPod plugged into little portable speakers. Frankie flipped over to sun her back. Midnight feast tomorrow, Sparrow! You excited?

Um, yeah, I said, even though I haven't been to a midnight feast since I was about ten.

Frankie went back to reading Legends of Tome, which she got from this weird little local bookshop. I've got a Jilly Cooper, Bella, that I found on the lending shelf at the caravan park.

That cover's so shit, Frankie said. (It's this woman with horrendous bouffant seventies hair and turquoise eye shadow.) Bella's a cool name though, she said, tapping my book's cover. You could call yourself that.

I asked: what's wrong with Alison?

She went: it's just a bit . . . where're you from again?

I said Streatham and she shrugged: just saying Bella's a cool name, that's all.

Next second she jumped up, pointed out to sea.

See that boat? One of the fishermen's looking right at us, perve—see his binoculars glinting? She ran inside and got Grandfa's telescope, looked through it and was like: oh, it's just some kid and handed it to me. It was that dark-haired boy from the beach, Shrimp. She grinned and went: I'm gonna give him something to look at. Pulled up her bikini top and flashed him. Just like that.

This is why I like hanging out with her. You never know what she's going to do next. The thrill. Just scared she's going to work out I'm not cool enough, get bored of me. Wish I could be more like the girl I met in the shower block here at the caravan park doing her make-up. Older than me . . . definitely cooler. Maybe late twenties, tiny wrinkles round her eyes. Amy Winehouse dark hair piled up on her head, lots of delicate tattoos on her hands and arms, bangles on her wrists. She must have caught me staring cos she grinned and I saw one of her teeth was broken in half which on most people would look minging but on her was kind of cool, cos she's so pretty I guess.

Hey, she said. I'm Cora. You staying here?

I said yeah. She drew some liner on the inner rim of her eyes which made her look like a beautiful cat.

I can't do that without it smudging everywhere, I told her.

Want me to do it for you? she asked. I said yeah and as she did it my eyes went all watery and this Celtic knot ring on her finger bumped cold against my cheek. Her breath smelt of fags and spearmint gum and she was like: suits you and I looked in the mirror and I felt like a different person.

What's your name? she asked.

Bella, I said.

AUGUST 1, 2010

Set my alarm for 11:30 tonight and snuck out of the caravan with some Skips and Dairy Milk (from Mum's stash of beach snacks). It was spooky walking along the cliff path on my own in the moonlight with the big drop on one side. When I looked at the dark sea I thought about Graham Tate's story about those horses being led over the cliffs one night.

I got a shock when I looked back at the path and saw three tall guys coming in the other direction. But then one of them was, like, oh hey, it's you, and I realized it was the guy from the beach, the one with the toffee-colored hair. He asked if I was OK or lost and I told him I was going to meet my mate.

From The Manor? He pulled this face.

Those posh wankers, said one of the blokes with him. And he went: shut up Nate. Then he said to me, well, if you ever get bored of that place, come down to the beach sometime, yeah? We could hang out? I was glad it was dark so he couldn't see my face. But I kept thinking about it the whole way to The Manor and grinning to myself like a total loser.

Frankie met me at the gates. The twins were there, too. They had this girl with them in a Kappa tracksuit, with the poppers down the side. When I asked Frankie her name she was like, oh, just some local skank. The twins were both larking about, showing off, trying to make her laugh.

We're going into the woods, Frankie said. Come on.

She had this little beaded bag over one arm and was carrying the fossil I found in the rockpool. I showed her the food I'd nicked from the caravan and she was like: ohmigod, Sparrow, you crack me up! It's not that kind of midnight feast but I guess we could use some snacks.

We walked into the woods. Never been anywhere so quiet. There was less moonlight as the trees are so close together but Frankie had a torch. I was trying not to think about Blair Witch. First we passed this dead white tree with two forked branches.

That's the Wishbone, Frankie said. This way. The twins followed us—showing off, doing wolf howls and stuff. It's weird though cos even though they're older Frankie is definitely the leader. I could hear that girl giggling. She kept going: what are we doing? But no one answered her.

Frankie led us through the trees to this clearing where all these stones were arranged in a circle around a tree. It reminded me of going to see Stonehenge with Mum and Dad, but a mini version.

We shouldn't be here, the tracksuit girl said. This is where they come.

Frankie was like: who? And the girl went: the birds, but the way she said it made it sound like: The Birds. I thought about Graham Tate's story. Started to feel a bit scared. Kind of giggly, excited too. But mainly scared.

Frankie just laughed and shone her torch up at the tree in the middle of the stones. It had all these weird shapes in the bark, hundreds of them. I was trying to think what they reminded me of when the tracksuit girl went: it's called the Tree with a Hundred Eyes. And yeah it did look like that, like all these eyes, all different shapes and sizes, staring out in all directions.

Frankie stuck out her hand. Look at this, she said, pointing to a long narrow slot in the tree. It made me think of a postbox or a mouth. She turned to me and went: dare you to put your hand in there.

I laughed. Said I didn't want to.

Go on, Frankie said. Do it.

So finally I did and I know it sounds stupid but I had this feeling like I might never get it back out again. And then the girl went: you're not meant to touch the tree unless you're going to use it.

Frankie turned to her. Use it?

Yeah. The girl sounded a bit embarrassed. You can, like, leave messages for them in the tree.

Messages?

If you want them to do something for you. Like, for revenge.

Frankie shone her torch right in the girl's face. Cute! You actually believe that stuff, don't you? And she laughed.

The girl laughed too but I don't think she found it that funny.

After that we walked to the old treehouse. I could see a rickety ladder going up into the tree and a dark shape kind of squatting in the branches. It was so dark up in there and smelt of old rotting wood and the floor was damp under my bum. The five of us hardly fit inside. Then Frankie opened her little bag and shone her torch inside.

Nice work sis, Hugo said. Oscar laughed. Fuck me you've cleaned her out. Frankie rattled the bag at me. <u>This</u> is our feast, she said. My mum's a cow but she's useful for something. Imagine her face when she gets to St. Trop with her toyboy and realizes she doesn't have her stash of chill pills. Serves her right for dumping us here every summer.

I kind of panicked. I've never taken drugs . . . only even been drunk once. I took one and put it in my mouth but when Frankie wasn't looking I spat it out so I only swallowed the coating.

The twins took theirs. So did the girl. Then Hugo leaned over and said something to Frankie and she grabbed my arm and was like, come on, let's leave them to it.

We walked back to the clearing. Frankie took all these little tealights out of her pockets, laid them down in the space between the stones before she lit them. She put the fossil in the middle. This can be our summoning tool, she said.

I asked what we were summoning. My voice had gone all wobbly. I could hear scrabbling in the bushes nearby. Told myself it was just a rabbit.

Frankie went: the Birds, silly. Thing is, what we really need is a human sacrifice.

I went totally cold.

She laughed at me. I'm joking! Ohmigod, you're so gullible, Sparrow.

She made me lie back down on the old dead leaves on the ground with her and it was damp and cold but she took my hand and hers was warm and dry.

Maybe I swallowed more of the pill than I thought cos I couldn't really feel the ground under my back and it was a bit like I was floating and I could feel my heart beating like crazy, couldn't breathe properly.

Then there was this sound, like a scream. And then Frankie was going ow, fuck's sake Sparrow, my hand! Hadn't realized how hard I was gripping.

What was that? I asked. Did you hear? And Frankie was like, ooh, I don't know. Maybe it worked. Maybe it was the Birds! Then she laughed and was like, it's probably a fox. They sound horrendous when they're having sex. But I had a bad feeling. Glanced at the treehouse.

The twins joined us after. The girl had gone home, they said. Then just before I left Frankie gave me a big hug and was like, that was fun right? And I said yeah, because it *was* kind of fun. In a creepy way. Then she said: but next time swallow the pill, Sparrow. It's no fun if you don't. It's kind of a letdown? I hate it when people let me down.

Francesca

I THOUGHT IT WOULD BE a good look, to mingle with the guests this morning. To show I'm one of them.

It was a little awkward when everyone turned to stare when I entered the restaurant; I suppose they all know who I am. For a lot of people I'm "the face of The Manor" (I think that may actually be a direct quote from the *Harper's Bazaar* article about me).

I take a sip of my drink: a vegan turmeric shake—we press our own almond milk here. Ugh, not great. I put up a finger and beckon over Georgina, the Seashard manager. "Georgina, darling—this is so watery? We can't be giving our guests something they could get out of any old carton! Yes?"

Georgina nods, meekly.

"OK, you're *amazing*! Run along and sort it, thank you my lovely. I so appreciate it."

She melts away.

It's not the almond milk, though. Something else is off. Similar to that feeling when you're in the sea and you swim into a patch that's much colder than the rest, with no obvious explanation. Yes, that's it: a cold current of bad energy on this gloriously warm day. I am *highly* sensitive to such things.

I glance around the breakfast room to ground myself, to remind myself that this is my space. Nothing can affect me here—

I stop short. Somewhere in the crowd I spotted a face. A face that . . . shouldn't be here. I try to find it again among the bustle of the room. It's like when a word on a page jumps out at you before you've read it, but you can't recall exactly where you saw it.

No, I remind myself. It's not possible. We've asked the guests to submit little potted bios "so we can best accommodate you and tailor your experience accordingly." I want to know who's staying with us. Nothing sinister, just so we have a true sense of community. I looked them all over myself, as I plan to do going forward. So I would know if anything were amiss. Then why do I feel so horrible, like I've been poisoned . . . ? I can just imagine the flood of cortisol through my veins.

I take another sip of the drink and almost spit it out. It tastes awful. A horrid metallic flavor in my mouth. I stand up and my chair clatters backward. The guests at the next table look up. I see the man glance at my mouth and wince. Instinctively, I put my fingers to my lips. I hadn't even been aware of it but I must have bitten into the flesh, because my fingertips come away stained with blood.

Owen

I PULL ON MY WORK boots, stride out in the direction of the woods. I'm looking forward to losing myself in the practicalities of today's work: preparing the ground for the Treehouse project. The Treehouses will have rope walks, tree bridges, wooden ladders, outdoor showers perched several feet up. They'll also have four-poster beds, state-of-the-art sound systems, and electronically retractable roof panels so guests can look up at the branches for the full "forest bathing" experience.

I can see the tree surgeon waiting at the edge of the woods in his chainsaw-proof overalls, tools lying on the ground beside him.

"Hey." He sticks out a hand as I approach. "It's Jim, I—"

"I've marked the trees to come down with a white X," I cut in, without any preamble. "See? There's this group here for a start."

"Yeah, er—" Something in his tone makes me turn and look more closely at him. He's standing with his arms crossed, something defensive about his posture. "I don't want to cut those down, mate."

"What?" I must have misheard him.

"I said I don't want to cut those down." At least he has the good grace to look a little sheepish.

I don't have time for this. "Why the hell not? It's literally what you're being paid to do."

A jerk of his head. "Those there, at the front—they're elder trees."

"Yes, I'm aware of that, thanks." The branches are heavy with the pungent white blossoms of the elderflowers.

"You know what they say about cutting down an elder?"

I am vaguely aware that there's some superstition attached to the trees. My mother was into stuff like that. But I'm not going to save him any embarrassment—I'm going to make him spell it out. "No. What do they say?"

He scratches behind an ear. "Well, it's bad luck, right? You can only cut a few branches and even then you have to—" He coughs, looking more awkward, as frankly a grown man talking about this sort of shit should. "Ask permission first."

"Ask permission?"

He looks more sheepish still. "From—er—the Elder Mother. The spirit inside the tree. But if you cut the whole thing down . . . well, that's properly bad luck, that is."

"Hang on. Let me get this straight. You've been hired to cut these trees down and now you're telling me you refuse to do so?"

"It does say it on my website, mate. 'No elders.' It's—you know—one of my conditions."

What is it with people in this part of the world? Still this backward insistence on witchcraft, and weirdness. True, Francesca is into all things spiritual. But there's a refreshing common sense about the way she approaches it. Selective, you could say. Useful in as much as it can benefit her. Some might say cynical; I see it as practical.

I realize Jim is watching me, presumably waiting for my reaction.

"OK, I'll do the elders myself. The oaks then: you can do the oaks. I've sprayed the ones that need to come down. The white Xs."

Jim frowns. "You're not the only one who's marked them, mate."

"What do you mean?"

"Take a look."

He beckons me forward. Points out a mark on the nearest tree. Not sprayed-on like my Xs; carved into the bark. They're fresh cuts, the exposed wood showing through raw and wet. They must have been very recently done. I step back to take in the mark properly. It's like a crude drawing of a bird in flight.

I can't help the sense of foreboding that surfaces like an unwanted taste at the back of my tongue.

"Right," I say, as much to myself as to Jim. "So some local vandals have had some fun. Tell me it means anything more than that."

Jim grimaces. "I think it means: 'don't cut the tree down,' mate. I think it means: 'something bad could happen if you do.'"

"For Christ's sake. They tried to block us via the local council, now they're trying this. It's pathetic."

We've made a few enemies, locally. That's the thing about these parts: a hatred of progress, of change. We've received some pretty grim post since the planning permission for The Treehouses went through—threats and insults. "And," I continue, "they've trespassed onto private property to do it. It will give me great pleasure to have these cut down. So, let's get to it."

"Yeah." Now Jim looks really uncomfortable. "See, I'm really sorry but I just can't, mate. Gives me the creeps."

"But you've been paid—"

He puts up his hands in surrender. "You can have your money back. It's not worth it. This is a strange place, you know? Tome. Stuff here you don't want to meddle in." He shoots a nervous glance deep into the trees. "Had a fry-up at the pub on the way over. People aren't happy about this place, are they?" He shakes his head. "Not happy at all." I wonder exactly what he's heard, but I don't press him. Best to remain detached.

"Look," I say. "You can keep your money, which I think is pretty bloody decent of me, but I'm going to use your chainsaw. Got it? The spirits aren't going to get you if I'm the one holding it, are they? And I'm happy to take my chances." I gesture for the machine. If bad spirits exist, they've already had their way with me.

After a brief moment of hesitation, he hands over the chainsaw. It growls as I fire it up. I position it against the bark of the near-est oak, feeling the explosion of splinters as it begins to bite and trying to ignore a tiny stab of unease. Suddenly, I seem to hear the tinkling melody of an old children's tune. "The Teddy Bears' Picnic," with its curiously menacing promise of a secret woodland gathering.

I grit my teeth and drown it out with the roar of the machine. When I glance at Jim he's turned his back, as though he can't bear to look.

AFTERWARDS I SIT down on one of the fallen logs to light up, the woods behind me. It's odd. I have the feeling of being watched, a prickle down the back of my neck. I glance over my shoulder a couple of times but there's no one there. Perhaps it's just the sweat trickling into my eyes that makes for the odd shiver of movement between the trees. But I can't shake the feeling of unease. The memory of the dead bird on the door floats queasily before me.

As I sit and smoke I become aware of something jabbing into the back of my thigh. I reach into my short pocket and pull out the little cream envelope. In the wake of dealing with that dead creature and being interrupted by Michelle, I completely forgot about it.

I read the name scrawled on the front: *FRANKIE*.

Who's Frankie?

A jolt as I understand. It must be addressed to Francesca, though I've never heard her called that. And maybe *because* I've never heard her called that, I can't resist turning it over and breaking the seal. The little piece of notepaper that slides out is familiar—*The Manor* printed in dark green at the top, the address beneath and a miniature line drawing of the building.

> *Meet me in the woods at midnight. Just like old times? Beneath the tree with a hundred eyes. It's been a while. We have a lot to discuss.*

I don't like it. That's my first thought. The nickname. The familiarity. The midnight summons to the woods. Was it left by the same person who nailed the cockerel to the door? If so, it takes on a really sinister undertone. Especially because whoever wrote it had access to hotel stationery, which makes it difficult to dismiss as the prank of a random local. And if it wasn't left by the same person who left the dead creature, I still don't like it. Because it suggests intimacy. A shared history. Reading through it again my eye snags on certain phrases:

It's been a while.

. . . a lot to discuss.

It preys on one of my insecurities about our relationship. How short a time Francesca and I have been together, how shallow our knowledge of each other really is. I'm aware of how little of myself I've revealed to her. But Francesca, with her wholesomeness, her emphasis on "radical honesty," has always seemed an open book. Now it occurs to me that there may be another deeper self, a history, that I know nothing of.

Frankie.

I fold up the note and shove it back into my pocket. But I can feel it there, the sharp ridge of the envelope cutting into my leg. I don't like it, with its suggestion of secrets. I *really* fucking hate anyone keeping secrets, especially those closest to me.

DI Walker

THE DAY AFTER THE SOLSTICE

WALKER CLIMBS INTO A PROTECTIVE suit, to match the other white-clad figures on the beach. At a little distance stands a group of fishermen: the ones who found the body and called it in. They form an uneasy, watchful audience.

A surge of fresh adrenaline hits as he approaches the victim. He can see the whole thing now because there isn't time to erect a tent over it, with the tide coming in. The blood-soaked fabric catching in the breeze. The obscene, broken-puppet angles of the limbs and neck. The ruin of the face. Features totally destroyed by the impact.

Not like it would have helped much to land on sand not rock. But it would have made less of a mess.

It's only when he glances up and catches Heyer's expression that he realizes he's spoken the thought out loud. She looks shocked. He's shocked at himself, actually, at his own callousness. He's usually so careful to be respectful of the victim and their dignity in death.

"Boss?" He turns and finds the crime scene manager standing there, frowning at him. She dangles a small clear plastic evidence bag with gloved fingers. "We found this," she says. "It was held in the victim's hand."

There's an exclamation behind them. Walker turns and sees that several of the fishermen are staring at the evidence bag. Who let them stand so close? They shouldn't even be near enough to see it but there's nothing he can do about it now. He watches one of them actually lift a hand to make a swift sign of the cross.

"Is that . . . ?" Heyer has come nearer to look, too. "Is that a . . . ?"

"It appears to belong to some kind of corvid," the crime scene manager says. "A raven or a crow—a bird of that species, anyway. We'll know exactly which later."

Walker studies it through the clear plastic. The oily sheen of it, the little puff of dark down at the base above the sharp quill.

A small black feather.

Bella

IT'S NOT YET NOON BUT I'm drinking a Manor Margarita as I sit on a green-and-white-striped sunlounger beside the pool, planning my next move.

From here I can see the bay and the beach just below. In the intense midsummer light the sea has turned aquamarine, navy where it meets the horizon and the cloudless blue of the sky. The steps down to the beach ten meters below are accessorized with a little painted sign and a rope handrail. Lackeys stand ready to carry down striped-green umbrellas and matching plush towels for the guests, coolers full of drinks and gourmet snacks.

The infinity pool is a piece of Owen Dacre architectural wizardry, giving the illusion of a steep drop from the cliffs into the open sea. The tiling is a muted grayish green. I remember, from many summers ago, the old mildewed flagstones, lichen-covered water nymph statues, and a pool house crammed with random odds and sods. The past shimmers like a mirage on the water.

I recall scrabbling about for a handful of pound coins. Her shout from the sunlounger: "If you find them, you can keep them!" Then lying to dry on the warm rough stones that snagged my bikini bottoms, feeling the heat of the sun caress, then begin to bite. The scent of chlorine a sting in the nostrils.

My sunlounger's near the "infinity" end of the pool, nearest the sea. Nearly all the beds are already taken. The ones that aren't strewn with Instagram-flawless bodies (mainly the women) and client-account paunches (mainly the men) have been marked out by towels: no matter how rich you are, no one's above staking out their territory like package holidaymakers.

I get up and move in the direction of the pool. I won't put my head under. Blonde takes care, the hairdresser warned me: chlorine turns it green. That wouldn't really work with the whole vibe I'm going for here. I climb down the steps, sink into the water. It actually *feels* expensive; the texture like silk. My toes touch the bottom. No slimy skin underfoot in this pool.

Afterwards, I clamber back onto the hot canvas of my sunbed. Sultry Euro house seeps from the speakers. Snippets of conversation drift over from the sunbed next to me.

"Jesus, look at the rack on that."

"More of a leg man, personally. That foxy little receptionist—now you're talking."

"So you're invested in this place, too?"

"Yeah. Put some cash into it when I sold the company. Thought I'd help sis out. We spent whole summers by the pool. Strange to be back at the scene of the crime. Of course, it was a hideous kidney-shaped monstrosity back then, nothing like this. But we thought it was the shit at the time."

Suddenly, all my senses are on high alert.

"You've got to give Fran credit: she's spruced the place up all right."

I hardly dare to turn my head. But behind my sunglasses I glance to the right. Enough to glimpse pink swim shorts, an unfortunate match for a developing sunburn. Soft puff of stomach above the band. My gaze climbs to the expensive haircut, receding a little at the front—but not enough to disguise that distinctive shock of white hair at the crown.

Hugo.

"Shit!" Margarita slops down my chest. I dab with the corner of my towel. I'm aware of the two guys turning to look, no doubt exchanging a glance at the crazy loner drinking cocktails at this hour.

I want very much to get up and leave. But I'm suddenly so light-headed with unease I'm not sure I can manage the walk. Instead I bow my head, letting my hair fall over my face, and sit with my heart thundering in my ears. Then, with clumsy fingers, I reach into my bag and pull out my poolside reading. The decrepit old notebook stands out a little next to the finance bro tomes and Booker Prize winners everyone else is "reading" (they're not, the books are just strewn about like sunlounger window-dressing).

I take a long slug of my drink. Turn the pages until I find the spot I'm looking for.

"Yeah, Francesca's done a great job," I hear Hugo Meadows's companion say.

Thank God: they're chatting again. I sense the spotlight of their attention receding.

"Yeah," Hugo says. "Had to laugh at those manicured little paths going into the woods, though. When I think how we used to run about in them like total reprobates!"

"Sounds fantastic."

"Yeah. Plenty of good outdoorsy fun in those woods."

That last line hits like a punch in the gut.

Summer Journal

THE CARAVAN—TATE'S HOLIDAY PARK
AUGUST 2, 2010

This morning, Frankie and I were by the pool with our books and she said: that was fun, right? In the woods?

Yeah, I said. Even though last night I had bad dreams.

Then she leaned over and tapped my book and went: you're reading Jilly Cooper for the sex, right? That's why I read Polo.

And I was like, er . . . maybe. Then she turned to me with her face so close I could smell her Juicy Tube gloss and went: you have had sex, right? Omigod (like she could tell from my face I've only kissed one boy) you haven't! Babe! We need to get on that. Slim fucking pickings round here, though.

I nearly told her about the guy with the toffee-colored hair from the day I found the fossil. I see him sometimes when I walk the cliff path. He has an orange paddleboard but I'd spot him without it. His body's <u>Heat</u> torso-of-the-week amazing. He and his mates swim out to The Giant's Hand and jump off sometimes. He does it like it doesn't scare him at all. Not in a show-off way, just super casual. The other evening he looked up and spotted me and waved and last night I thought about the line of his hips above the waistband of his green board shorts and back in my room alone I ————————————

Mum if you're reading this PUT IT DOWN.

Didn't tell Frankie about him in the end. She can be funny about locals. And also, maybe I want to keep him to myself?

AUGUST 3, 2010

Saw that Shrimp kid again this eve. There's a caravan that's a little away from the others, dirtier and older and looks like someone actually lives there—washing line, old pot plants and that. He was sitting there crouched on the caravan steps.

He was playing with this box of matches, lighting one after another, watching the flame all the way down till it must have been burning his fingers. You know how there's always a kid at school who gets picked on for being weird/poor/wearing hand-me-down clothes? Yeah, you could tell that was him. I felt bad for him.

I said hi and he mumbled something. And then I was like, it's Shrimp, right? And he just muttered: what's it to you? I mean, whatever. I was only trying to be nice.

Heard the match first, this SCRIIITCH sound that made me jump. Then I looked closer and saw the flame and his face lit up by it. Super creepy.

AUGUST 4, 2010

Two things happened today. Two bad things.

There was a storm last night. Proper electrical storm with lightning out to sea. But it was hot again this morning so me and Frankie went to the pool. The cover had a load of leaves and stuff on top of it. There was this bulge under it too . . . thought maybe one of the floaties had got trapped there. Frankie started winding it open and when it got halfway back I saw this thing poking out from under the plastic, like a little cluster of twigs. Then I saw it was a bird's claw. Frankie just kept winding until the whole thing appeared, all broken and mangled looking. It was so gross. It seemed huge. I didn't realize they were that big. They look much smaller in the sky.

Must have got blown in by the storm, I said.

Yeah, Frankie said. She stared at me. But then how did it get trapped <u>under</u> the cover?

I asked what she meant.

I think it's them, she said. The Birds. Maybe we did summon them after all. Go get the net, Sparrow. Pool house.

The pool house gives me the creeps. It's musty and dark and probably full of spiders. It seemed so dark in there, cos it was so bright outside. The light-switch doesn't work and I couldn't see the net anywhere. Just random stuff: broken jugs, empty plant pots, garden twine, dusty old paperbacks.

Then I saw it leaning in the corner. Stepped forward to grab it. That's when I felt hands on my waist. I made this sound, like our cat Widget does when you step on his tail. For a second I didn't know if I was excited or scared. Then he laughed and pushed me back into the corner. I was scared then. How much stronger he was as he spun me round to face him. I crossed my arms over my tummy but I couldn't cover all of myself and he was pressing himself against me. He was blocking out the light and all I could see was that white streak of hair and all I could smell was Lynx Africa and sweat. He shoved his tongue in my mouth and I gagged on Cool Original flavor Doritos and weed. Then his fingers were in my bikini bottoms. I pulled back, managed to say: let me out.

He went: don't give me that. I see the way you look at me. Parading round in your bikini. Dirty little prick-tease. Was doing you a favor. Not gonna get many guys coming on to you with a chest that flat.

When I came out I felt blinded it was so bright. Back at the pool Frankie pushed her sunglasses down her nose like a movie star and looked at me over the top of them. Oh, there you are, she said. Found what you were looking for?

AUGUST 5, 2010

Don't want to make the pool house a thing. Don't want to think about it too much. Don't want it to spoil The Manor for me. I went back today cos I want to pretend everything's normal. But I keep playing it over in my head. Keep remembering Hugo's tongue pushing into my mouth. Woke up this morning feeling like I couldn't breathe.

Maybe it's not that bad? Maybe I did give him the wrong idea? Maybe if I just keep my distance from him it'll be OK.

Just wish I could stop thinking about it. The things he said about my body. The word he used. Dirty.

Luckily he totally ignored me today. He was having this big fight with Oscar instead, something about a tracksuit. Hugo kept saying Oscar had nicked his but Oscar was like, it's got my fucking nametag in you bellend. Look!

Ugh, they're pissing me off so much, Frankie said. They've nicked half my stash of pills so now I've only got a handful to last me the summer.

Haven't told Frankie about it. Like, what if I do and she gets weird about it? Sees me differently, thinks I asked for it? Worse . . . what if I look at her face and see she already knows?

AUGUST 6, 2010

Frankie invited me to The Crow's Nest tonight. It's this old-worldy pub in Tome with low ceilings and wooden beams. Thought it would just be me and her but the twins were there too as they'd driven over in Oscar's lime green Golf GTI. Froze when I saw Hugo at the table. But he just went: Hi! Friendly smile like none of it happened, like he didn't do or say those horrible things or it wasn't as bad as I remember (if it wasn't, why am I still having bad dreams?). He even asked me if I wanted a drink. But the landlady wouldn't serve us cos no one had ID (even though the twins are old enough). Felt like everyone in there was staring at us.

We were about to leave when someone said, oh hey! It's you! It was Cora, from the caravan park shower block, with her Amy Winehouse hair and these leather trousers and a white vest. The twins were drooling and Frankie couldn't stop staring and I felt kind of proud that she remembered me. Cora was like, I work here—I've been painting the sign outside, look! She held up her hands and her palms were covered in gold paint. But I really need a bloody drink. When she smiled I saw the broken tooth and also the dark shadows under her eyes but they kind of suited her too.

Frankie said well, they won't serve us and she went: I'll sort you out. Asked everyone what they wanted. Hugo gave her a twenty. She came back with the drinks and said: yeah got myself a double G&T, hope that's OK? Hugo just nodded like a shy little boy. She sat down with us. She got us three rounds in the end, until this woman walked past and was like, Cora. Can I have a word? When she came back she went: fucking brilliant. Alcohol for minors, apparently. She's been waiting to fire me, I swear. Well there goes another job. But they can't stop me finishing my drink. She seemed a bit drunk by then and went on about going to Glasto "in my old life," the others hanging on every word. I got up to go to the toilet. Asked if Frankie wanted to go. She didn't even look at me when she said no.

Coming out of the toilets I crashed into someone tall and for a moment I freaked. Sure it was Hugo, come to find me, to show the whole nice-guy thing at the table was an act. Then I saw the silver neck chain. The boy from the beach. Hey, he said, I was just going to grab some fish and chips next door. Fancy it? It's Jake, by the way.

It seemed better than going back and sitting opposite Hugo so I said yeah. We left out the back.

I was deciding on haddock or cod when I saw the person behind the counter and just kind of froze. It was the girl who came to the woods with us the night of the midnight feast.

When she went to lift the basket of chips I saw her hand shake. Oil splashed up her arm and she did this little yelp. I asked if she was OK.

She went: like you fucking care.

But now I think I know what happened to her in the treehouse. I was about to do or say something to show I got it, but Frankie and the twins came in. Frankie went, what the hell, Sparrow? If you want a lift we're going now. When I looked back at the counter the door behind it was swinging shut and the girl had gone. I glanced at Jake about to make a lame apology but he just smiled and shrugged, said: another time?

In the car, Frankie said: who was that boy? I said, super casual, oh, Jake? I've just bumped into him a few times. But I think my voice went a bit funny. She wrinkled her nose. But you don't actually LIKE him, do you?

I asked why and she shrugged. Well, if you like that kind of thing. But that neck chain he wears . . . so tacky! And that yokel accent! Can you imagine when he comes? It would be like fucking the guy from the Ambrosia advert. Ooh arrr! Then she looked at my face and was like, babes, I'm only looking out for you, yeah? Anyway. Another midnight feast tomorrow?

When I didn't answer straight away she went: maybe if you can't make it I'll ask Cora. She's cool, isn't she?

I said I'd go.

When I got back to the caravan park Shrimp was sitting there next to the entrance playing with his little box of matches. He didn't spot me and as the flame lit his face I saw him staring out of the gates up the track. His eyes looked so big and dark. And yeah he was kind of a dick to me when I tried to speak to him that time and a bit of a creep watching us from that fishing boat through his binoculars. But I felt sorry for him, cos right then he looked like a lost little boy.

AUGUST 7, 2010

Last night was . . .

I'm just gonna write it here.

Frankie was like, I made brownies! Proper midnight feast. We ate them on the way over to the woods. Have another, Sparrow, Frankie said, shaking the box at me. Or I'll just eat them all myself.

It was so warm we were just in T-shirts and shorts and the stars were crazy beautiful and clear. Frankie looped her arm through mine and the twins were just doing their own thing ahead. Felt better about everything. Such a magic night I could pretend the pool house never happened.

By the time we got to the treehouse I'd started to feel a bit strange, like my feet weren't touching the ground. And Frankie was like, ha, Sparrow! You ate TWO hash brownies, what did you think was going to happen?

Then she gasped, grabbed my arm. Oh my God! Look! She shone the torch up at the treehouse. I actually stopped breathing. There were all these symbols painted over it. Hundreds of them. The color, a dark red . . . it looked like blood. I'll try and draw one here:

Holy shit, Hugo said.

And Frankie went: oh my God, I know what that is. I saw it in the <u>Legends of Tome</u> book. It's their mark. See how it looks like a bird? She was gripping my arm so tight it hurt. Sparrow! Shit . . . do you think we summoned them? I didn't think that would actually work . . .

Could tell the twins were as scared as we were: Hugo was all quiet and he's never quiet and Oscar was muttering something about getting out of there.

Then Frankie shouted: look in the tree! She pointed the torch up at the branches of the tree that held the treehouse. I saw these "nests" there, about ten of them. But they didn't look like any birds' nests I'd ever seen, cos they were so big and all ragged and they looked like they were tied together with black string. And wouldn't we have seen them if they were there the other night?

Let's look in the treehouse, Frankie said.

Hell no, Hugo said.

And she went: chicken.

He told her to fuck off and I guess to prove they weren't chicken he and Oscar went first. Frankie and I followed. Didn't want to go up there but <u>really</u> didn't want to be left on my own on the ground.

Before I even saw what was inside I heard Hugo mutter: what the fuck. He sounded properly scared then. And I saw what he was staring at.

There was a body in there. Just lying there, this big dark shape slumped against the back wall. I almost legged it there and then, but Frankie shone her torch on it fully and you could see it was like a Bonfire Night guy: some clothes stuffed with straw.

That's my fucking tracksuit, said Hugo, his voice all strangled.

Look at the face, Oscar said.

Frankie shone the torch there and screamed.

It had the head of a bird. A huge beak and what looked like real feathers and these big blank staring eye holes.

Hugo turned to Oscar and was like, you fucking joker, I knew you'd stolen my tracksuit and you could tell he was trying to kind of duke it out, and he shoved Oscar who was like, it wasn't me, I swear it wasn't me. Fuck's sake. He sounded scared. He went, do you think it's because . . . do you think she . . .

Hugo shouted: just shut up. Shut up. It's nothing. It's just some stupid party shop mask, look. He picked up the whole thing and shoved it out of the treehouse and it landed with this horrible FLUMP on the ground outside. It was hard to remember it wasn't an actual body.

And then Frankie shouted: wait. There's something there . . . look. She went to pick it up. It was a note where the body had been. This freakish, jagged handwriting. I said: THE BIRDS ARE WATCHING.

Bella

"SOMETHING'S BURNING," THE GIRL ON the lounger next to me says. I'm dragged blinking back into the present, from the cool dark of the woods into heat and sunlight. She's sitting up, nose aloft. Her partner glances over lazily. "It's probably the pizza oven," he says. "The outdoor bar has one."

"No," she says, "it's coming from the beach." And maybe the breeze shifts because suddenly we're surrounded by a stinging blue cloud of woodsmoke, so thick you can barely see the other side of the pool.

"Jesus!" says the guy, sitting up straight. "Who's lit a fire in this heat?"

"Look!" the girl says, shrilly, pointing.

The breeze shifts and the smoke thins a little, and I can make out figures down there on the sand next to a small inflatable dinghy. A little gaggle of kids in their late teens, early twenties. The smoke's billowing from a bonfire they've lit in the middle of the beach.

There's the putt-putt-putt of an engine and another small boat arrives, its board-shorted occupants—all male—jumping out into the shallows, dragging it to shore. I watch them from behind my dark glasses: the lean, tanned bodies. Do they have any idea how beautiful they are? I think of Eddie last night, his blush. Probably not. You'd have to be pretty cynical to know your power at that age. The male guests here probably spend collective lifetimes in the gym, and hundreds of pounds on those tailored swim trunks, but they're soft and pallid by comparison, no match for the raw glamour of these boys with their hard brown bodies and ratty board shorts.

Perhaps the only guy from The Manor who could compete is the one I met at the beach this morning: Owen Dacre.

A third boat appears, this one roaring in at a phenomenal speed, braking just before it hits the beach. Everyone around the pool is looking now. Then a girl with hair dyed the dark red of cherry cola saunters out of the waves in black thong bikini bottoms and nothing else. She looks like a punk mermaid or a Gen Z take on Botticelli's *Venus*, hair a wet slick down her back and skin pale as sea foam, tattoos inked in blue-black contrast. Never having had much in the way of boobs myself I'm amazed by hers: huge and gravity-defying on her slender body. She wrings out her hair, hip cocked, totally unselfconscious. She must know she has an audience.

"Holy shit," I hear the guy next to Hugo Meadows breathe, covering his lap with his *GQ*. I'm jealous of the girl's figure, sure I am. But most of all I'm jealous of her bravado or confidence or sheer brass balls: whatever you want to call it.

Now the kids on the beach—a crowd of about twenty—are getting into formation, stepping into a long line across the sand. Their leader looks older than the rest, almost middle-aged, wearing some sort of band T-shirt and holding something—a loudhailer—in his hand. Suddenly they all raise their heads in our direction. One guy makes a very definite gesture.

The chatter up here has completely ceased. It's so quiet you can hear the sounds of the pool's filtration system, birdsong. "They can't come up here, can they?" the girl to the left of me murmurs.

"No, darling," her partner says, "there's a locked gate."

But it suddenly doesn't feel like enough.

The first stone falls in the pool. It's almost like it happens in slow motion: the surface of the water bending to receive it, then the shattering of the smooth surface, the shockwaves spreading outwards.

"What the fu—" someone nearby says, before the next stone falls and the next and the next, until they're hailing down around us, landing in the pool, on the sunbeds, striking exposed flesh. There's a brief silence of total shock and outrage, and then guests are swearing, screaming, overturning sunbeds in their haste to get away. Glasses and coffee cups shatter, sunbathing spots and mobiles are abandoned, a pair of Oliver Peoples shades are trampled underfoot.

"Call the police!" a guy shrieks. But already the storm seems to have passed. One final pebble plops into the pool like a piece of punctuation and then there's the roar of several outboard engines gunning down below. Just before they leave a voice blares through a loudhailer: "More where that came from, you posh fucks! Enjoy your stay!"

Francesca

MICHELLE JUST CALLED TO SAY there's been a disturbance on the beach. Locals, again. She assures me it's all in hand, nothing to worry about now. Still . . . I touch my black opal ring. Normally I'm immediately soothed by its vibrations but at this moment it just feels like a cold, dead stone. Usually I would do an energetic cleanse and feel instantly better, but right now that's not going to cut it. I know what I need. I need Julie.

I pass some guests on my way to the Orangery. Give them my most serene smile. "Are you having a *nourishing* stay with us?" I ask. Is my voice slightly higher than usual? A little shrill?

They're on the way to lunch. At least, I think they said that. It's a little as though I'm listening to them through a buzz of static.

"Well, I'm so glad," I say. I *beam* at them. "I hope we'll see you at our solstice celebrations tomorrow night!"

The Orangery is tucked round to the west side of the main house. I've always thought there's something a little budget, a little Groupon voucher/Boots toiletries aisle, about the word "spa," you know? And the original part of the building used to be Granmama and Grandfa's orangery, so there's an amazing feeling of light and space, which Owen has cleverly replicated in the treatment rooms.

I'm so proud of having state-of-the-art wellness infrastructure here. Everything you might expect to get in London—or LA—tucked away in this little quaint corner of the English countryside. We also have our own skincare line, formulated from local moss and a tiny sprinkling of chemicals, sold exclusively here, though (on the downlow for now!) soon to be stocked by Space NK, Liberty, and Cult Beauty, so everyone can experience just a little of the magic. Quite democratic, if you ignore the price! It wouldn't be great for business to admit I get a medical facial every four weeks which probably has more to do with my glow than any serum. But do I use the products? Of course I do! Sometimes, anyway: my aesthetician is rather exacting.

As soon as I step inside the Orangery and inhale the scents of the local herbs infusing the air, I feel better. I go straight to the front desk, where they're all smiles, ready to welcome me.

"Hello lovelies," I say. "Suze, how's your family?"

Suze beams. "Good thanks, Francesca. Sol was three yesterday, so we had a party—"

"Oh, how wonderful! I'm sure that was a very special day." It's so important to treat your staff well. I read a fascinating book about it. Did you know, for instance, that people will actually accept lower pay if they think that they're truly valued at their place of work? "Right my lovelies," I say. "I need to see Julie."

"Hm." Suze frowns, consulting her bookings. "She's got someone in at one."

"That's OK!" I say, brightly. "I know you two will be able to work your magic. You'll be able to find them a different slot. Won't you?"

"Er . . ." Suze is scanning the screen. She'll make it happen. I mean, we would never actually acknowledge this, any of us, but she doesn't have much of a choice. ". . . I think so." That's not really good enough and she knows it. She rallies. "Of course I will. Leave it with me, Francesca. I'll sort it now."

"Super! I'll just go straight on through to her then, shall I?"

The moment I'm out of sight I feel my smile snag and falter like a sail losing the wind. But Julie will help me. Honestly, she's the best. I had Reiki with her when I was down here overseeing the renovations and needed a quick self-care boost. Her "clinic" was out of her house, a damp cottage on the outskirts of Tome: very much a last resort in the absence of anything else. But talk about a hidden gem. I sensed immediately that she had a gift—I'm pretty good at that, at "discovering" people, bringing out the best in them. Curating, you might say. Julie is older than most of our employees here—in her sixties—but actually that can be a good thing for this sort of role, you know? It suggests experience. People see wrinkles and think wisdom. And she looks a lot smarter, these days, in the ecru linens I've politely requested she wear. The M&S cardies and jeggings somehow didn't say "spiritual healer."

"Hello Francesca," she says now. Julie has a very direct gaze.

"I'm feeling a little . . . jittery," I tell her. "It's as though"—I search for a way to put the feeling into words—"as though I've just drunk four cups of coffee, even though I never touch caffeine besides a sprinkle of matcha."

She nods. "How long have you been feeling like this?"

"Only very recently," I tell her. I can't bring myself to tell her about the face I thought I saw at breakfast. "Maybe it's because there's so much on," I say, "with the opening, you know? It's only natural!"

She has me lie down on the bed. I close my eyes as she cups my head briefly in her hands and asks me to take three deep breaths. I find it surprisingly difficult—I feel like I've just run up several flights of stairs. She hovers her palms above me and immediately I sense the heat of them, as though she is somehow warming the air between her hands and my skin. As she moves slowly down my body, I hear her breath catch. I sit up, even though I'm not meant to interrupt. "What is it?" I ask. "What did you feel?"

"I heard something," she says, solemnly. "A voice."

I grip the sides of the bed. "What . . . what did it say?"

"They said"—the next words in an awful, keening pitch—" 'It's dark and cold down here. It's dark and cold.' Just that, over and over."

"I have no idea what that could mean. Perhaps the energies are confused," I say.

She doesn't answer, gestures for me to lie back down. I hear her take a deep breath, as though she's steeling herself. Her hands hover over me once more. But she soon stops again. There's a long pause, and my sense of dread builds. "You aren't safe," she says, finally.

"There is one nearby who would do you harm." She closes her eyes. When she next speaks her voice is lower in pitch—like someone talking in their sleep: "An enemy draws near."

I feel my skin prickle with cold, despite the heat of the day. "Who? Who is it?"

She shakes her head, as if clearing it. Back in her usual register, she says: "I can't answer that for you. It's a blind kind of knowledge: more of a feeling. All I know is what I've told you. I can't give you a face or a name."

"But—there must be something you can do to make it clearer?"

She frowns at me. "Not this way," she says. "But there is something. I don't have much experience in it. It's an ancient kind of . . ." She hesitates. ". . . of practice." For a moment, I wondered if she might be about to say "magic." "My grandmother taught me."

"Can we try?" I ask, a little desperately.

"Yes. I need a basin of water. And an egg."

"An egg?" She nods. I haven't eaten eggs for years, but at this point I'm not going to argue. I ring Suze from the phone in here and ask her to get the kitchen to send everything over right away. As we wait, Julie lights several candles and the scent of vetiver seeps into the space. She fills a large earthenware bowl full of water. A couple of minutes later there's a knock on the door.

A handsome young guy stands on the other side. It's more difficult than usual to remember what he's called, which is annoying as I've made such an effort to speak to the staff on a first name basis, talking about them all as "The Manor family." He hands Julie a little wicker basket of mismatched eggs, fresh from The Manor's own chickens. As he does he blushes, a stain spreading up his neck to his cheeks; the proximity to me in my towel, perhaps, or the dim candlelit intimacy of the room.

"Thanks," I say, and smile at him. His blush deepens. *Sweet.* "Thank you"—I remember just in time—"*Eddie.*" He gives a funny little bow, closes the door.

Now Julie turns off all the remaining overheads so the only light shines from the trembling flames of the candles. Suddenly there's a very definite atmosphere in here. I watch as she breaks the egg on the side of the bowl with a sharp flick of her wrist so only the white goes in. I glimpse a tiny marking on the inside of her arm before she pulls her sleeve down again. Some kind of symbol, a Chinese character, perhaps. Goodness, I wouldn't have thought her the type for a tattoo. It doesn't go with the grandmotherly image, somehow. A youthful folly? I can understand that.

She washes the yolk down the sink, then turns to me, holding the basin.

"Sit," she commands. I lower myself onto the massage table. She picks up a candle and sets it down next to me. Then she holds the basin in front of me. "Look," she says.

By the light of the candle, I can make out the jellyfish outline of the egg white, the thin meniscus separating it from the water.

"What do you see?" Julie asks. I can hear how her breathing has changed: it's low and harsh, as though she's been doing something that requires great effort.

I keep looking. "I can't see anything."

"Closer," she commands. "You must come closer."

I lower my face until my nose is practically touching the water. "I can't see anything."

"Stop trying. You must look, but not with your eyes. You must look with your inner knowing."

She begins to murmur, the words too low to understand: they might even be foreign. I feel myself start to drift, that moment just before you fall asleep. Odd, I'm sure I can feel a kind of heat coming off the surface of the water—even though I watched her fill the basin from the cold tap.

I still can't see anything special besides the egg white bobbing there, undulating, changing shape . . . morphing into—"I *can* see something," I say, "there's something there." Some kind of image—a face—beginning to reveal itself. There are eyes. Two small eyes, with no boundary between the white and the iris: more animal than human. And then . . . no nose, no mouth, but something that pro-trudes beneath the eyes. It looks like . . . a beak. Yes, I can see it clearly now: the face of a bird, with a cruel hooked beak and small, beady eyes.

A *bird*?

I'm beginning to lose focus. The image wavers, then disappears.

"It's gone," I say, looking up at Julie.

"But you saw something."

"Yes . . . but—well, it looked like a bird!" I let out a little laugh, which sounds more nervous than I had meant it to. "But that's ri-diculous, isn't it?"

She doesn't smile back. Her eyes are black and pupilless in the low light, her mouth grim. She's frightening me.

"The basin never lies," she hisses. "But whatever you saw in some way represents your enemy. It means you need to watch your back."

Owen

I RETURN FROM THE WOODS covered in flecks of bark and sawdust, sweating like a pig. Out of the shade of the trees, I feel the heat rising. Guests wilt on benches, fanning themselves. Soft London melts. This lot must go on several foreign holidays a year but apparently they have no tolerance for over thirty in the British countryside. And clearly the guys reckon the use of suncream in the UK is for pussies: most of them are already pink as Christmas hams. It's only meant to get hotter tomorrow: Christ knows how they're going to cope then.

I can't help thinking about the note inviting Francesca into the woods. I'm sure it's nothing, that when I ask her she'll have a perfectly reasonable explanation. Still, I don't like it.

A sharp cry jolts me out of my thoughts. I glance down. Just in front of me on the path are two huge crows, squabbling over the entrails of some small creature, dancing and bickering as they tear into the flesh. I'm reminded of the grisly present left on our door. I take a step closer and wait for them to fly away but they're too focused on their feast. I aim a kick at the nearest one. It doesn't even flinch. Instead it cocks its head to one side and glares up at me with what feels like pure malevolence. Unnerved, I step to one side. "Shoo! Fuck off!"

I look up and see Michelle advancing toward me along the path. No time to swerve her. Jesus Christ, is the woman stalking me? She gives a quick authoritative clap of her hands and both birds take flight instantly, one carrying the dead thing in its claws. A bloody smear left behind on the gravel.

"Hello, Michelle," I say: cool but civil. Not going to let her rattle me.

She looks me over from top to toe and I feel her taking in my sawdust-caked clothes, the sweat beneath my arms. "So they've come down?" she asks. "The trees?"

"Yes," I say.

"And the Treehouses are inspired by one Francesca had as a child?" she asks.

"That's right." I remember Fran talking me through her vision: "We had *such* larks in the woods playing in there. Real *Swallows and Amazons* stuff. Such happy memories!"

Michelle is silent as she looks toward the woods. Then she turns back to me.

"I never forget faces," she says. "It's what makes me so good at this job." A jerk of her head toward a couple of guests strolling across the lawns. "The Hodgsons, Seaview Cabin Fourteen," she recites, like a kid saying her times table.

"Very impressive," I say. "But I don't see—"

"It's you," she says. "Isn't it?"

I swallow, my throat dry. "I don't know what you mean."

"In your usual clothes you look so different. But now . . ." She gestures to my sweaty, grubby T-shirt and shorts. "I remember you both, coming in to drop off the catch. You and your dad. You were so quiet. You barely even looked at me. I suppose that's because everyone made fun of you. But just look at you now, Shrimp."

I feel myself sway on the spot. So much for keeping away from Tome, from locals, wary of being recognized. I've been rumbled from within the gates.

She's frowning at me. "You came back. Just like I did. It's the thing they say about Tome. Everyone returns in the end—" She breaks off and looks genuinely mortified for a second, covers her mouth with her hand. Perhaps remembering that not *everyone* does return.

For a moment I can't speak. Then I say, "And you're Shelly, aren't you? The girl from the fish and chip shop." I didn't realize it before, but it's why I've been so wary of her, why I've instinctively kept my distance. It's why I did everything in my power to dissuade Francesca from hiring her in the first place. Michelle, Francesca's uber-efficient assistant, is none other than the girl from the chippy where my dad and I used to drop off the morning's catch.

"But why *did* you return?" She seems somehow troubled.

"Well, if you must know," I say, drawing myself up, "it was Francesca herself who got in touch with me. She commissioned my work."

I try not to think about that strange phone call from Francesca's "office." The confusion at that first meeting. I'm certainly not going to share my doubts with Michelle.

"But it can't be a coincidence," she says. "You being back here . . ."

"What do you mean?" I say it more sharply than I intended.

"I—nothing." She's suddenly wary. "I shouldn't have said anything." Then, like she's drawing a line under it: "Well. Look at us now. Both reinvented ourselves, haven't we? Long way from trawlers and chippies, isn't it?"

No, it's not like that at all. I feel a hot sting of indignation at this conflation of our positions. No, Michelle, you grasping wannabe. I'm not like you. I'm not *staff.* I don't *commute.* And it's hardly "coming back" when I don't set foot in Tome. I live here. I sleep beneath Belgian linen. I'm Lord of the fucking Manor.

A memory hits me suddenly: seeing this place properly for the first time, through the blue light of dawn and a haze of nicotine and diesel fumes from the outboard engine. The house seemed to float above the cliffs, a shimmering pale gray in the morning light. Whole and perfect and untouchable. Another universe to a moldy broken-down caravan. And then I remember—crystal clear—coming back around The Giant's Hand in the trawler in the afternoon and seeing, through Dad's binoculars, a blonde goddess in a hot-pink bikini. I was thirteen years old and she was maybe several years older than me . . . it was like she'd walked out of my fantasies. A noughties take on a fairy tale. The princess in her castle viewed by the pauper fisherman's son. And then the craziest, most spectacular thing happened: she whipped off her bikini top—and I forgot to breathe.

"I know it's not the easiest," Michelle says, snapping me rudely back into the present, "overcoming the way people see you. The labels that get attached—"

"Stop," I bark. "I don't need to hear it."

I won't go back there. To being the weird kid, the poor kid. The one everyone took the piss out of, before. And then worse: after, the one everyone pitied when his mum upped and left without so much as a by-your-leave.

I feel like a layer of skin has been sloughed off, the true me exposed beneath the fancy clothes and the shell of Owen Dacre, celebrated architect.

"And I felt so sorry for you—"

"Fuck off." I see her take a step back, stung. Good.

"Thing is," I say, "I don't need you to feel sorry for me, thanks. You seem to have mistaken me for an equal. I'm your boss."

She frowns. "Actually, *Francesca's* my employer."

I take a step closer. "I'm going to strongly recommend to your *employer* that she terminate your employment with immediate effect. I'll tell her the local chippy girl really isn't cut out for a management role here. No wonder you're so unprofessional—"

"I don't think you want to do that, Shrimp," she says, quickly. The old nickname hits like a slap. "I've got much less to lose here than you. This place is everything to you, isn't it?" Suddenly her phone rings and she looks at the screen. "Oh," she says. "Would you look at that?" She turns the phone around so that I can read the name of the caller written across it. *Francesca*. She says the next words in a kind of hiss: "She's not what you think she is either, you know. Whoever brought you into this—I'm sure you weren't meant to fall for her. She's not a good person."

"What on earth do you—"

She holds up a hand. "Better get this." I watch as she answers the phone and switches into consummate professional mode so quickly it's unsettling. "Hello, Francesca. Funny thing. I'm actually here with Owen." Was there a weird emphasis on the way she said my name? Just a reminder that she's rumbled me? "Yes, yes, he's made some progress on the Treehouses! Isn't that exciting!" She wanders away in the direction of the walled garden, chattering busily into her handset.

But just before she disappears from sight, she turns and looks back at me. In the middle of this sweltering summer's day, I feel a sudden chill.

DI Walker

THE DAY AFTER THE SOLSTICE

IT'S A SHORT DRIVE FROM the cove to The Manor, the road looping inland for a mile before it rejoins the coast. SOCO are focused on moving the body before the tide comes in and DI Walker has had a call from DS Fielding, one of the team already over at The Manor, saying they've got the fire under control. Smoke still fills the sky, though. The sun's a pale thin disc through it, the light dull. Nothing like the crushing heat of yesterday.

"Dairy Milk?" Heyer asks from the passenger seat, pulling a bar out of her pocket and thrusting it at him.

"No thanks. Can't stand the stuff."

"That is *not* normal, boss."

"Never said I was normal."

She shrugs, pops a chunk into her mouth. "Low blood sugar. But for a moment I'd thought I'd never be able to eat again. After that . . . the face. It was . . ." She trails off, words failing her. Walker knows what she means. "Did you see a lot of that sort of thing, boss? When you were in the Met?"

"Lots of death. Nothing . . . quite like that."

"Yeah—I heard you were more cold cases."

He shrugs. "I've worked on a few."

"What's it like?"

He thinks. "Frustrating. Slow. Laborious. Often bloody thankless, picking over old ground."

"Sounds like hard work."

"Yeah, it is. You have to go back through all the evidence. Sometimes you have to be seriously creative, as you have so little to work with. But when you solve a case—there's nothing like it. Righting a historic wrong. Getting justice for the victim and their family when it's been denied for so long."

Walker's good at the attention to detail. Leaving no stone unturned, doing the legwork, going the extra distance—all the clichés.

"How come you transferred down here?" Heyer asks thickly, through a mouthful of Dairy Milk. "Pace-of-life type thing?"

He shrugs. "Felt a kind of calling, you could say. And something opened up."

"You live with anyone, or—" Heyer breaks off. It's the question you're not meant to ask, isn't it? Are you normal, do you have people, or are you a loner weirdo?

"Nope. Just me." There's no way to make it sound less sad. Less like the dysfunctional cliché of a police detective.

He's not desperate to get into an in-depth conversation about all of this and he's also sure Heyer regrets asking, so it's something of a relief when a figure materializes in the road, just ahead. In the smoke-filled light the girl looks like an apparition. Maybe it's the silver dress, torn and grubby at the hem. She's barefoot, carrying her shoes. Long hair, a dark red that can only have come out of a bottle. Her head's down but it snaps up at the sound of the engine and Walker spots the moment she clocks them: she mouths a silent "FUCK." He actually sees her shift her weight as though working out if she can peg it in the opposite direction, then realize she doesn't have a hope.

He pulls over, climbs out of the car, and shows her his badge.

"I don't have to speak to you," she says with a jut of her chin. "I'm not under arrest, am I?" The whole bolshy attitude is at odds with the smudged eye make-up, the sooty tear tracks down her face.

"No," Walker says, gently. "We just stopped to check you're OK. And ask whether you might have seen anything last night that might help us work out what went on."

"But that's just what you lot try and do, isn't it? Get people to say stuff without a lawyer present." Ah, Walker thinks. Someone's been watching too much TV.

"It's nothing like that," he says. "We're not trying to trick you. We're just on our way to the hotel and happened to see you. Were you there last night?"

"What makes you think that?"

"Well," he says, reasonably, "the road ends at The Manor. There's nothing else there. And you seem pretty dressed up. I heard there was a bit of a do there last night."

A short pause. She shrugs. "Yeah. I was there. What of it?"

"You're a hotel guest?" Heyer asks.

The girl runs a hand down her grubby face. Finally shakes her head. Gulps.

"Are you OK?" Walker asks.

"I was . . . we were . . ." Her voice trails off. Then she starts again. "He said . . . he said it would be a laugh. It was meant to be just a bit of fun—"

"What was just a bit of fun?" Walker asks.

"Nothing," she says abruptly, as though remembering where she is, who she's talking to. "Just . . . had a bit of a fight with my boyfriend. Why are you asking me all this?"

"There was a death," Walker says. "Last night. Someone went over the cliffs, not far from here."

He sees the sudden tiny dilation of her eyes, catches the hitch of her breath.

"We're trying to work out what might have happened." He softens his tone. "Perhaps you can help us. We'd just like to know whether you saw anything. The smallest thing could help."

The girl's eyes flit from Heyer to Walker and back. "Nope." She shakes her head. "I didn't see anyone."

Heyer shoots him a look. He gives a little nod. "You didn't see *anyone*?" Heyer presses, a subtle emphasis on the last word.

The girl's eyes widen. "I didn't see any*thing*," she corrects. "Just a frigging figure of speech, innit?" Suddenly all the fight goes out of her. Her shoulders slump and somehow the change in posture makes her look much younger. She starts to cry, fresh tears tracking clean paths through the grime on her face. "I just want to go home," she says, words hitching on a sob.

"Can we give you a lift?" Walker asks. "We're en route to The Manor now. Or we could send some of our colleagues—"

Her eyes widen. "Fuck no. I'm not getting in the back of any police car. *I* didn't do anything wrong. I just want to go home. I'm so frigging tired." Her shoulders slump. "Last night . . . it wasn't meant to be like that. It . . ." She catches herself, trails off, and then sobs, "It was meant to be . . . like, special."

"WELL," HEYER SAYS, as they climb back into the car, after they've managed (with some difficulty) to extract Delilah Rayne's details. "Did you see the look on her face? She's hiding something, for sure. What was all that about 'it was meant to be special'?"

Walker nods. "Yup. Definitely something off. We'll get her in for a formal statement soon as we can."

He drives past a five-bar gate. A peeling sign. A tumbledown barn housing a herd of watchful cows.

"Seaview Farm," Heyer says, reading the sign. "Think we should ask them if they saw anything?"

"Not now," he says. "It'll take too long."

"Look at the state of the place. What a dump. You'd think if you lived in such a beautiful spot you'd keep your gaff a bit nicer. Stinks, too."

Maybe it's the way she wrinkles her nose that makes Walker say: "You're better than that, Heyer."

She straightens in her seat like he's just slapped her. Did he cross a line? "Sorry," he says. "But compassion's underrated in this job. You never know about people's lives, what they might be going through."

Heyer doesn't answer, just sullenly bites off another chunk of chocolate. Suddenly her eyes widen and she shouts, "Boss, look!"

As they round the corner he can see it fully: the wreck of a very beautiful, very expensive silver Aston Martin convertible. Someone has plowed it into the bracken-tangled verge at the bend of the road, one front wheel reared up onto the bank. Shards of glass litter the tarmac. The bonnet's a mess of corrugated metal.

Walker crawls the Audi closer. Reads the numberplate. A fancy personalized one: D4CRE.

The driver's door hangs open, the front seat empty. No one in sight. And just visible through the shattered windscreen: a smear of blood on the pale leather of the steering wheel.

Bella

THE DAY BEFORE THE SOLSTICE

MY SHIRT'S WET WITH SWEAT by the time I enter Tome, the light breeze lifting sticky hair from the back of my neck. I'm heading for the village pub as I can't afford to eat in the hotel restaurant for every meal (only breakfast's included in the room rate). It's also the next spot on my treasure hunt into the past.

Tome is freakishly quiet. Thatched houses made from local pale gray stone cluster along its streets, some held in the clutches of a climbing rose or honeysuckle. There's no one in sight. Maybe everyone's inside hiding from the heat. But I can't help feeling there's something watchful about the emptiness. Several times I'm sure I catch a shiver of movement beyond the windows that glitter below their fringe of thatch like small, dark eyes.

Up ahead I see the village cross, an antique stone structure, and I step under its shade to get my bearings without the sun frying my brain. I sit down on the stone seat, cold beneath my sticky thighs, wipe the sweat out of my eyes and find myself looking straight at the stonework panel opposite me. The image of twelve hooded figures standing in a circle, heads bowed so you can't see their faces. Trees surrounding them, as if they're in the middle of a forest. My heart's beating a little faster. One of the figures seems to be holding a long, sharp-looking knife.

My gaze slides to the next panel. This one shows a man in medieval clothes: a belted tunic and pointed boots, a look of terror on his face, holding something in his hands. I step closer to get a better look.

"It's a feather," says a soft voice, close behind me.

I almost jump out of my skin. I thought I was alone under here. I turn and see a woman with a sensible gray bob, dressed all in black despite the summer heat. "Beautiful, aren't they? Very old. Fifteenth century, I believe." She's smiling at me, curiously. "They've affected you, I can see."

"Oh," I say, "I suppose they're just very . . . vividly rendered."

"Well, they were a way of reminding local people to behave themselves. Centuries ago, these were wild, out-of-the-way parts: no police to keep the peace. So a different kind of authority grew in their place. To protect the community, to satisfy grievances. To deliver justice."

"The messages in the tree. Did they always act on them?"

She frowns, cocks her head to one side. "I didn't say anything about messages in trees. Are you familiar with the legend?"

"Oh," I say, casual as I can. "Suppose I must have heard about it somewhere . . ."

"Well," she says, "it depends. Firstly on whether the messenger—the one who put the note in the tree—had a true grievance. The Birds had ways of establishing the facts. Then it would depend on the magnitude of the crime and whether the culprit showed due remorse, made reparations. And if not . . ." She grimaces. "Let's just say it was a different time. Bleaker, bloodier . . ."

I watch her, waiting for more, but she falls silent. I realize that what I assumed was a slightly eccentric black smock is topped with a white dog collar.

"You're a vicar?"

"Yes," she says, smiling coyly at me. "Does it seem odd, my taking an interest? In these parts the pagan and the church have always been closely linked."

I turn back to the panels to take another look.

"But they're historic," I say. "Aren't they? I mean, presumably this group . . . the Birds, whatever they are, they ceased to exist a long time ago?"

I wait for her to answer but nothing comes. I turn around, only to find that she has gone.

I feel jittery, spooked by the whole encounter, by the memories that are threatening to surface. Perhaps some food in my stomach will help.

On my way to the pub I wander past the sort of shops you'd expect in a village like this, a Spar, a post office, a bookshop called The Crooked Shelf. I pause to look in the window. Next to the usual bestsellers there's a standalone collection: *Wyrd West Country, Occult Britain, Runes: the Definitive Guide.* And there it is: *Legends of Tome.* I avert my eyes and hurry on.

Finally I reach the pub. It's not as I remember it. Only part of the old Tudor building remains: some of the old stone frontage, the low doorway and shutters. But the roof is tiled where once it was thatch, modern casement windows instead of mullioned glass—the new additions tacked onto the old parts like a bad skin graft. The sign, though, is the same, swinging back and forth in the hot breeze. And whatever's fixed to the bottom of the sign is making a tinkling sound—some sort of wind chime. No: looking closer I see that it seems to be made from lots of tiny bones.

As I step inside a hush descends. I can hardly see a thing; it's so dark compared to the white glare of midday. Cool too, probably due to small windows and thick stone walls, the air a fug of wood, vinegar, and spilled beer. When my eyes adjust it seems like all the people missing from the empty streets of Tome are in here. Quite a few of them watching me from the tables in the corners. I take a stool at the bar.

A couple sitting nearby catch my eye; they're younger than most of the other punters—or at least the pretty, maroon-haired girl definitely is. On second glance the guy is dressed like a teenager in bleached jeans and faded T-shirt that reads IT'S ONLY A CRIME IF YOU GET CAUGHT, but he's thinning on top and probably a few years older than me.

Suddenly I realize I know them: they were the leaders of the rabble on the beach throwing stones. Their heads are bent and they're talking in whispers, but a few phrases slide my way.

Him: "We're gonna make it a night to remember all right. Spoke to Gaz. He's gonna bring all the gear. It'll be fire."

Her: "Yeah . . . I just dunno if it's such a good idea, Nate."

"Nah, it'll be grand. Yeah? Come on, Lyles. It's just a bit of fun."

"It better be—" The girl glances in my direction and clocks me watching before I can look away. "Let's talk later, babe. People eavesdropping on private conversations. Rude."

There's a rap on the bar and I turn to see the landlady looking pointedly at my hotel-branded tote bag. "You're from The Manor?" She's early sixties with buzz-cut bleach-blonde hair and an open, suntanned face, smile lines scored white around her eyes. She's not smiling at me, though. As she reaches up to pull a pint I spot the dark shape of a small tattoo on the underside of her bicep, which underscores the ageing punk look lent by her haircut.

"Oh," I say, "yeah. Just thought I'd come and explore Tome." I can feel the maroon-haired girl and the guy watching me. In fact, I suddenly feel like everyone in the pub is looking at me, like I have OUTSIDER tattooed across my forehead.

"There's some here that'd say I shouldn't serve you," the landlady says, nodding her head toward the other punters. "Not much love for that place round here. Killing people's business. Barring us from the land. But I'm feeling friendly today. Maybe 'cause you pronounced Tome right. Out-of-towners always say it wrong. You said 'tomb,' same as we do. So what'll you have?"

I order a ploughman's.

"What happened to the pub?" I ask, when she brings it out. "All the original features?"

She frowns at me. "I mean, you're going back now. That was at least fifteen years ago. Someone tried to burn it down."

"Oh." I'm truly shocked. I think of it, packed full of people every night back then as now. "That's . . . awful."

"No one hurt or killed, so it could've been a lot worse. Never caught 'em. But at least the insurance money came through in the end." She peers at me. "Do I *know* you? I'm good with faces. Years could go by and I'd recognize someone."

My mouth has gone a little dry. "I don't think so," I say. "Thanks for the food. Can you point me to the toilets?"

"That way," she says, nodding to the right, but still studying me. "Corridor."

Actually, I remember exactly where they are. Out toward the pub garden.

In between the gents and the ladies is a third door, slightly ajar: FUNCTION ROOM, I see, in brass letters. FUCTION ROOM, actually, as the N's fallen off. Then I glimpse some sort of structure inside the room, visible through the gap in the door. I see hundreds—maybe even thousands—of woven, twisted branches. If I just step a little closer, I'll be able to make out the whole of it properly—

"Can't go in there, love," a voice says. "Private."

I jump and find the landlady standing a couple of feet behind me. Her tone was light but her gaze is chilly and that "love" had zero warmth in it.

"Oh, right, sorry. I was just looking for the toilets."

"Symbol of a woman in a dress on that door right there? Doesn't say Function Room—that's a fairly big clue."

"Of course—how stupid of me!"

I feel her watching me the whole way back down the corridor.

Summer Journal

THE CARAVAN—TATE'S HOLIDAY PARK
AUGUST 9, 2010

Been hanging out with Mum and Dad the last couple of days. Wanted a break from The Manor. Had nightmares about that thing we found in the treehouse. And there's Hugo—even though he was different in the pub I still feel sick and shaky when I see him. But it's kind of boring lying on the picnic rug at the beach, Mum reading Maeve Binchy, Dad passed out with Lee Child over his face. I'm never bored with Frankie.

So I went for a swim—and saw Jake. On his own, carrying his bodyboard. He waved and came over. I was cringing as I kept thinking about what Frankie had said about having sex with him. And I still feel grubby, after what Hugo said. <u>Dirty little prick-tease</u>. But Jake's got such a great smile. Kind. And I know what Frankie said but I like his accent.

He asked if I wanted to have a go on the bodyboard and when I lay on it he went, can I? And he reached round to adjust my position. At first I just froze, after Hugo. But it was different. So gentle. And he asked. I can still feel the tingle of the places he touched.

Then when we got out Shrimp was sitting on the rocks poking around in the rockpools. I asked the guy if he lived at the caravan park. Yeah, he said. They're quite poor. He's a bit weird but you can't blame him. He's got kind of shitty parents.

When I got back to the rug Mum was like, he's cute! (CRINGE) Maybe you'll hang out a bit more down here now instead of the big house?

I was like, what does that mean?

I don't know. It just seems such a different world. I wonder what she sees . . . and then she shut her mouth, looked all embarrassed.

What she sees in me? Cheers Mum.

I guess it got to me so much because I've wondered about that myself.

AUGUST 10, 2010

Went back to The Manor today because I missed it, in spite of everything. Felt like I was missing out somehow. No sign of Frankie when I got there. I texted: where r u?

She texted: tennis court. Seemed weird as she has zero interest in sport.

Got to the court and there was Cora from the pub, smoking on a sunbed, topless—wearing just bikini bottoms and an armful of silver bangles. Her body was like a girl from an MTV music video. Then Frankie appeared holding two iced coffees (she doesn't even like coffee!), wearing eyeliner, her hair all piled up.

Oh she said, like me being there was a surprise (even though we'd just texted), we've only got two sunbeds. Didn't know if you were ever coming back. She chucked down a couple of cushion pads.

When Cora went to the toilets I asked why she was there.

Frankie grinned: you jelly, Sparrow? She's cleaning for the olds in the mornings. She needed a job after she lost that one at the pub. But she's cool. So we've been hanging out. Like it's been three weeks, not A FEW DAYS.

I'm actually an artist, Cora told us when she came back, so this is a stopgap. But it's hard living down here in the sticks.

Grandfa could help, Frankie said. He knows plenty of rich old people with cash to burn on paintings.

Oh seriously? Cora sat up. But Frankie had already picked up her copy of <u>Heat</u> and was all like, OMG look at the state of her. Must be her fourth boob job.

AUGUST 13, 2010

I miss it being just Frankie and me. Cora's there EVERY afternoon. The twins keep finding excuses to drop by and stare. She and Frankie talk sex—or Frankie does, and about the raves she goes to in London and the different drugs she's taken. But Cora has this whole vibe like she's experienced stuff we could never dream of. I just sit there feeling like a total loser virgin. Like, what am I going to contribute? That one of Frankie's brothers tried to finger me in the pool house? Also: surely Cora has some mates her own age to hang out with? We must seem like stupid kids to her.

It's so hot on the courts. The air gets trapped by the hedges. But when I suggested we could go to the pool, Frankie went: Cora prefers the courts, don't you, Cor? It gets chilly with the sea breeze. WTF? They're literally calling it a heatwave summer.

Then Frankie went: and we're not sure how the olds would take it, you know? Hanging out with the staff? But we're safe here. Granmama hasn't played tennis since she got her new hip. And Grandfa works in his study in the woods and phones his important friends slash mistresses in the afternoons.

Do you think maybe you could have a word with him? Cora said again. About my art?

Frankie screwed up her nose. Yeah. Sure. Maybe. Can I have another fag?

Good luck with that one Cora.

AUGUST 14, 2010

Today Frankie poured half a bottle of Malibu into a jug of banana Nesquik. The others were talking about sex again so I couldn't join in. I texted Jake. Probably wouldn't have had the balls if I hadn't had two glasses of Frankie's cocktail.

Hey. What u up 2?

He messaged straight back. Working @ the mo. But wld be nice 2 c u soon. Beach?

Who are you texting? Before I could answer Frankie grabbed the phone and read the messages. It's that guy, isn't it? Fish and chips?

Ooh, Cora said, how exciting! So patronizing, like a grown-up pretending to be interested in kids' stuff.

But Frankie looked actually pissed off. She was still holding on to my phone like she didn't trust me with it. I told you Sparrow . . . you could do so much better. She described him to Cora. He's local. You know him?

Cora looked a bit uncomfortable and said: I don't really know many of the kids round here.

See?! So patronizing! The "kids." UGH.

I wish I'd never introduced her to Frankie. I wish she'd just fuck off.

AUGUST 15, 2010

Ran into Hugo today on my way out of The Manor. It's the first time I've been alone with him since the pool house. He grinned at me. Not flavor of the month any longer? Frankie cancel your membership card yet? Aw, no one wants to play with you. Guess it's because you're a boring frigid little bitch.

He looked me up and down like I was naked. It's hotties like the new one who should wear bikinis by the way. Stick to the Speedo, little girl.

Eddie

I'VE BEEN DOWN IN THE kitchens washing plates from dinner for hours. I glance up through the small windows and see it's getting late: the first stars on the horizon. I head up and out through reception to get some fresh air.

"Eds," Ruby hisses from the front desk. "Come keep me company a sec."

I wander over. A few minutes later two women walk past, both of them wearing the little velvet crystal pouches from their rooms around their necks. One of them is touching hers over and over.

Ruby side-eyes them as they leave. "I saw this meme," she says, "that was like: 'How can there be so many problems in the world when there are so many wealthy women with crystals?'"

Then she says, "Oh, have you heard? They're going to make us wear *costumes* tomorrow. For the feast. The guests have to wear white and, like, willow crowns or some shit. It's like they're going for this *Midsommar* aesthetic but haven't actually watched the film to see how it ends." She snaps off, straight into professional mode as an older man enters reception.

"Hey darling." The guy strides up to the desk then leans over it so his face is only a foot away from Ruby's. I'm genuinely impressed by how she manages not to duck away . . . or headbutt him. "Hugo Meadows. Know who I am?"

"Of course." Ruby smiles brightly at him. "How can I help you, Mr. Meadows?"

"Look. Got a guy arriving tonight—he's big news. Investor. Need you to really pull out all the stops for him. Treat him special, yeah?"

I wonder if he meant to make it sound like he's asking for something dodgy, like a certain kind of bloke might ask for a "special massage."

"You got it," Ruby says.

"Thanks gorgeous." He leans forward and chucks her under the chin.

Ruby watches him leave. Then she takes a deep breath and exhales: "*Fucking wanker.*"

I'm about to, I dunno, apologize on behalf of all men when there's a strange sound from outside, a kind of howl. We both glance out through the front doors.

Ruby points. "Hey. Do they look OK to you?"

I follow her gaze, spot the couple walking through the dusk, wheeling bicycles up the drive. They're hunched over . . . And then halfway up the path the woman drops her bike with a clatter and sinks to her knees, putting her face in her hands. You can see her shoulders shaking from here. The guy lowers his bicycle and crouches over her. Are they having an argument? Is he comforting her? I watch as he sort of hauls her back to her feet. She folds over again and—oh, jeez—vomits into the grass on her hands and knees. A few other guests turn to stare at the spectacle.

"Shit," Ruby says. "I should probably go see what's going on."

The Manor is very hot on "bad energy." Dan, from the gardening team, told me a couple got quietly asked to leave earlier because they had a big argument at breakfast. First full day of their booking and they got sent packing!

I follow Ruby outside as she marches up to the couple. "Hello!" I hear her call in her brightest tone. "Can I help you with anything?"

The woman shakes her head, trembling as she rises to her feet. But the man steps forward and mutters in Ruby's ear. I see Ruby take a step backward. Then she places a soothing hand on the guy's shoulder and says something to him. She's gesturing toward the restaurant. What the hell is going on?

Ruby turns and starts walking back in this direction. "I've just told them to go and order the forager's tasting menu, on us," Ruby says. "A bottle of wine, whatever they like . . . and their whole stay will be complimentary . . . but it's kind of crazy."

"What's happened?"

"I think we'll have to get Michelle. They found . . . blood in the woods."

I swallow. What the hell? "Blood?"

"Yeah. Not just a few drops either. The guy said it was 'like something from a horror film.'"

Francesca

I'VE COME TO THE WALLED garden, to soothe myself with nature. Guests love a vegetable garden, especially the notion that their supper has been plucked from The Manor's own soil. Quite a bit of it hasn't, actually—we have a delivery of fresh fruit and vegetables most mornings from a supplier in London—but it's the thought that counts.

This bench in the corner beside the runner bean trellis is a good place to sit—from here I can see anyone who comes and goes through the archway. All day I've had the feeling that someone is watching me.

I close my eyes. Breathe in, breathe out. Ah, that's b—

I open my eyes. Was that . . . a howl? It sounded like it came from near the kitchens. I stand up and hurry in that direction. It's actually rather a relief to have something to focus on.

I spot our receptionist, Ruby, and the boy, Eddie, with a couple of our guests. Ruby comes toward me and murmurs something sotto voce.

"They found what in the woods?" I ask, certain I misheard.

She repeats herself.

I didn't mistake the word. Blood. They found blood in the woods. For a moment the ground seems to go from under me. I've explored transcendental meditation in the past but I think this may be my first truly out-of-body experience.

Ruby chews her lip. "I mean, should I call the police?"

This brings me back to myself. "Oh goodness no," I say. "We can't *possibly* have the police here." Not on our opening weekend, not with reviewers from Mr. & Mrs. Smith and *Condé Nast Traveler* staying—the midnight feast is going to put us on the hotlist! I give Ruby my most reassuring smile. "I'm sure whatever it is, it's nothing. My grandmother used to keep chickens. Foxes can make a dreadful mess. Really grisly."

I certainly sound like the assured, self-possessed Francesca Meadows that everyone is used to. But I think of that face at breakfast. The image in the stone basin. The feeling I've had all day, of being watched. No. Whenever I have been faced with adversity in the past I have always triumphed. It's just who I am. Blessed. Bad things just don't happen to Francesca Meadows.

"What we don't want to do," I say, in a voice of utmost calm, "is upset the guests. So, Ruby my lovely, I would be so grateful if you could just *own* this one for me. You know?" I wait, beaming at her, until she apparently realizes she doesn't have a choice.

"Um, yeah. Sure. OK."

"Oh, great. *Thank you.* I knew I could count on you! You want to explain to the guests who stumbled across the unfortunate scene that we are investigating but it's all part of authentic country living and *absolutely nothing to worry about.*" As I say the words, I believe them.

She nods.

"You're a star Ruby! You're *my* star." I beckon the boy over. "It's Eddie, isn't it? You brought me the eggs in the Orangery!"

He coughs. "Yeah." That blush again, spreading up his neck.

"So Eddie," I say. "I'd like you to go into the woods. Take some water, perhaps. Just do whatever you have to do to clean things up. Nature may be red in tooth and claw but our guests would prefer their version of it green and clean. Sound OK?"

"Um—"

"And go when it's a little darker, so you don't run into any other guests."

"Is that—" He seems to falter. "Um. Is that, like, legal? What if—"

"Of course it is!" I say, smiling winningly. "This is private property."

"OK," he says, submissively. Thank you, dear Eddie, for being so blessedly thick and biddable.

I spot another member of staff pushing a wheelbarrow in the other direction. "Dan, isn't it?" I call. He stops in his tracks, clearly stunned that I know his name. "You'll go with Eddie, yes?"

He nods before he even knows what he's being asked to do. It could be quite heady, having this power over people—but I don't ever let that sort of thing get to me.

"And look," I say. "Just between us, yes, boys? But how about a little five-hundred-pound bonus each, as a mark of my gratitude?"

Their eyes grow round. Of course it must sound like such a lot of money to them. I've done a good job of making it sound like a gift, a boon for services rendered. Not at all like I'm passing a bribe.

I HEAD UP to the private apartment shortly after. I'm just in the kitchen prying open the Ayurvedic tea tin I keep for emergencies when I realize I'm not alone. Owen appears from the sitting room.

"Hey," he says. "I've been meaning to give this to you." He fishes in his pocket. "Someone slipped it under our door this morning and I forgot about it until now."

He holds it in front of me. A note, written on hotel paper.

Meet me in the woods at midnight. Just like old times? Beneath the tree with a hundred eyes. It's been a while. We have a lot to discuss.

"Who's it from?" Owen asks, casually enough, but I can feel him watching me.

"My love!" I say, brightly, "I have absolutely no idea. Probably just some local crank. It could just as easily be meant for you. You're the one working on the woodland project—"

"But it's not addressed to me. Look." Now—now!—he produces an envelope. The name written on it: Frankie.

No. Frankie no longer exists.

"It sounds like they know you pretty well," Owen says. "It doesn't sound like the other complaints we've had. What do you think it means: 'just like old times'?"

"Oh for fuck's *sake*," I hiss. "It's nothing. Just . . . just drop it!"

His eyes widen, he takes a step back.

"My darling," I say. "I shocked you. I shocked myself. Gosh!" The voice didn't even sound like mine. What's happening to me? I smile. "Ugh, it's the pressure of this weekend. It's just getting to me. Look, I have no idea who that note is from. It could even be one of my brothers playing a little prank on me. You know what they're like!"

As soon as he turns away, I allow the smile to fall from my face. I didn't take the note from him because I thought my hands might shake if I did.

I think of the image I saw in the stone basin earlier. A bird.

And I called *her* Sparrow, all those years ago . . .

It means that face I thought I saw at breakfast wasn't a mirage. After all these years, she's come back. And I know exactly where she wants me to go. Deep into the woods—to a place I haven't been for years.

Summer Journal

THE CARAVAN—TATE'S HOLIDAY PARK
AUGUST 17, 2010

The woods, Frankie said. Tonight. Cora's first time! You up for it?

I dunno, I said, because I keep having nightmares about it. Don't get why Frankie isn't more scared.

So Frankie went: OK, Cora, just you and me. So I said I'd go. Know it's childish but I didn't want them going without me.

The local kids pick shrooms in Tome woods, Cora said. Then went off on some story about how she took them at a festival this one time. YAWN.

Frankie got all excited. Let's find some! Then I won't care so much that the twins cleaned out my stash.

Cora was like, well I don't know if you'll find them this time of year. Frankie was annoyed by that, you could tell. She's like that when she wants something. No, she said, we'll find some.

It was just getting dark when we went into the woods but I brought Mum's little keyring torch this time. We walked past Grandfa's study—he was in there on the phone, looking serious.

As we headed deeper into the trees Frankie showed us a photo on her mobile (the new iPhone . . . so cool!!) so we knew what we were looking for. It sounds stupid but I really wanted to find some mushrooms, like that would prove something. Cora said she was going for a pee. I got super focused, poking around with a stick. When I looked up Frankie was gone, too. I shouted but no one answered. All I could hear were owls calling high up in the branches.

Actually cried a bit. Just knew they'd done it on purpose. That they were probably hiding somewhere, laughing at me. I was scared. And lost. Whenever I thought I'd found the right path I kept coming to a dead end: bushes, a stream I'd never seen before. Finally I found a different path and followed it till I came to a clearing and I realized it was the one with the stones and that tree in it, with all the "eyes." And then I saw the mushrooms. Just like the photo Frankie showed me, under a pile of old dead leaves. They were pale next to the dark soil and with the moonlight coming through the trees it looked like they were glowing. It felt like finding that fossil on the beach at the beginning of the summer. Like somehow they found me? These little brownish pointed caps, almost cute looking. Like a kid's drawing, not like something that could send you on a crazy trip.

Had this really intense feeling of being watched then. How you can just _feel_ someone's eyes on you? I shone my torch around. Thought I saw something move in the shadows. Someone? This dark figure, crouched over, half-hidden behind a trunk. Something glinting, like eyes caught in the beam. Maybe an animal . . . a badger or something? Looked bigger than a badger though.

I was properly scared then. Just wanted to get out of there. I started running.

That's when I heard music. This old-timey melody, all crackly like it was playing through a gramophone. A creepy, high-pitched man's voice singing the words. Then I realized it was that old kids' song "The Teddy Bears' Picnic." You wouldn't think a nursery rhyme could sound so sinister. But there in the dark woods it did. It seemed like it was coming from every direction, following me through the trees.

Owen

"I HAVE TO SEE TO a few things now, my darling man," Francesca says. "So busy . . . you know, with the celebrations tomorrow. I must love and leave you." She kisses her fingers, presses them to my cheek.

Why isn't she meeting my eye? Usually, she has the most intense eye contact of anyone I've known. I joke that she practically hypnotized me into taking on the project here.

What is it about that note that's rattled her so much?

It was a test, showing it to her cold without any warning. It worked. But I'm not sure what it means, other than confirming there's something she's not telling me.

The door closes behind her.

Maybe I'm blowing things out of proportion after all the disturbing shit that happened earlier. What was it Michelle said? "She's not a good person." But Francesca literally radiates positivity. There isn't a shred of darkness about her—

And yet I can still feel the sting of the scratches on my shoulder blade, chafing against my shirt. I think of that hidden side to her, the demon that's unleashed in the bedroom. But that's different, right?

I'm sure it's nothing. Perhaps it's because I have a specific dread of mysterious notes dropped on doorsteps. It's how Mum let us know her intentions all those years ago:

I'm so sorry. I can't imagine what you think of me right now, but I hope you understand.

A scrap of paper through the letterbox, two weeks after she left. Like that was all we merited. A Jiffy bag of cash arrived shortly after. Twenty grand, in fact.

"Well," Dad had said. "Now you see what she really was. Christ knows where she got it but she sure as hell didn't earn that money in any honest way." We left Dorset soon after. "I'm damned if I'm going to hang around here to be gossiped about and pitied," he said. "And I don't want her filthy cash. Take it as your inheritance, son."

I pull out my phone, it's a little habit of mine. I like to check several times a day. The accuracy is scarily good, and it works even where there's no 3G signal. Francesca's passing through reception, possibly on her way to a catch-up with Michelle. I continue to watch as she passes through the front door, across the lawns. I find it so soothing. It's—I don't know—my equivalent of all the meditation Francesca goes in for. That's my excuse, anyway, for downloading a tracking app onto her phone. She had to travel a fair amount up to London before the opening for interviews and the like. She went on research trips to stay at would-be competitors. And she was always, always where she said she would be. Of course she was. It gave me such peace of mind.

I installed it in secret, so she doesn't know it's there. No harm done. It's reassuring. You know? Just in case. And even though she's now back here most of the time I still check it, just out of good practice, three or four times a day.

I've felt some guilt about it. Course I have. But now I feel vindicated. Because it looks like there are secrets on both sides of this marriage.

DI Walker

"BOSS! LOOK!"

Walker slams on the brakes. A few feet ahead a pair of legs splays out onto the tarmac. Everything from the waist up disappears into the hedgerow. His first thought is *another body*. Then he sees it— *him*—stir. The top half of the man's body rises out of the hedge like something from *The Exorcist*, his head swiveling slowly to look at them.

He puts up a hand. Lurches to his feet, staggers twice, nearly falls and then manages to right himself. He's wearing a white linen shirt and matching trousers, stained with mud and grass and God knows what else. A headdress of twisted leaves just about clings to his head. All quite a contrast with the designer trainers and gold signet ring.

"Ah," he drawls as Walker pulls level and lowers the window, "shit. Thought you were my driver."

"Sorry to disappoint," Walker says.

"No worries," the man drawls. "Can't be helped."

Heyer shoots a look at Walker like, *Can you believe this guy?*

"Actually," Walker says, wanting to shock him, "we're investigating a death."

The man doesn't seem to have heard. Too busy checking his Apple Watch. "*Finally* got some bloody 5G. First time I've been able to sync my mailbox. Now I've gotta get back to London."

"I'm afraid that might not be possible for a while," Walker tells him.

"You're fucking kidding me."

"Nope. Can we give you a lift back to the hotel?"

The man scowls. "Fine."

He half falls, half climbs into the back seat. Slumps against the headrest with a groan.

"Bad night?" Walker asks, watching him in the rearview mirror as he starts the car.

"Fucking awful. I'm not really a hotel guest, you know. I'm a business associate. VC. Hugo and Oscar Meadows?" As though anyone in the right circle should have heard of them. "Anyway. Meant to be heading to Glasto this week: got a stake in a glamping collective called Camp Hedonist. Not crappy yurts—it's the whole works: Starlinked co-working zone, wellness center, world-class room service to your tent."

"Sounds . . . authentic," Walker says.

"Yeah yeah, it's the tits. Anyway, after this I need about a month of therapy instead. Total shitshow. The Meadows brothers disappeared halfway through the evening. Claimed they were off to find something better to drink, never reappeared. Couldn't find them fucking anywhere. Talk of unprofessional. And the architect, Dacre—total mess."

"In what way?"

"At the bash last night. Saw him near the gates. Definitely on something." Walker's guessing this guy hasn't looked in a mirror: his own pupils are the size of five-pence pieces. "Looked like he'd been sleeping rough for a month. Embarrassing, really."

Walker hears Heyer stifle something that might be a snort. He understands: it takes a special sort of arrogance to cast judgment while in that much of a state yourself.

"Last time I saw him he was running like his life depended on it, out of the woods. Honestly, the guy looked possessed. This . . . demonic look in his eyes. Yeah"—Walker actually sees him shiver, in the act of remembering it—"pretty bloody sinister."

Bella

A BLUE DUSK FALLS AS the last of the sun melts into the sea, but people are still on the grass tennis court when I pass by. The Manor offers padel courts, too—of course it does—but this evening tennis seems to be winning out. I hear balls being hit, laughter, a shout of: "You bastard!" I veer that way and sneak a look through the hedge. The court's in exquisite condition now, a glorious deep emerald green (no hosepipe ban for The Manor, apparently). Back in the day it was a desiccated yellowing savanna, the grass long and tufted by the net where the elderly gardener had missed it with the strimmer. A total suntrap. God how I hated being there.

A tipsy-looking mixed doubles match is finishing up: a lot of prancing around, cocktail swilling, tennis racket swishing, and groping. It's a little like watching a group of horny racehorses frolic in the pasture. The women have almost identical outfits (very short white dresses) and Instagram filter looks, save for one being blonde and the other brunette. At a quick glance I note that the two guys are of a type: plummy, tall, both slightly gone to seed. Oh no. Now I recognize them. A nasty little bolt of adrenaline goes through me. What are the chances, among a hundred or so guests, of bumping into Hugo Meadows twice in one day?

They're leaving the courts now. I press myself back against the hedge to get out of their way: they're walking four abreast with the entitled inconsideration of drunk people. And as they barrel past both men glance at me, appraise me in a way I remember so well. Up, down. Lingering on breasts and legs. Their gazes pressing heavy as fingertips. I barely manage to suppress a shudder. The shame, the fear: as close to the surface as if it were yesterday.

Now Hugo Meadows glances away—judging by the girl on his arm I'm way past my sell-by date. Is there a second of hesitation from Oscar Meadows? I steel myself, but then they're striding out of sight. I can still feel my pulse going double time. Thank God I look so different to the skinny, shy girl with the long dark hair of fifteen years ago. How much did they ever know? I've never been able to work out the answer to that question. They were there that night, after all.

I leave the courts and take the path between the Woodland Hutches. The shadows are lengthening, the moon rising. It's nearly time to enter the woods. My whole body is singing with adrenaline and there's a hard little knot of dread between my ribs. I can't quite believe I'm actually doing this. I can't believe I might be about to come face to face with her after all this time.

A little way into the trees I notice a kind of gap or scar on the ground where the brick foundations of a building are visible. It takes me a moment to understand what it is. Of course. Her grandad's study. Where he'd go and "take important phone calls": phone his mistresses more like. I read the obituary in the paper. Lord Meadows died here *still hard at work at his desk on the day his heart gave up.* No wonder she wanted it pulled down.

The light here looks as though it has passed through green glass. The air isn't just cooler, it's like I've stepped into a different climate. At first I follow the well-kept gravel track laid out for guests with quaint little signs pointing the way. In beautiful painted handwriting I read: THE SECRETS OF THE WOODS LIE THIS WAY . . .

Are you fucking kidding me?

Another remnant from the past that she's repurposed into her special brand of rustic chic. I bet I'm the only one who finds that innocent little sign so sinister. But I'm not the only one who knows what happened in the woods that day . . .

Eddie

IT'S GETTING DARK AS DAN and I pedal into the woods on two of The Manor's bicycles. The male guest saved a What3words location where they found the blood, so we've got that to work from. It's kind of fun at first, whizzing as fast as we can along the winding trails, dodging bushes and trunks: it beats standing at the sink any day.

But then we're farther into the gloom and the trees are closer together and the sounds from the outside world begin to disappear. Delilah liked sneaking into the woods to have sex. She said my single bed with the old football stickers on it and being able to hear Mum listening to *The Archers* in the kitchen downstairs didn't really do it for her. Even though I tried not to show it I always freaked myself out in here. Especially because Delilah would sometimes sing this song that most of us locals learned as kids—our own version of "The Teddy Bear's Picnic" about a different kind of surprise in the woods.

For every foul that ever there was
Is gathered there tonight because
Tonight's the night
The Night Birds make their mischief

I never actually knew whether it was meant to be "foul" or "fowl." Based on the legends, I suppose it could be either.

While Lila and I walked in the woods I'd remember Mum's warnings about never going after nightfall. I'd keep thinking I saw things—shadows, figures—moving among the trees. I couldn't shake the idea that we weren't alone. There are all sorts of noises in old woods when you tune in to them: rustles and creaks that might be a small animal or the wind or whatever but might also be the sounds of someone creeping about. And while we were doing the deed it was often a struggle to keep it up (which wasn't normally my main problem). Especially because Lila liked to whisper stuff in my ear like: "Imagine: *they* could be watching us. Kind of a spooky turn-on, isn't it?" Erm, no. I never said this but I much preferred it when we were at her house and she lit a scented candle and played Lana Del Rey.

But right now I'm thinking about that last time we came into the woods together. Finding old Lord Meadows dead at his desk. The look on his face. I'm starting to wish I could just give that five hundred quid bonus back.

I call out to Dan to stop so I can check our bearings. It seems like the guests came off the path around here, following the animal trails that lead farther into the trees.

Dan stops the bike with a screech of brakes and turns to me, saying in a big rush: "Maybe we say we just couldn't find anything. Or, like, say there's nothing there. That they were making it up. It's not like they're going to come back and check."

"Yeah," I say, "I don't think we can do that. If Francesca Meadows finds out we didn't do the job properly, or Michelle hears about it—" It's not even worth thinking about.

"But, like, this goes beyond the job description. Don't you think?" Dan darts nervous looks between the trees. He's scared. And yeah, I'm scared, too.

We carry on cycling, but then I hear the screech of Dan's brakes a second time. He's pointing straight ahead. "Eds," he says, his voice wobbling. "What's that—there?"

I slam on my brakes too, follow his gaze. A dark figure crouches on the ground a few feet ahead, face hidden in the shadow of a black hood. I can't breathe. It's like I've just taken a hard tackle to the stomach. And then the figure unfolds itself and stands up fully, and I see that it's Nathan Tate. He's wearing dirty jeans that hang from his skinny jutting hipbones and a black hoodie that reads: I'D

RATHER BE MASTURBATING. For a moment he goes still as a hunted deer, then he relaxes. "If it isn't my old pal Eddie," he slurs. I think he might be drunk. Dan shoots me a glance like: *er . . . how do you know this guy?*

"What are you doing here?" I ask Tate.

"Could ask the same thing of you, m'lad."

"This is hotel property," Dan says, finding a burst of confidence from somewhere. "So, like, it's private?"

"Oh is it now? Because to me it looks like a fucking wood that's been here for thousands and thousands of years, probably since before humans even existed. And now *I'm* just existing. Just doing a bit of *forest bathing*. Is that really a crime?"

"Oh my *God*. Not a-bloody-gain." Delilah appears from between the trees, one hand on her hip. She's wearing black denim hotpants and a purple vinyl halter neck top and her belly button ring peeks out between the two. I see Dan's mouth fall open.

"Like, how is it that you seem to turn up everywhere? Should change your name to friggin' Eddie Stalker."

"Let's get going," I mutter to Dan. "They're harmless."

Maybe Tate's hearing is better than I thought—or maybe he's less drunk than I thought—because as we ride off he shouts after me: "That's what you think, Eddie old boy! That's what you think!" The last thing I hear is Delilah's laugh, echoing among the trees.

"Come on," I say to Dan, sounding braver than I feel, "let's just get this over with." I check the What3words location on my phone. The signal's totally died but I can still use it as a sort of map and according to this we're pretty close to the spot. We leave the bikes on the trail as the undergrowth is thick on the ground but as we shove our way through we eventually find a path that's been trampled, like something bigger than a human has passed through here. On a patch of bare earth, I see a hoofprint. A deer? But it would have to be an enormous deer.

Then we step into a clearing and in the beam of the torch I see it. Oh God.

Blood covers the ground, shining wet and blackish red in the torchlight. I lift the torch and see there's some spattered up the bottom part of a nearby trunk and even on the leaves of the lower branches.

"Fucking hell," says Dan, hoarsely. I look over at him. He's crouched down like he's trying to make himself smaller, his eyes wild and darting about. "Fucking hell mate—that is a *lot* of blood."

I can't even find the words to reply.

Francesca

THE BLOOD IN THE WOODS. The image in the stone basin. The note that Owen found. I'm trying to stay grounded. Keep it all in perspective. Not let anything detract from all the positivity I have been feeling about this weekend. But it is *beginning* to niggle at me.

I walk into the library (one of a few private spaces in the main house) and find Grandfa's ledger, the one he kept in his study in the woods. Open it to the last couple of pages. The letters are faint and wobbly, nothing like Grandfa's usual, immaculate copperplate:

The Birds . . .
Must warn Francesca . . .
Must tell her where . . .

I remember his hand gripping my wrist, hard, nails clawing into the skin.

I shut the book quickly. No. The poor old thing was definitely not well—he'd obviously been losing his grip on reality at the end. Because the Birds *aren't* real. I know that for a fact. I refuse to be spooked by some crusty old myth.

I do believe someone might be meddling, though.

She always was the clingy sort. A hanger-on. Basking in the re-flected glory of others. Also a lurker, a watcher . . . a cipher without any substance of her own. So it's just like her to show up here under a false name. I suppose I should feel sorry for her. What a sad little life.

When I think about the past it all feels like it happened to some-one else. It's like I wasn't really there, you know? Maybe it's no surprise: we all contain multitudes. And one can't spend one's time dwelling on ancient history, feeling hung up over things that happened years ago. It would be totally self-destructive, wouldn't it? Self-love is the first step toward loving others. I'm a huge believer in practicing what I preach.

Back up in the apartment, I sit down at my laptop. I find the historic feeds from Woodland Hutch number 11 for the last twenty-four hours.

The footage is wonderfully clear. But the woman in the room looks like a stranger: the sharp blonde haircut, the fringe, the clothes. She looks nothing like the scrawny girl I remember from back then, all split ends and high street clothes. I almost *almost* begin to doubt myself. Then some noise must catch her attention because she looks straight up, a perfect shot. I see the heart shape of the face, the curve of the eyebrows beneath the fringe. And I know for certain. I remember thinking that nothing about that face should add up to much. The features all small, nothing remarkable. And yet she was rather beautiful, in a mousy way, sadly wasted on her.

You know, now I think about it, it makes sense that she's staying here alone—especially if she's been holding on to toxic energy all these years. That sort of thing isn't conducive to finding happiness with another person. She always was destined to be a lost, lonely soul.

Scrolling back through the feeds I find some footage from half an hour ago. And there she is: on the path that leads in to the woods. Silly little Sparrow. Always one step behind. I'm not going to let you mess this up for me.

Bella

GRADUALLY THE PATH DWINDLES TO a thin ribbon, then little more than an animal track. The painted signs disappear. I'm in the right place. Headed for the heart of the woods.

I actually shiver: for the first time today, I feel like I could do with a sweater. I can't hear the sound of the sea here, or any noise from the hotel. Nothing but the muttering of leaves in the breeze, the occasional secret scurrying of some small, hidden animal. The rest of the world feels a very long way away. But then, I'd known it would be like this.

The diary in my bag bumps against my leg. I pass huge trunks spotted with lichen, standing on ancient, moss-covered feet. I pass twisted yews, dark and witchy with their moldering churchyard smell. Whispering beeches. A couple of monkey puzzles planted by some eccentric ancestor, with their freakish, swaying branches. All about me I can hear a shivering, chittering sound as though the woods are delighted—excited, even—to have a human trespassing so deep in their midst. The scents are of pine and months-old leaf mulch and the occasional rancid stench where some animal has expired in the undergrowth. Unmistakable, scorching the nostrils. We know the smell of death on instinct.

At last I see it: the Wishbone, she called it. The dead tree looms pale in front of me: two bone-white, forked branches, leafless and stark.

The knot of dread presses harder.

Shadows swim and shiver at the edge of my vision. The path has become more and more overgrown, I'm not sure I'm even following it anymore. The trees crowd even closer. The air is cooler still, denser. I think I catch the crack of a twig somewhere up ahead and am suddenly on high alert. I stop and listen, but all I can hear is my own breathing.

Just when I think I'm truly lost I see it: a twisted old tree, the rough bark studded all over with strange knots and whorls. I stop and shine the beam of my torch at it. The whirls are almond shapes, the knots within them round and plugged. They look uncannily like eyes; it's hard to believe from a distance they haven't been scored into the bark until you get closer and see it's definitely the hand of nature. Hundreds of them, staring out in different directions.

The tree with a hundred eyes.

It's just as haunted-looking as I remember. And there: the strange dark hollow in the trunk. I peer forward to look, then freeze. I definitely just heard something moving behind me. An animal? No: it sounded heavier, clumsier than that. I'm hardly breathing, my pulse in my throat.

Am I really about to come face to face with her for the first time in years? My whole body is electric with adrenaline. And with fear. Of course with fear. I know what she's capable of, after all.

Summer Journal

THE CARAVAN—TATE'S HOLIDAY PARK
AUGUST 18, 2010

Cora wasn't at The Manor today.

Just Frankie and me. Like old times. Except not. I think I really messed up.

Something else happened in the woods. I didn't write it down yesterday. Couldn't get my thoughts straight. I've been feeling weird about it. Don't know if I did the right thing.

I've never run so fast as when I heard that creepy melody playing. It felt like it was following me.

I just wanted to get out of there. When I saw lights through the trees, I was so relieved. Grandfa's study. Yeah he's old and posh and scary, but he'd know the path back to The Manor. I was pretty near when I heard voices. Thought he was still on the phone but as I got closer I saw two figures. A man and a woman, the door halfway open, light behind them so they were cast in shadow.

Grandfa. And . . . Cora. All I could think was: what the hell was she doing in Grandfa's cabin? His hand was on her upper arm. He was bending down to her . . . To say something? To kiss her???? But just at that moment a twig cracked under my foot and Cora turned to look out into the wood. I backed away, I couldn't tell if she'd seen me. I'd gone quite a way when a figure loomed in front of me on the path, grabbed me tight round my upper arms. I screamed and screamed and tried to get away but their grip only got stronger.

Then I heard a voice saying, Sparrow, it's me you twat. Frankie.

Where did you go? I shouted, still totally freaking out.

Did you hear the music? she asked. I could just see her eyes gleaming in the moonlight. I lost you guys and . . . oh my God, Sparrow . . . did you hear the music too?

Yeah, I said. I heard it.

She dropped her voice to a whisper. I think I saw <u>them</u>, Sparrow.

Your grandad and Cora? I said, kind of relieved she already knew.

And she was like, no. These tall figures, dressed all in black . . .

Then she stopped. Wait. What do you mean, my grandad and Cora?

I had to tell her, right?

I saw them together in your grandad's cabin. That's all I said. But maybe if I <u>had</u> said more, it wouldn't have sounded so bad. You know? Then she wouldn't have been able to imagine other stuff into the silence. I think maybe I knew that.

Frankie was more angry than I'd ever seen her:

What the actual fuck? I invited her here. If Granmama finds out . . . Everyone from my fucking mother on has let me down. Then she glared at me. You better not, Sparrow.

DI Walker

THE DAY AFTER THE SOLSTICE

WALKER AND HEYER ARE NEARLY at The Manor now. What's left of it, anyway. They round the last bend. In the distance the two grand gateposts—each topped with a stone fox—seem to make a mockery of the state of the building beyond.

"Je-sus," Heyer says. "What a mess."

They stare at it for a moment, the only sound a loud snoring from their hotel guest passenger in the back seat, now sprawled as horizontal as the seatbelt will allow, with drool running down the side of his chin and stained loafers resting against the opposite door.

Smoke still plumes from the building in the distance. The top stories are split open to the elements. Jagged support timbers reach aloft like broken sticks of charcoal. It's difficult to believe this macabre specter was ever intact. It looks ancient and evil, as if it's squatted here like this for a thousand years.

"Hey," Heyer says, pointing. "There's something there. By the verge."

Walker stops the car. They climb out to go and take a look.

"It's some kind of old notebook," Heyer says as they stand over it.

It's lying with the open cover facing up. The front is stained and dented and it's covered with dust from the road but you can still make out the words SUMMER JOURNAL embossed on the front. Looking at it, Walker feels a small kick of something that might be excitement or foreboding.

Heyer kneels down. "Don't touch it," Walker says, quickly. "I know it doesn't look like much. But anything on this part of the road from The Manor to the cliffs could be evidence. It could even have belonged to our victim beneath the cliffs."

Heyer grimaces. Then she hunkers down on her heels. "Look, though, boss. You can see from here."

"What?"

"All the pages have been torn out."

Eddie

"I DON'T LIKE THIS." DAN'S voice wobbles as we stare at the blood. "Nope. This is messed up." Then he turns and sprints off into the trees before I can stop him.

I'm left in the clearing on my own. I could leg it out of here, too. But even though everything in me wants to it's like I'm stuck to the spot, just staring at the scene. Then I spot something that looks like a black leather belt, with shiny buckles. But it's not a belt, I realize, looking more closely. It's Ivor the bull's harness: the one that gets put on him when he's going to be led somewhere. And there, a couple of feet away, is the big metal ring he wears through his nose. At the other end of the clearing I see now that someone has made a fire and there are charred bones in the ash, way too large to be any human's.

I catch my breath. There's been a killing, but not of a person. Someone's killed Ivor.

IT'S GETTING PROPERLY dark as I try to pick my way back through the undergrowth. I couldn't find the bikes we borrowed from The Manor anywhere—I guess Dan took his anyway. My hand holding the torch is shaking so much the beam is bouncing around all over the place. Lucky it's nearly a full moon: I think that's helping more than my torch is, to be honest. I'm pretty much jogging now—as fast as the trees will let me, anyway—pushing branches out of my face. I suppose I'm not really concentrating on where I'm going because all I can think about is that horrible mess back there in the clearing, about who might have done that to Ivor.

Next thing I know I've crashed into something—someone. There's a horrible scream. Actually, come to think of it, it might have been me. The torch bounces to the ground.

"You!" I hear someone say, in a hoarse whisper. As I crouch to grab my torch and point it shakily upwards I see it's that guest, Bella, from Hutch 11. She peers down at me, holding a light of her own, the one on her phone. I'm so relieved I could almost hug her. She frowns. "I thought you were— What are you doing here? It's a long way from the path."

"I'm—well, I got sent by the hotel."

"To meet me?"

"Er, no. Why?" It seems like a pretty random thing to assume.

"Oh, no reason . . . I just, well, I just wondered."

I want to ask her why *she's* in the middle of the woods at night, but she's a guest: they can do whatever they want.

"I thought I knew the way back but everything looks different in the dark," she says. "You're heading back to The Manor, right? Can I walk with you?"

"Sure, no problem." I try not to sound as relieved as I actually feel.

We walk for a while in silence, just concentrating on not tripping over the undergrowth.

"I can't work out if we're getting closer to the path or farther away," she says.

"Yeah, neither can I."

"Shit—I was hoping you were going to say you knew exactly where we were."

"Sorry."

"Never mind. I'm glad to have some company, anyway."

"Yeah." So am I, but I don't want to sound like too much of a melt.

"Eddie," she hisses, suddenly, and grabs my arm. "Stop."

My heart starts racing again. "What?" I whisper.

"Can you see that?" she whispers back. "Up ahead . . . there's something—" She yanks at my sleeve. "Here, come here. Behind this tree. And turn that off. Your torch! Turn it off."

I can hear something moving nearby but I can't make out anything at first. I feel like I might pass out from adrenaline. I try to tell myself it could just be Dan wandering around, as lost as we are. Then I see what she's seen, and I stop breathing.

Francesca

MY SCALP AND MY FINGERTIPS tingle with something like excitement. Silly, gullible little Sparrow. Of course I'm not going to meet her in the woods! For one thing, to do so would be to journey back into the past and I am all about existing in the present. For another, I'm not completely insane! As though I would meet on her terms. I want to really prepare for our first proper meeting. I rather feel I owe it to her. She's made an effort, so I should, too. And it's been so long. I should make sure this reunion is everything it could be.

I dress carefully, quietly. I rub aromatherapy oil into my pulse points.

And then, just for good measure you understand, I slip a Japanese ceramic knife—in its silicone cover—out of the kitchen drawer.

I always did love sneaking out at midnight as a youth. There's something so alive about this hour: magical and elemental. As though anything could happen.

Owen

I HEAR THE DOOR TO the apartment close. Open my eyes, check the alarm clock for the time. Just after midnight.

I reach for my phone and open the tracking app. Francesca is still on the premises, not yet in the woods. In fact, she appears to be heading to one of the cabins—Woodland Hutch 11. What is she doing in a guest's room at this hour of night? We don't have a single empty room this weekend. Is she meeting someone there? I really don't like this.

I dress, then head down through the courtyard into the public part of the building. Stride up to the girl on reception: unlike many country hotels there's someone there twenty-four hours, ready to attend to the guests' night-time whims. "Where's Michelle?" I ask. "Is she still about?"

The girl takes a step back and I wonder what she sees in my face. "I think she's in the store?"

A few minutes later I push open the door to the wine store. The bar of light from the corridor illuminates a figure crouched on the floor, catches on the bent blonde head.

"I need to talk to you," I say.

"Oh!" Michelle startles at the sound of my voice. Stands and turns, smoothing dust off her skirt. It feels satisfying to be the one catching her unawares, for a change.

I close the door behind me. Her eyes go to the catch as it clicks into place.

"I was checking the supplies for tomorrow's celebration," she says, unnecessarily, gesturing to the crates of booze on the floor beside her. "What are *you* doing here?"

As though I have no right to be here. As though I have no authority over her. I hate that she knows who I really am. I hate that she looks at me and sees that grubby, lonely, unloved kid from the past. But for the time being I'm going to swallow my pride.

"What did you mean," I say, "earlier? When you said she's not a good person?"

"Oh," she says. She looks uneasy. "I—I just didn't like seeing you ashamed of where you come from. I don't want you to put her on too much of a pedestal."

There's something shifty about her body language, about the way her gaze slides away from mine. She looks guilty. I think of the way she leapt up when I entered.

"What were you doing just now, when I came in?"

"Nothing," she says, far too quickly. "Just checking the supplies like I said . . ."

"I don't believe you," I say. "Tell me now, or . . . or I'll go straight to Francesca." I take a step toward her.

She narrows her eyes, juts her chin a little. "No, you won't. I think you've put a lot of effort into becoming Owen Dacre. I doubt you want me to reveal you're really a fisherman's son who grew up too poor to live in a real house. Not just a local, but the family even the locals looked down on."

I feel like she's just punched me: the long-ingrained shame of it. But I try to bluff my way out. "Yeah," I say, "well maybe I don't care. It's hardly a crime, growing up poor."

"No. *That* isn't a crime, anyway." A flash of that steel I saw in her earlier. She gestures at me, at my clothes.

I feel a sudden apprehension. "What do you mean—"

She sighs. "The chippy was right next to The Crow's Nest, if you recall. We stayed open late, to mop up the drinkers after last orders.

So I was often there in the small hours, long after everyone else had gone home, cleaning it all down, taking out the rubbish, locking up. I saw you. You . . . and that box of matches. And what was it? A can of fuel from your dad's boat?"

Oh no. "Shut up." I just want to make her stop talking.

"Look," she says, in a reasonable tone. "I get it. I do. People were awful to you and it must have felt good to get even." And then she says, almost apologetically, "And if you try to get me fired from this job, I'll tell *everybody* what I saw, the night before you and your dad left Tome. I don't think it would look all that great for your profile, do you? Famed architect revealed as childhood arsonist. I don't think Francesca would like that sort of thing at all. To her, image is everythi—"

The last word ends in a gasp, because my hands are around her throat. I feel the temptation to squeeze, to stem the awful flood of words, to wipe the look of scorn and pity from her face.

No one else has recognized me . . . the buck would stop with her—

And then I come to my senses. I drop my hands. What just happened to me?

"Oh my God," I say, and something like a sob escapes me. "Oh fuck, I'm sorry. I don't know what . . ."

"It's OK," she says, in a whisper. "It's OK."

I stare at her. She looks back steadily.

And then something totally insane happens. I kiss her. Or she kisses me. There's a moment when we break off, maybe each as shocked as the other.

And then we're kissing again, and she's making a deep, almost animal sound at the back of her throat, and this is wrong on so many different levels. And yet at the same time there is something intoxicating about being known and wanted for who I am. Here is someone who knows me as the boy who grew up in a caravan, who smelt of fish, fag smoke, and disappointment. And who still wants me, in spite of all that. Who knows and accepts maybe the worst thing about me.

I'm fumbling the top buttons of her shirt open when I see the small inked mark just above her left breast.

"What is that?" I ask.

"Oh." She smiles. "Just a youthful mistake." Silences me with another kiss.

And it is good. It is really, really good.

Eddie

I CAN HEAR BELLA'S ROUGH breathing as we crouch in the dark undergrowth. I can feel her hand on my forearm, fingers clutching tight.

There's a rustling of dead leaves, a cracking and snapping of branches. And then we watch as something moves out of the trees into the clearing a few yards ahead of us. A dark hooded figure . . . tall, as tall as me. For just a moment I think: it's Nathan Tate again. Then other things register. That it's carrying a long stick or club and wearing some sort of long tattered cloak, bits of it moving strangely with a kind of rippling, a quivering—until I realize it's covered in thousands of black feathers that reach all the way to the forest floor, where the ends of it slither along the ground. And the worst part: inside the hood, where you'd expect there to be a face . . . it makes my skin crawl. Where the nose and mouth should be is a hooked black beak and it seems to have no eyes.

It has to be some kind of mask. There must be a person inside there somewhere. But there's nothing human about it. Even the way it moves, in that cloak—a kind of glide.

I think I might have stopped breathing.

"Oh my God," Bella whispers. "It's one of them." There's more rustling and now more of them are appearing: a second figure, a third, a fourth—all wearing the same dark cloaks, the same dark masks with hooked beaks, carrying the same sticks. I count eight—no nine . . . then ten, eleven—twelve, I think, though it's getting difficult to keep track. They're moving together into one black mass. Suddenly there's a loud *whoomph* and what I thought was a stick turns into a flaming torch. Each bird passes the flame to the next, until all of the torches are lit and held above their heads. The woods seem even darker now. All you can see are those flames and the horrible figures lit up beneath them.

This is worse than the blood. Worse even than finding that dead old man in the study. I think of the little boy I was once, scared of the woods at the end of the field, closing his curtains so that no chink of moonlight could get in. This is what I was afraid of. But in spite of all the legends, in spite of the blood I found, in spite of that feather on the old man's desk, I don't think I ever *really* believed. Not till now.

I'm scared to move an inch. Nearby, Bella's breathing is coming in fast pants and I feel like even that might be too loud. She's gripping my arm so tight it hurts.

Then there's a sound: a shriek that feels like it goes right through me. For a long time afterwards it seems to echo off the trees around us. Whatever that sound was, it wasn't human. And as if they're obeying a command, the hooded figures all move into a circle.

Now there's a rhythmic drumming and I see that all of them are beating the bottom of their torches on the ground so that the flames dance and surge and spark. The drumming gets faster and faster, the torches are a blur of light, and I'm finding it hard to focus with the brightness of it all against the deep dark of the wood. Then, all of a sudden, they stop and the silence on the other side is so intense I actually hold my breath, because I'm sure this time they're going to hear.

A figure moves into the center of the circle. Then it makes a gesture and two of the others step forward, dragging a sack that looks like it contains something heavy. And suddenly I am absolutely sure that something bad is going to come out of the sack. I don't want to watch but I do as they kneel down and the leader reaches into it and begins to pull out something very large and dark. And the other two go to help and then they are all lifting the thing from the sack together.

I hear Bella whisper "*Oh Jesus*" and by the light of the torches I see it properly. A bull's head. Ivor's head. Now the figures begin some kind of chant, a low, fast muttering. And they lift the head higher and higher until it's held above the clearing, as though it's looking down at them all and it doesn't look like Ivor anymore, who was quite a sweet bull as they go. In the flickering light it looks like something old and evil and powerful, the dead eyes reflecting the torches so it looks like they're lit from inside, the nostrils dark and flared, the lips curled back from the big white teeth, the black tongue lolling out.

Oh God.

It happens before I realize it's going to and before I can stop it: I sneeze. I hear Bella suck in her breath. For a moment I think maybe I've got away with it. Then the leader gestures with an arm and the chanting gradually stutters to a halt.

And then the figure turns this way and points.

They're all turning in this direction now. The circle is breaking apart and the Birds on this side of the circle are moving toward us, pushing the undergrowth aside, getting closer, closer . . .

For a moment I can't move and all I can hear is the blood beating in my ears. Then: "Eddie," I hear Bella whisper, her grip stinging my arm. "Eddie, when I say so I think we should . . ." She leaps to her feet as she hisses the last word: *"RUN."*

Francesca

I OPEN THE DOOR TO the Hutch with my master key. I don't think I have much time; she'll have realized by now that I haven't showed. Still, I pause on the threshold as I experience a strange frisson of energy. I'm particularly receptive to such things (it's both my gift and my curse) and there's a powerful essence of her here, though she's only been here twenty-four hours. I can sense her in the air, in all the possessions scattered about the room. I glide to the bed and pick up one of her pillows. Inhale. I'm half surprised not to smell the sickly sweet aroma of Tommy Girl.

I cast an eye around the room. It's really rather untidy in here. Shows a certain lack of respect for the gorgeous design I put so much personal thought into. But perhaps I shouldn't be surprised. She's been my guest before—and showed the same lack of gratitude back then.

I'm not exactly sure what I'm looking for but I *am* certain I'll know when I find it. I open the wardrobe and find a row of clear garment bags from a designer rental company. Just like Sparrow to disguise herself in the clothes of another life. That's what she was back then. A little colorless cipher, living vicariously through others. A parasitic little hermit crab, borrowing another's shell.

It was an act of charity, all those years ago, inviting her here. To share a little of what I had with that ungainly creature on the beach. To see whether I could make something of her. Transform her. It turns out, just as Granmama used to say, you really can't make a silk purse out of a sow's ear.

In the chest of drawers (the underwear, as expected, cheap and graying) I find a little stash of clippings about me, about The Manor. This is no surprise either. I always knew she was obsessed with me, my life. Covetous. Of course that's what happens when you radiate something that others want. It's a shame. It could have been such a beautiful thing, our friendship. But some people can be so ungrateful. As I say, I'm a giver by nature, so it's very easy for me to get taken advantage of—

Gosh. I do love these images of Owen and me, though, in the *ELLE Wedding* profile. We are so perfectly matched. *He's* obsessed with me too, of course—but in the best possible way.

I search through the minibar fridge. I peer under the bed. I look through her toiletries in the bathroom (nasty, chemical-laden stuff). And then, coming back into the main room, I notice the little safe in its recess in the wall. I don't think there are any valuables in there because I've already found her wallet and some (cheap) jewelry.

I try a couple of codes at random—neither of them works. I close my eyes and try to manifest the number behind my eyelids but there's just too much interference in my head to connect with my deeper knowledge in the way the guru I used to see taught me.

I pace the room for a few minutes. I could take the safe with me—it's not too heavy to carry away. I think we have a master key somewhere, in case a guest forgets the code they've put in. Michelle will know.

And then something occurs to me. Perhaps my powers of manifestation have worked after all. A date, fifteen years in the past. I punch in the numbers, press the key icon and the little light blinks green.

My fingers seem uncharacteristically clumsy as I try to open the door.

In the dim light the safe looks empty at first. If there's anything in there it must be small. I reach a hand inside. My fingers close around something squarish, metallic. I draw it out. Stare at it for a moment. It's a pink iPod, headphones plugged in.

I fit the headphones and press play as the words of "A Forest" seep into my ears. Lyrics about hearing voices in the dark, getting lost in the trees . . .

I stab the stop button. I don't need to hear any more. A memory of lying by the pool, listening to The Cure with her, an earphone each. (See: I shared everything with her!) But somehow I don't think that's the cozy memory she's trying to conjure. She's sending a message. It's about what happened.

For a moment the iPod trembles violently in my hand. And then, with an effort of will, I manage to still it. I am in control here. Just as I ever was. It takes more than this to frighten me.

Granmama, a keen gardener, always told me that if you want to get rid of a weed you have to pull it or burn it out by the roots. Expunge it entirely. I touch the black opal set into my ring. This time I can feel its power seeping into me, strengthening me.

I hate confrontation, but one must make exceptions at times. After all, self-protection is a manifestation of self-love. And self-love is so important. You have to love yourself before others. I know what I have to do.

I sit down at the little dressing table. Catch sight of myself in the mirror. I smile.

A FEW MINUTES later I step back into the apartment. Being in her space has drained me and I'm hungry for Owen. I need to nourish my soul with the warmth of another body, to join my essence with another. To lose myself in physicality, in carnality. I need a release.

In the dark bedroom I lie down and slide a hand across his side of the bed.

"Hello, beloved," I whisper. But my fingers encounter only space, the coldness of the slightly rumpled sheet, the dip in the mattress where his body lay.

Well, that's interesting. It wouldn't be the first time he's gone off on night-time wanderings. I know (because I've watched him via the feeds) that sometimes he goes and sits in the walled garden and has a secret middle-of-the-night smoke. Sometimes he simply wanders around the grounds, restless soul that he is. But now, unsettled by the events of the night, I have a sudden desire to know his exact location.

I open my laptop and scroll quickly through the feeds. There's the deserted courtyard, the walled garden luminescent in the light of the moon, the indoor bar, the wine store, the—

Wait.

What?

I flick back to the feed from the wine store. It looks like . . .

I zoom in. It's rather unfocused at this magnification. And yet I don't need perfect clarity to understand the pose of the two figures. And to know the second figure by the bright blur of her hair. Even at this level of pixelation I'd know a high street dye job from fifty paces.

White cold fury surges through me so powerfully that it feels almost invigorating, cleansing—an Ayahuasca-like transcendental, elemental rush. I am left trembling in the wake of it.

I suddenly remember the Japanese knife I took with me to Sparrow's Hutch. I slip it from its silicone cover and, gliding swiftly into the bedroom, I raise it high above my head (for a moment I have a rather pleasing image of myself as some ancient priestess performing an important ceremonial role) and then I plunge it into the pillow on Owen's side of the bed. I revel in the sound of rending material, in the sensation of the blade plowing through the soft innards as white feathers explode from the fabric in clouds. I lose myself in it. I am euphoric, almost, transported. I am breathing in hard animal grunts, I am sweating, I am alive, oh so alive.

Yes. Yes. This. This is the release I needed. More powerful, really, than any orgasm. Because when you've behaved for this long, it feels so good to be a little bad.

DI Walker

THE DAY AFTER THE SOLSTICE

WALKER PARKS THE AUDI TWENTY yards or so from the ruined building. Then the two detectives sit for a moment and take in the spectacle before them.

The hotel guest they picked up stirs in the back seat, rubs his bleary eyes, looking as disgruntled as a first-class passenger woken for breakfast against his wishes. "Christ," he says, peevishly. "Can't believe I'm back here and not halfway to London by now. What a bloody nightmare. Looks like a scene from Fyre Festival."

People are scattered about the lawns in front of The Manor, wrapped in foil blankets, many of them shivering in spite of the morning's warmth. Some of them huddle together talking in murmurs, some are sobbing, a few are curled up, fetal, on the grass. Most of them are in a similarly shambolic state to their passenger. Walker sees lots of stained white clothing. Lopsided green headdresses. Against the dark backdrop of the burned building and amidst the flakes of soot that continue to swirl down among them they look kind of otherworldly: a hundred forlorn specters.

Three long tables stand abandoned on the lawns in front of the cliffs, white tablecloths lifting in the breeze, held in place by the wreckage of some kind of feast. Chairs are scattered about haphazardly. A wicker arch has been pulled onto its side and statues are strewn about the grass. There's broken glass and squashed food everywhere the eye lands. The ruins of a stage.

Walker and Heyer climb out of the car and rouse the guy in the back, then hand their back-seat passenger, sputtering with indignation, into the care of some of the paramedics.

"DI Walker?"

Walker turns to see DS Fielding approaching. On the couple of occasions they've met, Fielding's been as groomed as a Premiership footballer: high-fade hair, looks like he moisturizes, Ronaldo levels of eyebrow tweezing. But he's in as much of a state as anyone else here: soot clings to a sheen of sweat on his face and he's clearly run a hand through that perfect style so many times that it's sticking up like a duck's tail. "Boss," he says, "glad you're here. They've finally got the fire under control. Luckily most of the guests were out on the lawns for some fancy do. We've been interviewing some of the witnesses. It's—well, you should try talking to some of them. If I had to guess I'd say a large majority are . . . I think the only way to put it accurately is 'off their faces.'"

"Yeah." Walker nods toward their passenger, now fighting off the advances of the paramedics. "Think we came across one of those."

"And a couple of them have spoken about seeing some pretty odd characters last night." Fielding looks sheepish. "It all sounds a little hocus-pocus. But: masked figures. Dark cloaks and—"

He breaks off as a hush descends over the lawn. Every face turns toward the smoldering building as two teams of paramedics carry a couple of stretchers out of the ruins. On each lies a supine figure, fitted with an oxygen mask. Every pair of eyes tracks their progress into the back of the ambulance.

The chief fireman approaches. "DI Walker?"

"That's me."

"We found them trapped inside. Some kind of wine cellar, it looked like. Paramedics are trying their best but it's not looking good."

That would make two more deaths. Jesus. Walker thinks, not for the first time: *that it should have come to this.* Then he becomes aware that the chief fireman is still speaking. Snaps himself back into the moment. "They were shut inside," the man's saying. "They couldn't have escaped even if they wanted to."

"Right," Walker says. "Yes, you mentioned they were trapped."

"It's more than that. The door was bolted from the outside. Someone locked them in there on purpose."

Bella

I'M SHIVERY AND NAUSEOUS WITH spent adrenaline by the time I reach my Hutch. I stab my key into the lock, stumble through the door. The Birds are real. I *did* see one in the woods, all those years ago. I knew it.

Two questions rattle through my mind: did they see us? Why are they here?

I pace, my mind full of looming shadows and flaming torches, and it takes me a few moments to notice the changes in my Hutch. The bedside lamps either side of the four-poster have been switched on. I'm almost certain I didn't do that. The curtains have been pulled closed across the windows, the bedclothes folded down. I think someone has even sprayed scent in here. I don't really stay in hotels where they offer this kind of thing, but it gradually occurs to me that this is a turndown service. Which is a little overzealous of housekeeping at this time of night. Especially as I hung a Do Not Disturb sign on the door.

Now, with a crackle of foreboding, I see that something has been placed on my pillow.

Stepping closer I see it's a piece of the hotel's headed notepaper. There's something on top of the note: an expensive-looking chocolate. Fuck that. I pick it up and toss it into the bin as though it's radioactive. Then, scalp prickling and heart beginning to thump in earnest, I read the note, written in carelessly flamboyant posh-girl handwriting:

Hi Sparrow!

Look at us writing to each other like the pen pals we never were. I'm so sorry I missed the reunion. It's been so long! And there's so much to catch up on. Especially considering how <u>involved</u> you were in everything here.

Don't worry. I'll make it up to you tomorrow.

xox

Fear and anger fight for dominance. The whole note is one elegantly veiled threat. But it's that middle part that gets me the most: "how <u>involved</u> you were in everything . . ." She's trying to frighten me into staying silent. Well, that worked once. But it won't now.

If she had any remorse she never would have created this place. She'd have sold up when she inherited the house and run in the other direction.

This summer marks fifteen years. A horrible little anniversary. And it's the year I have become a mother, which has forced a reckoning. I'm all Grace has. I have to be everything for her. But how can I be if I'm not whole myself? Something broke in me on a summer's night fifteen years ago. Maybe it can never be fully mended. It's the burden I'll carry with me for a lifetime. But I want to be able to look my own daughter in the eye. I need something—naff though the word may be—like closure.

There's still so much I need to understand about what happened. I've been living with the guilt of it ever since. It has been the thing that has defined my life. My career prospects, because I flunked out of my final year at college. My relationship with Grace's dad, because there was this huge thing I could never share with him. Every relationship I've ever had, really. My bond with my parents, even—I've kept them at arm's length ever since. I've had to. It's not an exaggeration to say what happened ruined my life. And yet I'm not sure it was even a stumbling block in hers. It took every ounce of courage I had to come back here. But I *am* back, like the Ghost of Christmas Past. I'm not going to let her forget. And I know what I have to do.

A scrabble of branches against the windows. I tiptoe to the door and double lock it, then loop the safety chain across. Then, after a moment's thought, I drag the heavy velvet armchair in front of the door. They're out there, in the woods. And she's been here tonight, in my room. Worse, she wants me to know it.

Summer Journal

THE CARAVAN—TATE'S HOLIDAY PARK
AUGUST 19, 2010

Well. Think my friendship with Frankie might be over. Not sure how to feel.

Thought without Cora it might go back to how it was. Just me and Frankie in the sun, reading. But Frankie wanted to lie in her room, watch <u>The Simple Life</u> reruns with the sound turned down. I brought her the magic mushrooms I found in the woods to cheer her up but she didn't even glance at them, just stuffed them in her bedside cabinet.

It was so hot in her room, kind of depressing. I said maybe we could go sunbathe by the pool like old times. She went, oh sorry, not up to your requirements? It's not a fucking holiday camp. Go back to the caravan park if that's what you want.

It stung, but I could see she was down. So I said, how about some music? Thought that might cheer her up, change the atmosphere a bit. I could see her iPod on the shelf, plugged into the speakers. I turned it on and the first thing I heard was that creepy old-timey version of a children's nursery song about going into the woods . . .

The same music I heard the other night in the trees.

The same music that's been playing on a loop in my head, ever since.

My first thought was: that's so weird. Why's she been listening to this?

But then Frankie lunged and snatched it from me, turned it off. And I saw her face and I got it.

I said: the music in the woods . . . that was you?

She was silent for a bit, like she was deciding what to say. Then she rolled her eyes. <u>All</u> of it was me, Sparrow.

My mind was spinning. All the stuff we found in the woods. I was like, what—but not the thing in the treehouse, though? That dead bird? The symbols on the trees?

Yes, you total cretin. I'm good at stuff like that. It was easy. Granmama gets blood from the butchers for Grandfa's black pudding. Nicked Hugo's tracksuit, stuffed it with straw. Kipling killed that bird, thought it could be a nice touch. Of course the Birds aren't real.

I felt sick. Then angry. Really angry. I still am now. When I think of how scared I was. Was she laughing at me the whole time?

Why? I asked. Why the hell would you do all that?

She shrugged. Ugh, I don't know. Because it was fun? Because I read <u>Legends of Tome</u> and it gave me ideas? Because the twins pissed me off stealing my stash and I wanted to freak them out that someone had set the Birds on them? Because I was bored? Ohmigod. Sooooooooooo fucking bored.

Guess she saw my face then.

Yeah, sorry. Even with your thrilling company, Sparrow. But you were a perfect little idiot. You were pissing your pants!

So I know now. What she saw in me. Why she picked me out on the beach that day. To be her gullible little idiot.

Eddie

SOLSTICE

I CAN HEAR DORSET FM blaring out downstairs.

"It's going to be a real scorcher today, folks! Hottest midsummer in half a century. What are you doing with yours? Phone in and tell me—"

It was so hot last night, too. I spent hours lying on top of my sheets, sweating, thinking about everything that happened in the woods.

The Birds are real. They killed Ivor. What if they'd caught us? I think of finding the old guy in his study. The look on his pale dead face. I get it now, Mum, I do—why you told me never to go in the woods after dark. What if they come for me now?

I'm trying to work out if I should tell my folks about Ivor. It would really upset Mum. Besides, it's not going to bring him back, is it? And what if Dad did something stupid like head into the woods and try to confront them about it?

I scroll through my phone to distract myself from all the images I keep seeing over and over like they're playing on a reel in my head: the masked figures . . . the bull's head.

Delilah's posted a new video to TikTok, talking to camera and swishing her new red hair.

"Big night tonight guys," she says. "Not sure how much I'll be able to share but I. Am. Excited! It is going to be FIRE." A wink and a big pantomime kiss to the camera. And then Nathan appears over her shoulder. "Oh yeahhhh! It's gonna be lit!" He gives a long, manic cackle. He is such an arse. But when I watch

it for the second and third time I think I see something in his eyes. Something dangerous. I wonder if I should tell Michelle? Warn her? But what would I say? I have no idea if it's all just bluff and besides, I don't want to connect myself with Tate in any way.

My alarm goes off for the third time and I drag myself out of bed. No one's about downstairs, even though the radio's still on, chattering away. I shovel down some Shreddies in the kitchen then go to the understairs cupboard to have a hunt around for Mum's sewing kit. I'm on another split shift: breakfast washing-up in the kitchens this morning, few hours' break in the middle, then later today we'll all have to change into our costumes for the solstice celebration. Mine's too small, so on my break I'm going to let it out at the shoulders. I'm pretty good at stuff like that, which pleases Mum. "I taught you well! I always wanted to bring up boys who would never expect a woman to mend their clothes or wash their dishes." Maybe I took it a bit literally, becoming an actual dishwasher.

The cupboard is full of cleaning products, plus a couple of bottles of creosote and big heavy bags of industrial salt for the winter. Even stuff of my brother's: a rugby ball he had signed by the Exeter rugby team, a couple of his old jackets.

The sewing kit's not on any of the shelves: I guess it could have fallen down behind the boiler. I stretch and reach down into the space, feeling cobwebs wrapping themselves around my fingers. Then I touch something that definitely isn't Mum's sewing kit. Something hard and shaped into a blunt point. I snatch my hand back quickly. The shape and texture of it felt like bone.

I kind of know, at this point, that this thing is probably something I'm not meant to find. It's like a darker version of the feeling I got when I was a kid finding the small stash of birthday presents hidden in the airing cupboard upstairs and *knowing* I shouldn't look at the boxes, but unable to resist peeking. And I know I'm going to look now.

I hoist myself farther over the boiler, reach down and grab hold of the thing, which seems to be wrapped inside something soft. When I pull it up I see the material is a heavy dark fabric. I'm fumbling around with it when the thing inside thunks onto the floor. For a moment I just stand and stare at it. I think I know what it is. But it can't be . . .

I take a deep breath and pick it up with hands that have gone all shaky.

A black mask. Nothing like the sort you'd get off Amazon or from a party shop. There's a beak and it's long and curved and sharp and pretty realistic, with nostrils carefully molded into it. It looks so old: an antique thing from a time when everything was made by hand. I turn it over. It ties at the back with two thick black ribbons.

I know that mask. I just can't understand what it's doing here.

I look down at the big heap of black material on the floor. I'd been so focused on the mask I hadn't noticed the feathers sewn onto it. Hundreds and hundreds of them. I give it a poke with a toe. It falls open and I see the long black cloak, with its hood. A pair of black leather gloves.

It all looks very different here in the cupboard under the bright naked lightbulb, without a body or a face inside any of it. It still has a kind of dark power, though.

My mind's racing. It all fits. Dad coming in late the night before. How weird and guilty he was about Ivor yesterday. I couldn't work it out. Now I understand why: he knew exactly what had happened to the bull.

The Birds aren't just a story kids scare each other with. They're real. They're up to something. And my dad is one of them.

I think for a moment. That was some messed-up stuff last night, in the woods. I don't want my dad having anything to do with it. I think of that night with the locked garage, the tractor . . . I have to protect him, even if it's from himself.

I snatch up the whole lot and run the bundle out to my bike, stuff it deep down into the pannier on the back. If I hide them here, he won't be able to use them. Yeah, I suppose he might miss them. Wonder what's happened to them. Well, let him.

Owen

THE MORNING DAWNS, HOT AND bright. The day of Francesca's feast. I'm lying in our bedroom drenched in sweat. It's early and yet I can feel the heat ratcheting: the air as heavy as a wool blanket. The weight of my guilt is far worse.

What have I done?

I look over at Fran, lying next to me. Hair strewn across the pillow. She looks like a fucking angel, sleeping the sleep of the innocent, the blessed. There are even a couple of white downy feathers from somewhere caught in the strands of her hair, like the finishing touches to the whole picture.

And here I am: a foul, despicable creature, unfit to lie beside her.

I have no excuse. Whatever she was up to last night, my own actions are unforgivable. I've gone and endangered the best thing that has ever happened to me because I'm so bloody insecure, because I've never felt like her equal. I'm such a cliché.

And Michelle? How could I even go there? She's a viper in our nest.

I need a smoke and a walk to clear my head, to think about my next move.

It's ten past seven, meaning the guys should be arriving with the excavator soon for the next stage in the Treehouse project. Though we won't start the work until the solstice celebrations begin tonight, the plan is to get the excavator positioned in the woods early this morning, to avoid most of the guests having to witness the unsightly spectacle of a construction vehicle crawling up the drive.

I inch from under the sheet; I don't think I can face Francesca yet. But as I slide out of bed she turns toward me and opens her eyes. She stretches luxuriously, then gives me her most radiant smile as she reaches out a hand to cup my jaw. It's everything I can do not to flinch away—I feel so unworthy of her touch.

"Good morning, my beloved," she says, gaze boring deep into mine. "I do hope you slept well?"

Bella

WHEN I WAKE IT'S SUFFOCATINGLY hot. The pillow's damp and creased. My hair is a wild tangle, like I've been thrashing around in my sleep. I only got a couple of hours but my nightmares were wild and dark. I dreamt of the trees, of roots pushing up through buckling floorboards to twist around me and drag me down with them. Soil filling my mouth . . .

I feel like this place is actually choking me—sapping all my strength and courage. I have to leave its orbit for an hour or so. I stride out on the cliff path only a short while later, the sun floating huge and orange-pink from the horizon and blushing across the limestone stacks of The Giant's Hand. I can think a little more clearly here with the slight relief of the sea breeze. I gave her a chance to come to me, in the woods. Now it's time to act.

I'm jolted out of my thoughts by a cackling sound: loud and vicious. It takes me a moment to realize what it is: a flock of black birds—crows, I think—circling overheard. Hundreds of them. Their dark bodies a strange sight, incongruous somehow; I would have expected to see seagulls. For a moment they settle along the edge of the cliff in front of me. And then, as though a signal has been given, there's an explosion of movement and sound and they're all taking off, seeming to act as one, croaking and flapping, launching into the air and disappearing in a black swarm around the headland. Westwards, in the direction of The Manor.

I pick up the pace, a touch of foreboding in my gut.

After I've climbed down to the beach, I scan the waves quickly, remembering the bright kitesurfing sail that appeared yesterday. I want to make sure I'm alone. Then I force myself to go inside the cave again. I'm here to remind myself. To muster the courage

I need. The dark interior is shockingly cold compared to the heat of the morning, but I don't think that's why I'm shivering uncontrollably.

I press my forehead against the damp wall of the cave and rest here a moment, let the ghosts of the past envelop me.

Summer Journal

THE CARAVAN—TATE'S HOLIDAY PARK
AUGUST 20, 2010

Today was a good day.

Had a text from Frankie this morning. Sry Sparrow. Didnt mean 2 b a bitch. Feeling rly bad about it all. Come hang?

But I feel so weird about all that stuff she did. All that effort she went to. Dead birds and blood. It's so messed up. And it was so hot and the sea was glittering away while I ate my cereal in the deckchair by the caravan. It was like: freedom! I could do exactly what I wanted. So I grabbed my bikini, my book, started walking to the beach. Halfway along the cliff path, I bumped into Jake. He went: you never replied to my text. But smiling. And I was like: er, you never replied! Then he pulled out his phone and showed me. Did so. See? It was from a week ago.

Free tmrw. Beach @10?

I call my phone a piece of shit cos the battery's always dying. But it's never had a problem with texts, far as I know. Frankie took my phone off me that day, when I was texting. Before I'd have said: no way would she do that. Now I don't know.

He shrugged and said: no big deal. We could go now?

I said yes.

Went with him along the path until he swerved off to one side like he was about to jump off the cliff. He laughed at my face. Best beach round here. There's a path. You just can't see it from there.

I followed him down. To not look at the drop I stared at the patch of sweat on his T-shirt between his shoulder blades, silver chain brushing the hairs at the back of his neck. Tripped and had to grab a bramble and made a stupid squeal. He turned round and took my hand and put my thumb in his mouth and sucked the prickles out for me, his hair brushing my wrist. The hottest thing that's ever happened to me. Till we mucked about in the sea. Didn't care about my flat chest or my orange Holiday Skin streaky knees cos of how he looked at me in my bikini. He kept grabbing me and pretending to dunk me and our legs tangled under the water and his skin over his shoulders was like silk and he pulled me up against him and I could feel . . .

Then I looked up and could just see The Manor, looming above the cliffs a little way down the coast. All the windows glinting. I had this idea she could look down and see us. Asked if we could go back to the sand.

Maybe he saw me looking as when we were on the beach again he asked, so what's it like, the big house? They never mix with us peasants. We lay there with our toes in the shallows to stay cool but letting the sun burn the water off the rest of us and I told him about it. Told him about the woods. What Frankie did. And he was like, what? That's so fucked up. It felt kind of good to have someone else say it.

But I thought I saw one of them, I said. One of the Birds. When we were picking shrooms.

He went—you were picking shrooms?

Yeah. A few days ago.

He sat up then and went: yeah, no way those were magic mushrooms.

I said they were just like the photo I saw.

Nope. They only grow in the autumn. You gotta trust a farm boy. What you found . . . that's something else.

I asked him what.

He said: dunno but you should be careful. Mushrooms can fuck you up.

I thought about Frankie stuffing them in her bedside drawer and had this horrible thought that she might try them. And even though things are weird with us right now I texted her straight away: Bin the shrooms!!! DO NOT TAKE. Cld be super dodgy.

She's wrong about the Birds though, he said then. They're real. They just act on the big stuff. You don't get big crimes happening round here that often. Last time was maybe five years ago? Local guy sneaking up on girls at night, flashing them. People knew who it was but the police never caught him doing it. Don't know what the Birds did to him but they fucked him up proper cos he left town one morning, never came back. His house is still empty. But your mate wouldn't know any of that . . . she's not a proper local. There's things you can't understand if you're not from round here. It's not some fairy tale. You don't want to get on the wrong side of them.

AUGUST 21, 2010

Even hotter today. In all senses of the word. Oh my God, that sounds so naff. But it was.

Down on the secret beach again Jake said: hey. Want to see something cool? He led me back toward the cliffs but halfway across the beach he stopped, squinting up at them. I asked him what it was and he was like, dunno, thought I saw someone up there. We watched for a bit. Nothing. He was like, nope, must have imagined it.

The thing he wanted to show me was this cave. More of a tunnel, actually, going deep into the cliffs. It was properly cold in there after the heat of the sun and there was water running down the walls and it smelt of eggs and was a bit creepy but in a fun way, with him there too. He was like, look: at the back it goes even further. You up for it?

Promise you haven't brought me here to murder me? I said, just to be funny.

He laughed. I like you way too much for that. Felt properly nervous then, but in the best way. He lifted me up so I could see into the tunnel at the end and I could feel his breath warm against the back of my neck. Who thought you could get that turned on in a cold smelly cave? And then he let me down but he didn't move away when I turned toward him so for a moment we just stood there pressed against each other, noses brushing.

I don't know who kissed who. But I was the one who slipped my tongue in. He did this low groan then and I could feel, you know, pressing against me. And his hands were in my bikini top and for a moment I froze cos all I could think about was Hugo and the stuff he said about my flat chest. Then he said: you're so fucking beautiful.

All I could think then was: I'm going to lose it in a cave and I don't care. Then he broke off.

Did you hear that? Footsteps.

He was kind of laughing, kind of annoyed. Would be just like Nathan Tate. Or worse, the twins—would they know this place exists? Or maybe Shrimp. Know he comes down here sometimes.

He pulled away, ran to the cave entrance. Where are you, dickhead?

I heard the footsteps then. Somewhere up above us, on the roof of the cave.

He came back. Think they've legged it. Perv. Doubt they could see much. And it's not like we had our kit off. Yet.

But it sort of killed the vibe.

Then he went: hey, this is kind of cheesy. But you want to come and get fish and chips tomorrow night and drive to Seafarer's Point with me on my moped? Going to be a supermoon. We'd have the best view.

I laughed. Are you asking me on a date?

And he went: yeah, I think I am.

Got back to the caravan late, feeling sunburned and salty, this stupid smile on my face. Then I stopped short cos Frankie was right there, sitting in the deckchairs with my parents, holding a bottle of Coke. Mum and Dad laughing at something she was saying.

I almost turned and walked away but she called over to me, hey, Alison! Can't think of the last time she used my actual name.

Mum was grinning at me. Can't believe we've never actually met Frankie! She says we must come round for a drink, meet her grandparents. She was doing this funny voice, posher than normal, pronouncing all her words really carefully.

Frankie got up and came over to me. She whispered: I want to make it right, Sparrow, please. I'm sorry. We had fun, right? The stuff in the woods . . . it was meant to be a laugh, you know? But I see now it was fucked up. I went too far. I do that sometimes. But I _miss_ you. Look, the olds are going to some geriatric dinner party slash orgy down the coast tomorrow night. Got the place to ourselves. She put out a hand and touched my arm.

Then a bit louder she said: how about it? Barbecue tomorrow evening?

How fabulous! Mum called. I have literally _never_ heard her say fabulous. I'm sure Alison would love to go! You could bring some sausages, sweetheart.

I didn't say anything. I was thinking about Jake and fish and chips and the supermoon.

And then Frankie looked straight at me and grinned. Oh, she said. More the merrier . . . bring your boyfriend if you like. Your secret one.

Bella

I COULD THROW THE JOURNAL out to sea, let its secrets dissolve into nothing. I could climb back up to the cliff path and walk in the other direction, to Tome. I could get on a train to London and never look back. I'm at a crossroads, just as I was on a summer night fifteen years ago.

As if in answer, the breeze ransacks through the pages of the journal in my lap until it falls open on the last page. The biro-drawn map. X marks the spot.

No. I can't let it fester inside me anymore. This is why I'm here. Why I came back.

I'm hurrying back along the part of the footpath that hugs the road, nearly at Seaview Farm, when I see someone opening the gate. I stop dead, heart thumping, and manage to press myself into the hedgerow where hopefully I'm slightly concealed. I can't face meeting anyone coming out of that place. It's a young guy, tall and broad-shouldered, long-legged, wheeling a bike, and at first I think . . . I think . . .

My thoughts are spiraling, scattering. I'm struggling to breathe, struggling to make any sense of it. He's too young. He looks the same age he was back then—fifteen years ago. Then he turns in this direction—fuck, I press myself further into the hedge—and I realize it's not him. Of course it's not.

I do know this boy, though. And suddenly a lot of things fall into place. Why I was so drawn to Eddie the barman that first night. His strange familiarity. Why I totally took leave of my senses and found myself trying to seduce him.

He's his brother. He's his little brother.

Francesca

TODAY IS GOING TO BE a triumph.

It's the day of our solstice feast, the jewel in the crown of our opening weekend. And it is going to be perfect.

I walk to the windows and throw them open, bathing myself in warmth and sunlight. The hot air streams in laden with the scent of sea salt and blossom. Honestly, if you could bottle it you could make a *killing*. Perhaps I should look into that, actually—the next iteration of our wellness line.

On the lawns beneath me I watch staff scurrying hither and thither, planting stakes for the hanging lanterns, building the stage for our musical entertainments, lifting the fire pit for the spit roast into place, setting up three long tables a few meters back from the cliff edge. The tablescapes will be arranged atop them shortly: the woman designing them (theme: "midsummer cornucopia") is a genius. She doesn't like to discuss her other clients as she's so wonderfully discreet, but let's just say that she accidentally let slip the words *Amal* and *Como* while we were brainstorming my vision.

I feel a thrill of anticipation as I imagine the view my guests will have as they make merry: of the sun sinking beneath the waves and the stunning limestone formation of The Giant's Hand. I have created something truly unique here. I have thrown off the shadows of the past, manifested a new future for myself and this place.

Ah! And here come my willow sculptures, carried on the broad shoulders of the boys from the gardening team. Arguably my pièce de résistance, they will form an enchanted sylvan scene for my guests to wander through as they sip their fine cider and listen to the first strains of the music.

Everything beneath me is gilded by the morning sun—a scene of such perfection it seems hardly real. The epitome of "pagan chic." I've always been good at curating an experience. Hosting a party, too. We had a couple here when we were teenagers, actually. Of course, it was rather different then. A barbecue, some speakers, the pool. A little youthful horseplay. But the basic principles are the same. In place of alcopops we'll have fine cider, in place of the barbecued sausages we'll have a high-end spit roast (they play the pigs Bach and feed them hand-selected acorns), and in place of tinny tunes from my portable speakers we'll have our live acts. We've been very hush-hush about the line-up—to stop anyone alerting the press and because The Manor doesn't boast about such things—but we have the sort of talent performing tonight that could be expected to appear on one of the main stages at Glastonbury. All *begging* to be included!

Oh, we are totally going to make the Condé Nast Hot List. No: we are going to *destroy* it, grind the competition to dust beneath us—

I'm just so excited.

And surprisingly calm. Or perhaps not so surprising, considering how much work I've done on myself over the years. Once upon a time I would have allowed my rage at what I witnessed in the wine store last night to overtake me, cloud my judgment. Now I know it's much better to be clear-eyed about these things.

The simple truth is I need them both right now: Owen for his work on the Treehouse project; Michelle for the preparations for the evening's celebrations. I need her diligence, her attention to detail. Still, it is really so disappointing. I do *hate* it when people let me down.

Well, no matter. For today at least nothing and nobody is going to send my Mercury into retrograde.

I close my eyes to better enjoy the warmth of the new day upon my face. Goddess, but it is hot. But hopefully it won't get *much* hotter. Almost in answer to this thought I feel the heat ease a little. The rosy glow of the light through my eyelids dims. Did I actually make that happen? I open my eyes. A shadow has fallen across the sun. Some of the staff below are pointing at the sky.

I look up. Huge black storm clouds have appeared overhead. It's impossible. It's meant to be entirely clear today. Nowhere—in either the forecast or my manifestation—was it to be like this. I stare up at them, willing them to disperse.

Yet the way they're moving, shifting . . . they're no ordinary clouds. I shield my eyes and squint up at them. And now I see that they're . . .

Birds.

Darkening the sky. Blotting out the sunlight. Filling the air. Black seething swarms of them. They're everywhere I look: arriving in waves, surging together, their wing tips brushing as they circle, settling on the lawn until I can see barely a shred of grass for their black bodies. They're landing on the tables, too, the backs of chairs, the wicker sculptures. They look like a giant spillage of tar. The noise comes to me now: the cackling and chattering building to a roar of sound. Suddenly I can't even hear my own thoughts. I go to shut the window to drown them out and just as I do one flies right at the glass, hits the pane with a thud and ricochets away. A little scream escapes me.

I fumble for my phone, I need Michelle . . . I need her to sort this *now*. I stab at her name on my screen, clutch the phone to my ear as I wait for her to pick up. She isn't answering. *Why isn't she answering?*

Of course I am all about harmony with the natural world, but this is the limit. This doesn't feel natural at all. It feels personal. It feels like a haunting.

Bella

HIS *BROTHER*. JAKE'S BROTHER. SEEING Eddie like that has given me a jolt. A new sense of urgency. A reminder of what was lost. What she took.

As I march toward The Manor's gates I become aware of a sound behind me: the low grumble of heavy machinery. I turn and see a yellow JCB and a white van crawling up the road in this direction. They must be here for the construction work on the edge of the woods: the reason I got such a huge discount for my stay.

As I stand and watch them approach, an idea occurs to me. It's at once wildly audacious and so simple it feels like it was meant to be. My heart starts to beat very fast in my chest.

I open the journal. With trembling hands I flick to the biro-drawn map at the back, making sure. Then I turn and walk back toward the JCB, raising a hand to flag them down.

X marks the spot.

Eddie

"I MEAN, IT'S KIND OF sinister," Ruby says, as we watch the hundreds—thousands?—of birds flocking onto the lawns. You can hardly see the grass for their bodies. Ruby and I and a few of the others have been summoned to deal with them. "Have you ever seen them do this before?"

I shake my head: no. I know what she means, it *is* sinister. They look sort of like one of the armies in *Game of Thrones*, gathering before a battle.

"You all right, Eds?" Ruby's watching me.

"Oh . . . yeah." I was thinking of the scene last night in the woods. Of the cloak and mask I found at home. My own dad: one of them. And now these real birds acting in such an unnatural way . . .

But I can't mention any of this to Ruby, so instead I say, "There's this film where the birds start, like, attacking people, isn't there? It's definitely famous. Old, but famous. Can't remember what it's called, though."

"It's called *The Birds*, Eddie," Ruby says, with a bit of an eye-roll. "And the original story's better." I nod, like I know what she's talking about. I always feel a bit thick around Ruby. "Anyway," she says, "let's do this."

Together we wander onto the lawn. We try shouting and clapping our hands but the birds don't seem scared of us at all. They barely even move as we walk among them. There's something about the way they're eyeballing us that I really don't like. They've got very sharp-looking beaks and claws. I wonder how that film ends.

Out of nowhere there's a loud *bang!* and both of us jump. Francesca Meadows has burst through the front door of The Manor. Her hair is all wild and loose down her back and she's wearing a long silk dress that I think might actually be a posh nightie because it's a really pale nude color and you can kind of see everything through it, even though I'm trying very hard not to stare (I don't think it's professional to check out your boss's nipples). Her feet are bare.

I catch Ruby's eye. She mouths *what the fuck?* A part of me wants to snigger but another part is rattled as it's all so weird. The Night Birds couldn't make *this* happen . . . could they? That would be actual dark magic or something.

We watch as Francesca Meadows rushes into the middle of the flock and starts waving her arms around to try and scare them away. She doesn't seem to notice or care that the hem of her dress is trailing on the ground and getting all manky with the greenish bird crap that's staining her bare feet, too. As she approaches them groups of feathery black bodies rise up into the air and twist and corkscrew around her like miniature tornados, then resettle on the ground once more. She lets out a cry of rage that mingles with the screeching of the birds and kicks out at them and *then* goes for them with her hands—almost like she's trying to grab them out of the air. I have this horrible feeling that if she managed to get hold of one she might actually tear it to pieces.

"Oh my God," Ruby whispers, sounding kind of awed. "She's totally lost it. I *knew* that Goopy yoga princess thing was an act . . ." She trails off as Francesca Meadows turns to look at us. Flecks of foamy spit run from her mouth down to her jaw. One of the birds must have nicked her with a claw as blood is smeared above her eyebrow. Dark patches of sweat have appeared under the arms of her silk nightie thing. She's visibly panting.

Ruby and I stand here watching from a few meters away, kind of frozen to the spot. Then she turns toward us and there's a moment when we all stare at each other. Ruby nudges me and we both start moving among the birds again, trying to shoo them away, while nearby Francesca Meadows is doing some kind of demented dance-fight with them.

"Hang on," Ruby says, suddenly. "Look. They're eating something, aren't they?" She steps forward and crouches down to get a better look. "Yes! I think it's birdseed." She bends down and scoops a handful into her palm to show me. "Someone's scattered it everywhere. All over the lawns. Holy shit . . . That's why they're here. It's no random freak of nature."

I think again of the cloaked figures in the woods.

The bird mask tucked away secretly at home.

Someone planned this whole thing.

Owen

I COLLECT MY TOBACCO STASH from the wall. Scratch a match along the strip on the box. Enjoy the feel of it the same way I did as a boy all those years ago. The sense of control, conjuring flame out of the air. The same way I did just before my dad and I left Tome for good, when I lit that match and threw it into a pool of petrol siphoned from the outboard engine of the fishing boat. Watched the flames climb quickly up the ancient timbers and then onto the old thatched roof of The Crow's Nest, which went up in one huge burst of flame, showering sparks. The pub was the heart of everything. The place they all gathered. The people who had bullied and judged and then pitied my family. They could go burn.

As I watched I experienced something new. I felt powerful for the first time in my life.

Now, dragging on my rollie, I take the path that leads into the woods. There seem to be birds everywhere, all of a sudden. I see them lifting out of the topmost branches of the trees, joining the others already filling the sky. It's as though there's something malign at work here. I catch myself. For Christ's sake. I'm not a superstitious man. My dad was, which is the precise reason I am not. My dad, rest his troubled soul, wouldn't have liked this at all. He would have called it an evil omen.

I become aware of another sound, beneath the chattering of the birds. I stop short on the path and stand still, listening. I could swear that I can hear the sound of heavy machinery coming from deep in the woods: the grinding, tearing noises of what sounds unmistakably like excavation work. But that's impossible. They're not meant to start until the evening. They don't even know where they're meant to be digging.

And yet what I'm hearing would very much suggest otherwise. I'm jogging now. Along the winding path that zigzags between the Woodland Hutches, feeling an urgent need to know what's going on.

Sure enough, when I burst into the clearing, I see the JCB's articulated arm rising upwards, carrying a full burden of earth.

What the fuck?

They *have* started. And not only have they done so without my permission, they've also begun digging in the wrong place, thirty yards away from where they should be. I start running again, waving my arms above my head, yelling to try and catch their attention, but I can see that both the guy on the ground and the one in the cab have their backs to me, intent on their work. As I get closer still, I can see that there is already a sizeable cavity in the ground. The metal jaws rise from the pit, spilling a huge mouthful of soil and grass.

Gesticulating like crazy, I try and alert the guy up in the driver's seat but he *still* hasn't seen me. He dumps the load on the growing pile beside him, then works the controls to plunge the shovel back into the earth.

Finally the guy on the ground must hear my shouts because he turns and looks as I stride toward them. He signals the guy in the cab. Finally, the excavator stops moving.

"What the hell are you doing?" I yell. "You're not meant to have started! And Jesus Christ, you're not even doing it in the right place! What the fuck is going on here?"

"The boss came and met us," the guy says, a little defensively.

"*I'm* the boss!" I shout.

"She said she was the owner."

"*Francesca* told you to start?"

"Yeah!" He seizes on this. "Francesca Meadows. That's what she said. The boss lady."

I feel dazed. Francesca's still in bed. At least, I'm pretty sure she is . . . but it wouldn't be the first time she's gone sneaking around without explanation recently.

"She asked us to start digging here. Didn't she?" he calls up to the guy in the cab who leans out and nods.

"Yeah. She said to get going. Pointed it all out to us."

I stare at the hole in the ground. "But this isn't the right place at all. It should be over there—where those trees have been felled. Are you sure that's what she told you?"

"Sure as eggs is eggs." The guy on the ground folds his arms. "Seemed *very* certain of what she wanted. Had some kind of map."

This is all really fucking weird. I have no idea what's going on, but I don't like it. "Look," I say. "I have to call Francesca." I gesture to the JCB. "Just turn that bloody thing off. All work stops until I say so, OK?"

They look at each other, shrugging, nodding. "Whatever you say, boss," says the guy on the ground.

Maybe it's not the end of the world. They've made a bit of a mess, that's all. Nothing that can't be filled in. It's just a bloody stupid waste of time. But that's not what's eating away at me. It's the strangeness of it all.

I try and call Francesca but the signal's particularly patchy here. I walk a little way back toward the main house, until a couple of bars flicker into life, but her phone rings out. I bring up my tracking app, wait for the little flashing dot to load. There she is: out on the lawns in front of The Manor.

I jog back to the guys.

"What did she look like?" I ask. "The woman who spoke to you?"

"Er . . ." They look at each other; a smirk passes between them. They found her attractive. The first one coughs. "Blonde, thirty-something."

I walk back toward the house and try her again. No answer. I hang up. I'll just have to go and talk to her. But one of the guys is striding toward me now. "Guv," he says, almost apologetically. "There's something there. Where we've been digging. You might want to come and have a look."

Christ, I think. What now?

I walk back with him toward the trees. Peer into the hole. I can't see anything at first, just debris and broken roots and stones and earth. Then a color that doesn't make any sense: a long slash of vivid blue. I hunker down to get a better view. It looks like tarpaulin sheeting, I think, just showing through the earth. It looks as though it might have been used to wrap something—a large object, still concealed just beneath the soil.

I stand back up, trying to rationalize my sudden sense of unease. It's just some material. It could be absolutely nothing. And yet I don't like it at all. I'm aware of a prickling feeling at the base of my skull. An animal dread. Because suddenly I am certain that whatever is down there in that pit is not nothing.

DI Walker

DI WALKER IS CONFERRING WITH the fire brigade, checking no further casualties have been found inside The Manor, when a uniformed officer approaches. "We've just come across something else, in the woods, boss. I think you'll want to come and have a look."

Walker leaves Heyer in charge of the scene on the lawns. He and Fielding follow the uniform toward the woods, along a path that winds through a series of wooden cabins.

"They put the guests in those," Fielding says, nodding at them. "Look like jumped-up rabbit hutches, don't they? *Five hundred quid* a night." He looks agonized. "The missus was on at me to book one for our ten-year anniversary. Give me Premier Inn any day. And if I want to have a bath outdoors I can stick one in the backyard . . ."

Walker's barely listening. He's looking at the trees. He tunes in as he hears Fielding say: "Funny thought . . ."

"What's that?"

"No one's going to stay in them now, are they? Never again. Got to be some kind of record, right? A hotel open for one weekend only."

They're nearly at the woods. Fielding glances at Walker, frowns. "You cold?" He must have clocked Walker's involuntary shiver.

"Fine," Walker says. "Think it's cooler in this part of the grounds. Must be those long shadows."

"Speak for yourself. I'm sweating like Bojo at a paternity test. Still, least it's not as hot as it was yesterday. That was something else. Unnatural." The branches of the trees on the edge of the woods suddenly convulse and fifty or so black birds explode into the air with a vicious cackling. "Christ!"

Walker manages to suppress his shudder this time.

"Lots of legends about this place," Fielding says as they enter the wood. "Suppose it'd sound like total guff to a Londoner. But you gotta admit there's an atmosphere."

"Yeah," Walker says, "I'll give you that."

Soon they're passing through a clearing where several trees have been recently felled, the wood of the stumps wet and raw. Fifty yards ahead, Walker can see a small gaggle of officers, the bright flash of police tape being unfurled. Within the taped area he can just make out something that looks like a deep shadow on the ground. As they get closer, it's revealed as a cavity. The length and depth of the rectangular hole are somehow universally recognizable.

His breath feels a little labored.

"Here we go," Fielding says, quickening his pace.

A few steps farther and Walker can fully make out the ragged dark pit, clawed out of the earth by the jaws of some large machinery. The uniforms step aside for the detectives. And even though he is half prepared for what will greet him within, he takes a deep breath as he approaches.

He's hit by the powerful scent of fresh-turned soil: a secret history just unearthed.

Francesca

SOLSTICE

THE WAY THE BIRDS ARE staring at me with their gleaming black eyes. The malevolence. The knowing. As though they can see into my very soul. I think of that shape I saw in the stone basin and I think of Grandfa's ranting at the end and I put a hand up to my stinging cheek and see blood on my fingertips. I feel dread seeping through me.

Then I spot Ruby, the receptionist, scooping something up from the ground and letting it trickle back through her fingers. I look down at the grass, look properly this time where before I had only been able to see the birds and the mist of my own fear, and I see the seed scattered there. My horror converts instantly to rage.

Someone is trying to sabotage me and everything I've created. It's Sparrow, I'm sure of it.

"Michelle," I gasp at Ruby. "Go and find me Michelle. Now."

A few minutes later she appears, looking irritatingly pristine in her white shirt, not a badly highlighted hair out of place. "Francesca," she says solicitously, giving me a swift look up and down. "Are you . . . feeling all right?" She points to my brow. "You've, ah, got a little something just there."

"The birds," I hiss. "I need them gone, *now*."

"Of course," she says. "As you can see the staff are doing their best—"

I look at her smug, common little face. How could he? *Ugh.* Another wave of rage courses through me.

"For God's sake you stupid bitch!" I shout. "It's not good enough. I need *every* member of staff here. I need *every* single fucking bird gone. Can I not trust anyone in this bloody place to do their job properly?"

There's a stunned silence. I feel the staff watching me. I have the odd sensation I am watching, too, hovering above myself. Gradually the mist begins to clear. This is not Francesca Meadows. Francesca Meadows never speaks like that—not even inside her own head. It's like Francesca lost her grip and someone else briefly took over the controls.

I take a very long breath in. A very long breath out.

"Goodness!" I say, brightly. "I think I need to take a time-out. Ha ha! All the pressure of the day is getting to me. It's nothing to do with you, Michelle!" I don't actually apologize, because someone once told me that to do so is an admission of guilt and putting yourself in that position is dangerous. I feel shaky, drained.

"Leave it with me, Francesca," Michelle says, calmly. "It will be done."

Goodness, she's so efficient. I almost wish I could keep her.

Owen

WE DIG IN SILENCE.

We've managed to clear more soil off the top of the tarpaulin. One of the guys has managed to lower himself into the pit and he's using a shovel, lifting up spadefuls of earth. More and more blue tarpaulin is gradually revealed beneath the soil, the color bright in the gloomy shadow of the trees.

It's slow progress but a shape is emerging. It's largish and long. A bulk inside it. A certain word keeps presenting itself to me. I keep pushing it away. No need to rush to any crazy conclusions . . .

And then I glimpse a small tear in the fabric, revealing something smooth and off-white.

This is when I heed the premonition that has been taking shape in my mind.

"I'll take it from here," I say.

I pay the men. Tell them to leave the JCB, come back tomorrow. Trying to act like it's no big deal. They've been paid already but I pay them more, cash. A lot more. Each throws a final glance toward the pit but on balance they seem only too happy to get gone.

I do the remaining work on my own. Finally all the soil has been cleared from it. I take a deep breath and then with clumsy fingers I lean forward and undo the ropes tied about the tarpaulin. The thing falls open surprisingly easily, as though it has been waiting for some time to reveal its secrets.

Jesus fuck.

I can't tear my eyes away. It's so familiar—the stuff of Halloween costumes and horror films. Yet I am not sure I have ever seen a full human skeleton before. To think that this is all we are beneath the skin.

THE EVENING OF
THE FEAST

Bella

AN EXCITABLE HUBBUB OF VOICES outside: I peer through the windows and see the other guests leaving the Woodland Hutches for the evening celebrations, dressed in their white outfits. In the rich, golden light they are like ghosts drifting out of the trees. Strains of music float back from the direction of the front lawns. I need to get out there.

I've spent the last few hours hunkered here in the sweaty confines of my Hutch, feeling sick about what I've put in motion. Waiting, shivery with anticipation, for something to happen. Commotion, sirens, blue lights appearing up the drive, maybe. Feeling I had to stay nearby, but unable to bear getting any closer.

But so far . . . nothing. Was it the wrong spot? No: I'm certain it was the place.

As I pull on a white Toteme linen shift—another rental, obviously—I'm reminded of getting ready for another party. For a moment the girl I was feels near enough that I might almost lean through time to whisper in her ear. Then I place the willow crown on my head. Instantly a grotesque shadow looms on the wall in front of me: a dark figure with a huge Medusa-like mass where the head should be. I have to turn to check it's being cast by me. I glance in the mirror. Beneath the fringe of greenery my eyes are dark and pupilless: the eyes of a predator. I look freakish. A pagan cultist, a zealot. Definitely nothing like myself. Good. Because tonight I have to step outside myself, be more than myself. I have to leave that frightened little girl of the past behind. I try a smile, just to check the effect. It contrasts horribly with my eyes. I look like a Manson Family member in the dock. I bare my teeth. Better.

I leave the Hutch and walk against the flow of guests in the other direction, toward the lawns. Lanterns have been lit along the paths, many-colored wildflowers strewn across the gravel. I follow the path that winds toward the woods until I see the bright yellow JCB, sitting still in the small clearing, its claw frozen above the ground. There's no one in sight. There's an abandoned look to the whole scene.

I step closer, my heart leaping like a fish inside my ribcage. They've definitely been digging: I can see the dark shape of the void in the ground now. Closer still and I seem to be choking on my own breath. I think I might actually vomit. But I force myself forward. Force myself to approach the edge of the pit, to look and—

Nothing. It's empty. I stare down into the pit. Did I get it wrong? But I was so sure. Of course, after all this time—

No. There's something there. Something left behind, glinting at the bottom of the pit: a flash of silver bright against the dark soil. I get down on my hands and knees to look. It's been so long but I'd know this particular accessory anywhere: so closely associated in my memories with its wearer. I lie down on my belly and reach right down into the pit to pluck it out and shudder as my fingers close around the cold metal.

Summer Journal

THE CARAVAN—TATE'S HOLIDAY PARK
AUGUST 22, 2010, 7 P.M.

Frankie's BBQ tonight. Told Jake about the invite. How, in spite of every-thing, I feel I owe her this last night, after spending the whole summer there. Like closure or something. Then I never have to see her again.

He was like: personally I'd tell her to do one. Don't feel like you owe her anything. Then he shrugged. But hey, if it's important we could go for a bit? Then he grinned. And I guess I've always kind of wanted to see behind those gates. How the other half live.

Bit worried about bringing Jake (but definitely don't want to go with-out him). Can't help thinking about what Frankie said. About his accent, his "common" silver neck chain, etc. Is she going to mock him? Will I be embarrassed by him? Will it make me like him less? Urgh. I know this sounds super shallow. But that's what a diary's for, right?

Also, half an hour ago I came out of the shower block and Cora was standing there. Gave me such a shock I dropped my shampoo. She looked kind of rough. She went: hey. I've been looking for you. Can we talk? I thought she might be about to confront me, about how I saw her in Grandfa's study. But she just said: I really liked hanging out with you guys, you know? I can't tell you how much I loved that. Just chatting away about stupid stuff, not a care in the world. I don't get to do that sort of thing ever. It was so great, wasn't it?

I said yeah, even though it wasn't always so great for me.

She went: and I need that cleaning job. There aren't so many to go around down here. Girls like us, we don't normally get a break. I think she meant me, like we're in the same boat. Then she said: I texted and wrote and stuff but I don't know if Frankie got them. Could you have a word? Cause it was you, wasn't it? In the woods? Shit. She did see me then.

She said: you know it wasn't anything, right? I would <u>never</u>. But I've been trying to get ahead with my art. Frankie said she'd talked to him, but then . . . She shrugged. So I thought I'd ask myself. And I guess old blokes like that, they think they can, you know, touch you—the arm, back, bum. But it was nothing more than that. I <u>swear</u>. You know that right?

I nodded, even though I don't know if I do. But the crazy thing is I don't even care either way. Even though that moment in the woods was only about a week ago I feel like a different person. Since Jake, I guess. The me before seems like this silly, jealous little girl.

Looking at Cora I just felt bad for her. And guilty that she lost her job cos of me. I told her about the plans tonight. Said maybe she could come along a bit later when Frankie's mellowed out a bit? She was so grateful it made me feel even worse. Not sure anything is going to change Frankie's mind now. She was different yesterday, though, at the caravan park with Mum and Dad. So maybe?

Anyway, Jake's coming to pick me up at eight and I'm making an effort. I've got my silky yellow Miss Selfridge dress. I can't wear a bra under so I'm going to wear it with my bleached denim jacket on top so Dad doesn't freak out. I've borrowed Mum's No. 7 palette, done cat flicks with eyeliner. I want to blow his mind.

And maybe we only go for a bit? Maybe when it's not too rude we can sneak off together. Go sit on the cliffs and look at the supermoon . . .

The last true night of the summer.

Eddie

"IT'S DEFINITELY GIVING *MIDSOMMAR*," RUBY says, looking at the guests who have already arrived on the lawns in their headdresses and white outfits. Ruby and I are serving champagne glasses of cider as they pass beneath a willow arch and join the crowds on the grass.

It's so hot that all the ice in the crates for cooling the cider bottles has already melted. I keep fantasizing about pouring the freezing water left behind over my head. "And can you believe they're making us wear these fucking things?" Ruby adds, gesturing to her get-up: the little horns and the flowing green robes all the staff have been told to wear. On her it looks like high fashion. I'm mainly concerned about whether you can see my bits, because the material's pretty thin and the breeze keeps blowing it against me. It reminds me of being a Lost Boy in *Peter Pan* at school, when I had to wear a pair of too-small tights. Dad seemed to think it was the funniest thing he'd ever seen. I remember, because my dad never really laughs. That gets me thinking about what I found this morning. My dad: one of the Night Birds.

"You all right?" Ruby looks at me. "Eds? You've kind of glazed over there."

Before I can answer—*am* I all right?—a couple wanders up to us. The woman gestures at the tray of drinks I'm holding. "Does that contain sulfites?"

"Er . . . it's cider?" I say.

Ruby rolls her eyes at me once they've drifted away (they each took one anyway). "That's not what you say, Eddie. You say 'No, of course we don't allow any nasty common sulfites here,' and smile."

"I can't! She might have some sort of reaction."

"Guaranteed, Eds, a few years ago she would have been asking if it was gluten free. Sulfites are just more on-trend these days. Besides . . . would it be *so* much of a tragedy? One less of this lot?" She wrinkles her nose. "You know, sometimes I think this job's OK. The pay's all right. And then other times I think I'd really like to headbutt someone. Or just, like, torch the place." She pauses for a moment. "Though maybe not tonight because did you hear the rumor about Nick Cave doing a set? And Wolf Alice. Oi! Are you listening?"

I just caught sight of a face that has no business being here.

"Yeah? Sorry . . . I thought I just saw someone."

I search among the faces in the crowd. Now I can't see any sign of him, just more guests arriving, flocking onto the lawns in their white outfits. Maybe I imagined it. But why the hell would I hallucinate *Nathan Tate*, skulking round the edges of everything like some underfed wolf?

DI Walker

THE DAY AFTER THE SOLSTICE

HE STEELS HIMSELF. LEANS FORWARD to look into the pit and . . .

Nothing. Just the dark of the soil.

"There's nothing there." He turns to the uniformed officer who led them here. "I thought you said you'd found human remains."

The officer nods. "Yes. But we found the remains themselves some way further into the trees. If you'll come this way."

Walker and Fielding follow, deeper into the wood. They walk for several minutes, the trees growing thicker, darker, denser.

"Just there." The officer points, eventually. Another little boundary of police tape. Within it, a heap of blue plastic. Something pale, whitish, gleaming inside. "It's like they've been dragged—an animal or something? But I can't think of any animal large enough to do this."

However many years of experience Walker has under his belt, however cold the case, it never loses its sting, this stark confrontation with death. You can never really be prepared to look upon the remains of a human being.

And there's something so pitiful about these jumbled bones wrapped in their blue plastic shroud. This was once a person. With a life. Loved ones. No one should lie like this, abandoned, alone, in a patch of unmarked woodland.

This. This is why he's been drawn to cold cases: to the unavenged, the disappeared. This is why he leaves no stone unturned. Because everyone deserves their funeral rites. To be properly mourned by their family. And everyone deserves justice.

Francesca

SOLSTICE

I CAN HEAR THE CLAMOR from the lawns, the microphone being tested, the boom of the speakers. I'm nearly ready to make my entrance. This is my moment. I am the moment.

I'm feeling a *lot* better now. I'm feeling *much* calmer about everything, honestly, now that those beastly birds have gone. I . . . lost myself there for a brief spell. But I'm not going to dwell on it.

I've done my affirmations. I've haloed myself with sacred mist. I've rubbed clary sage into my pulse points and placed four separate crystals into the velvet pouch attached to my necklace: rose quartz, tiger's eye, and selenite for calm, citrine to ward off negative energy. I've performed a quick Qigong facial massage. I'm feeling *so* much more grounded.

I've also had five shots of vodka. It's from the emergency supply I keep in a bottle that previously contained the dragon-fruit-rose pick-me-up beauty water I get sent from Erewhon in LA. Vodka is a really clean spirit, so it's the best if you're going to drink anything. Oh, and I used it to wash down a couple of the little pills I keep inside my old Ayurvedic tea tin. Sometimes the most important thing is that you regain your equilibrium. It doesn't necessarily matter how you get there. Yes, I have certain lifestyle guidelines for myself but no rules: rules are dangerous!

I practically float down the steps and out onto the lantern-lit lawns. The guests milling about look glorious in their willow crowns, their white garments. As expected, the willow sculptures look stunning. Best of all is the glorious wicker archway that the guests walk through as they join the celebration, as though they're passing through into another realm.

It's perhaps a *teeny* bit hotter than ideal, but that just adds to the overall sense of otherworldliness, of transcendence. I am certain that this will be a night everyone talks about for years to come. My moment of greatest triumph. I have created something truly beautiful here, in this place that has always been my sanctuary—

A little poison dart of a thought: she's here, somewhere. The bitter interloper at the feast. I search carefully among the faces in the crowd. Where are you, Sparrow?

No sign of her. Then something occurs to me. I actually let out a little gasp of surprise at the realization, so loud that a couple of guests turn to look at me. *I have been looking for the wrong person.* Even though I know what she looks like now from seeing her on the video—the blonde hair, the sharp fringe—I've been looking for a sixteen-year-old girl with long dark hair straggling down her back and a yellow slip dress. Just as she was on the last night I saw her.

Bella

I WALK THROUGH THE WICKER archway and find myself surrounded by dancing hares and foxes, leaping stags, even the odd wild boar, all made of twisted willow.

But my thoughts are back in the woods, beside that dark pit. So, she got rid of the body. Of course she did. I should have known. Should have expected no less. Unusually sloppy for her, though, to leave something behind. My discovery is now a small weight in the safe confines of my bag.

Where is she? I look around me in a kind of daze. Staff flit back and forth wearing emerald-green cloaks stitched with fabric leaves, and tiny oddly realistic-looking horns. Lanterns hanging from metal stakes bob in the hazy dusk like so many fireflies and ahead, in front of the cliffs, stand three long tables, each to sit perhaps sixty guests. They're spilling over with a tablescape of green-leaved branches, moss, heaps of fat red berries and flowers, and long tapered candles in glass jars. I look to the right and see a small stage built from wood and greenery.

All so tasteful, so stylish. It's so hot though. I bet she didn't plan for this. No pleasantly warm English midsummer evening: this heat is unnatural, punishing. My dress sticks to my shoulder blades. All around me guests waft themselves with the white-feathered fans that are being handed out, but every face still bears a sheen of sweat. As I get closer to the tables I wonder if it's my imagination or if the table decorations really are already wilting in the heat: the leaves curling, the petals browning, the berries splitting and running with juice.

I jump at a sudden reverberation from the speakers. There she is, stepping up onto the stage in her long white robes, her hair rippling out behind, her feet ostentatiously bare. She looks like a pagan priestess. She surveys the assembled crowd, gaze roving busily over the faces beneath her. As though she's looking for something, or someone . . .

I feel suddenly exposed. Pluck a fan from the basket held by a nearby server, hold it in front of me as a kind of shield.

"Just look at you all," she says, smiling. "I want to say thank you for choosing us. Thank you for electing to spend your precious time here. Because I see you. I know how much you deserve this time to pause, to reset. I can only imagine how incredibly hard you all work. How much you need this break."

As though everyone around me works for Médecins Sans Frontières.

"And I feel this enormous sense of connection, of *oneness* with you all right now. We are bound tonight by something truly significant."

And that would be . . . what? The hundreds of pounds everyone here has forked up for the privilege? I think once more of the dark pit on the edge of the woods. My stomach clenches. She and I *are* bound by something more.

"I'm so proud of this place. So proud to share it with you all. And I am so *very* proud of the transformative creative vision of our architect. Owen, my darling, here's to you—"

She shields her eyes from a slant of evening light, looking out at the crowd. Her smile never falters as the pause stretches just the wrong side of awkward. This is clearly the moment Owen Dacre is meant to come forward for an acknowledgment. There's no sign of him.

She recovers gracefully. "No doubt he's still hard at work on the Treehouses. I can't wait to share them with you! They're already booked for this autumn—goodness, you wonderful people can't get enough of us!—but I think we have a smidgen of availability next year . . ."

Several guests around me take out their phones, begin urgently tapping.

She beams. "But for now, let's all take a pause to give thanks and inhale the cleansing sea air." She closes her eyes and holds up the microphone to the crowd, as though to absorb its shared breath. Then she opens her eyes again.

"I couldn't resist a little nostalgic touch tonight. A nod to the midnight feasts of my childhood. The glorious golden hours I spent in this place. When you hear the sound of the gong, we'll all take our seats to eat. In the meantime, enjoy yourselves and this gilded evening."

Another radiant smile. I have a sudden urge to rush up and storm the stage, to rip the microphone out of her hands, to denounce her in front of all of them. But I know it's not the right way. There's something else I need to do first. I scan the crowd. There he is, standing behind a makeshift, greenery-adorned bar that's groaning under the weight of dozens of glasses. Eddie. I can't believe I didn't see it before. Jake wasn't quite as fair and his build was a little slighter, but so much is alike. I try to remember. Did he in fact mention a brother, just a little kid at the time?

I start moving in Eddie's direction but a wood-nymph server blocks my path, offering a tray of drinks. "Would you like some sparkling cider?"

Isn't most cider sparkling? "Er, yes . . . thanks."

I take a sip from the flute and regret it. It tastes off—earthy, almost rotten. But maybe it's the heat or the penchant of the wealthy for a freebie because everyone else is knocking theirs back like it's water. I watch one guy halt another tray-wielding server and glug down three glasses, one after the other, liquid spilling over his chin and soaking the front of his shirt.

When I next look at the bar Eddie's vanished from sight. But through the milling crowds, I spot another face I know. Hugo Meadows. Holding forth about something to the group surrounding him. His hand cupping the arse of the woman next to him who's wearing the blingiest version of the dress code I've seen yet: a clinging floor-length sheath of white paillette sequins, its sparkle a good match for her impossibly shiny dark hair. The same Hugo Meadows I saw yesterday lounging by the pool like some kind of medieval king, arrogant and entitled as ever. Next to him—like a strange optical illusion—stands his double, Oscar Meadows. As though he feels the pressure of my gaze, Oscar turns in my direction, frowning, but his attention's caught by the woman approaching them. The hotel manager: so sensible-looking in her white shirt and black skirt, like the only adult in the place. Does *she* look familiar, now I come to think of it? Or am I now imagining shadows of the past everywhere?

Moving a little closer, I hear her say: "Mr. Meadows, Mr. Meadows. I understand you're not a fan of our cider. Such a shame!"

"Don't understand why you're serving it," Hugo Meadows drawls. "Tastes like rotten apples and piss to me. My sister's idea of rustic chic, I suppose. What's wrong with a nice white burgundy? Frankly it's embarrassing—got a prospective investor here and he's not a fan of the stuff either." He mops his brow with a handkerchief plucked from his top pocket. "And it's too bloody hot. Can barely *think* in this heat." Like it's something the poor woman has any control over.

"Well, look," she says conspiratorially, with a tolerant, nothing-too-much-trouble smile, "why don't you both follow me to the wine store and take your pick instead? It's nice and cool down there if you need a break from the heat. And we've got some fairly fabulous English vintages—"

"As *I* should know," Hugo cuts in. "Maybe you're not aware, darling, but I'm actually responsible for half of them being there—put Francesca in touch with my contacts in the biz. Wine's kind of my thing? Think we will, thanks. Come on Osc." He turns to Oscar, who nods, ever the follower. Then Hugo gives his wife/girlfriend/escort's arse a little slap, like a piece of punctuation, and I watch as the two of them follow the woman toward The Manor.

I carry on past them, still searching for Eddie. I find myself wandering in the direction of the pool, which has been lit with hundreds of floating lanterns.

Suddenly, like a strange optical illusion, all I can see is what was there before—when the pool was kidney-shaped and bright turquoise with that stone nymph at the end. Glimpsed through a fug of barbecue smoke, a little cluster of teenagers sprawled about as dusk began to fall, with no idea how the night was about to unfold.

Summer Journal

THE CARAVAN—TATE'S HOLIDAY PARK
AUGUST 23, 2010, 2:15 A.M.

Can't stop my hand shaking. Can't stop crying. Oh God. It doesn't feel real. I keep thinking, hoping, maybe it isn't? Like, maybe I imagined it all? I need to get it down but my hand won't stop shaking.

I feel so far from the girl I was before tonight. That girl worried about whether it might be awkward, bringing the boy. Or about how he looked like he'd made too much effort in his blue shirt and silver chain which made him look mega fit but also like a farm boy dressed for a posh night out.

I'd give anything to go back to that girl. She's gone forever now. She died tonight, too.

Got to go back to the beginning. Can't tell anyone. Can only get it down here.

It started with Hugo meeting us on the driveway which made it uncomfortable straight off the bat. He gave Jake the once-over and was like, mate the cocktail party's that way? Ugh. I wanted to kill him then, the way he looked at us.

Imagine if Jake had got offended, even punched him or something, and we had to leave. That would have been the end. But he was cool about it. Just looked at Hugo's hoodie and baggy shorts, smacked his palm against his head and was like, sorry mate. This must be the virgin gamers' convention?

Then this awful moment where I had no idea what was about to go down. Finally Hugo went ha! Where did you find this guy? I like him. Then he looked me up and down and went: well you look fucking delicious, if I may say so. Losing that cherry suits you. Can see you're a bit chilly there.

I felt Jake tense and gripped his hand, like: <u>don't say anything</u>. Again, we could have just turned around then . . .

But we didn't. We followed Hugo round to the pool. Oscar was there, plus a couple of local girls. Frankie, stretched out on a lounger. Her get-up made me feel like a little girl in a party dress: lime-green bikini, hot-pink mules, see-thru crochet top. But Jake squeezed my waist then. I saw Frankie's eyes flick to his hand, back up again. Then she grinned. So good to meet you, she said to Jake, standing up and walking round the edge of the pool like a supermodel on the catwalk. Oh, I love your shirt. Goes so well with that neck chain. Her eyes flicking to me. Sparrow's told me so much about you.

My stomach flipped then. I've told her basically nothing.

Then she says to him: come help me with the ice. I want to bring a whole load out for the booze and you look nice and strong.

Jake shrugged at me and followed her into the house. I took a beer and stood by the pool like a lemon while Hugo and Oscar showed off to the local girls and I wondered if I should find some way of warning them about the twins.

Finally after I'd drunk that first beer, and another, Jake and Frankie reappeared, Jake carrying a big freezer box of ice.

Jake nodded at the pool, grinned at the others, and said, can't believe none of you are swimming! I'd have brought my trunks.

Next second, there was this huge splash and Jake came up spitting water, looking totally confused. It took a moment to work out what had happened.

There you go, fella, Hugo said, big smirk on his face. Knock yourself out.

Fuck you, I thought. Maybe it was downing two beers on an empty stomach, cos I'm never normally that brave. But I didn't overthink it. Just took a deep breath and jumped straight in. My dress floated up all around me. Jake smiled, pulled me close. The steam from the water lit up by the pool lights like a smokescreen. Felt like it was just him and me in that moment so I kissed him. Felt his arms go round my back. When we finally broke off I saw her face turned in our direction. Watching us.

I knew then it had been a big mistake to come.

Eddie

IT'S NEARLY EIGHT O'CLOCK BUT it's still crazy hot, maybe even hotter than earlier. The guests can't get enough of the cider, there's a huge queue behind the bar. They're getting drunker. A lot drunker. Everyone seems to be shouting. Everything's got really loose. Like a house party, that moment where it feels like anything could happen . . . only with a load of sunburned rich millennials pissed on posh cider as opposed to teenagers wasted on White Ace and molly.

"Hey, look," Ruby says. "This must be the first act." She points. I look at the stage. Do a double take. *What?*

There he is: Nathan Tate, in his stupid I AUTOEROTIC ASPHYX-IATE ON THE FIRST DATE T-shirt (doubt he's washed it since two nights ago), his guitar looped over one shoulder. One of his mates, Gareth Turner, sits behind the drums, grinning out at the crowd and looking bombed out of his mind. They must have gatecrashed as there's no way they're *meant* to be here.

It takes me a moment to work out who the other person is, the one who's just walked into the middle of the stage. Delilah looks incredible. She's wearing a long silver dress that seems to be made of some kind of really fine chainmail, which ripples like water when she moves. You can tell she's not wearing a bra or maybe anything at all underneath the fabric. Her face and her arms and even her hair are all silver-colored, too. She's actually glowing, like she's somehow giving off this electric energy . . . or maybe it's just that she's reflecting every bit of light in the place, the candles on the dining tables, the tealights in the pool, the flaming lanterns.

All the chatter around me has hushed. Everyone is looking at her. "Fuck me," I hear one guy whisper and I can't tell if he's swearing or begging her out loud.

She steps up to the mic. There's a scream of feedback and a few people in the crowd wince and giggle. In spite of everything, I think: *come on Lila. You've got this.* She glares out at everyone, her trademark look: like she's going to punch the next person who laughs. Then she opens her mouth and begins to sing.

The crowd falls silent. All I can think is: how did I not know this about her? She always sounded all right when she sang along to Lizzo in the car or whatever, but this is different. I've never heard her like this. I don't think I've heard *anyone* sing like this. It doesn't sound like a voice at all: more like an instrument. And it's a feeling as much as a sound, something you feel everywhere from your scalp to your fingertips.

"Jesus, she's like a new Kate Bush," a guy nearby says to his companion. "But a sexy Kate Bush, not, you know . . . a crazy little girl in a nightie."

"Yeah," his mate says. "Terrible band name and shame about that vagrant with the guitar but she's got it. The whole package. Wonder if she's signed with anyone. I should get Otto on the phone."

And then suddenly the microphone goes off with a pop and Delilah stops singing, looking around in confusion. The lights on the stage go down and the speakers crackle back into life, The Prodigy's "Firestarter" blasting out so loud I can feel the bass vibrating in my ribcage, at the back of my skull.

The guests around me start whooping and dancing about like they're at a rave. But I can just make out the silvery glow of Delilah on the dark stage. She's standing totally still, staring out at us. When the music ends and the lights finally come back on she looks both completely shocked and even angrier than when I broke up with her.

Then I notice something else. She's alone on the stage: Nathan Tate and the other guy have vanished.

Francesca

I MOVE AMONG THE CROWD, smiling, smiling, smiling, as though everything that just happened was an entirely expected part of the evening. Certainly the guests around me seem to think it was.

"That was insane!" I hear one say. "Her voice . . . out-of-this-world ethereal, and then BOOM! Felt like I was at Burning Man."

"Yeah, yeah, or on a come-up at Ushuaïa. Ibiza this year was unreal . . ."

It's like wearing a mask, this smile, the muscle memory hewn through all my years of training. But my cheeks are beginning to ache.

And Owen is still nowhere to be seen. I need him by my side. And that moment in the speech was more than a little embarrassing. Where can he be? I try his mobile, but it rings out. It's making me a little uneasy . . .

And where on earth is Michelle, for that matter? I can't see her anywhere. She is supposed to be on top of everything. I think of the footage from the wine store last night. A bolt of pure rage shoots through me.

No. That's not the way.

Inhale for four, exhale for . . .

It's not working. I snatch a flute of cider from a passing tray. I'll just take the tiniest sip. This evening, it seems, I am going to have to let my standards slip just a little. Besides, apples are full of poly-phenols. And it's barely more alcoholic than juice . . .

Everyone will be taking their seats for the feast shortly, they're already plating up the food in the kitchens. But something seems to have got into the guests . . .

I gaze around me. One woman is sitting alone on the grass a few yards away, staring at the palms of her hands. And just over there, a man has pulled one of my beautiful wicker stags over and appears to be . . . humping it, like a dog in heat.

Vandalizing shit.

I think I just whispered that out loud. What's happening to me? I clamp a hand over my mouth. Calm, Francesca. It's fine.

In for four, out for—

I can feel sweat trickling between my shoulder blades and seeping out around my hairline. I do hope my make-up isn't beginning to run. I took such time and care perfecting my celestial glow. I beat my fan and more white feathers float free, but I don't seem to be able to conjure any breeze.

Of course, bad energy can be quite powerful, too. Perhaps it's not the weather after all but the current of poisonous karma floating from Sparrow. I am very sensitive to such things. And she's here, somewhere. Close by. I can sense her. I can almost *smell* her. And yet try as I might I can't see her. Something odd happens as I search for her in the crowd. I'm almost positive it's a . . . trick of the eye, something like that. An effect of the deepening shadows. But every so often, looking between the white outfits and green coronets, I seem to glimpse a figure all in black. A masked face. Dead still in the midst of the movement and chaos of the festivities. Each time this happens I get a nasty little shock. Because they are always turned in my direction. Looking straight at me. I gaze around and see them now toward the cliffs, now near the long tables, now beside the willow arch. But no single person could move between so many different spots so quickly. It must be a trick of the eye.

Or there's more than one.

I feel a touch to my elbow and start with alarm.

It's just Michelle. *About bloody time.*

"Ah," I say tightly, "Michelle." Deep breath. "I've been looking for you, my lovely. Where have you—"

"It's all under control," Michelle says, obsequiously. "That first act—I have no idea how it happened, them gatecrashing like that. But you know, the guests really liked it. Everyone's saying how amazing it was. I think they assume it was all planned."

"Yes," I say, "but that's not really the *point*, is it, Michelle? Imagine if they *hadn't* been good? Imagine if they'd been terrible? The point is that I've put together a carefully curated evening—everything tailored to our guests, to what we know they will enjoy. We can't just have some local yokels blundering up to bash their drums. It's not good enough." I shake my head. "It's just. Not. Good. Enough, Michelle."

For a moment I think I catch a gleam in her eye: a little mutinous flicker of something. Defiance? Even excitement? But just as quickly it is extinguished and she is all subservience and perhaps I imagined it after all. "I'm very sorry, Francesca," she says, earnestly. "We will find them and ensure they are removed from the premises."

She is capable. I'll give her that. It's why I chose her in the first place. That aura of control. It *is* a shame.

"Good," I say. "Thank you Michelle."

She hurries off. I watch her go. As I do, a couple of guests pass me by, and I hear the man say to the woman: "Yeah, that's my favorite, the thing on the beach. Something so raw about it. Pagan. The rest of them are a bit pedestrian, wouldn't you say? A bit . . . Covent Garden piazza."

"Yes," his partner says. "That one pushes the envelope. I like that they've really gone for it. It's pretty creepy. But you know me, I love anything folk horror."

What?

The woman gives me a nervous glance. I realize I'm scowling at them. With a great effort of will I haul my smile back into place.

I'm not going to dwell on the Covent Garden piazza comment.

Some people, sadly, have money but no taste; he's a forty-year-old man still wearing Yeezys. But what can they be talking about? I didn't order anything for the beach. I oversaw every single installation this morning. They're all up here on the lawns.

I try to suppress the fear rising within me as I make my way to the cliff edge. What is waiting for me down on the beach?

Eddie

A QUEUE IS FORMING AGAIN behind the cider bar; the guests wanting their next hit after the first music set. I can't hand the glasses out quickly enough.

"Eddie!" I hear a voice whisper. I must be imagining it because there's no one near me or behind me when I turn around. "Eddie! Down here, you twat!"

I glance down and nearly jump out of my skin. A silver face glows up at me out of the darkness from beneath the tablecloth and then a pair of silvery arms are reaching for me.

"*Lila?*" I stare. "What are you doing down there?"

"I . . ." She glances around like she's checking for someone or something, her eyes wide and kind of wild. "Come down here," she gestures.

I just have time to look around, checking Ruby's preoccupied with the cider orders, before she reaches out and yanks me down under the table with her. I'd forgotten how strong she is; she once nearly beat me in an arm wrestle. Here in the warm darkness I get a sweet, heavy hit of Chance by Chanel (I used to buy it for her birthday) and strawberry vape.

"What is it, Lila?" I ask. "What's going on? Your set, by the way—I didn't know you could sing like that. It was amazing! You're—"

"Yeah, yeah, I know I am," she says, cutting me off. "But we can talk about that later, OK? I'm down here because I'm hiding from Nate."

"Why?"

"I—I'm worried, Eddie."

This gets my attention. There's not much that worries Delilah. I have a horrible thought. "Did he . . . do something to you?"

"Nah, nothing like that. He's been talking about some sort of . . . plan. I thought at first it was just us gatecrashing this evening, you know? Turning up onstage like that. But I think there's more to it. He's—he's so angry, Eds. Underneath it all. Everything with his dad. And now he's disappeared. I think he's got something else going on tonight. And I don't want to be part of it, Eds. I just don't want to be part of anything illegal, yeah? This singing thing, you said it yourself. I'm amazing, right? I'm *fucking* amazing. I could be major. I could be the next Dua."

I almost smile at this; it's so totally Lila.

"I'm not just saying that, Eds: a guy gave me his card, told me to give him a call Monday. This could be it. My moment. And I don't want anything to mess that up. You heard about the thing with the stones yesterday: the swimming pool?"

"Yeah."

"That was his idea. We were just going to chuck some seaweed, you know. Kind of gross but harmless. Just a warning to that witch. But he was the one that picked up the first stone. He always goes too far . . ."

I hear a voice above us. "Eddie? Eddie—for God's sake, where's he gone?"

"Shit," I say, "that's Michelle—my boss. I have to go, Lila." I try to slide back, away from her, but she's grasping my wrist.

"Seriously Eds," she hisses. "Just keep an eye out for him, yeah?"

"Er . . . OK."

Small problem: I have no idea where Nathan Tate has gone. But I remember him in the woods. On the beach the other night. The gleam in his eye as he said, "You know what I reckon? It's time someone turned the tables." I think of the real anger that flashes under all his swagger and stupid T-shirts, like a switchblade hidden in a party cracker. How he always seems on the edge. Ready to cross the line. What if this is the time he finally does? How far would he go?

DI Walker

IT'S A RELIEF TO BE out of the trees again, back in daylight. The air's still filled with smoke but to Walker it seems easier to breathe here, out on the lawns in front of The Manor.

Heyer strides over.

"You OK, boss?" She peers at Walker. "You're looking kind of pale."

"Yeah. What was it you had before in the car? Low blood sugar. Think that must be it."

"If you're sure." But she doesn't look convinced, and there's also something deliberate about her stance that suggests she has news to break. "They didn't make it," she says. "The two they found trapped inside the building. Stopped resuscitation attempts a few minutes ago. So that's three now. One at the bottom of the cliffs, two locked inside in the wine store."

"Four," Walker says, but quiet enough that he doesn't think she hears it.

"And they've found some accelerants round the back of the property. Clear signs it was started deliberately."

"Right," Walker says, "so our arsonist also has blood on their hands. I'll come and take a look at the victims."

Walker follows her over to the ambulance where the two gurneys stand. The oxygen masks have been removed now and the paramedics are readying the body bags. He glances from one body to the other. Back again. Checks and rechecks. He's right.

The bodies—the faces—are identical. Except for one thing: a macabre spot-the-difference. The one nearest to him has a distinctive streak of white hair.

Eddie

SOLSTICE

"EDDIE," MICHELLE SAYS, FROWNING AT me. "What were you doing under the table?"

"Oh," I say. "I was just . . . checking supplies." I silently beg Lila to stay put beneath the tablecloth. "I think we're nearly out of cider," I say. "I could head to the wine store . . ." And have a look for Nathan at the same time.

"I'll deal with that," Michelle says, sharply. "Perhaps you could—" She scans the scene. "That guest just there. She looks like she needs looking after. See what she wants?"

I turn and see Bella watching from a few feet away, a strange expression on her face.

Now she's striding toward me, her eyes not leaving mine.

"Hi," I say. "Can I help you with anything?" It sounds a bit formal, after everything that happened in the woods last night, and everything before, but I'm not really sure how to play it with her.

"Eddie," she says, "can I talk to you?"

"Er, I'm on duty," I say. "I've got to—"

She reaches out and puts a hand on my arm. "I can't believe I didn't see it before. You look so like your brother."

What? My heart starts beating very fast. Why is this stranger talking about my brother? No one talks about him. Not my family. Not people around here, either—at least not to our faces. Not unless they want to make my mum cry.

I try to take a step back but she's still holding my arm. "I knew him, Eddie," she says.

"Jake?" I say, eventually, voice hoarse as I speak his name. It's so long since I've said it out loud.

"Yes. I was sixteen. He was two or three years older, I think . . . about nineteen."

Nineteen. That was when it happened. What is this?

Her grip on my arm gets a little tighter.

"Please, Eddie. I need to speak to you, somewhere private."

I look over my shoulder, trying to think of some excuse to get myself out of here. "I dunno," I say, "it can't make any difference now—"

"It's why I'm here," she says, urgently. "What happened back then. I want to tell you . . ." She closes her eyes. "Look, this sounds dramatic. But I know what she's capable of. Francesca. She's doing it again. Covering her tracks." She plows on, "I want you to know all of it . . . in case something happens to me."

I picture Jake's empty room, kept just how it was. The photographs in the albums I've looked at so many times. Trying to understand. Trying to remember who my brother was, coming up blank. Not being able to ask my parents because of the pain it would cause them.

Maybe I do need to hear this, after all. Maybe the woman is standing here holding a missing piece of the puzzle.

I think about all the stuff I'm meant to be doing out on the lawns. Of Lila, pleading for me to keep an eye out for Nathan Tate. But all of that can wait.

"OK," I say.

"Somewhere quiet." She looks around, points to one of the clifftop private dining cabins. "One of those."

I follow Bella into the cabin. I've never been in one of them before. They're circular, with panoramic windows the whole way around. I dimly register how you can see all the way along the coast to Poole, the houses lit up like Christmas lights. It feels like we're floating in mid-air, caught somewhere between the sea and the land. An amazing view, I guess. But right now it just makes me feel kind of light-headed. I grip hold of the doorframe to steady myself.

Bella sits down at the big round table; I take a chair opposite her. It's pretty dark but even so I can see she looks pale and scared. She starts talking as soon as I close the door. Fast, almost a whisper.

"I made the connection when I saw you coming out of the farm this morning," she says. "Jake told me how he was meant to take over from his—your—dad."

"Yeah." I swallow. "That was what was meant to happen."

Bella meets my gaze, then her eyes slide away. She looks . . . guilty.

Then she reaches into her bag and takes out a ratty old notebook. I notice her hands are shaking. She fumbles her way through the pages and then grips it for a second, staring at whatever's written in front of her, knuckles tight and white like she can't let go. Then she takes a long, shaky breath, puts it on the table, and slides it across to me.

"Here," she says, tapping the page. "Read from here."

Summer Journal

If I'd listened to Jake none of it would have happened. We'd never have gone to the party in the first place. Can't stop thinking about that.

Once we got out the pool the twins had gone off somewhere with the girls. I hoped the girls were OK. Frankie was all friendly and chatty while we ate the burned hot dogs (had half mine before I saw it was black on the outside and raw and pink on the inside). She asked Jake all these questions about his dad's farm, all like, oh, I can't believe we've never met you being so close, like she never said he was a tacky yokel or whatever. Smiling and smiling the whole time, all this intense eye contact.

Jake caught my eye. Smiled and shrugged like, she's not so bad. I couldn't smile back. It was too much. Too different from her usual self. Was she high? Her eyes looked wrong, pupils huge.

Had this bad, crampy feeling in my stomach. But I guess at the time it could just have been the gross hot dog.

Oh, she said, suddenly, jumping up. I forgot—I made some brownies! Little midnight feast, Sparrow, like old times.

She reached down and grabbed a Tupperware box, popped off the lid. I took one but I knew I wasn't going to eat it, partly cos I made that mistake before and wanted a clear head and partly cos I felt so sick from the hot dog. Jake took one too. I tried to think of a way to signal that he shouldn't eat it.

Then the buzzer to the gates sounded and Frankie went, who the hell's that? Can't be the olds, they've got a clicker . . .

I'd totally forgotten. I think it might be Cora, I said. Frankie . . . I'm so sorry, I forgot to say. I told her about tonight. She's got some stuff she wants to say . . .

I thought she might kick off, after that stuff with Grandfa. But this new Frankie gave a little what-the-hell shrug and pressed the release for the gate. Smiled her new smile and said: well, the more the merrier.

Eddie

I GLANCE UP FROM THE page.

"Jake came here?" I ask, confused and playing for time a little. "To this house? For some sort of party?"

"Yes." She grimaces. Still that pained, guilty look on her face. "Jake was my guest, that night. What happened to him—it was my fault." She covers her eyes with a hand. "Please. Just keep reading. This can explain it better than I can."

I look back down at the diary. Dreading what I'm going to find now. My brother disappeared for good, fifteen years ago.

I think I'm about to learn why.

Summer Journal

THE CARAVAN—TATE'S HOLIDAY PARK
AUGUST 23, 2010, 4 A.M.

Cora came to sit with us. She was wearing even more eyeliner than usual. She gave Frankie this nervous smile and whispered to me, thanks. I could just see her broken front tooth. There was a weird moment when she looked at Jake and he looked back at her and I saw him do a kind of double take. Hey, he said, looking a bit confused. Hey, she said back. So they knew each other. I guess it made sense, they were both locals.

Cora was like, Frankie, could I have a word? I want to explain some stuff. But Frankie had her head cocked to one side and was like no, let's not. It's . . . whatever. Let's live in the moment, yeah? That big smile again. She opened the Tupperware box and was like: have one of these, my lovely.

Frankie played some music. We listened for a bit and drank some more. The others came back from wherever they'd been and jumped in the pool, the girls screaming. Jake traced circles on my leg through the dress. I wanted it to be just us. I wanted to be away from this weird atmosphere. And then I looked up and saw that Frankie was watching his finger on my thigh. I thought of my cat, Widget, letting a spider run around in front of him before he pounced on it.

Then Frankie jumped up, clapped her hands. I'm bored. Let's go into the woods. And, like . . . take off all our clothes and commune with nature. She winked at me. Promise there won't be any surprises this time, Sparrow.

My heart started beating faster. I said, I dunno. It's getting late?

And she went: aw come on Sparrow. It's the end of the summer. Just once more. For old times' sake? She grabbed one of the solar-powered lanterns hanging by the pool. We'll take one of these so we can see the way.

And then we were all just following her like we didn't have any choice, through the walled garden to the woods.

But when we got to the end of the garden I got Jake to hang back, let Frankie and Cora go ahead. I don't want to go in there, I said. Not after everything. I don't know what she's playing at but it feels off.

Sure, he said. Let's not. Let's peel off when she's not looking, have some fun of our own. His lips right next to my ear, breath warm. Lots of places for us to get lost. He grinned. She _did_ talk about taking off our clothes.

I could see Frankie's lantern bobbing off into the dark trees, but it was still pretty light cos of the supermoon.

So we turned and legged it, giggling like little kids. Couple of minutes later, I could hear Frankie calling us. I didn't even feel that bad. I took him to the tennis court cos it was close and I knew we'd be hidden by the hedges.

That's what this would all be about, if the other stuff hadn't happened.

How we lay down on the grass court. How we _did_ take off our clothes (or some of them, anyway) and laughed at how the grass prickled us. How afterwards we lay there together, my head on his shoulder. Looking up at the huge moon. It sounds so corny but it was so nice. I have to write that. To try and remember it. It might be the last happy moment of my life.

Don't know how long we lay there like that (maybe we even fell asleep?) before the screaming started, from the woods. I can still hear it now. I knew then something was horribly wrong.

Owen

WHEN I OPEN MY EYES, it's dark. I feel the coldness of earth beneath my cheek, the bristle of fallen twigs, of dead leaves. Roots nudge my ribcage and thighs. I hear the lonely cry of an owl, somewhere high above me, and strains of faraway music, and the rasp of my own breathing, half muffled by the soil. For a moment I have no idea where I am. How long I've been here. How I got here.

I think I must have passed out from the shock.

Beneath my hand I feel a crackle of plastic. There's just enough light leaking through the trees for me to make out the vivid blue of the tarpaulin. The white of the bones inside.

Bella

"I CAN STILL HEAR THEM, even now: the screams," I tell Eddie as he sits across from me, the diary splayed open. I can still see the scene, too. Both of us lying there semi-clothed in the warm, quiet darkness on our bed of grass like babes in the wood. And then those agonized sounds, shattering the silence. Panic and terror crashing through me. Jake and I scrambling to our feet. Jake saying: "What the fuck was that?"

Then something that sounded slightly less animal, slightly more human. Something that sounded like a groan of "Help."

Summer Journal

THE CARAVAN—TATE'S HOLIDAY PARK
AUGUST 23, 2010, 4 A.M.

We pulled on our clothes. Ran into the woods, crashing through the leaves and branches. Jake's torch bouncing along the ground. The screams getting louder all the time. Then (much worse) they got quieter. Stopped.

Felt like hours before we found them. It was probably only a few minutes. Frankie, crouched on the ground. Cora curled up on her side, knees tucked. The moonlight across her. Guess I wasn't thinking straight—all I could think at first was how weirdly beautiful she looked, like she'd been born out of the forest floor. How small and young, even though she's older. Then Jake shouted, what the fuck happened? He sounded so stern, so grown-up: it shocked me back into the moment. Frankie's head snapped up and she went: I didn't do anything, she just . . .

But Jake was already shining his torch on Cora and the patch of sick next to her. Then he turned the torch on Frankie and went, so loud and cold, like an interrogation: what did she take? Frankie just stared back. I could see the shape of her skull. Her eyes glittering in the sockets.

I looked at the sick, Cora, Frankie's face. I thought of her smile as she handed out the brownies.

What did you do with those mushrooms? I asked her. This long pause. And then she went: I just wanted us to have some fun. Like a little girl whose party game had gone wrong. Then her face went dark, cos Jake had dropped the torch and was crouched over Cora. He went: I'm going to try mouth-to-mouth. That's when it hit, how bad this was. That she wasn't breathing. I picked up the torch then. I needed to see Frankie's face. What did you do? I asked her. She didn't answer but she didn't need to. You put them in the brownies, didn't you? I said. I told you to get rid of them. Told you they weren't magic mushrooms.

Quick as a flash she went: no you didn't. Too quick.

I texted you.

From your piece of shit phone?

She was lying, I knew it. I know it.

But then Jake was shouting, for fuck's sake can one of you call an ambulance? And I realized I'd left my phone by the pool. But Frankie already had hers out: walking away from us, talking quickly into it. For a moment I thought maybe it would all be OK.

Then Jake was saying: oh fuck. I can't feel a pulse. I think she's gone.

Owen

I HEAR A LOW MOAN and realize that it has come from my own lungs. The horror floods through me anew. In fragments, I remember:

The JCB. The men calling me over.

A dark pit—the bright tarpaulin-clad shape emerging.

The tarpaulin falling open.

Stepping back from the pit, my shadow leaving the bones.

The skull, with its gaping mouth. Inside the mouth: the teeth. One of the teeth broken in half. I knew a crooked smile like that, once upon a time.

The chipped left front tooth. Unmistakable. Fifteen years since I've seen it—when she smiled at me waiting for her by the caravan park gate. Or crying in despair at her lot: stuck in a tiny life, her big dreams stifled.

I remember how I wrenched my eyes away from the tooth and saw the jewelry. All the cheap little pieces with which she adorned herself. The silver bangles, the tiny studs and rings from her ears, all bright against the darkness of the soil.

The last time I'd seen her she'd cupped my chin. Smiled that wonky smile. "I know I'm a rubbish mum, Owen. I was such a baby when I had you, that's the thing. I hadn't lived. I know I drink too much, stay out too late. But I'll try harder, I promise. You're everything to me. You know that, right? I would never do anything to hurt you."

I fell to my hands and knees. Lifted her out, wrapped in her horrible blue shroud. Carried her with me deeper into the trees. Just to get her into the air, the light. I couldn't leave her for another moment in that dark, cold pit of unmarked earth where she'd lain for so long, all alone.

She didn't desert us. She didn't leave me. I was the one who abandoned her. No wonder I felt pulled back here. She's been here waiting for me all this time.

Bella

EDDIE LIFTS HIS EYES FROM the page. All of a sudden he looks a great deal older than his nineteen years, like someone who's aged in a very short space of time. "There's nothing left," he says. "It looks like . . . it looks like the diary ends here."

"Yes," I say. "I couldn't write any more."

"So she gave the brownies to all of you," he says. "To you and Jake, too. She could have killed you all."

"Yes, but I didn't take one. And Jake hadn't eaten his, it turned out, because he hated—"

"Chocolate. Yeah. My parents told me that about him." He shakes his head. "That poor woman. And Jake. Oh God. What it must feel like to see someone die in front of you like that."

"I can tell you," I say. "It ruins you."

"And he was my age. I can't imagine . . . we never knew . . ."

"He was amazing," I tell Eddie. "You need to know that. He was the only one of us thinking clearly. He wanted to call 999."

"And did he?"

I hesitate. "No."

I tell him the rest. How Jake carried Cora out of the wood, set her down gently on the lawn. I was blinded by headlights on the drive, dazzlingly bright after the darkness of the wood. The ambulance was here, then . . . maybe the police, too. I longed for someone to take over, to determine what would happen next . . . whatever that might mean.

But when the lights turned off I saw it wasn't an emergency vehicle after all. It was a Range Rover, burgundy red. The same one that always sat in the driveway of Tome Manor. Frankie ran round to the driver's side and I saw a tall, white-headed figure step out. The two of them began conferring in urgent murmurs.

I think that's when it dawned on me that this wasn't going to go as I'd expected.

At that moment I remember turning back, sharply, at the sound of a sudden commotion from the woods. An explosion of movement in the topmost branches of the nearest trees. A hundred horrible, hoarse, cackling cries as a flock—a murder—of crows rose up from the treetops into the sky. And beneath them crouched the dark woods, silent and watchful.

I REMEMBER FRANKIE and her grandad breaking up their little conference, walking toward us.

"Is the ambulance on the way?" Jake asked.

"You can rest assured that the right and proper course of action is being taken," her grandad said. "But what we definitely don't need is any meddling." He turned to me. "I hope you're not thinking of doing anything stupid."

"I've told Grandfa everything," Frankie said. "How you were the one who picked the mushrooms and gave them to me."

Jake took a step toward her. "You were the one who cooked them into some fucking brownies and fed them to her."

"And I *told* you we couldn't take them," I said. "I texted you."

Frankie rolled her eyes. The fear I'd seen in the woods was gone. "Yeah, like I said. I never got it."

"Why didn't *you* eat one, then?" Jake asked. "Because you didn't, right?"

Frankie shrugged. "You always need a spotter. I was being responsible."

"I think it's quite clear neither of you ate yours either," Grandfa said. "Otherwise you'd be in the same unfortunate predicament. On that count you appear just as culpable."

"I felt sick," I said. Jake said: "I hate chocolate." Both answers sounded so stupid, so arbitrary. This wasn't lost on Grandfa. "I'm sure that would all sound very convincing to the authorities," he said, laconically.

"You *hated* her," Frankie said, rounding on me. "I saw the way you looked at her. You were so jealous."

I swallowed. I hadn't realized I had been so obvious. "I would never have—"

We all startled at a shriek from the direction of the swimming pool—a cackle of laughter. "Frankie," Grandfa said. "Go and tell your brothers it is time to end the party. I will deal with this."

I supposed by "this" he meant us. Also, I realized, the lifeless form on the lawn. I couldn't bring myself to think of it as "Cora."

When Frankie had gone, Grandfa turned back to us. To me. "I don't think you'd want to throw it all back in our faces, would you?" he said. "Not after everything we've given you. I don't *think* you'd show that kind of ingratitude. You've been very happy to swim in our pool, eat our food, sun yourself in our garden . . . Step up in the world from Tate's Holiday Park, isn't it? You've done very nicely for yourself." I hated how he made me sound: grasping and calculated. "And now we're asking something of you. There's nothing anyone can do for this woman now. I think we all see that. What happened tonight was a terrible mishap. We can agree on that too, I think?"

Mishap. That word. How it diminished everything.

"If you did feel tempted to go off on a folly of your own," he went on, speaking slowly enough that every word landed, "I can tell you now it would be very unwise. As we have established it could look far worse for you than for Francesca if the police were to become involved. This family has certain—resources. We will not hesitate to use them. I know people at the very highest level in this country."

I could see why he'd been such a successful Whip; he'd encircled me python-like with his words. No doubt he'd done the same with rebel MPs, bringing them back into line with threats and coercion. And we were just frightened children. No match for him at all.

Then he turned to Jake. "And I happen to know that your father has contravened the law in several ways with his farming practices. Practices that could get him thrown off his land if I were to speak to the right people." He let this sit for a moment, then: "Here's what I propose," he said, so measured, so reasonable. "No one will call anybody. And both of you will stay here tonight. It's late. You're tired. You should get some rest."

I sensed it, even then: he was running the clock down on us. Every minute that we didn't call the police made it a little less likely that we ever would.

We were shown into the library downstairs. He left us for a few minutes then returned to hand us each a thick envelope.

"Take a look," he said. "Please."

Inside was more money than I had ever seen in one place. Three thousand pounds, it turned out. Such a lot at sixteen. A serious, adult sum. Just the physical act of receiving our envelopes, accepting them from his hand, had changed something. Even if we'd thrown them back at his feet that simple, split-second act made us in some way complicit.

"Get some rest," Grandfa said, before he shut the door. The silent coda to his words: *and keep your fucking mouths shut.*

Jake turned to me. In the dim glow of the standard lamp he looked drawn and pale. Like the night had washed away all traces of the tanned, happy boy I knew.

"Cora. I was so confused when she turned up here tonight."

"Why?"

"She has a kid," he said. "She's a mum."

"*What?*" My first thought was he'd made a mistake. Cora couldn't be a mum. The tattoos, the piercings and eyeliner, the topless sunbathing . . . surely not?

"Yeah—you know him. Shrimp, from the caravan park. She had him when she was like, sixteen. Oh my God."

Then he doubled over and I could hear him sobbing. But after a while he stopped and when he next looked up his face was white, angry. "We can't let them get away with it," he said. "She should pay for what she's done."

"But you heard what her grandad said," I told him. "They'll say it was us just as much as her." What I really meant was: they'll say it was *me*. I was the one who picked the mushrooms after all. "And he threatened your family."

I saw the fight go out of him then.

"I can't do this," I remember him whispering into the dark, over and over. "I can't do this."

I LOOK AT Eddie. "I don't think I slept at all," I say. "But I must have done, at least for a few minutes, because when I woke up your brother was gone. That was the last time I saw him."

Eddie swallows. "So that's what it was," he says, hoarsely. "I'd always wondered. And my parents. They never knew . . ."

"I texted him the next day," I say. "I never heard back. Thought maybe it was my phone, after all. Tried to call. And then eventually—the day we left—I went to talk to him. I felt like I was going crazy. Trying to act half normal in front of my parents. Wanting to check the news somehow—and dreading it. But when I got to the farm I saw the police car, the blue lights flashing. A woman was at the gate, sobbing; a man had his arms around her. Your parents: it must have been. I thought—he's told them. He's told the police. And I ran all the way back to the caravan park and waited for it to be over."

Later when Dad came back to the caravan he looked somber. I hid in my little cabin, my heart thumping so hard I thought my parents must be able to hear it, and listened through the paper-thin door.

"Graham told me something awful," I heard him say to Mum. "It almost makes me glad we're leaving. Puts a bit of a cloud over everything. I mean . . . God. It's just tragic." And then I seemed to hear the rest in fragments. "Young lad from the farm—moped went over the cliffs last night—searching for the body right now . . ."

I'VE RECOUNTED THE last part to Eddie without meeting his eye, because I won't be able to get it all out if I see his expression. "So you see, it was my fault," I continue. "I brought him to The Manor. I got him involved with this place and Frankie's fucked-up little game." Finally, I look up and hold his gaze. "So that's the truth. If it hadn't been for me, your brother never would have died."

Francesca

I GLIDE THROUGH THE THRONG of people, toward the cliffs, beaming radiantly all the while but I'm feeling sort of jittery, a little . . . blurry. Almost pleasantly so, actually. A little like I've just had a hit of something except I've barely had anything beyond a few sips of organic cider—oh, and those little pick-me-ups in the apartment beforehand—because Francesca's body is her temple *yadayada whatfucking-ever.* Whoopsie, I seem to be talking in the third person again. But there you go, we all contain multitudes!

My phone buzzes in my hand. I look at the screen. Owen. *Finally.*

Well, I don't actually have time right now. I need to see what's down there on the beach. Besides, he's been perfectly happy to ignore my calls. It might be no bad thing to give him a taste of his own medicine.

As I pass among the guests I notice more strange behavior: a man lying full-length on the ground, just staring up at the starlit sky, a woman plucking the leaves from her headdress and . . . is she *eating* them? Something utterly bizarre is going on. Oh—a nasty shock goes through me. Another masked face, staring right at me. Then dissolving into the melee.

I move on. Let my feet carry me forward. Breathe through the rising bubble of dread. All is well.

There!

At the other side of the crowd, appearing behind two dancing women. A dark-cloaked form, stark between their white dresses. Then seeming to vanish like smoke into the shadows.

I shut my eyes. It must be the stress of the moment. They're not real, they're not real . . .

"Look at that!" I hear a man just ahead of me shout. Several guests are clustered with him at the cliff edge, peering down at the beach. I move toward them. I can just about make out something down there. Something monstrously large—the top of it almost level with the clifftop. But I can't see it properly: it's so dark down there on the beach. A cloud has drifted across the moon and, more than that, my eyes seem a little unfocused. Sweat from this unnatural heat, perhaps. There's a chattering, cackling sound all around. Where is it coming from? It's horrible. And it's so close by. I press my hands over my ears but I can still hear it. Is it inside my head?

There's a streak of light on the horizon, far out to sea. Lightning, a long way off. But the air is dry. So heavy, so hot. But dry. Another small spasm of light briefly illuminates more of the shape. I see a distinct head. A body. What look like vast outstretched arms. No . . . wings. The cackling sound grows louder still. I feel every hair on my head begin to lift away from my scalp as the air prickles with static. It must be some electrical disturbance: the same force that's causing the lightning.

The chattering grows to a roar. It's almost unbearable. But the others around me don't seem to be affected by it. They're all looking down at the vile thing in wonder, pointing, making noises of excitement and awe.

The moon slides out from behind the clouds and I suddenly see the whole hideous shape of it. My breath catches in my throat. It's three times the height of a man, built on a completely different scale to the other sculptures: the graceful, delicate ones *I* commissioned. This is a hulking colossus. The cowled head with its dark eye-sockets, the menacing hooked beak, the vast black outstretched wings almost as wide as it is tall. There's a grotesque movement to it: as I watch, the surface seems to quiver and convulse. I look more closely and see that thousands of feathers are woven into the very structure.

I can smell it too: an acrid stink that catches right at the back of the throat.

"Is there someone down there?" a woman close by says to her partner. "Look!"

I think she's right. I glimpse a shadowy figure near the base, a tiny spark. Then a rush of flame and it goes up in one soft *whomp*. The guests around me gasp. The whole thing must have been drenched in lighter fluid.

The heat from it almost knocks me over. Sparks and burning debris fill the air, flying everywhere, even up the clifftop . . . falling over the guests. Now, as the flames rush up inside it, the eyes appear to glow with a concentrated malevolence. It seems to be staring straight at me.

Eddie

I SIT HERE DAZED BY everything I've heard. Trying to make sense of what Bella has just told me.

"But that's not what happened," I say.

"What?" Bella frowns.

"My brother, Jake. He didn't die."

She looks totally floored. "But I don't understand. I heard—"

"Maybe he *wanted* to die," I say. "I mean, I was a little kid and my parents *never* talk about it. But I do know he somehow got hold of a load of drugs and tried to ride his bike over the cliffs. Suppose he changed his mind at the last second or something. The bike skidded off the edge, landed on the rocks at the bottom. It was a total wreck. At first I guess they thought the worst, like maybe his body had been washed out to sea or something, because he was AWOL for several days. When he finally turned up . . . even I could see something was different. Like the old Jake was gone. Like there was . . . a demon inside him or something. And it just got worse and worse."

I tell her about the drugs. The stealing. "He sold my dad's tractor. Just drove it off one day and sold it. It would have fetched, like, tens of thousands of pounds, money my parents couldn't afford to lose. They could never get out of him what he did with it. More drugs, probably. My parents had to remortgage the farm to buy a new tractor. They nearly lost everything."

Bella's staring at me, pale and stunned. "All this time," she says. "I'd thought . . ." She trails off. "But then— Where is he now?"

"I don't know."

"What do you mean?"

"He's—what's the word? Estranged? He could be anywhere." He could be dead, actually, the way he was going. But I've never let myself believe that. "After the tractor . . . Mum had to talk Dad out of having him arrested. Dad said he never wanted to see his face again. He said as far as he was concerned he no longer had an older son. He's got a temper, my dad. Thing is, I'm sure he regretted it afterwards." I know he did. That night he locked himself in the barn with the replacement tractor, engine running. "But by then, Jake was gone."

And so in a way it is like he died. I think about all those years we lost as a family. All the nights lying up in my room, hearing Mum sobbing in the kitchen below. "I don't even know where he is, Harold. My baby boy. He could be lying—oh God—he could be lying dead in an alleyway somewhere."

I think about the dad that I can just about remember who used to sing local shanties and even—if he'd had enough to drink—get out his old fiddle. I think of how I never hear him laugh that big belly laugh I once heard. I think of how my parents hardly talk to each other anymore.

I think of all the times I've walked past the door of my brother's old bedroom, kept just the same as it was when he left, Mum hoovering every week to get rid of all the dust that settles on every surface with no one moving around in there to disturb it. All the times I've looked at his bodyboard or his football or his rugby trophies or his books or the photos of him when he was younger and thought about all the things he could have taught me: the sort of things a big brother teaches a little one. All the things we could have done together, all the adventures we might have had.

I think about sneaking into Jake's room once and taking a jumper from his cupboard, which still had the smell of him, and trying it on and the sleeves dangling down over my hands. And then, years later, trying on the same jumper and it fitting, but the smell being gone.

I think about lying in bed at night when I was younger trying to remember him, the sound of his voice. Trying to feel him out there, somewhere, trying to imagine where he might be, what sort of life he might have. And then feeling so angry at him because if he was out there, why didn't he just come home?

Now I know. I understand. Because a local woman died in the woods and he was there and he couldn't save her and he couldn't tell anyone. And then Dad said he never wanted to see him again. And none of it was actually his fault. Like Bella said, she got away with it. Francesca Meadows. She got away with it while my family broke apart.

"There was no explanation," I say. "Maybe if we'd known . . . if my parents had known . . ." I can hardly get the words out. I taste salt on my lips and realize I'm crying.

Bella reaches across the table and covers my hand with hers. Then she says: "*This* is why I'm here, Eddie, because of the lives she destroyed that night. You get it, don't you? You can't walk away from something like that as though it never happened. And you sure as hell can't come back." I'm not sure she realizes how hard she's gripping my hand, my fingers hurt. The look on her face scares me a bit. I know it's not me she's this angry with, but it's almost a relief when the door of the dining pod crashes open and Ruby barges in.

"Um. Hello." She flashes her dazzling professional smile at Bella. Her gaze falls to Bella's hand on mine and then she shoots me this look, like: *just signal with your eyes if you've been trapped by a crazy.* Then she frowns. "Er, Eds? There's something I need your help with . . ." I sense she's choosing her words carefully, but there's a nervous energy coming off her.

"Oh," I say, my voice sounding a very long way away. "Yeah. Sorry. I'll come now . . ." I turn back to Bella.

"You go," she says. "I've got something I have to do." Her voice is hard, determined. She's staring out through the windows at the night, as though she's already somewhere else.

As we walk away from the dining pod Ruby grabs my arm and mutters: "*Who* was that?"

"Oh," I say, still feeling dazed, "no one. Just a . . . a guest." A guest who has just taken everything I thought I knew about my brother and exploded it and formed a whole new picture. He had no choice. He must have been so scared, must have felt so alone.

"She seemed crazy intense," Ruby says.

I manage a shrug. "Probably too much to drink."

Luckily she seems too distracted to press any more. "This way," she says, marching toward The Manor. "There's a—situation I need your help with." She waves a hand in the direction of the crowds on the lawn. "Oh, and it's got *wild* out here."

"What?" I say, not really able to focus.

"Er . . . everyone's acting, like, seriously fucking weird. They're all meant to be sitting down by now. But look at them!"

Now I do look and I see what she means. The food has been served: platters upon platters of fancily arranged salads and whole grilled fish, roast vegetables in posh arrangements, slices of pork from the spit roast, everything scattered with brightly colored edible flowers . . . but it's just sitting there in the light of the half-burned candles. Not a single guest has taken their place at the tables and several of the chairs have been knocked over. Before I went into the dining cabin it had definitely got looser, but nothing like this. Guests are running, crawling, swaying on the spot. A lot of them are clustered near the cliff edge, looking down at something on the beach.

Ruby points and I see the cloth covering the nearest table lift slightly and catch sight of naked, twisting limbs. "Are they . . ." I squint, trying to make it out, and then quickly look away. "Oh." Yeah, I think they are.

"Shit," Ruby says, suddenly, pointing. "They're in the pool, too."

I see writhing bodies lit by the pool lights, hear strange cries and whoops. More and more guests pile in as we watch, not a care about the people they're landing on as they jump in.

"What's . . . happened to them all?" I ask. "I don't get it."

"It's like everyone here is high," Ruby says. "But that doesn't make any sense. I mean, yeah, I clocked a couple of them powdering their noses in the toilets. But they can't *all* be on something, can they?"

We're nearly at the main building now. Ruby's leading me round to the back, near the staff entrance.

"Where are we going?" I ask.

"He says he's a mate of yours. He said you invited him. I mean, clearly that's bullshit, but if he is your friend I wanted to give you a chance to talk to him first, before I call the police."

Ah, crap. I have a bad feeling about this. Like I need this on top of everything else.

"There." Ruby points and I see them now: a couple of shadowy figures in the flowerbeds. I hear sniggering, whispers. A "Fucking hell, mate!" that sounds all too familiar.

"Nathan?" I call.

The two of them freeze and look up, eyes gleaming in the light from the lanterns along the path. It's Tate and the other guy, Gareth, from the band, the idiot who was grinning away on the drums.

As I look back at them I remember Nathan the other night on the beach: *"Heard they're having some sort of bullshit solstice celebration? Mate of mine works for an organic cider farm, says they've put in the biggest order ever."*

And I think about the fact that if you want to get hold of any gear around here, Nathan Tate is your man.

"Ruby," I say. "I think I know what's happened to the guests."

Francesca

AS I STARE DOWN AT the monstrous thing on the beach a burning feather floats toward me; I feel the red-hot kiss of it sting my cheek. That *hurt*. My skin crawls. My vision blurs. They're real. This is what the thing on the beach means. Those masked faces I keep seeing in the crowd. Grandfa's warning, the last time I saw him. *The Birds* . . .

They came for him. Now they're here. They're coming for me—

I turn from the vile thing, unable to look at it a moment longer. And this is when I see her. I don't know how I could have missed her. She's standing stock-still while the rest of the guests cluster along the cliffs. She's not looking down at the beach like the others. She's staring straight at me. It's almost a relief. Here is a problem I can actually deal with.

Stupid little Sparrow. Shouldn't fly this far from what you know. Shouldn't fly this close to the sun.

DI Walker

WALKER'S PHONE BUZZES IN HIS pocket. It's the crime scene manager from the SOCO team on the beach.

"Just wanted to keep you abreast of everything."

"Sure. How's it looking there?"

"Tide's fully in," she says. "We got everything we could on site beforehand. The body's on the way to the mortuary now. And we've moved on to the car—the Aston Martin, at the top of the cliffs."

"OK," Walker says. "Anything of interest?"

"There's the blood on the steering wheel. And we've also found a bag in the footwell containing some personal effects. A piece of silver jewelry, a ring. A key, too—looks like a posh hotel key. It reads," she clears her throat: "Woodland Hutch Eleven."

Eddie

SOLSTICE

"HI NATHAN," I SAY. HE glares back at me. He's in a black hoodie now even though it's about a hundred degrees, the hood pulled up over his head like he thinks he's some kind of gangster.

"I'll leave you guys to it," Ruby says, in an undertone. "I'm meant to be getting people to the tables. But call me if you need help. Yeah?" She looks at me pointedly before striding off toward the lawns.

"Ah," Tate says, when she's gone. "My old mate Eddie Eddie Eddie. What you up to, my old mugger?"

But his eyes don't match his tone. His eyes are like a wounded animal's, like the deer Dad once had to finish off with a shotgun after someone hit it on the road by the farm. The lighter in his hand, clicking and flickering away. Then I realize that he's also trying to hide something behind him, something bulky. I feel a kick of adrenaline.

"What have you got there, mate?" I ask. He shifts to hide whatever it is. I shine the torch past him: three jerry cans of petrol.

"What are you going to do with those, Nathan?" I ask.

"Oh come on, old Eddie. You can't really give a shit about this place? These people? You seen them all by the way? Off their fucking rockers on something. Fucking *hilarious*."

"What are they on, Nathan?" I say, trying to sound as stern as possible. "I know it was you."

"Anyway." He turns to the other guy, ignoring me. "Gaz and I just thought we'd enjoy the party a bit, have a little look around, didn't we Gaz? All very innocent. Then we just happened to stumble across these, which someone has so carelessly left lying around. Just wanted to make sure they didn't get into the wrong hands, you know? Cos that would be a *real* shame."

"Come on Nathan."

"Nah, don't think I will, thanks. She took everything. You've seen my dad. He's a mess. This place has good as killed him." His voice is low and raw now. "We'll never get him back." Then he pulls himself up to his full height (not very tall) and hisses: "I want to see it fucking burn. You're not telling me you choose these rich wankers over Tome . . . your own people?"

I don't have any love for this place. Definitely not now. But innocent people could get hurt. "Just leave it, Nathan," I say. "I'm sorry about your dad. But this won't make it better. Just . . . just go home, yeah?"

He picks up a can of petrol. "Pass me the lighter, Gaz."

"I won't say it again," I tell him, taking several steps closer. "And I know you spiked the cider tonight, too."

"Dunno what you're talking about."

I don't believe him for a second. Telling Bella about my brother has brought something else back too, something I've always kind of known but have never said out loud. "And I know you were the one who supplied Jake, back then."

"Don't give me that," he says, mockingly, "he was a big boy. Did all that by himself. Fucked up his own life. Not that it wasn't kind of entertaining to watch. The golden boy, all that."

I punch him. Didn't even know I was going to do it before it happened. I've never actually punched someone before and it hurts, but I think it hurts Tate more. He staggers backward clutching his face. My whole body's trembling. But I'm not going to lie: after everything I've heard tonight, all these feelings churning inside me, it's also a kind of release.

"Fuck!" Gaz whispers, sounding almost impressed. "Maaaate!"

"You little shit!" Nathan moans through his fingers. He takes his hand away and it's now I see the blood trickling from his nose. I'm so shocked at what I've done I start half-stumbling, half-jogging away.

"Yeah, yeah!" I hear Nathan shout after me, "Pretty clear which side you're on, narc! But you can't stop us now. We'll keep coming for her like the fucking tide!"

Bella

"OH MY GOODNESS," FRANCESCA SAYS, gliding toward me. "Is it really you? Do you know—I *thought* I saw you at breakfast yesterday! But then I thought 'It can't be!' The hair, that threw me off. It suits you! How have you been, my lovely? What are you up to these days? It's been so long."

For a moment I'm totally at a loss. Of all the things I'd expected, it wasn't this. It's utterly shameless. But then she always was. People don't change that much. All of this, the soft curling locks, the rural goddess photoshoots with farm animals, the flowing linen: it hides something steely and unyielding. Beneath it all she's always been hard as fucking nails.

I take a step toward her. Her eyes skitter away from mine, unable to hold the contact. The only tell.

"I need to speak to you, Francesca."

She tosses her head. "Oh," she says, smoothly, "funny thing, I'd also been hoping for a catch-up with you!" Her broad smile is Cheshire-cat sinister. I swallow my dread and move toward her, all the same. Too close, right into her personal space. And it works. She takes a step back and I see a spasm of something cross her face. Fear.

I feel a surge of triumph. Apparently she's registering the fact that I'm no longer the timid little girl she remembers, that she can't just push me around. To really ram that home I take a step closer and grab her by the wrist, gripping the fragile bones tight beneath my fingers. I'm vaguely aware of faces turning to look at us. "You'll come with me, now," I say. "Or I'm going to make a big scene. Bigger than this. Way bigger than this."

Again, that shimmer of alarm in her expression. "Let's go some-where else," she says, placatingly, her gaze darting to the watching guests. "Somewhere quieter, to talk."

I follow her into the main building, past the entrance to the bar where I first met Eddie. "In here," she says, opening a door. "I think you'll remember this room. It's barely changed. It's so cozy, don't you think?"

It's the library: antique tomes and pieces of curios filling the book-shelves that line three walls, the grand old fireplace. I don't think she's chosen it by accident. Last time I was in this room, I was with Jake. We'd just been paid three thousand pounds for our silence.

She closes the door and then, I see, she turns a key. I feel a stutter of alarm. Brush a hand against my tote bag to touch the reassuring shape of the half bottle of gin I took from my room. Carefully, though, because just before I left the dining pod I smashed the neck against the table so the top is lethally sharp. You can take the girl out of South London . . .

Once the lock clunks into place, she rounds on me. "*What* are you doing here?" she hisses. Francesca Meadows has disappeared in a puff of sage-infused smoke and the Frankie I knew stands before me. In a way it's a relief. The whole creation of Francesca Meadows has felt like a kind of gaslighting. Because Frankie—Frankie was bitchy and cool and fun, Frankie smoked Marlboro Lights on the tennis courts and drank Malibu-spiked banana Nesquik. Frankie with her cool-posh-girl voice—husky, lethargic. Frankie with her tall tales of sex at raves in London warehouses. Frankie who made me long for a bigger, more glamorous existence, who made me feel at times that I could almost taste it.

Frankie who ruined my life.

"What have you come here for?" she asks. I blink. I realize I've been so lost in the shock of the transformation that she's put me briefly on the back foot. But not for long. I clutch the bottle's stem, for courage.

"I've come to remind you of what you did. It seems to me you could do with some refreshing."

She gives a little sigh. And when she speaks again her voice has changed and she is Francesca Meadows, high-end woo-woo goddess, and Frankie has slipped into the shadows again: "Oh, Sparrow. You can't spend your whole life living in the past. It's just not good for you. You have to live in the *now*."

"Well, I disagree. I think you've moved on a little too easily. It didn't touch you at all, did it? Not then. Not now. Not one iota of remorse. You shouldn't be able to *stand* being here. It should make you ill. How could you talk to journalists about your idyllic summers here . . . about getting up to fucking 'high-jinks'? Like it was all some lark? Some childhood mishap?"

"Oh, Sparrow. We've been over this, no? It was a terrible tragedy. No one's fault."

"No. You killed her. Maybe you meant to kill all of us. And honestly, in a way it doesn't matter whether you meant to or not. Because what you did afterwards, how you all covered it up: that was evil. She didn't matter enough, did she? She was local, poor. She wasn't a real person, not to someone like you.

"The thing is," I continue. "For all these years you've made me feel like a killer. You and your hideous *Grandfa*, making me and Jake complicit, palming us off with cash. But we weren't the guilty ones. You are, Frankie."

"Don't call me that," she hisses. Another whiplash change from the airy, aloof creature of before. Then she closes her eyes and inhales deeply. "Sparrow. You should get some help. Go to a retreat for a few months. Meditate. Honestly. It changed my life. Gave me purpose."

"I've got that," I say. "It's why I came."

"Are you here to kill me?"

She asks it lightly, almost conversationally—like we're at a drinks party having a polite catch-up. Again, I'm wrong-footed. But I carry on. "I'm here for justice. And it doesn't even matter that you moved the body."

She frowns. "What on earth are you talking about?" For a moment she seems genuinely thrown. I press on.

"There'll be evidence there, all the same. You weren't as thorough as you could have been." I think of Cora's silver Celtic knot ring, hidden in my bag.

"There *is* no body," she says, her voice a touch higher than usual. For the first time she sounds uncertain. "Grandfa dealt with it all— he told me. The . . . the tragedy: he made it go away."

I look at her. She seems truly unsettled. Could it be that she really doesn't know?

It's possible. She left the next morning, after all.

"I came back," I say. "The day before I left Tome, all those years ago." It took all my courage. "I wanted to talk to you. I wanted to look you in the eye, just the two of us, and ask if you'd meant to do it. But you'd already gone."

I plugged in the code at the gate. I was met at the front door by Grandfa. "Francesca and the twins have gone away for a time with their grandmother," he told me. "I thought I already dealt with you. You've done enough, don't you think? There's nothing for you here. Leave us alone." And the words that he was far too well-heeled to speak out loud: *or else.*

He shut the door in my face. I turned and walked back down the steps. I would have walked away and never come back except that halfway down the drive my eye was drawn to something on the edge of the woods. A disturbance in the ground. A heap of earth. I knew that he might be watching from the house, so I kept walking. Pressed the button to open the gates. And then, right at the last second, rather than going through them, I slunk into the shadows beside the wall. I walked along the perimeter, staying in the shadows, and then when I reached the woods I used the trees as cover, walking right along the boundary.

The spot I had seen from the drive was bare and raw looking. Several feet long. I stood there for a long time and stared at it, trying to work out what to do with this knowledge. Perhaps if I had been older, braver—perhaps if Jake had been with me . . . But I was alone and scared, in the grounds of a grand house occupied by a grand old family with money and power and threats.

I knew I could do nothing except mark it out in my memory: the precise location, the trees beside it. When I got back to the caravan I drew my map in the back of my journal. This seemed important. That someone would remember. I sent a text to Jake, too. I know where she is.

"Is it possible your darling grandad wasn't quite as thorough as you thought?" I ask Francesca. "After all, he was pretty sloppy about hiding his affairs, wasn't he?"

"Be quiet," she says, pressing the flat of her palm against her brow so it's almost as though she's talking to herself as much as she is to me. "Just—just SHUT UP."

But I can't stop now. It feels too good to make her feel a tiny measure of the pain I've experienced for fifteen years.

"I want you to say it. I need you to acknowledge what you did to her—to us. I want to be able to look my daughter in the eye. I want to be able to look in the mirror and know that, in spite of my many flaws, I am a good person. That I'm someone who does the right thing. Because that"—I'm crying now—"that's what you and your *grandfa* took away from me that night." I start walking toward her, reaching for the bottle inside the tote. I see her eyes flit to the bag. If I'm lucky she'll think I'm holding a knife.

"I saw them," I whisper. "Last night, I saw the Birds."

She begins to laugh, a little manically. "The Birds? I told you that was all me, you stupid cow!" She sweeps her hand out toward the festivities. "I've always been good at creating a spectacle, haven't I?"

"But that's where you're wrong, Frankie—"

"Don't call me that."

"I saw them back then—"

I think I glimpse a tiny spasm of fear. Then she seems to gather herself. The mask comes back down. "What, while you were high on prescription meds I'd filched from my mother's stash? Yeah, course you did."

"And I saw them last night. In the woods—"

She actually rolls her eyes. "Oh for God's sake, Sparrow. I've moved on from childish games and fairy tales. You're wasting my time."

But as I step toward her she's backing away, into the corner, until she's pressed right up against the bookshelves. It's then that I see it, on one of the shelves above her head: my fossil—the one I found on the beach that first day, unwittingly setting off this whole chain of events. That little haunted relic of an ancient past that has had so much bearing on my present.

Her eyes are wild and trapped. "You've always been a leech," she hisses. "A taker. And I'm not going to let you take any of this away from me."

The pain comes first, before I can work out what has happened. The pain, the outrage of the impact. And then I feel my legs give way and I fall to the ground like a puppet with its strings cut. It takes a moment or two of lying here in a blind red static of pain, reduced to my most animal, diminished self, to work out what just happened. She's struck me with something heavy and blunt. I'm lying on the ground in front of her, head throbbing. Blurrily I can just make out her sandaled feet a few inches from my head, the immaculate nude pedicure. And in spite of everything I can't help making the absurd observation: of course she wears a bloody diamond-studded toe ring.

Suddenly I feel overwhelmingly, irresistibly tired. It wouldn't hurt, would it? Just to rest here for a while. Just to gather my strength.

"Sleep tight, Sparrow," she whispers, close enough that I can smell her sweetish breath. "I won't let you ruin this place for me. Just like I wouldn't then. I've created something beautiful here. Something for the now, for the future. So much bigger than anything that happened in the past."

I feel her ease the tote bag from my shoulder. And as though from a very long way away, I hear the door open, then click closed. The turn of the key.

I shut my eyes.

Francesca

I STEP OUT INTO THE boiling air. I smell burned wood and scorched feathers. Guests are pouring down the steps to the beach now, capering around the monstrous bonfire like demons in a medieval fresco, screeching and whooping. Some of them are tearing off their clothes and rushing into the sea, the waves lit up by the flames, the water seething around the naked bodies. Some are crawling and dancing and weeping and almost certainly copulating on the lawns.

But for the moment I don't care. I'm feeling almost triumphant. I reach for a glass of cider on an abandoned tray and drink the whole thing in one go. I have dealt with Sparrow. I have extinguished her toxic energy. I can't believe how easy it was in the end, no matter the broken bottle—found in her tote—that I suppose she'd brought as a makeshift weapon. That's the problem with some people, you see. They just lack the clarity and focus, the self-belief, to really see something through.

Now I feel equal to almost anything. There may be gatecrashers and saboteurs here this evening, but I refuse to be intimidated. They have no idea who they are dealing with. I'm no frail, weak-hearted old man. Sorry Grandfa, but it's true. I have darkness within me, a violent darkness I have kept at bay for so long: an inky bottomless well of it like crude oil buried deep, deep beneath the ground. I close my eyes and inhale the smell of burning wood and feathers from the beach and I smile.

Owen is calling me again. This time, I answer.

"Darling?" I say. "Sorry I couldn't pick up before. It's been . . . manic. Where on earth are you? I've been wondering and wondering . . ."

"Fran." Owen's voice sounds odd. "I found—" His voice is muffled on the third word, almost as though he's holding a hand over his mouth. Or perhaps the line's just bad.

"I didn't catch that, darling. What did you find?"

He repeats himself.

I laugh lightly, to show how foolish I know my next words will sound. "This connection must be truly terrible, darling. Because it really sounded like you just said 'a body.'"

Again his voice is oddly muffled, incoherent. But this time I'm sure I catch the word *bones*. And then a series of strange noises that again—if it wasn't Owen—I would say sounded like someone sobbing.

I feel a tiny dart of unease. Sparrow spoke of a body. But no. Grandfa would never have been that careless. He promised to take care of it, that he would make it all go away. "It's done," he said. "I have taken care of it."

And yet . . . I think of a time I overheard Granmama on the phone to a friend about one of his affairs. "Of course he always thought he covered his tracks. That was the most insulting thing. I nearly divorced him on that basis alone. Men are so sloppy about these things, aren't they? They're lazy, that's the problem. Like a dog always burying a favorite bone in the same bloody flowerbed."

I feel an electric thrill of panic. I try to do my breathing. It's not working. It just makes me feel like I'm suffocating.

"I'm sure whatever you've found is very old, darling," I say. "You know, there's lots of ancient stuff around here." I almost convince myself. I'm so good at this. You'd never know I was struggling to breathe.

"No," he says. He takes a shaky breath. "No—fuck. Fran, it's not old. It was wrapped in tarpaulin. And . . . oh Christ. I think . . . no, I know. There in the ground all this time . . . it's my mother, Fran."

"Your mother was Cora the *cleaner*?"

It's out before I realize what I've done. That I've actually uttered the words aloud. I was just so thrown. Because it would mean that everything I thought I knew about Owen is completely false. The enigmatic glamour, the urbane polish—everything that attracted me to him. And it turns out he's a . . . *local*? The son of Cora Deeker, the skank from the pub?

It's only now, in the silence that follows, that I understand the significance of what I have revealed. A chill spreads from my scalp to my fingertips.

There's still silence on the other end of the phone. Perhaps he's hung up. I hope wildly that the line cut out before I said it. That perhaps he simply didn't hear. Six little words. They could have been blotted out by a drop in signal, couldn't they?

But no, now I can hear him breathing. "Where are you Francesca?" His voice is changed. Hard and cold. He never calls me Francesca.

He heard it all.

Owen

YOUR MOTHER WAS CORA THE CLEANER?

I stare at the screen of my mobile.

My mother: dead. And Francesca . . . knew.

It's the hottest night of the year, yet my teeth are chattering together.

I open the tracking app on my phone.

Francesca

I GAZE AT THE TEEMING crowds, fear climbing my throat. Owen's voice at the end of the call—the coldness in it. I've never heard him like that.

"Where are you?" he asked. Is he looking for me at this very moment? Hunting me down? If so I suddenly feel very exposed here, standing right in the middle of the lawn.

I need to give him space, until he's had time to calm down. I hesitate to use the word "hide," but that's what I need to do.

Then, well, perhaps I can think of a way to persuade him of my innocence. Surely it's not insurmountable. Nothing is. I learned that a long time ago. Everything will come well. It always does. I feel the stranglehold of fear loosening, my breath coming easier.

Michelle crosses in front of me holding a walkie-talkie, heading into the melee. In a sudden vision I see the coupling in the wine store last night, all the vile things she did to my husband: a kaleidoscope of pure filth.

Fear transmutes instantly to rage. Yes . . . rage I can work with! The outlet I need for all this bad energy.

"Oh. Hello, Francesca," she says, looking in my direction, as though we're not surrounded by scenes of utter chaos. She appears totally unflustered. Her practical, ugly bun doesn't have a strand out of place and hers must be the only face not shining with perspiration. Does this woman not feel the heat? How *dare* she not be sweating, when everything on the lawns has descended into mayhem?

I want to smack her.

"Michelle, my lovely," I say. "I think we need to have a little chat." I cast a glance toward the crowds on the lawn. "Not here. Somewhere private." Best that we are not observed. I beckon.

Obedient little thing that she is, she trots along behind me. Yes. I feel an energetic release coming on. A purging of toxic emotion.

I lead her away from the hubbub and into the walled garden. It's nice and quiet here. Also, crucially, I have a view of both entrances. I turn to face her but she clears her throat, nods toward the bench in the corner where a couple of guests sit, visible only by the white glow of their outfits. Wait. Not just sitting. One appears to be straddling the other.

Oh for God's sake. But she's right. I lead her on, through the walled garden and onto the path that leads to the Woodland Hutches. It's very dark and quiet here, away from the chaos and noise on the front lawns. This will do.

Except that I'm feeling a little . . . peculiar. A little untethered. Something strange seems to be happening to my vision. The Hutches seem to grow taller and taller: I blink, and they shrink back to their normal size. But the next second they seem to lean in toward me. I put up a hand to fend them off and close my eyes for a little longer. When I open them again—the relief!—they've returned to their usual positions.

"Everything all right, Francesca?" Michelle asks.

"Absolutely," I say, regathering myself and my clarity of purpose by visualizing that footage from the wine store once more. Francesca Meadows can rise above that sort of thing. Francesca doesn't experience true jealousy. She understands that sex and attraction are important natural urges that sometimes just cannot be suppressed.

But Frankie . . . Frankie is pretty fucking angry with Michelle, the sneaky, ungrateful little cunt.

I think I'm actually going to enjoy this.

"Michelle," I say. "It's quite clear to me you're out of your depth here. It's time for you to go now, my lovely. I'm afraid you've rather let me down and I hate it when people let me down."

Michelle juts her chin and I see again that mutinous flicker in her eye. Not quite what I had expected. "No," she says.

"What do you mean, no?" I actually laugh. Of all the—

The laugh sticks in my throat. Something has caught my eye by the trees. Something strange is happening to the shadows. They appear to be shifting and expanding toward me, out of the deeper darkness of the wood. I shake my head.

"Thing is," Michelle says, reaching up to smooth back an imaginary strand of hair. "It's time for you to leave, Francesca."

For a moment I'm so astonished I can't speak. It's like a tame pet has just turned and bitten my hand. For Christ's sake. I chose Michelle partly because she's so beige. The most basic of bitches, someone I could own like a lapdog.

I catch more movement by the trees. Over Michelle's shoulder I seem to glimpse freakish, otherworldly forms coalescing and dissolving into the shadows of the wood once more. Dark figures with the heads of birds. Demonic, scythe-like profiles. Blank staring eyes.

Not real not real not real.

"Oh very real," Michelle says.

Did I speak aloud?

"You see them," she says, "don't you?"

I take a step back from her.

"You thought you were the worst thing in the woods," she says. "Didn't you?"

"Stop it," I say.

"You always did show disrespect for this place. For our traditions." She pulls aside her collar to reveal a mark just below her collarbone. I know that mark because I once painted it all over the woods to frighten others.

"You're . . . one of *them*?"

"Your disgusting brothers locked me in that treehouse," she says. "What they did . . ." For a moment she breaks off, closes her eyes. Then she opens them again. "I wasn't the first, either. And probably not the last."

I stare at her. "You're—"

"Shelly. Not that you bothered to ask my fucking name back then."

I'd say I recognize her but the truth is I barely glanced at her that night. She was just some girl from the chippy in a tracksuit, awful gold hoops. "That wasn't even me," I say. "That was my brothers—"

"You were very happy to let them get on with it, though, weren't you? But you're right, my personal grievance is against them."

As she's been speaking everything has fallen into place in a very sinister fashion. "This whole time, you've been—"

"The seed on the lawn. The cider." She makes a little bow. "Yours truly. The dead cockerel pinned to your door yesterday—that was another of our number. And I do hope you appreciated our installation on the beach."

I have no idea what she means about the cider or the cockerel. But the birdseed? That was her? The thing on the beach?

Once more, I feel more angry than afraid. I put her in a position of trust, I overcame my reservations about her terrible personal style and dodgy accent. And this is how she repays me? How fucking dare she? I don't try to stem my feelings this time. I have no need of any calming breath. My rage is my dark power.

"Well," I say. "It all makes sense now. Once a slut, always a slut. Yes, I saw you, you stupid cow. Last night, in the wine store. I only kept you on today because I thought you could prove useful. But now you've quite clearly outlasted your use to me."

I step toward her. As I do I sense the grotesque shadows seeping forward, out of the trees. The cowled heads appearing, the vicious beaks. Reaching toward me as though ready to envelop me. With them an unholy snickering, chattering, building to a roar. I put my hands over my ears but I can still hear it. Is it inside my own head?

"Someone left us a message," Michelle says. "In the old place. The old way. Accusing you of a worse crime. The taking of a life. The killing of a resident of Tome. Right here, in these woods. You covered it up. You and the old man."

Slumped in his study in the woods . . . the door open to the night. The terrified ravings before he died . . .

The ground beneath me seems to pitch and sway. This cannot be happening. "I didn't do it," I say. "You have no proof."

She smiles. "We don't need proof. Don't you understand? We take care of things in our own way, as we've always done. But we'll give you a chance. Leave now, within the hour, and don't come back."

The outrage of it. The absolute barbaric insolence of ordering me from my ancestral home.

"This is *my* land," I hiss. "My inheritance." It is now that I remember the broken bottle in the tote I took from Sparrow. I reach into the bag and feel the severed glass nick my fingertip. Yes. Sharp enough to do the job.

My hand closes around the stem. I am about to withdraw it when I see a new figure, stepping into the clearing from another part of the woods. Very real, definitely human. But utterly changed from the man I know, face transfigured by rage.

Owen.

I turn and run.

Owen

FOR A MOMENT I SIMPLY stand and watch her run, as though my feet are nailed in place.

I followed the blinking dot to the edge of the woods. Hurtled through the trees, until I came to the Woodland Hutches and saw Francesca standing there. I wanted her to look me in the eye. I needed her to explain. Part of me desperate to be convinced that in spite of what she'd said on the phone she was somehow innocent. The alternative . . . unthinkable.

But the look on her face when she saw me just now told me everything. The guilt, beacon bright.

That, and the fact that she ran.

I created this place for her. For the girl-goddess I first saw all those years ago. For the dream of perfection that she and this building represented. The woman who gave meaning to everything. My love. My light.

Murderer? My mother's killer?

Now everything is dead clear: clear as it was when I stood as a boy holding that lit match. Foreseeing the change I was about to make in the fabric of things.

I know what I have to do.

Francesca

I BOLT TOWARD THE MANOR. I'm nearly at the main building, crossing through the staff car park, when I look across the gravel and see two of the grubby locals who gatecrashed the stage standing there. The older one—some desperate spectacle of a middle-aged man dressed like a teenager in a disgusting sloganed T-shirt—holds one of my flaming lanterns. I stare at them for a moment and they gawp back at me, two cornered rats. The stink of petrol, the naked flame, the gleaming pools of liquid on the ground between them and the building. And in the same moment it occurs to me that Sparrow, the only true witness to what happened back then, is currently locked inside the house. What did I say? The universe always delivers for me.

"Go on!" I say. "Do it. I dare you. I *dare* you."

Still they hesitate. They look frightened. I think they're afraid of me. Perhaps that encounter beside the wood has changed me in some way, lent me an otherworldly power.

"Oh for God's sake," I shout. "Do I have to do everything myself?" I lunge toward them and grab the lantern and I toss it toward the shimmering pool of fluid and it rushes in a liquid chain of fire toward the building faster than the eye can track and it may be the most beautiful thing I have ever seen.

This place has been the creation of a lifetime. It's the only place I have ever felt truly happy. Truly myself. But it is poisoned now. Contaminated irrevocably. This could be the answer. A terrible fire started by bitter locals. If they try to say otherwise I will batter them in the courts. One of Grandfa's maxims: never go anywhere under-lawyered.

A new start. A cleansing of all that has gone before. Yes: I can see it clearly now. Purification by flame. A rising, phoenix-like, out of the soot and remnants of tragedy.

And besides, I've got excellent insurance.

Briefly I hunker in the shadows of the house and watch as the flames begin to climb. Then I turn and race back toward the staff car park, where Owen's Aston Martin sits gleaming like a silver chariot ready to whisk me away.

I need to get away. A little distance from all of this, to reclaim my headspace. This is all—well, it's *a lot*, you know?

A plan is starting to form. *Of course* I knew nothing about the body buried in the grounds. A nasty little surprise inheritance. But I *did* happen to know Grandfa was having an affair with the woman, I'll say that. He had form, after all, with those earlier scandals that drove Granmama to her wits' end. And perhaps things got out of hand one night, out in the woods where he had his study . . .

Grandfa was a pragmatist, after all. *You can't libel the dead*, he once said, when he'd published his memoirs and thrown several deceased peers under the bus. You can't convict the dead of anything either. Do you know, I really don't think he'd mind? I certainly think he'd understand. Might even approve? And Grandfa was resourceful, like me. When I told him about a note Cora had left for me, trying to get back into my good books after she'd snuck into Grandfa's woodland study, he told me he'd use it to our advantage:

I'm so sorry. I can't imagine what you think of me right now, but I hope you understand . . .

What could be more simple than repurposing the note? Posting it to Cora's husband and pretending she'd run away? Left her shitty life in that caravan park behind. It was probably only a matter of time anyway.

I take a deep, restorative breath. I'm feeling better already. I am beginning to see how it's all going to work out. Grandfa will take the blame, posthumously. I'm the injured party. The sins of our fathers, grandfathers, etcetera. The poison of the patriarchy. We can put a whole feminist spin on it. No, perhaps we'll make it less angry than that, more sorrowful. All about healing.

I refuse to be punished for something that happened so long ago. The girl I once was feels like a distant relative. I suppose the only thing I have in common with her is that we are both survivors. Surviving all those moments people have let us down.

I skid to a stop on the gravel and jump behind the wheel of the silver car. I slip the key from my phone cover and it roars into life as everything behind me begins to burn.

Bella

I OPEN MY EYES TO a dense, red static of pain. I crawl to the door: locked. She . . . hit me, didn't she? Yes: I can see the bloodied fossil, discarded on the antique rug. I move on instinct through the pain, all thought pared to the essentials. Reach for the fossil, heft it in my hand, then use it to smash the window. I knock as many of the remaining shards from the frame as possible then step onto a chair and clamber through the gap. I'm vaguely aware of the sting of broken glass against my flesh, but it's nothing compared to the agony of my head.

The drop onto the gravel path outside is farther than expected and I land badly. I stagger shakily to my feet, then half-run, half-stumble round to the front of The Manor, my vision blurring as though waterlogged. I can smell smoke. The heat seems even more intense now.

Then I hear the growl of an engine and glimpse the silver car, gliding along the driveway. The blonde figure behind the wheel.

All I can think is: she's leaving. She's escaping. It feels very important that I stop her. But I can't think straight—everything's clouded by the pain in my head. Could I jam the gates from here, somehow? No, there's no time—

I begin to stagger toward the driveway, but it's useless. There's no way I can catch up. Someone's gaining on her, though. A figure running from the direction of the woods. As they get closer I see Owen Dacre sprinting after the car, looking like a man possessed. And now I can make out the shadowy forms seeping from the other end of the trees, approaching the gate. After last night I'd know those macabre silhouettes from any distance.

"Oh my God," someone says. I turn my head and see Eddie. "Are you OK? Your head—your arms . . . you're bleeding. Come on, I think you should sit down . . ."

"Eddie . . ." I gasp, reaching for his arm. "She attacked me. And now she's leaving. Look—"

The silver car slips inexorably toward the gates.

"I can't let her go," I say. "It has to be now, tonight. I have to stop her getting away with it again."

Eddie

I JOG QUICKLY TOWARD THE rear of The Manor. I've told Bella I'm going to grab an ice pack for her head. I've seen plenty of concussions playing rugby and hers looks pretty bad. I tried to get her to sit down but she was still on her feet when I left her. I really hope she isn't thinking of doing anything stupid.

I round the corner and run smack into Nathan Tate. His eyes are wild—he looks even more tapped than before.

Then there's a muffled boom and a window somewhere above explodes outwards, glass raining down around us. I look up and see flames leaping through the gap.

"Oh my God," I say. "Nathan, what have you done?"

"It wasn't me," he says. "It was that mad fucking witch. I swear." Then he lurches forward and grips me by my upper arms. "Eddie. I was coming to find you actually." He screws up his face. The next words tumble out in a rush. "So—here it is, right? I did supply Jake with the H all those years ago. I've . . . yeah, look, I've felt shitty about it ever since. It's eaten me up. And . . . I'm sorry, mate. But you should have seen him. Could tell he just needed it, for whatever reason. Something to make him feel better. He was just so fucking sad."

He looks down the drive. "Can't believe she just torched her own gaff. What a frigging psycho." His voice hardens, eyes feral, fists clenching at his sides. "She had to take that away from me too, didn't she? And now she's getting away with it. Nah. Fuck that." And then I turn and watch as he starts to run.

Owen

I WATCH THE TAILLIGHTS OF my own car vanish along the drive. But I feel superhuman, infused with abnormal strength and speed, my entire body twitching with adrenaline and rage from scalp to soles, as though I could tear a person limb from limb with my bare hands.

I get it now. This is why I was brought back here.

The thought of Francesca living a life of light and luxury beneath the sun while all this time my mother lay here forsaken in the cold, dark ground. Escaping justice for all these years.

That ends tonight.

She won't get away with it now.

Francesca

I APPROACH THE GATES. IN the rearview mirror I see flames uncoiling from the lower windows. Secretly, almost sneakily. I almost wish I could stay around to watch. A little thrill of anticipation. The same thrill I felt all those years ago in the woods, ready for the terror to appear on Sparrow's face. Or as I handed out the brownies I'd made that night, waiting for the consequences to unspool.

Then I glance through the windscreen and think I glimpse several of those horrible hooded figures ebbing swiftly from the farthest end of the woods. Another glance in my rearview mirror and I can see a running figure, gaining on me. Owen. And as I near the gateposts someone steps out of the shadows. I catch the gleam of bright blonde hair: Michelle, her face grim, determined.

But the gates are opening to release me and I press my foot down on the accelerator and speed through, leaving them behind. The gates are closing now and I can breathe again. I'm going to get away with it. Just like before.

And now it's all behind me and I'm moving faster than anyone could travel on foot, even along this winding country lane, and I feel I have all the time in the world. As I brake for a sharp bend something falls out of the bag I took from Sparrow and into the footwell. I stop the car, allow myself a moment to pick it up. It appears to be some sort of diary. Leafing swiftly through I see the dates. My name. I tear the pages from the spine and feed them to the hot breeze. Fling the empty shell of it behind me, robbed of any power it might once have contained. It feels good. A physical purging of the past.

Then I press my foot down on the accelerator once more.

Now I'm rounding the bend that leads toward that terrible, stinking farm beside the cliffs, the eyesore of a caravan park beyond.

I'll need a new site, obviously. Somewhere abroad. Perhaps we can pivot slightly: offer therapy sessions, week-long mental resets. A Mayr Clinic minus the masochism. I can practically see the deep-dive interviews now. You'd think this sort of thing—this kind of scandal, because I suppose that's what it will be—would put people off. Far from it.

The wind is warm in my hair, the summer night air velvet soft upon my upturned face. The stars are so bright. In fact, they seem to be shining just for me. Glowing, vibrating almost with this crazy beautiful energy as though the universe is speaking directly to me, as it often does. I look down and I can see that some of them are scattered in my lap, sparkling up at me. I blink. How strange. How wonderful!

I grab a handful and toss them into the air. They land in the midnight sky like strewn glitter, like the flecks in my black opal ring. I laugh and my laugh is carried off on the warm breeze like wind-blown blossom. I feel a little odd. Not bad odd, though. Just . . . unleashed. I let my gaze drift out to sea, dreaming of new horizons.

When I look back at the road there's a figure in the middle of it. I wave my hand to brush it away, like I scattered the stars. Nothing happens. I close my eyes and open them again. The figure is still there. A dark apprehension trickles through me. *A bad feeling.* I try to get back to the stars, the warm wind. I know it must be a trick of the shadows creating a blot on my vision.

No: they're not real.

But even when I blink it's still there: the tall figure in black, the cloak billowing up behind it like a deeper patch of night. Arms raised as though it's signaling me to stop. As I speed closer I see the hideous shape of the head, the hooked beak.

The dark feeling billows up, a mushroom cloud of dread. Something strange is happening to my vision because the figure, too, seems to be swelling, growing in front of me. The outstretched arms become two black wings opening to envelop me whole. I'm nearly upon it but it's not moving. I turn the wheel a little, try and swerve. I honk my horn. But it moves further into my path. It looks as if it's going to spring at me, on top of me: jump right onto the bonnet of my car. I fling myself, the car, sideways and there's a thud and a scattering, tinkling sound. When I press my foot on the accelerator nothing happens beyond a terrible grinding noise. I fling open the door and glance up and it is coming for me.

There is a howling all around me—I am howling, the universe is howling. I think I can hear *her* howling, too, all those years ago, as she fell to the woodland floor.

I shove out at the dark figure and a small soft fragment comes away in my hand. I am running now, running away. Am I in the woods? There's something—branches?—tangling around my legs. No: it's brambles, twining themselves around me. I push through and suddenly they give way as easily as if they were clouds of smoke. And now there is nothing beneath me, nothing in front of me, but warm midsummer night air. I am sailing, soaring, into the star-lit sky.

Oh. Now I am no longer soaring I am plummeting and—

THE SHADOWS MELT BACK INTO *the woods. Swarm and coalesce around the tree with a hundred eyes. Shadows with form, with substance. They haven't failed yet to find justice. They are one with nature. And nature always finds a way.*

AFTER

Eddie

THE DAY AFTER THE SOLSTICE

IT'S GETTING LIGHT. THE SMOKE is clearing now and beyond it there isn't a cloud in the sky. Everyone's sitting on the lawn, mostly wrapped in foil blankets from the paramedics, even though it's already warm. But like, I get it. After the shock, all of that.

My back is killing me. My shoulders feel like they've been ripped out of the sockets. It still hurts to breathe. They're calling me a hero, because of how many people I got out of The Manor before it burned to the ground. When I looked up and saw the building, totally swallowed by fire, I didn't stop to think. Like I was on autopilot I ran to help. Grabbed hold of people as they emerged from inside. Some of them were totally out of it—I don't know if was the cider or the smoke or what. I dragged one of them after another across the lawns to safety, away from pieces of falling stone and glass. I went in again and again.

I hear the crackle of a walkie-talkie. A couple of police—one in uniform and one in ordinary clothes—are standing a few feet away having a murmured conversation. But I catch the words: "So it's a question of the sequence of events. How she ended up a mile away from here at the bottom of the cliffs while this place burned—"

"Oh my God, Eddie," Ruby says, stumbling toward me, and I lose track of what the policemen are saying.

"You all right Ruby?"

She just shakes her head, lost for words. I get up and she steps into my arms for a hug and maybe I hug a little too long or a little too tight because she pulls back a bit and looks at me.

"Are *you* all right, Eds?"

I open my mouth but I can't find the words to answer her. I can't work out where I would even start.

"You were amazing, Eds. What is it? That there were two people you didn't get out? You can't let yourself feel guilty. You couldn't know there was anyone else inside. I can see it in your face, that it's eating you up."

It's true that I wanted to save as many people as possible. That's why I ran back into the burning building so many times. Not really caring what happened to me.

There were the two I didn't manage to get out. We've all seen the body bags in the back of the ambulance. But I don't feel guilty about that. I know there was probably nothing I could do. I guess Ruby does know me pretty well. And I suppose she *can* read me, too. But what she thinks she sees isn't quite the whole picture.

Bella

"HOLD STILL," THE PARAMEDIC TELLS me, as he places the last butterfly stitch on the wound above my eyebrow.

I sit here wrapped in my foil blanket, squinting with pain, trying to eavesdrop on the conversations around me. Rumors swirl around me about deaths, maybe several of them.

The police are here now. I watch them moving among the groups of guests on the lawns, speaking to everyone. I don't want to talk to them. Not yet. I can't get my thoughts straight about what happened last night for a start. My head is agony: I have a pretty serious concussion, apparently. The last thing I really remember is seeing Francesca drive off in that silver car. Knowing I couldn't let her get away.

Did I pass out after that? I think I must have done. Everything afterwards is a blank.

All I can think of now is my daughter. I just want to go home to her, to my baby girl. My small, safe life. But I sense it's going to be a little while before I can do that.

I understand Cora better now. You don't stop wanting things or wanting to cling on to an earlier version of yourself just because you've become a mother. All the more so, I'd imagine, if you had a child when you were still a kid yourself. We saw Cora as cool and sophisticated, and she saw us as two teenage girls who'd never imagine the responsibilities she might have at home. At that magical place—the place I once thought of as a Narnia, a Neverland—she could escape into a different world for a few hours each day.

I glance up at the crackle of a radio. Uniformed officers are everywhere you look, plus a select handful who I think must be plain clothes. My eye's drawn to one figure in particular. A man around my own age with close-cropped hair, graying at the temples. He's the tallest of them and seems to carry the most authority. He turns in this direction, the sunlight hits his face.

But it can't be.

DI Walker

"IT'S A MIRACLE THERE WEREN'T more victims," Fielding says to Walker. "I've started trying to make a list of key witnesses, like you asked. I keep hearing that one guy—member of staff, kitchen pot-wash lad—was a real star. They're saying he helped get a load of people out. He's a nice lad. Bit shell-shocked. Doesn't seem to think of himself as a hero either, which is always the case with the ones that really are. Should put him forward for one of those public bravery awards or something. Look. He's sitting just over there. Come and meet him."

Walker follows DS Fielding over to where a strapping young guy sits on a patch of grass staring into the middle distance, pale and worn and hollow-eyed beneath his suntan.

"Here he is," Fielding says. "What was your name again, mate?"

"Eddie," the boy says. "Eddie Walker."

Fielding turns to DI Walker. "Huh. That's a coincidence. Suppose it's a common enough name." He looks back to the boy. To Walker again. "Funny. If I didn't know better I'd say . . ." He trails off, looking confused. Walker can see his brain trying to assimilate the impossible.

Now the boy, or rather something between a boy and a man, is getting to his feet, staring at Walker the whole time. Walker sees the exact moment it registers.

"What the fuck," Eddie says. From the clumsy way he says "fuck" Walker can tell he doesn't use the word very often.

Mum brought her boys up not to swear.

"If you could give us a moment," Walker says, turning to DS Fielding.

"Yeah. Sure . . . boss." But even as Fielding walks away he glances back over his shoulder once, twice, as though trying to make sense of what he's seeing.

Walker knew there would be a moment like this. When he would have to withdraw from this case, too compromised to continue. When he'd have to reveal his deep connection to this part of the world. To admit that while he came down to these parts from London it's not where he *comes from*.

He can sense Fielding watching from a little distance away. He knows he has some explaining to do. A lot of explaining to do, in fact. There's a chance this could mean a disciplinary—worse. But he can't worry about that now. Because most of all he needs to explain himself to the boy standing in front of him. He swallows.

"It's me," he says. "It's Jake, your big brother. I've come back."

Eddie

"NO," I SAY. "IT CAN'T be you."

It's some sick joke. It has to be. It doesn't make any sense. Jake was messed up, a druggie. He stole Dad's tractor. He went off the rails. There's no way he's just turned up like this—a *policeman* of all things.

But it *is* him. Even though his face is thinner, older. Underneath it all I can see the boy from the photos in the albums. I should know. I've stared at them enough times, up in my room, trying to remember him as he was, trying to imagine what he'd be like now.

Now I know.

I also know, after last night, that no one is what they seem.

"Eddie," he says, his voice thick. I can see tears bright in his eyes. "I can't believe it. I know it's stupid . . . I know how much time has passed. But in my head you're still that little blond boy. Splashing about in your paddling pool. You really bloody loved that paddling pool."

He covers his eyes and I see him take a deep, shuddering breath. Then he coughs, squares his shoulders. I see him pull himself together. "I'm sorry. I've thought about this so much. But I somehow can't can't get my head round you standing in front of me like this, a grown man. And they're saying you're a hero, Eddie. My baby brother! I heard what you did. How you saved people last night. Look . . . I know it isn't my place. I know I don't have any right saying this, after all this time. But I'm so proud of you."

"No," I say, quickly. "I'm not a hero."

"But—"

"I'm not."

"OK." He nods, like he's going to let it go for now. "Look. I—can imagine you have a lot of questions."

I'm feeling so many things all at once, have so many things to ask, that I don't know where to start. "But— But where have you been?" I say. "I thought you were in prison . . . maybe even—" I can't say it: *dead.* "But, but . . . look at you. You're *fine.*" It comes out angry. Well, I *am* angry. If he's fine, what was it all for?

"Oh Eddie," he says. "I'm not fine. I'm better than I was. You could say that, I suppose. I was in a very bad way back then. After what I did to Mum and Dad. After Dad chucking me out. But that wasn't all of it. Something really bad happened, Eddie. There was no way I could come back here after it. Not just like that."

"I know," I say. "I know about the woman who died."

The color leaves his face. "How?" he whispers.

"She told me." I point across the lawns to where Bella sits having her head patched up by a paramedic. She's staring back at us. No: she's staring at Jake.

"So she came," he murmurs, almost to himself. "I didn't know if she would. After all this time. I wondered how she'd coped, whether it had affected her like it affected me. See, I had to find a way to live with myself. This job, it's been good for me. Solving murders. It was like . . . penance, I suppose. I specialize in cold cases, Eddie. Uncovering the truth in crimes that have gone unsolved for a long time. Seeking justice." As though he's still speaking to himself, he says, "Maybe I should have known this was the only way it could end."

He runs a hand across the short bristles of his hair, looks at the ground. He's breathing fast, chest rising and falling. Finally he seems to steel himself. He looks straight at me, meets my eyes. "I've seen it myself. I know the chances of bringing a charge in a case like this, fifteen years later, are almost zero. Mud doesn't stick to these sorts of people. They have the best lawyers, high-level connections. This . . . belief in their own invincibility. It's like they inherit that along with all the rest."

He grimaces. "They threatened me back then—threatened our

family. But there was this stupid irony about my job literally being about solving murders, for God's sake—and never being able to do anything about a killing I witnessed with my own eyes." His voice changes now. Harsher, angrier. "I knew I couldn't let her get away with it—" Then he breaks off, looks over my shoulder. I turn to see Bella Springfield standing a few feet away.

"*Jake?*"

He nods. Clears his throat. "Hi," he says. "It's been a while." If he's going for light-hearted it doesn't work. I wonder if the two of them are remembering the last time they saw each other. Two terrified teenagers.

For a moment they simply stare at each other. Then Bella closes her eyes and sighs, like she's just understood something.

"It was you," she says, looking at him again. "Wasn't it? You sent me that clipping. You brought me back here."

He nods. "You knew what they'd done with the body. I'm sorry I never replied to your text, back then. I was in a pretty bad way . . . But I always regretted it: not doing anything, not saying anything. Especially after I became a policeman, especially when my job became about solving cold cases. Then *she* waltzed back here, like none of it had happened, whitewashing this place, the past. Coming after Mum and Dad's land. She started making claims on it, via the local council. It's literally there on the website. Alleging it's really hers. So I found you."

Now he points in the other direction and I turn to see where Owen Dacre sits with his head in his hands. His face is hidden, but he looks utterly broken. "He was the first one I contacted," Jake says. "The first one I brought back here, before you. It seems so cruel in a way. But I couldn't bear the thought of all those years he spent, thinking his mum had just upped and left him."

"Oh . . . God," Bella says, staring. "I feel so stupid. How did I not see? It's him, of course it is. I see it now. But I only ever knew him as Shrimp. I suppose it was the clothes, the name." She grimaces. "And the fact that he married her—"

Jake shakes his head. "When·you open up the past like this . . . it can have repercussions you never imagined. I never thought he'd conceal from her who he was. I still thought perhaps there'd be some way to reach out, to tell him about what happened. But then he fell for her, so quickly. That was when I realized I needed more. When I brought you in."

Bella just shakes her head, looking lost for words. Then she says: "But you didn't *know* I'd come. You didn't know any of us would."

Jake nods. "Of course I didn't. But I did what I could to set something in motion. I didn't know exactly what would happen but I thought *something* might. See, that's what you do with a cold case. You return to your main witnesses, you bring back the key players. You do everything you can. Pull at every thread. Try all the angles. Turn it all inside out again." He frowns. "I'm not sure I could have foreseen all of this, though. I . . ." He trails off.

"What?" Bella prompts.

He snatches a look over his shoulder, toward his police colleagues. Lowers his voice. "I shouldn't tell you this. It could get me struck off. But perhaps it doesn't matter now. There's a body, at the bottom of the cliffs . . . We have to wait for a formal ID but it's her, I know it is."

I hear Bella's sharp intake of breath.

"It was the Birds," Jake says. "Old Graham Tate swears he saw them. There was a black feather in her hand."

"She's dead?" I swallow, because it's like something's stuck in my throat. "Are you saying . . . are you saying Francesca Meadows is dead?"

"Yes." Jake nods. Then he looks at me more closely. "Eddie? Are you OK?"

His voice seems a very long way away. Because suddenly it's like I'm not really here. I'm back there. Last night . . .

Eddie

I WATCH THE SILVER SHAPE of the car moving through the darkness along the driveway toward the gates. Nathan Tate's words echo in my head. "But you should have seen him. Could tell he just needed it, for whatever reason. Something to make him feel better. He was just so fucking sad."

I think of my lost brother. My broken dad. My family, destroyed by what she did. I understand what Bella means. Francesca Meadows is rich and posh and she's got away with it for fifteen years already. Of course she'll get away with it again.

What can I do? But I have to do *something*. I've never hated anyone in my life before. But after what I've learned, what she did . . . Yeah. I think I hate her.

There isn't much time. *Think, Eddie.* The road winds inland a way before it meets the sea again and you can't go much more than twenty miles an hour . . . the cliff path is much shorter, more direct. Maybe there's a chance—

I sprint to the bike lockers, only a few meters away. Grab my bike. As I pedal like crazy I pass Nathan Tate, who hasn't a hope of catching up with her, then nearly lose my balance at the sight of Owen Dacre sprinting toward the gates, looking deranged with anger. I wobble a little as I pass Michelle, too, staring down the drive with a face like thunder. And as I leave through the gates I think I glimpse several dark figures at the edge of my vision: watching me go.

But then they're all left behind and it's just me. Out on the cliff path I cycle like my life depends on it, skidding over pebbles and into potholes, legs pumping, lungs burning, sweat running into my eyes. The moon lights my way, hanging huge and heavy above the black water. My chest burns, I feel like I might throw up with the effort. But I can't stop. All I know is I have to get there in time.

Finally I reach the place where the road meets the cliffs again by the caravan park. I leap off the bike, panting. I'm scanning in both directions, trying to catch any sound over the thud of my heartbeat in my ears. There's no sign of any car. I'm too late. She must already have gone past. But then . . .

Yes, I can hear the growl of an engine. Can see the gleam of the headlights over a little rise in the road, coming from the direction of The Manor. A flash of silver. It's her. My heart's beating even harder. This is my chance.

But I need something else, something more. *I* need to be more. More than plain old Eddie Walker who can't even squash a spider when his girlfriend asks him to. I need something that will stop her in her tracks.

The roar of the engine gets louder. I don't have much time. I throw down my bike and as I do the pannier lands on the tarmac with a soft thud and I remember the mask, cloak, and gloves hidden inside. I think of the terrifying sight of those dark figures in the woods.

I lift up the mask, except suddenly it seems more than just a mask. It's like it's vibrating with a strange power . . . or maybe it's just the trembling of my hands. There's this moment outside time when I pause and stare at it and think: do I dare? But now it feels like it is meant to be. The only way.

I fit it over my face. I pull the cloak around my shoulders and though the air's crazy hot and the black fabric is thick and heavy it's oddly cool against my shoulders. I shiver, the first chill I've felt all night.

I stand here, waiting. I hear a shout from the direction of the caravan park. I glance behind me. And by the light of the moon I see old Graham Tate clinging to the outer fence and clutching a whisky bottle and staring right back at me with wide, frightened eyes. It takes a beat and then I realize: he doesn't see me, Eddie. He sees one of the Birds. And he is terrified.

This thing I'm wearing . . . it's more than just cloth and feather now. It's changing me into someone—something—different. A dark power seeping into me. And as the headlights swing around the final bend I step out into the middle of the road and I put up my hands and the cloak whips out behind me and I shout "STOP" but even my voice isn't mine any longer. It comes out like a shriek—like no sound I've ever made, like no sound any human should make.

And I catch sight of her face through the windscreen and she, too, is terrified.

Good.

Because I'm not Eddie anymore. The fear is gone, the doubt is gone. All that's left is anger. More than just my own anger, about my family, which is a sad, dull, bruise-like feeling. This is bigger than that, bigger than me: more powerful, more dangerous. Exciting, almost. Like somewhere deep inside me a fire has been lit. And I can hear a chattering in my head like the chattering of the hundreds of birds on the lawns this morning.

And the car's coming closer and closer but she has to stop. I'm here. I won't let her pass. She's racing toward me and I can hear the growl of the engine growing louder and louder and maybe she's *not* going to stop, after all. I don't have time to get out of the way. I see her pale face through the windscreen, her wide screaming mouth. At the very last moment she swerves to one side and the silver car thunks into the bank at the side of the road with a tinkling of breaking glass. There's a moment of total silence and stillness. And for a moment I think that's it. Is she . . . ?

No, now she's throwing open the door, climbing out of the driver's seat. She turns and looks at me and she is so scared, I can see it. But it's not enough. It's not enough for her to be scared. I need more. The *Birds* need more. The chattering grows louder, building to a roar. And she is sprinting away from me and maybe this is how a bird of prey feels when it sees a field mouse running through the grass because at the sight of her running I only feel the anger grow, the need grow. I am chasing after her. And now I'm gaining on her but she's pushing through the brambles at the side of the road and a small voice in my head, what's left of Eddie, thinks *why that way? Not that way . . .*

I shove through the brambles after her and feel them tearing at the cloak and I have nearly got to her—just a little farther—and I sense darkness on the other side, darkness and space and *nothing* and at the last moment she turns back to me as though she's just changed her mind and snatches out a hand and I feel her pluck a feather free.

Another scream. I don't even know if it's her or me or real or inside my own head but suddenly she is gone.

I'm alone on top of the cliffs.

The smell of smoke from somewhere.

And everything quiet save the sound of the hot wind tearing in across the sea.

Oh, God.

Epilogue

Owen

I INHERITED IT ALL. NEXT of kin. A local, a boy who grew up on a caravan park, a boy once ashamed of being so poor, turned Lord of the Manor. Or what was left of it, anyway.

The really messed up part is I miss Francesca, sometimes. Or rather, I miss the Francesca I thought I knew. Her radiance. Then I remember: that person was mostly a phantom. An ingenious—entirely cynical—creation. Then it's like I experience the loss a second time.

My first instinct was to sell up, get rid, have nothing more to do with this place. It went on the market and prospective buyers crawled quickly out of the woodwork. All of a species: developers looking to build luxury new properties, hedge funders in search of a down-from-London bolt-hole, the odd high-end hotelier undeterred by all the drama and tragedy. Because a spot like that—with a view to die for—doesn't come along very often.

But I couldn't do it. For better or worse, it was my mother's final resting place. It had to be something worthy of her.

It will be my first public-orientated project. In place of the imposing ancestral block of stone will be an ultra-modern, light-filled gallery, exclusively displaying the work of local artists. A new cultural destination in this out-of-the-way place. A community center, too, for local families: a swimming pool, tennis courts. The walled garden has been converted to allotments. The woods are entirely open to the public once more.

I built it for her. For the boy I once was. And for this place. Because Tome came through for my family in the end. They brought my mother back to me. They looked out for their own. The local people, the little people. The true inheritors of this land.

Eddie

I SIT HERE IN MY room and stare out at the dark. The stars are so bright tonight. I can see them up there: the Great Bear, the Little Bear. The stars: the same. The woods: the same. Me . . . changed forever.

There's a murmur of voices from the living room, down below. A big rumbling belly laugh. Was that . . . Dad?! It's such an unfamiliar sound. Then Mum saying something. And then another voice, a new-old voice. Jake.

He's come home. After fifteen years my big brother's come home. All of us under the same roof again—a family. Just for a couple of hours at a time. Baby steps. But today he came over for Sunday lunch, then stayed to sit by the fire in the living room. And it's weird and super awkward at times, like we're all trying to play the parts of family members without having learned our lines. Jake and Dad reaching for the gravy boat at the same time, apologizing to each other like strangers.

We are strangers. We're never going to get the lost years back. Sometimes I catch Jake shooting Dad the odd glance when Dad's not looking and I think: he hasn't forgiven him. Not yet. Maybe he never will. And at other times: Dad watching Jake with this raw, ashamed, sorrowful expression on his face. And I know that there's more to come . . . difficult, messy, angry, sad stuff that has to be dealt with but can't until they've got past the polite stranger stage.

But today everyone wanted to get along, and so we did: chatting over blackberry crumble, everyone's bellies full of food and booze. Jake saying how much he missed Mum's homemade custard,

Mum getting all glassy-eyed and actually reaching out to ruffle his hair . . . then Jake joking that he'd even missed the lumps and Mum pretend cuffing him on the ear. That—the happy part—was when I had to make my excuses and come up here to be on my own. Because I'm OK with the awkwardness. I much prefer it, actually. I can hide behind it, hide the change in me.

I've caught Jake looking at me funny once or twice. And when it's just been the two of us he's opened his mouth like he's about to say something, then closed it again like he's changed his mind, or just can't find the words. I guess he's seen it before plenty of times in his work: guilt.

The worst part is everyone round here thinks I'm a hero. Telling me what a good job I did during the fire, getting all those people out . . . after I cycled back to The Manor because there was no way I could go home after what happened. What I did.

Did I mean to do it? Did I know what might happen when I put on that cloak? When I stood in the road to stop her in her tracks? When I, Eddie Walker, became a killer?

I jump at the sound of a soft knocking on my bedroom door. Mum pokes her head through the gap before I can respond because she never waits even though you'd think having had two teenage boys she'd have learned to give it thirty seconds at least.

"Alright, love?" She steps into the room. Stands looking down at me. I feel like I've been caught out doing something dodgy, even though I've just been sitting here on my bed looking out at the dark. I guess it's because I haven't had time to get my mask in place . . . the old version of Eddie I have to put on these days like a costume.

"Yeah," I say. It comes out a little hoarse.

"I'm just heading out to my book club," she says. "I think Jake's leaving in a little bit, too, if you want to say bye."

"Sure."

Just like I've seen Jake do a couple of times, Mum opens her mouth like she wants to say something. Closes it again. I wish she'd stop looking at me. I wish she'd just leave so I don't have to try so hard to pretend.

And then she drops something. Something that falls to the floor with a muffled *flump*. Both of us look down at the small dark shape on the floorboards.

"Whoops," Mum says. But there's a pause before she stoops to pick it up. A pause that gives me time to see what it is: a long, black leather glove. Not at all the sort of thing Mum usually wears (I know, because I once saved up to buy her the beige cashmere mittens she uses all autumn and winter). But that's not the reason I suddenly feel cold all over. It's because I've seen gloves like that before.

"Mum," I say, "what is that?"

Mum holds the glove for a moment in both hands as though weighing it, as though deciding what to say next. "It was you," she says, finally. "Wasn't it, love?"

For a sickening moment I just stare back at her, heart thumping, feeling like I'm going to vomit. Is she saying . . .

Then Mum says, "I mean, it was you who took the . . . the things from the understairs cupboard, wasn't it?"

I'm half relieved, half totally confused. I took those things to stop Dad using them, to protect him. Dad, one of the Night Birds. Dad who hid his mask and cloak and gloves there.

Wasn't it . . . ?

"That was such a silly place to leave them," Mum says, shaking her head. "I needed somewhere I could grab them quickly and somewhere your dad wouldn't look, as he never does any cleaning. Luckily, there was a spare I could borrow. One of our number wasn't wearing hers that night."

Not Dad. *Mum.* It's my mum who was—*is?*—a Night Bird.

But—no. It can't be. It just can't. Mum is home and safety and comfort and cottage pie and watching cooking shows together.

Mum doesn't go into the woods in the middle of the night dressed in a cloak and mask.

But maybe nothing should surprise me now. The whole world has turned on its head. No one is what they seem. Including me.

"But . . ." I say, trying to find the words, not knowing where to start. "I thought . . . I was so sure that it was Dad . . ."

"You thought your dad was a Bird?" Mum gives a little sigh. "Your father, of an evening, would go to one of the outbuildings and play Fortnite—I think that's what it's called—into the small hours with strangers on the internet. We both had to find a way to live our lives, you know? After everything."

"You . . ." I still can't cope with the size of this new knowledge. I start with the first thing that comes to mind: the blood in the woods. The black-cloaked figures. "It was you," I say, "*you* killed Ivor the bull?"

Mum gives a little sigh. "Ivor was old and sick. He had arthritis in all his joints, he was in constant pain. He had a good life and his time had come. We needed a sacrifice, for the solstice. For Samhain, too, Beltane . . . all the others. It's tradition. A blood-letting, to bring us good fortune in our endeavors. And we especially needed it this solstice."

I stare at her. She doesn't even sound like herself. It's like someone else—something else—has possessed Mum's body. Then she looks at me and says in her normal voice, "Honestly, Eds. Every time I looked into Ivor's poor old face he seemed to be saying 'Help me.' Far kinder than being sent off to the abattoir."

"But . . . but Dad seemed so guilty . . ."

"Oh, your father *did* feel guilty, because he couldn't remember if he had left the gate open. He thought it might have been his fault that Ivor escaped. He'd been drinking and you know what your father is like when he drinks."

While she's been talking another piece of the puzzle has fallen into place. "Wait. *That's* why you were working at the hotel?" I see her in her white uniform pushing her cart, the laundry inside speckled with blood. "The sheets," I say, "with the blood on—"

Mum shrugs. "Ah, well. Yes—I was on my way to . . . deliver a message when I ran into you."

My head is spinning as I remember that night in the woods, with Delilah, much longer ago now. The black feather on the desk. "And the old man? Lord Meadows?"

"We simply paid him a visit . . . or two. You know what they say about a guilty conscience. Who knows? Perhaps there is such a thing as being frightened to death after all."

Francesca Meadows's face that last night. The staring eyes, the screaming mouth—

"This," Mum brandishes the black glove now like it's more than just a glove—which I suppose it is, "*this* gave me a purpose. When I put on that mask and cloak—I am something different. I am powerful. I am something more than myself."

Her words hang in the silence for a long moment. I can sense her looking at me but I can't bring myself to meet her eyes.

And into the quiet comes a sound from beneath us: another deep belly laugh from Dad.

Mum steps forward, puts her hands on my shoulders. Eventually, I manage to lift my gaze to meet hers. "That laugh," she says. "Do you understand what a miracle that is? I thought I'd never see your father happy again. Finally, *finally*, our family can start to heal. And Tome, too—rid of a deadly parasite. Because the Birds are like nature. And nature always finds a way."

Now she takes my face in her hands. "Oh my lovely boy. Don't cry. Please don't cry."

AFTERWARDS I'M LEFT here in the dark and silence with only the stars looking in at me. And I get it, what Mum said about becoming someone—something—else. I get it because I felt it that night.

But I killed her, all the same. I know that, too. I can feel it like a wound deep inside of me that no one else can see. For all Mum's talk of healing I don't know if or how I'll ever recover from it. Probably I never will.

But would I do it again, if I had the chance to go back in time? Yeah. I think I would.

Bella

I SIP MY HALF PINT at the sticky bar and listen to the pub owner talking to the two regulars at the next stools along.

"Heard the inquest found she had it in her system, same as the rest of 'em," the guy two down says. "So she was driving while high and had some sort of bad trip, a hallucination or something. Ran off the cliff into thin air."

Even Francesca Meadows couldn't manifest her way out of that one.

I never got the confession I came for. The reprieve from fifteen years of gnawing, life-altering guilt. But perhaps it was a naïve hope. Turns out a leopard doesn't change its spots, even if it's covered them up with some wellness bullshit and white linen.

But it wasn't really about my absolution: I know that now. I was brought here for the woman—the mother—buried in an unmarked grave in Tome woods. Funny. As it was Francesca herself who said I lacked a purpose. And for the last fifteen years she'd have been right. But in coming back here, I found one. I can look my daughter in the eye now. Perhaps I'll never be quite whole myself but I can pass something better on to her.

It's time to say goodbye to this place. It's why I'm back for this one night. In an hour I'll meet Jake Walker to stroll along the cliff path, for old time's sake. Just two people briefly reunited, finally freed from the shadows of the past.

I need a jot of Dutch courage first, though. It's been a while— and the rest. I take another sip of my beer and tune back in to the conversation along the bar.

"You heard what old Tate's been saying of course," the guy next to me says. "He swears blind it was *them*—"

"Graham Tate wouldn't know one end of a bottle of Bell's from the other," the landlady says, cutting him off, "so you'll forgive me taking his fairy tales with a big pinch of salt. Besides, for what it's worth his own son testified that he saw her set fire to the place. Torching your own hotel—if that doesn't sound like someone off their rocker on drugs then I don't know what does."

With Hugo and Oscar Meadows left to suffocate inside. Even for her that seems beyond the pale.

"Course . . ." the guy next to me says, turning to his fellow with a grimace (and maybe a touch of excitement?), "you saw the body, mate."

"Yeah." His drinking buddy shudders. "Coming in from the morning catch. Nasty business. Wasn't a fan of that place or the family but I wouldn't wish that end on anyone."

"Oh and you heard about the prodigal? A policeman of all things! Thought we'd never see hide nor hair of Jake Walker again. That's going to be a strange family Christmas."

"Shh." The other guy nudges him. "His mum's here this evening, look."

I follow their gaze to the long table at the back. A table of women, slightly incongruous in this fairly masculine space. Most of a certain age (lots of gray hair, a few untouched roots), talking in a low, respectable murmur.

Now I'm looking closely there are a couple of faces I think I recognize. Wasn't the blonde one, the youngest among them, the manager from The Manor? And is that . . . ? Yes, I see the dog collar: the vicar I met at the village cross. And now the landlady steps out from behind the bar with a tray of drinks, sets them down at the table to a chorus of appreciation. Pulls up a chair to join the others.

The first guy turns back round. Shrugs. Takes a sip of his pint. "What's with all the old birds in here this evening? Place is overrun with them."

ACKNOWLEDGMENTS

HOW TO BEGIN? SO MANY dedicated, creative people have helped this book come into being, and I am more grateful than I can express to all of them. I think, though, that I have to begin with peerless editorial team of Kate Nintzel, Kimberley Young, and Charlotte Brabbin for working SO HARD: tirelessly, speedily . . . and crucially, with such good humor. No query or sudden, mad middle-of-the-night thought has been too small or too random, and you've taken all my panicky/last-minute amends and what-ifs in stride. Thank you. I am so grateful to you all, and never has it felt more unjust that there's only one name on the cover!

NEXT, TO MY DREAM LITERARY agents, Cathryn Summerhayes and Alexandra Machinist. You are total rock stars—so driven and brilliant and also such fun. Thank you both for your peerless wisdom, intelligence, and flawless instincts. I feel so privileged just to spend time in your company, let alone to be represented by you both. Bring on the tour!

CATH, THANK YOU SPECIFICALLY FOR traipsing round Icelandic volcanoes with me while sick as a dog and for rescuing me in the middle of LA crosswalks. I love every moment of working (and plotting!) with you.

ALEXANDRA, THANK YOU FOR ALCOHOLIC Soho lunches and fabulous, gossipy catch-ups. I want to be you when I grow up.

TO THE GLORIOUS JASON RICHMAN. Everyone raved about you before I met you and now I know why—you are such delightful company and so, so brilliant at what you do. I've had the best year working with you—bring on the rest!

TO KATIE MCGOWAN AND AOIFE MACINTYRE, thank you for all your tireless work in finding my books homes around the world.

TO ANNABEL WHITE AND JESS MOLLOY, thank you for everything you do and for always doing it with huge good cheer and peerless efficiency. It's always such a joy to see you in the office.

TO ANNABELLE JANSSENS, THANK YOU so much for your hard work and your patience with this disorganized, wayward author!

TO MY WONDERFUL PUBLICISTS EITHER side of the pond, Emilie Chambeyron and Eliza Rosenberry, thank you for your ingenuity, diligence, and stamina and for doing everything with such grace and humor. It's a joy to be working with you each of you again after a one-book hiatus.

TO THE DREAM MARKETING TEAMS of Sarah Shea, Abbie Salter, Vicky Joss, Kaitlin Harri, and Amelia Wood: thank you for embracing this book so wholeheartedly and imaginatively. Hopefully we can have some fun marketing this one! CBD cocktails all round?!

TO THE FABULOUS HOLLY MARTIN: what a wonderful, unexpected thrill to be working together. Let's sneak off for lunch and start speaking in code and make Al and Harry jealous.

TO THE BRILLIANT FRANKIE GRAY: thank you for taking the reins with such grace and confidence. What a treat to be reunited again. Headline girls for life.

TO THE STELLAR TEAMS AT HarperCollins US and UK: Brian Murray and Charlie Redmayne, Liate Stehlik and Kate Elton, Roger Cazalet, Tom Dunstan, Bethan Moore, Emily Scorer, Vicky Joss, Ben Hurd, Fionnuala Barrett, Sophie Waeland, Jennifer Hart, Kelly Rudolph, Maya Horn, Jeanne Reina, Andrea Molitor, Pam Barricklow, Jessica Rozler, Michele Cameron, Marie Rossi, Rhian McKay, and Linda Joyce. Thank you for all your hard work and your belief in me and my books.

TO GRAHAM BARTLETT, FOR YOUR brilliant police expertise. Any mistakes (and a small sprinkling of artistic license!) I've made with regard to the DI Walker sections are my own. I'm so grateful for your help. And readers, check out Graham's books—they're fantastic!

TO JORDAN MOBLO, FOR ALL your belief in me and my books. Thank you.

TO JUNIPER AND LA FOLLIA, for making a large portion of the writing of this book so delicious!

TO MY WONDERFUL PARENTS, SUE AND PADDY, and my fantastic parents in law, Liz and Pete, for all your support, love, and help with the small people!

TO SAID SMALL PEOPLE, MY mad, funny little boys, for filling life with pure joy.

TO AL. I DON'T REALLY know where to start with you because it starts and ends with you. You are my co-plotter, my first reader, and wise counsel all in one. You have held the babies, soothed the anxious creative, and kept the show on the road. I am so lucky to have you by my side and I'm going to put it down here in writing so you can't brush it off and make light of it or pull a face! Thank you, for everything.

Turn the Page

For a letter from Lucy Foley
and three deleted scenes . . . all
exclusive to this Barnes & Noble
edition of *The Midnight Feast.*

Dear Reader,

Here are three scenes that hit the cutting room floor between drafts: two from Eddie's point of view, one from Bella's. I had my characters (Eddie was first of all of them, in fact!) and my setting from the outset. I always knew that in *The Midnight Feast* I wanted to play with pagan mythology and folk horror elements against the backdrop of a luxury countryside hotel and for everything to feel very slightly heightened, but still plausible.

All three scenes touch on those themes and I had such fun writing them. Ultimately, though, while I liked the atmosphere I felt they weren't advancing plot and intrigue as they might—or as well as I felt other scenes did. They had to go! By the final draft every scene in the book has to really "sing for its supper," and these just didn't sing loudly enough. Yet I never feel the writing of such pieces is a waste—in a way I think of them as like scaffolding for the final, leaner manuscript: they needed to be there at the beginning in order for me to understand my characters and setting better.

I (and my brilliant editors!) also went back and forth a great deal on how much to "show" the Night Birds. They were a new writing challenge for me: a strange, slightly otherworldly, cultish presence. I wanted to touch on magical realism and hopefully make them truly spooky at times yet retain a real-world, human groundedness—I always think humans can be far more frightening than anything otherworldly! In the end it transpired that the way to best achieve this was a less-is-more approach; as soon as they started "speaking" they seemed to lose some of their menace and mystique. I needed them to be shadows on the edges of things, rather than down on the beach chanting round their bonfire . . . much as I had some (evil) fun writing those "burn to the bone" incantations!

I hope you enjoy!

Lucy

Eddie

I'M CALLED UP TO HELP a couple of the others build the bonfire on the front lawns. Apparently it's going to be an important part of the Solstice celebrations. Dad actually told me once about the fires they used to light here along the coast at this time of the year: "In the olden days they used to put bones on them too, lad. That's where the word comes from."

The wood for it is all going to come from the trees that have just been chopped down. So Dan, Ruby, and I are at the edge of the woods, throwing the chunks into wheelbarrows. I can't shake the feeling that we're being watched while we stand here, the others larking around. It's the woods: the shadows between the trees. It's last night, what I saw in there. I notice Dan throw a couple of nervous looks in that direction, too. He doesn't know the half of it. I haven't given him any crap about doing a runner, though. I wish I'd done the same.

It's sweaty work, as it's even hotter this afternoon, and after a few minutes Dan takes his top off—I'm pretty sure he's trying to impress Ruby, who could not look less impressed. I keep waiting for Michelle to storm out of the hotel and tell him to put it back on as she's pretty hot on that sort of thing, but she's been kind of absent since earlier. I guess she's pretty busy with the preparations for later.

I pick up a piece of wood and then stop and look at it more closely. There's a strange mark on it. Something carved into the bark. It looks pretty new, the cuts fresh and clean. And it looks like someone has taken a lot of care over it, too, like they've been creating a work of art.

"What've you got there Ed?" Ruby says, noticing. "Chuck it here."

I pass it to her and she frowns at it. "Looks like a picture," she says, turning it round. "Or a symbol or something." She shows it to Dan, who pulls a clownish face. "Spoooky!" he says, then laughs. "Nah, they probably did it to show which trees to cut down." He lobs it over his shoulder and it hits the wheelbarrow with a clang. "Get in!" he shouts—little fist pump, pleased with his aim.

But I feel weird about it, like we're doing something we shouldn't be. I think what also gets me is the fact that Dad was livid about the trees being cut down, like a lot of people around here were.

"I don't know what the hell she's playing at," he said. And: "everyone knows you can't cut down elders. She's a bloody fool, that's what she is." Whenever Dad trims the elders on the farm or on our side of the woods, he asks permission first. I've actually seen him do it: get down on his knees and bow his head, muttering to himself the whole time. I know all that stuff is just stupid superstition, but it's also the kind of stuff I've been brought up on. If Dad knew I was here, what I was doing right now, I don't think he'd speak to me for a month.

"Hey," Dan shouts. "Look, I've found another. Oh shit, look at this!" He drops it on the ground like it's burned him.

We all circle round to have a look. Above the symbol is a plait of silvery-gray hair, pinned onto the wood.

"Fuck me, that's minging," Dan says, nudging it with a toe. I definitely don't want to pick it up. In the end Ruby gives a big sigh. "You guys are total wimps." She grabs it and flings it into the wheelbarrow too.

WHEN WE'VE BUILT the bonfire, out on the front lawns in front of the sea, it doesn't want to burn, despite the fact that all the wood is really dry. There are just these clouds and clouds of black smoke billowing from it that sting your eyes and the back of your throat.

"Weird it's not taking," Ruby says. "When it's so hot. You'd think it would go up in seconds."

"There's some sort of chant, isn't there?" Dan says. "Something you're meant to say to get it going. Yeah . . . I remember my dad teaching it to me. It's the one they say the birds sing. Er, something like"—he clears his throat—"on wing of fire, burn to the bone, sparks fly higher, burn to the bone—"

"Stop," I say. Hearing it makes my skin crawl. Makes me think of the bones in the woods last night, the flaming torches, the masked faces. Makes me think again of my worries about Dad. Maybe he hears something in my voice, because Dan trails off. "I can't remember the rest, anyway," he says, shrugging.

"I mean, top marks for creepy pagan effort, Dan." Ruby says. "But we're going to have to tell Michelle. Because this ain't happening."

"Er, you volunteering for that?" Dan asks. "She's in a pretty shitty mood today." He can't help a quick check over his shoulder—I don't blame him. Michelle likes appearing out of nowhere.

"Right," Ruby says. "Wait here." She disappears round the back of the main building. A few minutes later he comes back with two big jerry cans of petrol. "This should do the trick." She sloshes it everywhere.

"Ugh," Dan says. "That shit reeks—smells like a petrol station."

It does; it stinks. I'm not sure it really works for the whole vibe of The Manor, which is all about being as "green" as possible, but I suppose beggars can't be choosers. Then Ruby takes out a lighter and holds it out. The whole thing goes up at once, like some sort of special effect in a war movie.

"Fuuuck!" Dan shouts. "I think I just lost my eyebrows!" And then the two of them are giggling like kids, kind of dancing around the flames. It's like the fire has done something to them, changed something in them. It's almost animal. I don't feel it, though. I know it's probably stupid old superstition but I can't help thinking about those marks on the wood and how it refused to burn. I feel like we've just done something we shouldn't.

Eddie

THERE'S A CROWD OF PEOPLE along the cliff edge, pointing and looking down.

"I thought it was part of the entertainment at first," Ruby says, "but from the way Michelle's freaking out, I don't think this is planned." She points. "Look."

Down there on the beach are eleven hooded, cloaked figures, holding lighted torches. All wearing masks with huge hooked beaks. The same figures we saw in the woods last night. The same ones that probably killed Ivor. The light from their torches throws their shadows down the beach, huge and flickering, so it's like there are a further eleven monstrous forms dancing behind them on the sand.

All of them are looking up here, at The Manor, at the celebrations on the lawn. In the middle of them I can see this massive, hulking structure. It's some sort of wicker sculpture, I guess, but it's nothing like the ones up here. It's about five or six times the size, for a start, and it's much darker and sort of shaggy-looking. It's a massive bird, I realize. The head outsized. These two giant black wings, which I think might be decorated with actual feathers, woven into the wicker. A giant, curved beak. It's a giant night bird.

Suddenly all the noise has stopped up here. No one's laughing or shouting anymore. The music has broken off too. Some of the guests are clutching tight to each other, some are pointing. Every is staring down at the beach. Their faces are smeary, sweaty, sunburned. They seem disoriented, confused. Are they trying to work out whether this is part of the celebrations? They look like a load of frightened children, and in their white outfits they suddenly seem raggedy and lightweight compared to the dark cloaked figures down below, like a puff of wind might blow them all away.

Everyone seems to be waiting for something to happen. There's this strange, powerful pull of energy: like the moment just before a huge wave crashes onto the beach, or in the seconds leading up to the first roll of thunder. It feels like it's got several degrees darker, too. I have to look up and check the sky is still clear because I wouldn't be surprised to see storm clouds gathering up above, ready to break the intense midsummer heat.

Because it's suddenly so silent you can hear that down on the beach they're all saying something. No: chanting. One of them stands a little way in front of the rest and you can tell that they're the leader, all the others taking their cue from them. I can just make out the words. But their voices don't sound like human voices at all— more like the rasping of a flock of angry crows. Their voices starting low, but growing louder and harsher and angrier with each line:

> *On wing of fire*
> (Burn to the bone)
> *Sparks fly higher*
> (Burn to the bone)
> *Flame in the lung*
> (Burn to the bone)
> *Solstice begun*
> (Burn to the bone)
> (Burn to the bone)
> (Burn to the bone)
> *BURN TO THE BONE*

While some of them are still shrieking out the words, others are just shrieking and swaying on the spot, arms in the air, reaching upward, like they're lost in some kind of trance. It seems crazy that just eleven people could make so much noise: the sort of volume and pitch that hurts your eardrums. Some of the guests are actually covering their ears. And then just when it really feels like it's too much, like it has to stop, it does. It's completely silent. And then all of them but one—the leader—stick their lighted torches into the sand and move into a perfect circle around the huge wicker bird in the middle. They put up their hands to complete the ring, each gripping the wrists of the Night Birds on either side. And then the leader, who is in the middle of the ring, next to the wicker bird, bends and touches the tip of their flaming torch to the sculpture and there's a rush of flame. There's a gasp from everyone watching. They must have covered the whole thing in lighter fluid, like we did with the bonfire, because it goes up in one go, *whoosh*. Sparks and burning feathers are suddenly in the air, flying everywhere, even up here on the cliff top . . . scattering over the guests who shout and bat them away.

The one I think must be the leader steps forward again. They're a little smaller than a couple of the others but there's something about the way the others gather round them that shows they're the boss. They open their mouth and the voice that comes out definitely isn't a human voice. It's warped and rasping and several times louder than it should be.

And what they're saying is: "Send her down. Send her down now."

And then all of them are chanting at once in the same strange, distorted rasps: "Send her down. Send her down. Send her down."

Bella

I NEED A SWIM, TO wash off the grime from the cave, the feel of
having the diary in my possession once more. I peel off my clothes
down to my bra and panties and as I do think of my self-conscious
teenage self, crouched on a sun lounger beside a swimming pool,
folded socks tucked into each cup of my balconnette bikini. Shivering on the edge one night, full moon bright on the black water,
embarrassed by my pale bowed legs despite the warmth of booze in
my belly. The only body shape that seemed desirable then was the
girl in a music video on MTV: DD boobs and endless golden limbs.
I didn't realize how beautiful I was. I care a lot less now. Growing
a human inside you and being carved open to get them out tends
to do that. I skim my fingertips along the scar just above my bikini
line, the slightly stippled ridge of it.

I step into the water, gasp at the cold against my warm skin.
Caught off guard I'm gripped by the muscular tug of a wave, toes
scrabbling for the sandy bottom. For a moment I feel panicky and
out of control. No; I can do this. I'm a good swimmer: I go to
the council pool every week. It's one place I feel close to calm,
because if I push myself hard enough I can almost outswim my
own thoughts.

Quickly I find a rhythm, moving alongside the beach, enjoying
the burning sensation at the base of my throat as my breath comes
harder. Then I head a little farther out, swim until I can make it out
there up beyond the cliffs: the imposing grey block of stone. I tread
water to stay in one place as I look and breathe. In this moment I
feel less jittery, less afraid. I feel resolved. Capable of everything I've
come here to do.

AFTERWARD I WALK across the beach, feel the wet grit of the sand between my toes. The tide is out and has left behind little pools trapped among the flattish rocks on one side. I climb up onto the rocks, where someone has left a backpack and a small pile of clothes. I clamber over to the nearest pool, the rough pumice of the barnacles and slither of seaweed beneath my soles, and look into the glassy surface. A whole universe is contained inside. I watch for a flicker of life to appear among the weeds: a crab or tiny fish. A little distraction while I work up the nerve to do what I need to.

And there it is, behind me: the cave. Just where I remembered, set into the steeper rocks on the far side. Still moving like I'm possessed I walk to it and peer inside. The dank cool of it is such a contrast to the heat of the morning. The dim interior feels full of ghosts.

As my eyes adjust I see something, tucked into the shadows. Or what looks like the beginnings of some kind of structure, made from lots and lots of long, thin twigs plaited together like the weave on a basket. I take a step back. My skin prickles. Then I see the black feathers scattered across the floor of the cave, some of them sticking together in tarry clumps. Lifted by the breeze several of them float up and one settles against my collarbone, soft as a kiss, sheening with iridescence. I brush it off, sickened by the touch of this living-dead thing. And now as I continue to look I take in the rough white symbols scrawled onto the walls in what I guess must be chalk; there's enough of it scattered about. There's something witchy about the sight, something ancient and strange. But familiar, too. I've seen symbols like this before. I shiver, in spite of the heat of the sun on my back.

•